BOOKS IN THIS SERIES

School for Psychics (Book One)

THE ASTRAL TRAVELER'S DAUGHTER

A SCHOOL FOR PSYCHICS NOVEL

K.C. ARCHER

Simon & Schuster Paperbacks

NEW YORK   LONDON   TORONTO   SYDNEY   NEW DELHI

Simon & Schuster Paperbacks
An Imprint of Simon & Schuster, Inc.
1230 Avenue of the Americas
New York, NY 10020

First Simon & Schuster trade paperback edition April 2019

SIMON & SCHUSTER and colophon are registered trademarks
of Simon & Schuster, Inc.

For information about special discounts for bulk purchases,
please contact Simon & Schuster Special Sales at 1-866-506-1949
or business@simonandschuster.com.

The Simon & Schuster Speakers Bureau can bring authors to your
live event. For more information or to book an event contact
the Simon & Schuster Speakers Bureau at 1-866-248-3049
or visit our website at www.simonspeakers.com.

Manufactured in the United States of America

1   3   5   7   9   10   8   6   4   2

Library of Congress Cataloging-in-Publication Data is available.

ISBN 978-1-5011-5936-7
ISBN 978-1-5011-5938-1 (ebook)

To VB, AG, EM, ES:

Thank you for seeing what is invisible to others.

THE ASTRAL TRAVELER'S DAUGHTER

CHAPTER ONE

TEDDY CANNON SAT ON THE FLOOR IN THE LIVING room of a cramped apartment in San Francisco's Tenderloin District, reading about the assassination of a Ukrainian drug lord. Foreign newspapers weren't her typical summer reading (she preferred dystopian thrillers, to be honest), but there was something unusual about this assassination. It wasn't the bullet hole in the Ukrainian's head. That would be pro forma in most assassinations. It was the fact that there was no exit wound. And, once the autopsy was performed, there was no bullet.

Teddy folded the copy of the *Ekspres* and placed it in the ever growing stack to her right. She didn't need to keep consulting Google Translate to know that this incident definitely belonged in the "suspicious" pile.

When she'd called her parents at the end of the school year to tell them she'd be staying in San Francisco (using the magic words *summer internship*), they'd been disappointed that they wouldn't see her, but proud that she was on some sort of career track. A major improvement from her situation last year, when she'd been living in the apartment above her parents' garage, hundreds of thousands of dollars in debt to a Vegas loan shark. At least she didn't have that to worry about anymore.

The front door opened, then slammed, stirring the dust that had settled in the apartment over the last few weeks. A reminder that she—or preferably, one of her roommates, since she was obviously busy—really needed to do some tidying up. (In retrospect, maybe her mother's weekly cleaning "intrusions" weren't such a bad thing after all.) Teddy heard footsteps. A pair of scuffed black Converse sneakers entered her peripheral vision.

"What a surprise," a deep voice rumbled. "Still sitting here. In the exact same place. Doing the exact same thing."

Teddy glanced up. Lucas "Pyro" Costa was another student at Whitfield, a former LAPD detective. Dark haired and dark eyed, he took smoldering-hot to a whole new level. Teddy and Pyro had hooked up their freshman year. Now, however, their relationship was strictly business.

She shrugged, gesturing to the stack of clippings spread in front of her. "Yeah, but my pile is bigger."

"And that matters because?"

"Because I'm trying to find connections. Patterns. The answers are buried in here somewhere. I know it. I just have to keep digging."

"It's time to move on," Pyro said.

If she'd been returning to any other school in the world in September, that may have been the title of her "how I spent my summer vacation" essay. But Teddy Cannon wasn't going back to just any other school. She was going back to the Whitfield Institute for Law Enforcement Training and Development. And they didn't train just any law enforcement recruits. The Whitfield Institute trained psychics. So, the title of that summer essay? "How I Spent Three Months Combing Through International Papers Identifying Mysterious, Inexplicable Events That Could Possibly Be Linked to an Über-Secret Squad of Psychics Who Call Themselves the Patriot Corps and Still Have Absolutely Nothing to Show for It."

Pyro settled into a chair across from her, a greasy take-out bag tucked under his arm. "But let me guess," he said. "You're still not there yet?"

"Your powers of deduction never cease to amaze me. Are you sure they didn't kick you off the force?"

He tossed a wrapped burger in front of her. "Eat."

She put down the newspaper and picked up the fast food. She couldn't remember the last time she'd eaten. She'd probably starve if not for Pyro.

"Thanks," she said. Then, "Don't mess up my piles."

"Yeah, you've got a real system here. I can tell."

She took a bite and tried to suppress a moan.

"Okay there, Teddy?" Pyro was smirking. That smirk got women into trouble. Even she wasn't completely immune to it. As he studied her, Teddy felt something in her chest move. Acid reflux, probably. She should stop eating cheeseburgers soon. Then again, why not enjoy them while she could? Once she was back at Whitfield, the school diet was strictly vegan, which supposedly kept their bodies clean and their minds focused.

"You know I have a thing for cheeseburgers," she said, mouth full.

"What about the guy who brings you the cheeseburgers?"

There was a conversation she didn't want to have. At least not now. Pyro was one of the most dangerously seductive guys she knew. And once that heat was kindled, it was only a matter of time before the whole building went up in flames.

Teddy ran her hand through her hair—which was considerably longer than it had been when she'd started at Whitfield last year—and stared at the wall, her eyes darting from one article to the next. It had been Pyro's idea to tack the more pertinent articles on a corkboard. Probably a cop thing. Organized and efficient. But ultimately unhelpful.

Despite weeks of dead ends, Teddy's determination to track down the Patriot Corps (shorthand: PC) hadn't diminished. Everything that had happened in the final days of school last year—the betrayal of her classmate and supposed friend Jeremy Lee and the loss of her friend Molly Quinn—was linked to the vigilante group. Teddy was desperate to understand the organization's inner workings. She had another reason, one she didn't want to admit to Pyro, in case he thought she was going soft. In Teddy's final encounter with former PC member Derek Yates, he had suggested that her mother was alive and with the PC. He'd promised to help Teddy find her. A promise that remained unfulfilled.

Part of her had wanted to stay in San Francisco all summer because she'd thought that Yates would make contact. But now, weeks later, that idea seemed the most foolish of all. So she'd done the only thing she could to feel productive. Try to learn what she could about the PC. Find connections. Patterns.

Pyro cleared his throat. "I asked a cop friend to help me get to San Quentin. See if anyone on the inside had heard from Yates. I didn't want to get your hopes up, Teddy. But . . ." He trailed off.

Teddy wouldn't have gotten her hopes up. She knew that playing nice with others wasn't Yates's style. He was a lone wolf. And now he was in the wind. Teddy and the other Misfits—her group of friends from school—had helped Yates escape scot-free. He'd used them, and they'd served their purpose. He wasn't coming back.

"Thanks anyway." She crumpled the burger wrapper and went back to the Ukrainian newspaper. Her phone buzzed. Dara. *On my way up. Need anything?*

Nope, Teddy texted back. She closed her laptop, stood and stretched her cramped muscles, then went to unlock the door to the fifth-floor walk-up that she, Dara, and Jillian had sublet for the summer. Although he spent almost every day with them, Pyro slept across the bay in Tiburon on a friend's couch, though there were stretches when he went back to L.A. to see his family.

Teddy turned to find him watching her. "Dara's back," she said. "She and Jillian promised they'd help me go over those bombings from the nineties again. See if they could get any psychic reads."

"Again? You've gone over those, what, five times this week alone?"

"What's your point?" Teddy heard the edge in her voice but couldn't help it. An *entire year* spent at Whitfield Institute, and she still couldn't further their research. Teddy Cannon's psychic abilities—astral telekinesis and telepathy—allowed her to do amazing things: blow a steel door off its hinges, see inside someone's mind, slow down time, but locate someone long gone? Delve into the inner workings of the PC? That would be a big N-O.

Pyro rolled his shoulders, let out a breath. "Look. I want to find the PC as much as you do. I want to find Molly. But don't you think you're taking this a little—"

"Taking this a little *what*?"

The front door opened and Dara stepped inside. Dara Jones seemed to dress the same way year-round: silver bangles up to her elbows, ripped jeans, band tee. She'd bleached her hair blond over the summer, providing a sharp contrast to her dark skin. Gothic glam. A platinum-haired version of Rihanna in her *Anti* phase. Teddy often wondered if she dressed to look the part: she could predict how people would die. All Teddy knew was that Dara had no control over how or when the death warnings came. Like Teddy, Dara was still learning to harness her abilities. Unlike Teddy, she came from a long line of Louisiana psychics who'd been practicing the dark arts (in layperson's terms: voodoo) for years.

Dara stopped at the threshold. Read the tension in the room. "Am I interrupting . . . *something*?"

"No," Teddy said, shooting Pyro a look. She picked up the article from the Ukrainian newspaper and placed it on top of a thick pile of clips by the window. The bombing folder. She dumped everything on an ugly Formica-topped table in the kitchen, then looked at Dara. "There's more here. We're missing something. I can feel it."

Dara glanced at Pyro before looking back at Teddy. "We're supposed to go back to school the day after tomorrow."

"I know," Teddy said. "That's why it's important that we find something before—" She stopped rifling through the pages in the folder. "Wait a minute. What are you saying? School's starting, so, what, we're done? A few dead ends, then we walk away? What we've been looking for could be underneath our noses. We just need to try a little harder."

"You think this is about trying harder?" Dara said.

Pyro lifted his hand as if to touch Teddy's shoulder, then seemed to reconsider. "Listen, what about some fresh air? A walk? When was the last time you went outside?"

Teddy's gaze shot from Pyro to Dara. Were they *patronizing* her? They were the ones with the problem, not her. They were the ones giving up. She'd been out yesterday for coffee. Hadn't she? Or the day before, when she'd been to the library to look at microfiche. Or was that last week? She rubbed her temples, trying to remember specifics, but the days were fuzzy and running together.

She could keep the events of the past in line for the assassinations, the bombings, the unsanctioned rescues, the foiled kidnappings, the toppled regimes—all events in which the United States government claimed no involvement. But she couldn't remember the last time she'd left her apartment. Her friends had long since given up asking her to take a break and grab a pizza or go see a movie. She'd refused them every time.

Teddy's thoughts were interrupted by a crash from behind her as Dara stumbled against a cabinet and tried to steady herself. By Dara's feet, a newspaper. *The New York Times.* October 27, 1998. Teddy knew that date. A bombing at an office building on Forty-Seventh Street. Twenty people had been killed, including eight suspected members of Al-Qaeda, and dozens more had been injured. The incident had occurred months after a bombing in Saudi Arabia killed nineteen Americans. It wasn't until years later that intelligence had officially connected the New York City attack to Al-Qaeda.

"Dara?" Teddy navigated through the stacks to the kitchen, where she filled a glass with tap water. She handed it to Dara, whose hands shook so badly that the water sloshed on the floor.

Last year, Dara had seen their friend Molly's death. Or what would have been Molly's death had Teddy not been able to put the pieces together at the last moment. Still, Molly had been seriously injured. And that injury had led to her disappearance. Teddy thought the prophecy had made Dara feel responsible for Molly; while they were all eager to find out what had happened to their friend, it was different for Dara. More personal. In any case, Teddy had learned to take Dara's prophecies seriously—no matter how illogical they might seem.

"Dara?" she said. "What is it? A death warning?"

Dara struggled to take a breath.

"Is it about Molly?"

Dara shook her head. "Something else. Something . . . different. It's been happening more and more since school ended."

"What's been happening?" Pyro asked.

"I'm not seeing the future," Dara said, her eyes once again focused. She glanced down at the paper. In the photo, a burned-out office building. "I think I'm seeing the past."

"The past?" Pyro said. "That's incredible, Dara."

"It's not incredible when every damn object you pick up makes you see a dead person," Dara snapped, wiping her brow with the back of her hand. She grimaced. "Sorry. It's just . . . They're harder than the warnings. Those I can act on. These, I can't, you know, *do* anything about."

That made sense. But it *was* incredible. With the training they'd received at Whitfield, each of their psychic skills had increased. Teddy had discovered she had more than just one ability—why not her friend? "What did you see?" she asked. "The PC?"

Dara shook her head. "I saw the building in the picture as the bomb was going off . . . people screaming, running, bleeding." She gave a small shudder. "God, it doesn't get easier."

Pyro put his hand on Dara's shoulder. "It's not supposed to."

"Did you see anything else? Anything that might help us?" Teddy knew the words sounded callous the moment they left her mouth. But it was too late to take them back. Besides, the real question she wanted to ask, she'd managed to hold back: *What about my mother?*

Dara's hands were finally steady enough to hold a glass. She took a sip of water and shook her head.

Teddy's phone buzzed, breaking an uncomfortable silence. Jillian: *Be there in five. Eli coming with.* Teddy thought, *Ugh, Eli Nevin.* She wanted to scream. Jillian had promised to go over PC research. That was particularly critical in light of Dara's newest vision. But if Jillian was bringing her new boyfriend along—a new boyfriend who didn't, and couldn't, know anything about their psychic world—they wouldn't be able to talk about anything important.

Jillian and Eli had met at an animal shelter at the beginning of the summer. Teddy had never seen anyone as besotted as her former roommate. She'd thought that word irrelevant in this millennium, but Jillian had proved her wrong. Eli, with his *Save the Earth* T-shirts, and hemp oil and nutritional yeast, and twenty-seven different animal rights petitions he'd made Teddy sign since she'd met him. And he went on and on about HEAT, the nonprofit he ran: Humans for Ethical Animal Treatment.

Teddy didn't have time for Eli and his causes. None of them had time for Eli and his causes. She—they—had their own cause, their own mission, this summer. And time was running out.

"Hey," Jillian called out from the hallway. "Eli's just grabbing some veggie wraps. What'd I miss?" She shucked off her signature fringe jacket. You couldn't help but notice when Jillian walked into a room, not because the girl was practically six feet tall and built like a brick house, but because she radiated sunshine and puppy dogs and sugar cookies and all the good things that people like Teddy Cannon didn't.

"Oh, you know, just the fact that Dara had a vision of a PC bombing," Teddy said. "Nothing too important."

Jillian paused in the middle of twisting her long blond hair into a topknot. Teddy noticed a new pair of dainty bar studs on her earlobes—a gift from Eli? He'd asked Teddy what to get Jillian for her birthday. *Crap.* She'd forgotten Jillian's birthday. It had been, what, last week, the week before? Well, she'd make it up to her. Margaritas at the Cantina as soon as they were back at school. Teddy had just been distracted this summer. Her friends would understand. Jillian, especially, would.

"There's going to be a bombing?" Jillian asked, eyes wide.

"*Was* a bombing," Pyro said. "Past vision. Dara can see past deaths now."

"When did you start seeing the past?" Jillian asked Dara. "Are you okay?"

That was the right reaction, Teddy realized, making a mental note. Not asking what the vision in particular was about or, worse, how it might help her.

"It's a new thing," Dara said. "I didn't want to tell you all until I was sure. But then I saw this." She held up the newspaper. "It's hard to know if something is past or future unless I'm looking at an actual live person in front of me." She glanced at the photograph on the front page. "Or a dead one."

Teddy slumped into a chair. "Bottom line, we aren't any closer to finding the PC," she said. "Sure, we know some of what they've done. But other than Yates and our old classmates, we don't know who the PC actually are."

"Well, Yates, our ex-classmates"—Jillian paused to take a fortifying breath—"*and* your birth mother."

Teddy's chest constricted. No one—not even Jillian—had brought up the topic of Teddy's birth mother all summer. Let alone directly insinuated that she'd been involved in the inner workings of the

PC. "That's not what this is about. I'm"—Teddy paused to correct herself—"*we're* trying to find Molly."

Her friends stayed silent, as if they knew pressing her on this issue could cause her to erupt.

"Besides," Teddy continued, "just because my mother is with them doesn't mean she's *with* them." Her eyes went wide as an awful realization struck her. After a summer of researching the past, did they believe her mother was actually a participating member of the PC? Not just a prisoner being forced against her will? "Wait a minute. You can't really think—"

"We don't think anything yet," Pyro said. "We need proof. We need to ask ourselves what Clint would do."

But thinking about what Clint Corbett would do—dean of Whitfield Institute, ex-cop, friend of Teddy's birth parents—made Teddy feel even worse.

Clint had personally recruited Teddy last year. And though she wanted to trust him, he'd made that nearly impossible by keeping secrets from her. Secrets about her past. He'd known all along about Sector Three, the covert government training facility where her parents and Derek Yates had worked—or, rather, been experimented on. The facility where her father had died. So yes, she respected Clint. Liked him, even. But on some level, she remained as wary of him as she would be of a crooked Vegas dealer. When it came to doling out the truth, somehow the cards always fell in Clint's favor.

"All we have are conjectures and—" Pyro said.

"Veggie wraps!" Eli shouted from the hallway.

Teddy shot Jillian a look, then sprang into action. Turned the corkboard around to face the wall and threw one of Jillian's tapestries over the pile of papers on the floor. Eli had been told the same cover they used for close family and friends: they all attended a school for government and law enforcement trainees. It wasn't untrue. And certainly nothing in the apartment screamed *psychic*.

But Teddy didn't like that Eli was always around. "How much do you think he heard?"

Jillian shrugged. "It's fine. I told you, we can trust him."

Teddy rolled her eyes.

"Hey," Eli said, stepping inside.

Teddy couldn't blame Jillian for being attracted to him. He was taller than Jillian, with strong shoulders like a swimmer's, and curly dark brown hair that fell over his forehead in a way that made him look more like a member of a boy band than an activist. Today he was wearing a Greenpeace T-shirt and cargo shorts. Teddy loathed cargo shorts. And anyone who wore them.

"Hey, man," Pyro said. "We were kind of in the middle of something."

"No problem," Eli said. "I can come back later. Just wanted to give Jill her lunch."

Teddy clenched her jaw. Jillian wasn't Jill. She was Jillian. Naked-yoga-doing, patchouli-wearing Jillian Blustein. *Her* roommate.

"Thanks, babe," Jillian said, kissing him on the cheek.

"Oh, and Teddy, this is for you." He put down the take-out bag and fished around in one of the pockets of his cargo shorts (*All those stupid pockets! What is he hiding?*) and handed Teddy a folded piece of white paper.

Teddy glanced at the paper and froze. In a voice she barely recognized as her own, she choked out, "Where did you get this?"

Eli shrugged. "Some guy on the street asked me to bring it up to you."

"When? Just now?"

"Yeah, like five minutes ago."

Teddy rushed to the window. She took in the usual people who called the Tenderloin home. Dealers staking out corners for the night, gangs of teens, men and women staggering home after twelve-hour shifts. Dozens of people, but not the one person she wanted to see.

"What is it?" Pyro asked.

Teddy showed him the note. On the outside, in a distinctive scrawl she'd recognized right away, was a single word. Her name. *Theodora*. But no one ever called her that.

No one except Derek Yates.

Pyro swore, leaning toward the window to search left and right. "He's gone."

"Who?" Dara demanded from behind them. "Who's gone?"

"Should we go down?" Teddy said. "Start looking? Maybe—"

"Waste of time," Pyro said. "He was gone two seconds after he passed Eli the note."

Teddy reluctantly agreed. No one was better at disappearing than Derek Yates. Turning away from the window, she unfolded the paper. "Numbers," she said, scanning the missive. "Just random numbers."

"If that's from who we think it is," Dara put in, "there's no way those numbers are random. They mean something. What?"

"A phone number?" Jillian suggested.

Teddy shook her head. "Too many digits."

Suddenly, Eli was over her shoulder. "Those are coordinates. I know because this one time, when we were protesting in . . ."

Teddy didn't listen to whatever came next. She rushed to get her laptop and keyed the numbers into Google Maps. Heart pounding, she watched as the screen moved from California to Nevada. A small town called Jackpot pinpointed on the map.

"Jackpot," Dara said. "Anyone heard of it?"

Teddy hadn't. Although she'd grown up in Vegas, the only association she had with the word *jackpot* was a generic come-on to lure tourists into handing over their hard-earned cash. The town itself meant nothing to her. She scrolled through her mental time line of suspected PC events. No bombings or assassinations had ever been reported there.

"Maybe he's messing with you," Pyro said. "Jackpot, you know. *Winner, winner, chicken dinner*, except not at all?"

"That saying is messed up," Eli said. "Poultry farming. Did you know they use arsenic laxatives on chickens?"

God, what is Eli Nevin still doing here?

Ignoring him, Teddy said to Pyro, "Yates isn't like that. He doesn't mislead on purpose. He's giving me a specific clue. I'm just not seeing it."

"So switch your screen view," Dara suggested. "What's *at* the location?"

Teddy clicked on the street view, and her heart stopped. The computer screen filled with a familiar picture. A cottage. A yellow cottage. The house that she'd dreamed about for as long as she could remember. The dreams had become increasingly vivid as she'd seen, heard, practically *felt* her mother in the abandoned rooms. Those dreams meant something, Teddy had known, but what? Last year, Clint had told her that the yellow cottage was where her parents had lived while they'd been at Sector Three. The last place they'd called home before her father had died, before her mother had gone missing.

"Teddy? You okay?" Pyro asked.

"We have to go to Jackpot," Teddy said. "Now." Turning, she began to grab things she knew she'd need. The bombing folder, for sure. Water bottle. Backpack. Clothes.

Her friends watched, looking bewildered. "I'll call you later," Jillian said to Eli. For once, Eli took the hint. He gave Jillian a quick kiss goodbye and left the room.

Once the door closed . . .

"School starts the day after tomorrow, Teddy," Dara said.

"Which means we have to get to Jackpot tonight."

"Teddy," Jillian started.

"Yates wants me to go there. I don't know why you all aren't seeing this. It's what we've been waiting for all summer!"

"Teddy," Pyro said. "Hold on a minute. Yates sends you one slip of paper, and you go running off into the desert? Just like that?"

Her friends looked at her, arms crossed and brows furrowed. Teddy struggled to rein in her impatience. "It's their house, okay?" She took a shaky breath. "My parents' house. *My* house. It's where we lived while we were at Sector Three. It's probably a wreck now." At least in her last dream, it had been. "But if there's something there that leads me to her . . ."

"Her?" Dara repeated. "You mean Molly?"

Teddy took another breath. Her chest felt tight. "Yes, of course Molly. But also my birth mother." She shot a glance at Jillian. There. She'd finally said it. What she didn't want to admit to her friends or even herself. Right now, Yates was her only path to Marysue Delaney.

Pyro, Dara, and Jillian exchanged a look—one that preceded a conversation starting with "We need to talk." And not the good kind of talk that ended with ice cream and trashy TV.

Pyro spoke first. "Aren't you taking this too far? I mean, I know it sounds harsh, Teddy, but if your mother wanted to get in touch with you after all these years, she would have done it by now."

Teddy's stomach dropped. "Whatever," she said, turning away to refocus on packing. "This is the only solid lead we've had all summer. It may help us find the PC, it may not. But there's only one way to find out." She zipped her backpack and tossed it over her shoulder.

"Hold on." Pyro caught her arm. "If I thought I could talk you out of it, I'd try. But that doesn't mean I'm going to let you go alone. I'm coming with you."

"So am I," Dara said.

Teddy sighed. Despite her show of bravado, the thought of facing Derek Yates alone was terrifying. Realizing Jillian had remained suspiciously silent, Teddy turned to her roommate.

Jillian bit her lip. "I promised I would go to a HEAT meeting in half an hour."

"Are you saying HEAT's more important than the PC?"

"No, of course not. I'm saying that I made a promise, and . . . well, I have other commitments."

"Other commitments? Derek Yates just gave me the exact location of the house where my parents lived, the house that's haunted my dreams for decades, and you don't have time?"

Jillian looked at her feet. "I told Eli I'd go. It's important to him. To me, too."

"How's this," Pyro said. "Teddy and I will leave now. We'll take my car. And then Jillian and Dara will follow tonight after the meeting. You'll be, what, an hour behind?"

"At the most," Jillian said, obviously grateful for the solution. "I'll pop in and out really quick."

"Fine. But it's like a nine-hour drive," Dara said. "We're not listening to any Grateful Dead."

Their discussion of logistics faded into the background. Finally. After months of waiting, poring over newspaper clippings and tracking dead ends, at last they had *something*. A lead. A clear direction. Teddy followed Pyro down the flight of stairs and to his truck.

Only one problem.

Even though she knew they were driving to Jackpot, to her childhood home, she had no idea what waited there, or what kind of trap Derek Yates might be leading them into.

CHAPTER TWO

TEDDY JERKED AWAKE WHEN HER HEAD BOUNCED against the window of Pyro's truck. They'd left the smooth blacktop of Highway 93 behind and had turned onto the rough streets of Jackpot, Nevada. She rubbed her head and looked around. Not much to see. Desolate desert landscape stretched for miles in all directions, and plopped down in the middle of it was a rinky-dink town desperately aspiring to Vegas glamour. A smattering of ramshackle businesses, a single casino, and a few hole-in-the-wall bars. Dice Road and Aces Lane. The Royal Flush trailer park.

Neon lights flickered off as they drove past, their arrival coinciding with sunrise. They'd split the driving, Teddy taking the leg from San Francisco to Reno, Pyro hauling in the remaining four hundred miles to Jackpot. Normally, the proximity to poker tables would have made Teddy's palms itch, but now there were more important things at stake.

Pyro pulled in to the first restaurant they came to—Cactus Pete's. A perfect match for her prickly mood. Her head hurt. Her shoulder was numb. And her mouth was dry. Nine hours on the road would do that to a girl.

"This okay?" he asked.

She nodded. Sent a text to Jillian and Dara with their location. Jillian replied instantly: *About thirty minutes away.*

Pyro parked and cut the engine. It was barely five a.m., but gamblers were awake, and that meant there were diners to serve. A waitress left them with menus they didn't need. Teddy shoved hers aside, too agitated to focus on food. She picked up a paper napkin and began tearing the edges, a nervous habit. A tell if she ever had one.

Pyro studied her over his menu. "How you feeling?"

Teddy put the napkin down, dragged her fingers through her hair. "About as good as I look."

He took a long moment to look her over. "So, pretty good, huh?"

Teddy allowed a small smile and shook her head. She hadn't been fishing for compliments. Besides, Pyro knew she'd been nursing a broken heart all summer. More like a broken heart, a bruised ego, and a flattened sense of self-confidence, all courtesy of a failed and ill-considered *whatever* with Nick Stavros—the FBI liaison at Whitfield. Teddy's brain told her that she was over Nick. Over his fancy suits and his cute butt and the future they could have had, but her heart—well, her heart was still on the mend.

So, yeah, she could give Pyro another shot, see if he was the medicine she needed to be cured of Nick once and for all. But was that really fair to either of them?

Teddy took a deep breath to fortify herself. Time to put up a roadblock before things went an inch further. It was the Right Thing to Do. "I know things have been a little weird between us," she began.

He leaned back in the booth, his body causing the plastic of the banquette to wheeze. "Definitely wasn't the response I was hoping for."

"Let me guess. You just assumed that we'd sit down here at"— Teddy glanced at her watch—"five-twenty-seven in the morning, you'd say a magic line, and then I'd throw myself at you?"

"Why not? We had a pretty good thing last year, and now that Nick's out of the picture . . ."

Now that Nick was out of the picture, what? They'd go back to hooking up until someone else caught his eye? Or someone else caught hers? That wasn't what she wanted. That wasn't what either of them deserved. Pyro thumbed the edge of the menu, quiet now. Teddy swore she could smell plastic burning. At last he muttered, "What do you want me to say, Teddy?"

"You were the one who brought it up," she said. "I think it would be best if we agreed to keep things platonic."

"Best for who?" he asked.

"For both of us. Things are complicated enough as it is. And we're good friends. I don't want to lose that."

"Yeah, friends," he said. He moved his hand from the menu. Reached under the table, placed it on her knee. The heat traveled from his palm and radiated up her thigh. She needed to move, put a little distance between them before her best intentions went up in smoke. It felt good. Too good. But then chemistry had never been their problem.

She crossed her legs, dislodging his grip. "Trying to change my mind?"

"Depends." The right side of his mouth ticked up. "Is it working?"

Yes.

"No."

He laughed.

"What?" she asked.

"For an ex–poker player," he said, "you're totally losing your game face."

She felt her phone buzz in her pocket. Jillian: *15 minutes away.*

Teddy cleared her throat and sat up straighter. "We need to focus, Pyro. There's a reason we're here. And it's not about you and me." She tucked her phone away and looked at him. Even if he said her poker face currently sucked, she wasn't playing him. "I'm scared," she confessed. "All this time searching. Now I'm finally here. Truth is, I'm terrified about what I might find." She felt in her pocket for the photograph she had of her birth parents. The one that included both Clint and Yates. Taken back when the four of them were young, hopeful, bright eyed and bushy tailed, and whatever. When they'd first met at Sector Three. She pushed it across the table toward Pyro.

Pyro picked up the photograph, then turned it over so the image faced down. "I know what it's like to want answers. After my partner died, I couldn't let it go: Why didn't I see the gun sooner, why didn't I react faster? I spent years torturing myself that it was somehow my fault. And after this summer . . ."

"What happened this summer?" Teddy asked.

Pyro lifted his shoulder. "The guy was up for parole. I had to testify. I didn't follow protocol that night, and they used it against me. Now he's out on a shorter sentence."

"Lucas—" Teddy reached out across the table.

"All that time beating myself up about it didn't change anything. Sometimes the past is best left alone. The only direction we can move is forward."

Teddy pulled her hand away.

And that was where they left it. With absolutely nothing resolved as the waitress appeared to take their orders. Coffee. Omelets. Western for her; bacon, cheddar, and avocado for him. Rye toast and home fries for them both. The door to the diner opened, and Jillian and Dara strolled inside, drawing stares of open curiosity from the locals at the counter. But then, it was hard not to stare. They stood out. Even looking wrecked from hours of driving.

They slid into the booth with Teddy and Pyro. Dara announced she wasn't getting back into that car without coffee. And maybe a couple eggs. Also hash browns, toast, grapefruit, and a few cheese Danishes, just to keep their strength up.

"I couldn't sleep at all," Dara said, and groaned. "Jillian chants while she drives. She *chants*."

"I was clearing the animal energy from the road," Jillian protested. "Warning them we were coming. What if I'd hit a squirrel?"

Teddy tuned out the ensuing argument. After what felt like the longest breakfast of her life—though in reality it was probably no more than twenty minutes—all four of them piled into Pyro's truck, leaving Dara's car at the diner to retrieve later, and got back on the road.

They drove through the town of Jackpot, leaving its cheesy casino, auto parts stores, shuttered movie theaters, and broken-down dive bars behind. The downtown dropped off as quickly as it began. Then the GPS directed them into the suburbs. A few miles more and the houses spread farther and farther apart until they disappeared altogether. It felt like they were leaving civilization. Just barren ground, miles of shrubs, rocks, and early-morning sky. It may as well have been the end of the world.

At last they drove onto a crude roadway. Nothing more than a long, worn patch of dirt on Teddy's right. A turnoff so inconsequential they would have sped right past it had the GPS not alerted them to the coordinates they'd entered.

Pyro slowed, shifted gears, and took the turn. Teddy swallowed hard. This was it. It had to be.

When Pyro came to a stop, so did Teddy's heart. It took a long, shocked moment for her to reconcile the house that had haunted her for years, one that had been so full of life and warmth, with the dilapidated structure she saw now. Even though, rationally, she knew the house had changed over time—she'd seen as much in her most recent dreams—she was nonetheless unprepared for how badly deteriorated the once charming home had become.

The exterior paint was no longer a warm golden yellow but faded and cracked. Weather-beaten asphalt shingles peeled off the roof. The front shutters swayed off the window hinges, which protected nothing but broken panes of glass. Tangled weeds replaced the carefully tended garden. And the front door? The door that her mother had opened time and again in Teddy's dreams and beckoned her inside? Gone. Nothing left but an ugly, gaping hole.

Pyro's hand landed softly on her shoulder. "Hey," he said. "We've seen it. We can go if you want."

"No." Teddy steeled her nerves and reached for the door handle. "I'm going inside."

Pyro shook his head. "This is probably Yates's idea of a joke."

Teddy shook her head. "Dara was right. That isn't like Yates. If he brought me here, it's for a reason." She slipped out of her seat and heard the other doors slam behind her in quick succession. And then her friends were at her side.

"So, this is it," Dara said, sizing up the house. "Definitely worth nine hours driving with Jillian."

Jillian, as though she'd been waiting for her cue, chose that moment to squeal, "Oh my gosh! Look!"

Teddy nearly jumped out of her skin. Pyro wheeled around while Dara shrieked, "What?"

"There! Just beyond that bush—a greater sage grouse! Do you have any idea how lucky we are to see one? They're just off the endangered list!"

Teddy let out a shaky breath. Beside her, Pyro did the same. "C'mon, Jillian," he said, "could you just give us a warning next time?"

If Jillian heard him, she gave no indication. She went down on all fours, trying to coax the startled bird out from behind the bush where it was hiding.

"That's it," Dara said. "I'm done. I am not driving back with her. I'll ride in Pyro's back seat. I'll skateboard. I'll hitchhike. I'll walk. But I will not spend another moment in the car with her."

Teddy ignored them all. She approached the house and climbed the rickety front steps. She passed through the threshold, and she was inside. Dust, mold, and animal urine assaulted her nose. Although the interior was too dim for her to make out much initially, she heard the scratchy panic of mice scrabbling against the floorboards. Then her eyes adjusted, and she took in the rooms around her.

Bare of nearly everything. Stripped and neglected. Nothing left in the entryway but a broken wooden chair and pieces of shattered pottery that might have been a vase or a bowl. Faded rose-patterned paper, half-peeled from the wall. Teddy took it all in. Every despairing detail. This had been her home. She'd hoped to see something familiar, something that triggered a memory—an echo of her mother's voice, an image of her childhood—but all she saw were stripped walls and broken floorboards. There was nothing left. Nothing whole. Everything was wrecked, destroyed, abandoned.

She scanned the room, searching for clues to what had happened here, as if the place were a crime scene. Like she'd learned in her classes at school.

Having finished with her sweep of the lower level, she moved toward the staircase and proceeded upward. When she reached the second-floor landing, a voice greeted her.

"I was wondering when you'd show up, Theodora."

CHAPTER THREE

DEREK YATES STOOD IN THE DOORWAY OF AN UP-
stairs room, mere feet away. For months, he'd remained elusive. And
now that the man stood in front of her, it felt, well, anticlimactic. In
prison, he'd appeared polished and put together. Despite his circumstances, he'd emanated power and control.

But the Yates standing before her wasn't the Yates she remembered. His beard was overgrown, his hair unkempt, his clothes un-
washed. He'd lost weight. And though he appeared a shadow of the
person she'd met in San Quentin, one look into his eyes told her
that he wasn't someone to be trifled with. There was no mistaking
the glittering intelligence lurking there. She sent a pulse of energy to
her mental shield, willing the electric walls higher. She wasn't letting
Derek Yates into her head, whether he took the guise of a psychic spy
or a panhandler who slept beneath highway underpasses. Either way,
he was dangerous.

"Welcome home," he said.

Teddy laughed despite herself. This wasn't her home. There was
nothing for her here. Nothing but Derek Yates and his games. She'd
been played by him once again. He'd passed on a kernel of hope, and
she'd devoured it like a last meal.

"What do you want?"

"It's about what we both want, Theodora."

"Oh? What's that?"

"Information."

He held her gaze, and she stared right back. She expected him to push into her head, or try to, but . . . nothing. Nothing on top of the piles of nothing that she had already collected early this morning.

Then he took a step toward her. As he moved from the doorway, Teddy could see into the room behind him: a sleeping bag on the floor, a pile of clothes, a neat stack of canned food, a cache of water bottles. Derek Yates had been living here. Not just waiting for her. She stashed away the piece of information as he closed the door behind him.

"Teddy?" Pyro called up the stairwell.

"Good, you didn't come alone." Yates brushed past her and walked briskly down the stairs. "We have work to do."

He left no choice but to follow. Down the stairs, back to the entry-way. Yates looked between her friends. It was then that she realized they'd never seen him in person. She'd told them about her encounter at San Quentin, about the note she'd received at the Cantina. But they'd never met. "Pyro—I mean, Lucas—Dara, and Jillian," Teddy said, gesturing to each of her friends. "This is Derek Yates."

He scanned them dismissively, as if he'd sized them up and found them wanting. "I suppose they'll have to do."

Pyro gave one of his signature smirks. "We don't have to do anything, you—"

Yates narrowed his eyes. Pyro stumbled back as though an invisible hand had shoved him against the wall.

"What the hell was that for?" Pyro said, catching his breath.

"Respect," Yates said. "Show some."

Pyro lunged for Yates, but Teddy grabbed hold of his jacket to stop him.

"If we're finished with theatrics, we have business to attend to." Yates smoothed his shirt deliberately, even though Pyro hadn't been close to laying a hand on him. "I brought Theodora here—"

"You sent a cryptic string of numbers via Jillian's boyfriend," Dara interrupted.

"You figured it out. Anything else would have led them straight here."

"Who?" Teddy said. "The Patriot Corps?"

Yates's eyes flashed, but he didn't reply. As if on cue, a rumbling in the distance. Trucks. "There's been activity at the base nearby. I need to confirm who's behind it. And why."

The base nearby. Teddy didn't know why it hadn't hit her sooner. She'd known she'd be returning to the yellow house that haunted her dreams. But her subconscious had resisted putting two and two together. If she was going to Jackpot, that meant she was going to Sector Three.

She raced through the entryway, out the door, down the steps. The morning desert air was cool against her suddenly flaming skin.

"Wait," Yates called from behind her. "Wait."

Teddy felt him at the edges of her mind, but her shield held strong. He caught her wrist, jerked her to a stop. "Not yet. You're not ready."

Teddy pulled free. "Which way? Where is it?" She was probably less than a dozen miles from where her parents had been tortured. Where her father had died. In the anticipation of seeing her childhood home, where her story began, she hadn't realized that she'd also be within reach of where her father's story ended.

"All in good time, Theodora. Come back inside. We have matters to discuss."

Time wasn't good. Time wasn't on her side. "No," she said, "I'm tired of waiting. I've waited all summer. I've waited my whole life."

Yates scanned the horizon as if following the sound of the trucks in the distance. He glanced at the doorway, where Pyro, Jillian, and Dara huddled together, watching them. Then his gaze settled on Teddy. "You look like your mother," he said. "But you sound like your father. Impatient. Impulsive." Birds chirped around them. The sun had risen and broken through the ghost of desert mist. It would be a good morning for a hike, or some other normal outdoorsy hipster activity, if she didn't have other shit to deal with.

Yates continued, "When I finally decided to abandon the Patriot Corps, I asked Marysue to come with me. But she wouldn't." He studied Teddy. "After all they had done to her. After what they did to your father. She still wouldn't leave. She told me she had chosen her path."

Teddy felt her body stiffen. For years she'd been desperate to learn *anything* about her birth mother. All summer, she'd been trying to rationalize why Marysue had stayed with the PC. She didn't want to believe Yates. Didn't want to believe that her mother could have committed the crimes she'd read about, been a willing participant in a group that had caused such atrocities.

"You're lying."

"I'm many things, Theodora. But I'm not a liar."

She thought back to when she'd met Yates in San Quentin and acknowledged the truth in that. Derek Yates was manipulative, self-serving, cunning. But he wasn't a liar.

"Before we went our separate ways," he continued, "Marysue asked me to find you. To give you something. The fact that I've been in prison for years has delayed her request, but we find ourselves in an interesting situation: now, I think, we find ourselves on the same side."

The same side? Absurd. Last year she'd thought he was innocent, but he'd used her. He probably would again. She should turn and walk away. Jump in Pyro's truck and head back to school.

But Yates had something for her. *Something from her mother.* She had nothing from her birth parents. Only an old photo. Another object delivered by Yates. Another move to manipulate her into doing his bidding when the timing seemed right. And still she felt herself yearning for it, for some connection to her past. "What is it?"

"If you agree to help me, I'll give it to you."

Teddy narrowed her eyes. "That wasn't the deal. That's not what you said. You said my mother gave you something to give to me."

"A promise I intend to honor—with certain conditions, of course." *Naturally.* "What do you want?"

A quick shake of his head. "I don't like having these conversations in the open. You never know who may be listening. We'll talk inside." He turned and made his way back to the house, clearly confident that she would follow.

Teddy dug her nails into her palms. Ever since starting at Whitfield, she'd felt like everyone else held all the cards, and no matter how many moves ahead she tried to play, she was always playing from behind.

No longer. That ended now. With each step toward the house, Teddy's resolve hardened.

"You all right?" Pyro asked, as she followed Yates into the house.

"I'm fine." She was done with Yates parceling out information at his own pace. She wanted to know why she was here. Now. "Enough with the games, Yates. Whatever my mother wanted me to have is mine. So give it to me."

"Agree to help and it's yours. Trust me, Theodora."

"Teddy, what's he talking about?" Pyro asked.

Ignoring Pyro, she held Yates's gaze for a long, steady beat. Trusting Yates was about as likely as a royal flush on a flop. But using him the way he used her? That she could do. So she'd give her word, agree to help him. Maybe she would, maybe she wouldn't. Not the most honorable move, but that was exactly what Yates would do. He'd use her and then disappear.

She thought for a moment, then said, "What would be different this time? You'd get what you want and then vanish."

"Couldn't you find him telepathically if he tried to get away?" Jillian said.

The corner of Yates's mouth twitched. Teddy knew that breaking in to his head was like breaking out of Alcatraz. He reached into his pocket for a pencil and a scrap of paper. Wrote something down, then passed it to Teddy.

She glanced at it. "A post office box in Santa Fe?"

"Write me and I'll come to you. And don't for a moment consider staking out the post office for my arrival. That will be forwarded to another city, and then another, until it comes to me. No email, no phone numbers. We're going old-school, Theodora. Safer for everyone that way."

"And I'm supposed to trust this?"

"It's more than I've given anyone else before."

Not perfect. Not even close. But at least she had some link to Yates. A string she could pull when she needed it. "You have a deal," she said.

Yates nodded and disappeared into the kitchen, leaving the Misfits alone in the hallway. Her friends stared at her in appalled surprise.

"Teddy, what are you thinking?" Dara said.

"She's obviously not," Pyro said, "if she'd willingly make a bargain with Derek Yates. Jesus, Teddy."

She shook her head, ignoring their concerned stares. No time for explanations. Yates returned with a small bundle wrapped in beige muslin and passed it to her. She studied it for a moment in agitated silence. Something from her mother. It should have been hers years ago. But would she have been ready for it? Before she'd known about her birth parents, Whitfield, Sector Three, psychics? She wanted the moment to be private. Instead, her friends and Yates looked on as she carefully unwrapped the yellowing fabric. Inside, a familiar object: a large purple stone in a silver setting, hung on a matching chain. Teddy recognized it from the photograph she had of her parents. "It's her necklace."

"What does it do?" Dara asked. "Or is it just sentimental?"

"Crystals help certain psychic abilities," Jillian said. She stepped closer, peering at the stone. "Ametrine. It's a combination of amethyst and citrine. Rare to form together in quartz. Every stone is different. It has properties of both, but it harmonizes them, too."

"There wasn't a note?" Teddy asked. But a note would have been too easy. And Teddy Cannon's life was anything but. She held the pendant between her fingers, felt the smooth surface of the polished crystal. She'd expected answers, not a memento. She turned the stone over in her hands, studying it for a clue, waiting for something, anything, to happen. But nothing did. Her frustration rocketed. Essentially, she'd just made a deal with the devil for an accessory.

"So, what, that's it?" Pyro asked.

"That's it?" Yates mocked. He looked ready to push Pyro through the wall, not just up against it. "Marysue Delaney was a powerful psychic. An astral traveler."

Astral travel. The ability to move through both space and time. Clint had mentioned her mother's skill last year, but so far, Teddy hadn't shown any aptitude for it.

Yates continued: "I don't know how that stone works, but she always had it on her, Theodora. I never saw her take it off. Not once. Not until I told her I was leaving. And then she begged me to get it to you."

"But how do I use it? I'm not a traveler, I can barely—"

A low groan interrupted her. Dara stumbled, clutching her head. "Crap. It's happening again."

"A death warning?" Jillian said, worry in her voice.

"I'm not sure. It's jumbled. Fire and explosion. And—" Dara's knees buckled. She reached for the wall to steady herself. "I see the Sector Three symbol."

"A past vision," Pyro suggested. "The explosion. Teddy's father—"

"Old news," Yates interrupted, his cool demeanor back in place. "There are larger things at stake here. What concerns us at this moment is the present—what's happening on that base *today*."

An echo of her conversation with Pyro in the diner ran through Teddy's mind. Pyro had told her to forget the past and focus on the future. Yates was telling her the same thing. But she had to understand her past in order to move forward. That was the point of all this, wasn't it?

"I have a plan," Yates said. "But you'll have to follow my instructions exactly."

Teddy watched him look around the room, sizing up her friends. And that was when it hit her. Yates needed her. Needed them. He hadn't brought them here just to deliver her mother's necklace. His next words proved her assessment correct: "We've got to move fast if we want to get in before the guards change shifts."

"Wait a minute," Pyro said. "What guards? Get in where?"

Yates delivered a withering look, then unzipped a slim backpack. Teddy watched as he loaded in a small camera, a knife, water bottles, and a heavy piece of rope—supplies, she realized—before zipping it closed and putting it on. He walked to the door, then paused. "I thought you would have figured it out by now. We're breaking in to Sector Three."

CHAPTER FOUR

TEDDY FOLLOWED DEREK YATES OUT THE BACK DOOR
and down a path that ran east, carrying them deeper into the desert.
As soon as she'd realized that Sector Three was mere miles away,
there'd been no question that she'd do anything to see it. But her
friends? She tried to guess without going into their heads what had
motivated them to agree to join Yates's mission (that was psychic
friendship 101, after all, and especially frowned upon for a student at
Whitfield Institute).

It hadn't been necessary with Jillian, anyway. When another
greater sage grouse ambled in the direction of the reactivated base,
Jillian proclaimed the bird's appearance as a sign. Teddy didn't know
much about signs, or the endangered wildlife of the Nevada desert, but
anything that turned her once reluctant friend in the mission's favor
worked for her. Dara, Teddy guessed, wanted to see the source of her
latest vision, or maybe search for Molly. As for Pyro, he'd probably
come to make certain they didn't get caught, hurt, or, considering
Yates was involved, worse—killed.

To Teddy's left, a mountain range loomed in the distance, its stony
peaks rising somewhere across the Idaho border. To her right was
nothing but stark desert plateau, interrupted only by an occasional
scattering of large rock formations. Yates directed them due south and
then east again, cutting across flat, miserable ground rife with prickly
scrub brush and thorny cacti. Even if she'd wanted to, Teddy couldn't

have tracked their location. It just looked like the damn desert. The perfect breeding ground for snakes and other slithering creatures.

Her combat boots proved to be more than an interesting fashion choice.

Although it was still early morning, it was late August in Nevada. Which meant it was hot enough to burn a polar bear's butt. They walked for over an hour, covering what Teddy calculated must have been almost three miles. Three miles into the middle of the desert. Though Yates looked worse for wear, he moved with lithe, effortless grace. In contrast to Teddy—out of shape after a summer spent sitting on the floor of a dusty apartment reading newspaper articles—who struggled to keep up in the heat.

"Remind me why we didn't take Pyro's truck?" Jillian asked, straggling behind.

"Because I'd prefer not to announce our presence to everyone within fifty miles," Yates replied, gathering the group behind the shelter of a dense desert sumac. "It doesn't matter. We're here."

He lifted his chin, directing their attention to a primitive wooden structure draped with camouflage netting. Two armed guards, dressed in regulation tan fatigues, stood on opposite sides of a secured gate that allowed vehicle access. The facility was surrounded by an eight-foot chain-link fence, topped with ribbons of razor wire. Caged within the fence was the sort of basic no-frills complex common to military bases and prisons. Ugly two-story structures distinguished only by their state of disrepair. Buildings that appeared to have been hastily constructed, then abandoned and subsequently beaten down by the intense desert heat. Apart from the guards, there was no sign of life anywhere. Earlier, they'd heard vehicles. Trucks rumbling across the desert landscape. But now, nothing.

"Sector One," Yates announced. "Or what's left of it."

"Looks deserted to me," Pyro said.

Teddy shook her head. "Then why are there guards?"

"Maybe they're using it as a storage facility or something," Dara said.

"We should find out." Pyro rubbed his fingers against his thumb, then held them against a brittle weed, clearly intent on starting a small brush fire. "I'll create a distraction. Then we'll slip inside."

Yates knocked Pyro's hand away from the smoldering twig. "So dramatic. So unnecessary."

"What would you suggest?" Pyro said, lip curled.

Yates turned his attention to the guard station. If Teddy hadn't known to watch for it, she would have missed it. The hard look on Yates's face, the brightness in his eyes . . . Seconds later, a dull thud, then another, as the two guards fell to the ground, guns scattering.

Jillian gasped. "What did you do to them?"

"It's only temporary," Yates said. He took a step out from behind the overgrown sumac. "Follow me."

They crossed a barren field and strode through the entrance, past the unconscious guards. Teddy had seen mental influence before, but the ability to knock someone out cold with just force of mind? She shuddered. And sent another surge of power to her mental shield.

Teddy remembered Clint telling her that Sector One had been an army training facility, a base used to prepare troops for the conditions they'd encounter once deployed to Desert Storm. But as she and her friends made their way deeper inside the base, nothing she saw gave any indication of the facility's more sinister purpose. She peered inside one of the ravaged buildings, desperate for a glimpse of what had happened there. To see firsthand what her parents and the other psychics had endured. But all she could make out were abandoned desks and chairs, assorted dirt and debris.

"We're missing something," Dara said. She turned to Yates. "The government wouldn't conduct secret experiments where anyone could see what they were doing, right? The facility would have been hidden. Entry allowed only with high-security clearance."

"Very astute, Ms. Jones." Yates surveyed the dilapidated structures surrounding them. From Teddy's perspective, they all looked the same, but he zeroed in on one and moved toward it. He identified a spot on its exterior wall and kicked aside some sagebrush. As he did, another sage grouse scurried free.

Yates pointed to the ground beneath the overgrowth. A padlocked metal double door, sunk low into the ground. Similar to the exterior Bilco doors that allowed access to basements. Yates bent and brushed away the sandy soil coating the metal surface. Though the design was rusted through in places, Teddy could make out the pattern etched on the surface: a number three surrounded by three overlapping concentric circles. Just like the screw she'd seen in Clint's office. The symbol on her parents' jackets in the photograph she had in her pocket. The symbol Jillian had seen in her vision.

The symbol for Sector Three.

Teddy bent down, grabbed the padlock, and tugged, but it wouldn't budge. Not a problem. She'd broken through a metal door before. She could do this. She stood up, centered her breath, readied herself to use her telekinesis to break through. Pyro stopped her. "Don't," he said. "Save your energy." He looked toward Yates. "Just in case."

Pyro stepped past her and rubbed his hands together, generating heat. Then he pressed his palms against the surface. He focused his gaze on the thick metal padlock. Within seconds, the lock began to glow red, then white, as the heat built. Tiny sparks shot from his hands. Like watching a smelter pull something out of a fire, only Pyro manipulated the metal with his bare hands. At last the lock began to warp and twist, breaking away before their eyes. Pyro removed his hands, put them in his pockets.

Teddy cautiously felt the metal door. It was still warm. "That's amazing," she said.

"Just something I've been working on." He smiled.

"We done?" Yates said, his voice dripping sarcasm.

Ignoring him, Teddy gave Pyro's arm a quick squeeze and pulled open the Bilco door. She peered down into a black, gaping hole. A sheer drop of at least two stories, maybe more. Bottom line: even if they survived the fall unscathed, they'd never get out. She wheeled around to glare at Yates.

"Fire exit," he said. "They're not expecting us, so I thought it prudent not to use the front door."

"How are we supposed to—"

"Patience, Theodora." With that, he removed the length of rope he'd carried in and secured it around the base of a charred stump. "I'll go first."

He grasped the rope in his hands and centered himself over the open Bilco doors. Gave a light jump and rappelled down the interior of the shaft, disappearing into the waiting darkness.

Pyro peered into the hole, then back at Teddy. "You sure about this?"

"I have to know."

The rope snapped taut.

"All right, then. It's clear."

Teddy grasped the rope and turned around, centered herself over the hole. Using the same technique Yates had employed, she began her descent. Once her feet reached solid ground, she gave the rope a snap and stepped back, signaling her friends. She waited beside Yates in the gloom of a narrow corridor, neither of them speaking. It was dark inside but not totally black, which Teddy found interesting. Light seeped in from connecting passageways. She allowed herself a second to wonder if partial electricity had been recently restored, or if no one had ever bothered to disconnect the secret government facility from the grid.

Not that there was much to see. Teddy could make out a few details of their surroundings: narrow hallways, linoleum floors, caged bulbs overhead. No sound except the steady hum of machinery operating in the distance—a generator, she guessed. The air smelled acrid, as though she were detecting a faint residue of smoke, and it felt hot and dry against her skin.

Dara rappelled down to join them, then Jillian. Pyro brought up the rear. Once they'd assembled, Yates shouldered past Teddy. "This way," he whispered. "Stay together."

He led them through the long, dim passageways. Every so often, the hallway splintered, forking into another offshoot. Teddy tried to keep count of the pattern of lefts and rights, but as they made their way deeper into the belly of Sector Three, she lost track of the route. She'd go crazy down here, she knew that for certain. Like a rat trapped in a maze.

As they walked, she noted wooden crates whose labels indicated food, water, clothing, and cleaning and medicinal supplies stacked neatly against the walls. Evidence of future occupation, she supposed. But by whom? As far as she could tell, none of the crates had been opened.

Eventually, they came to a single metal door. For the first time since they'd entered Sector Three, Yates hesitated. Shadows played over his face, making his naturally stark features even more grim. He gave a terse nod and opened the door. "I believe this is what you wanted to see, Theodora."

Teddy stepped through the doorway, squinting. She sensed that she was in a relatively large room, but it was too dark to make out any details. She ran her hand over the rough surface of the wall until she made contact with a switch. She flicked it on.

A dim overhead bulb sputtered to life. Some sort of operating room, she surmised. Two broken metal gurneys rested on their side. Shattered medicine bottles, thick leather hospital restraint cuffs, and twisted surgical tools littered the ground, accompanied by syringes, scalpels, and assorted medical equipment. Clearly, the space hadn't been touched since whatever had happened here. The walls were charred black and pockmarked with bullet holes.

Though the room was destroyed, its use was evident. But if the rumors about Sector Three were true, the type of medical procedure that had occurred there belonged more in a horror movie than in a hospital. She looked at Yates.

He returned her gaze. "In your worst nightmare, you couldn't imagine."

The problem was, she could. Only then did she realize how tightly she was clenching her fists. Squeezing so hard, her fingers had turned numb. She shook them loose, then stuffed her hands into her pockets. Her fingers grazed her mother's necklace. She wrapped her hand around it. The stone felt cool in her palm, comforting.

"Tell me what happened here," she said to Yates.

"I would think that's obvious, Theodora." He moved away from her, ran a finger along the twisted metal door of a medicine cabinet. "Certain people wanted to know how psychics . . . worked."

"The government, you mean?"

"Initially."

"What about the PC?"

"The PC was formed after we left Sector Three . . ." He trailed off as he studied a bullet hole in the wall, then turned back to face Teddy. "Imagine it: the kind of research the government conducted—if you could call it that—in the hands of my former organization, untethered by law or accountability."

"If the PC was so bad, why did you stay so long?" Dara challenged.

Something flared in Yates's eyes. "They had ways to make us cooperate."

"Meaning?"

Yates ignored Dara's question. Looked at Teddy. "The things I saw Marysue do with that necklace . . . Teddy, if you could harness that power? You'd could be unstoppable. It could change everything."

He looked as though he wanted to say more, but an echo of distant voices suddenly drifted toward them. Pyro reached for the light switch and flicked it off. They froze in the darkness, listening to the noise recede. Whoever had been there was moving away. A lucky break.

As they waited for the silence to become complete again, Teddy became aware of the stone in her hand. She rubbed her thumb across the pendant and found it no longer cool but burning hot. She tried to release her grip but couldn't. She opened her mouth—to alert her friends, to ask for help—but she couldn't speak, couldn't catch her breath. It felt like the wind had been knocked out of her.

Then she felt a sharp tug, as though an invisible hook had latched underneath her rib cage, dragging her somewhere she didn't want to go. Panic flooded her. She wanted to scream, because how was this happening and how did she stop it, and then everything went dark. Not just dark but a bottomless blackness. And then she was in pain. Like her head was in a vice. Like she was simultaneously being thrown from a great height and squeezed through an invisible tunnel the size of a drinking straw.

She may have lost consciousness—she wasn't sure—but when she opened her eyes, she could breathe again, and the pain was gone. She was still deep within the bunker of Sector Three . . . and yet it wasn't the same place she'd been moments ago. The walls were gleaming white and brightly lit. The medical equipment was neatly displayed, and the metal gurneys shone. She was alone.

No sign of Yates or her friends.

What kind of trick is this?

A trick. Yes. Yates. He'd been looking at her, talking to her. He must have gotten inside her head. Was he trying to show her what had happened in the past? Was she in his memory?

A nurse stepped into the room and strode right past her to collect supplies, as if she couldn't see Teddy at all. *A memory, then, if she can't see me. But if that's true, where is Yates?*

A sound echoed from the hallway—the squeak of wheels and a male voice saying something about "the next subject."

"He put up a hell of a fight," a second voice responded. "But he's out cold now."

Two orderlies pushed a gurney into the operating room. Lying atop it was a man. His hair, dirty and streaked with gray, was damp with sweat and hung limply across his forehead. As she studied him further, Teddy took in other details—the thick leather straps at his ankles and his wrists. The ligature marks up and down his arms (this obviously wasn't the first time he'd been bound).

The man looked up, looked right through her. She could see him, but he couldn't see her. His skin was sallow, even under the harsh lights. And his face—bloodshot eyes encased by dark circles, sunken cheeks—ravaged but familiar. She knew the man before her.

Richard Delaney. Her father.

She staggered backward, overcome. Bile rose in the back of her throat. Although only two years had passed since Richard had posed with Clint, Yates, and Marysue for the photo Teddy carried, he looked as though he'd aged decades. The click of a lever, and the lights in the room surged and flickered. Her father's hands gripped the metal arms of the chair, forearms straining against the bindings. As the electricity surged, he cried out. She felt the noise inside her, felt the vibrations burn in her own chest.

She couldn't watch this happen. She backed up, desperately edging away from the scene unfolding before her. She'd barely made it out the door when she heard footsteps racing down the hallway.

"What have you done to him?" the woman shouted, her voice hoarse with terror. She flung herself onto one of the orderlies. "Where is he?"

The orderly caught the woman's fists and spun her around, away from the operating room. In that instant, Teddy saw her face.

A face she recognized—her mother's.

From within the operating room, another agonized cry, followed by a surge of electricity that caused the hallway to go blindingly bright. Teddy had barely had time to shield her eyes when a second scream echoed through the corridors, and then, with a pop, the hanging lightbulbs exploded, raining shards of glass. One razorlike sliver pierced the skin on Teddy's right index finger. She was bleeding.

She refocused on the scene before her to see one of the orderlies dragging her mother away. An alarm sounded. Before Teddy could identify the source of the piercing whine, the pain was back, pulsing behind her eyes, worse than any migraine imaginable. The hallway tilted sideways, and Teddy felt her knees give. She reached out, trying to grab hold of something to stop her fall, but she was too late. The room spun, and once again she plunged into bottomless blackness.

CHAPTER FIVE

TEDDY WOKE WITH A JERK, OUT COLD ON THE FLOOR. A piercing alarm screaming down the hallway and Pyro's hand supporting her head. "It's all right, Teddy. You're okay. But we have to get out of here."

She blinked as Pyro's face swam into focus. She was back in the bunker, surrounded by her friends and the ravaged remains of the medical room. "What? Pyro? Where—Yates—"

"Yates is gone," Dara said, her expression strained. "You passed out. You have to get up now."

Teddy glanced down at her right index finger, where the glass shard had pierced her skin. She touched it, then looked at her hand, the blood still tacky. But there was no evidence of broken glass anywhere. It didn't make sense. How could she be injured if she'd been inside Yates's memory?

"Someone's coming," Jillian hissed from the doorway. "We have to hurry."

Pyro tucked his arm beneath Teddy and brought her to her feet. She swayed. "Can you run?" he asked.

"Run? What—"

"The guards Yates knocked out must have woken up and called in reinforcements." Anger darkened his gaze. "Yates bailed on us the second the alarm sounded."

Teddy shook her head, struggling to make sense of what her friends were saying. Yates had abandoned them. He'd led them inside Sector Three but hadn't stuck around to get them out. Typical. She should have known better.

She shoved aside the horror of what she'd seen in Yates's memory. She'd deal with that later. First they had to get off the base.

They shrank back against the wall as an armed guard raced down the hallway, past the operating room. Teddy braced herself for more, but none came. After a beat, Dara checked the corridor and gave the all clear. They ran opposite the direction the guards had taken, sweeping left and then right through the narrow hallways, relying on Pyro's sense of recall to bring them back to the Bilco doors. They stalled at a T intersection.

"What now?" Teddy asked.

"The air's different," Pyro said. "I feel the heat coming in. We must be near the exit."

"But which direction?"

Pyro snapped his fingers, creating a flame. He watched it flicker and dance toward the left, where the exit created a draft. "This way." They sprinted down a long corridor. Then, in the dim light of the bunker, Teddy saw the rope. Still attached to the tree outside the Bilco door.

Relief poured through her. Yates hadn't taken away their means of escape.

She lunged for their lifeline and shoved it at Pyro. "Go!"

"I'll go last!

They didn't have time for this. "*Go*—it'll be faster this way."

Pyro looked ready to argue, then seemed to understand what she meant. Once he reached the top, he swung around, his body flat on the ground, his arms extended.

One by one, Teddy, Jillian, and Dara climbed the rope. Pyro grabbed each of them the moment they neared the surface and pulled them up, saving seconds they desperately needed. Once they were clear, he dragged the rope up after them, hid it behind the shrub, and shut the Bilco doors.

The scene aboveground had changed dramatically. Half a dozen military jeeps rolled through the grounds, prowling for intruders. The Misfits crouched behind what was left of a burned-out wall. They could hide, but not for long.

"That son of a bitch," Pyro swore.

Later, Teddy thought, trying to focus. No sense pointing fingers. Besides, if anyone was going to shoulder the blame, it had to be her. She'd agreed to help Yates. And now she and her friends faced the consequences.

"There's an opening in the fence about fifty yards to the west of us," Dara said. "If we can make it there, we have a shot."

Fifty yards. A fast sprint over flat ground roughly the width of a football field. Since Rosemary Boyd didn't step into the gym without a stopwatch, they all knew exactly how long that took. Ten seconds. Which was nine seconds too long—they'd be spotted.

"Influence?" Pyro said.

Teddy shook her head. She still felt weak from what had happened earlier. She didn't have enough strength to focus on controlling one person's mind, let alone a troop of armed soldiers. She looked at Pyro. "How about some drama now?"

He nodded. "Whatever happens, keep moving." His brow knitted in an expression of intense focus.

Teddy, Dara, and Jillian angled toward the direction of the fence and knelt in a crouch, ready to run. Pyro swiveled to face the opposite direction. Half a minute passed, then he roared: "Go!"

Teddy took off, Dara and Jillian racing beside her. She knew she shouldn't look, but a quick glance back showed Pyro sending a jet of blazing fire toward a truck. Eyes closed, hands up, he looked like a god of old. Teddy swung her attention around, focusing on the path before her. Fifty yards became forty, and then an explosion behind them nearly sent her flying. She didn't have to look to know he'd succeeded in blowing up the truck. A second later, Pyro was at her side. Shouts filled the air as nearby soldiers tried to extinguish the explosion.

They'd nearly made it to the fence when the sound of a motor revving caused Teddy to stumble. A jeep gunned into view on her left, a lone soldier behind the wheel. Teddy knew her options were limited: peel off from the others and give them a chance to get away, or freeze and risk them all getting caught.

She filled her lungs, gathering the last of her energy. But the screech of tires caused her to stumble once more. She watched the jeep swerve hard and crash into a pile of debris. The driver slumped over the steering wheel, unconscious.

From the corner of her eye, she caught a glimpse of a slender figure emerging from behind a nearby building. They locked gazes for a second before Derek Yates took off in the opposite direction. She vaulted to the fence, caught up with her friends.

"Was that you?" Pyro asked, breathing hard.

"No. I think it was Yates."

They slipped through the fence and kept running until Sector Three was a speck in the desert behind them.

The Misfits trekked back through the desert in silence. They found their way to the yellow house thanks to some quick thinking on Jillian's part ("Birds were basically the first GPS"). When they finally reached the cottage, they found water bottles, which they greedily guzzled. But no Yates. He and his possessions were gone. Teddy interpreted his leaving the water as a sign that he'd known they'd make it back in one piece. That even though he'd abandoned them in Sector Three, he was somehow on their side.

"What are you talking about?" Pyro protested. "Bastard didn't care if we got caught."

Teddy wasn't so sure. She'd seen how he'd intervened with the jeep. And it couldn't have been an accident that he'd left the rope behind. Yates didn't do anything by chance. Every move he made was calculated twenty times over.

"You're actually trying to defend him?" Jillian said.

"I'm just trying to understand what happened out there," Teddy said.

"Yeah," Dara replied. "The guy ditched us to save his own skin."

Teddy shook her head. Derek Yates was a pragmatist. He'd brought them to Jackpot because he needed their help. But not for breaking in to Sector Three. Obviously, he was capable of doing that on his own. So he must have lured them there for something else. According to Dara, Yates had bolted when the alarm sounded. Not even a moment's hesitation. As if he'd been waiting for it.

As if that was exactly what he'd planned.

"We were a distraction," she said.

Jillian looked at her. "What?"

"That's why Yates needed us. Not to break in to Sector Three. If anything, we held him back. We were there to distract the guards while he slipped off to do whatever he was actually there to do."

Dara blinked. "Holy shit."

Teddy gnawed her bottom lip, thinking. "I don't know what he's up to, but he wants something from us. Or, rather, me. Otherwise he wouldn't have given me the necklace—or a way to contact him."

Pyro extended a hand to Teddy. "If I were you, I'd burn that address he gave you. The guy's bad news."

The subject of Derek Yates wasn't one they were likely to ever agree on. Teddy turned the conversation to the logistics of returning to Angel Island. Before they left, Jillian took a minute to fuss over Teddy's finger, rinsing her cut and wrapping it in gauze from a first-aid kit Pyro kept in his truck. Then the Misfits drove back to the diner, picked up Dara's car, and headed back to Highway 93.

Hours earlier, Teddy had been filled with reckless, agitated excitement. Now she felt drained and deflated. Visions of what she'd seen in the operating room at Sector Three hovered at the edge of her mind—a shadow she wasn't ready to acknowledge. Not until she understood what had happened. She purposely volunteered to drive the rest of the way with Jillian, just so the sound of her friend's chanting would provide a distraction from her swirling thoughts. She'd come to Jackpot for answers. But when she finally saw the waters of San Francisco Bay on the horizon, she wasn't any closer to finding them.

CHAPTER SIX

THE NEXT DAY, MONDAY, THEY ALL OVERSLEPT.

"What about your circadian rhythms?" Teddy growled at Jillian.

"I'm sorry my internal alarm clock failed," Jillian replied, rolling off the couch. "It's not like my body has spent the last forty-eight hours in a stress-induced environment or anything."

They staggered around, heaving their belongings—and all of Teddy's "research" (air quotes were Dara's, of course)—into duffel bags. Dara dropped the key in the mailbox for the landlord. Then they piled back in her car and drove to the docks. Pyro resigned himself to making a trip to Tiburon to gather his things from his friend's place at a later date.

They reached the dock and rushed to catch the ferry that would shuttle them across the bay to Angel Island, home of the Whitfield Institute. As the boat carried them toward school, Teddy couldn't help but think of her first year at Whitfield . . . and the first Whitfield student she'd met. When Molly Quinn had introduced herself on the ferry, Teddy had believed Molly was in control of herself, of her power. That turned out to be far from the truth. If Teddy had learned anything over the last year, it was this: things were never as they seemed.

And where was Molly now? It was a question that once looped over and over in Teddy's thoughts. But as she'd looked deeper into her past, and her mother's, she had let one investigation supplant the other.

The ferry bumped against the dock at Angel Island, jostling Teddy from her thoughts. She grabbed her gear and trudged the half mile to the campus with her fellow Misfits. The Whitfield Institute sat atop a hill behind a massive iron gate topped by an arch engraved with the school's name. To a casual observer, it looked exactly as it was presented on the official website—a facility for law enforcement training. Whitfield's mission as a training ground for psychics remained a top-level secret. Even within the federal government, few knew the true nature of the facility.

Aside from the guard checking identification at the gate, the campus appeared deserted. Which could mean only one thing—opening-day assembly was already under way. Teddy and her friends hurried to Fort McDowell and into the auditorium, slipping into seats in the back.

Clint Corbett, dean of students and Teddy's mentor, stood at the microphone. He paused, noting their late arrival, before continuing his speech. "Sometimes a student's desires and skills are perfectly aligned," he said, holding his hands in parallel as illustration. A former football player, Clint knew a speech was never great without accompanying hand signals. "But sometimes they're not. And our goal, of course, is to guide you to the position that will enable you to use your gifts to best serve your country."

During their time at Whitfield, Clint explained, they'd spend each semester training in different divisions (in addition to their regular coursework of military tactics, seership, and casework). First up: Secret Service. Clint stood in front of a PowerPoint slide listing the different law enforcement tracks available to Whitfield students: DEA, FBI, NSA, Department of State, Treasury, or Defense, Military Intelligence, Homeland Security. He explained that while students would have the opportunity to indicate their top three choices, the faculty ultimately made the final call.

Teddy tried not to roll her eyes. If her fate were left up to Sergeant

Rosemary Boyd, she would be working for City Sanitation. In Juneau, Alaska. In truth, Teddy knew little of how the selection process worked, and she only half listened as she scanned the panel of instructors sitting onstage.

Because there, right next to Boyd, was Agent Nick Stavros, Whitfield's FBI liaison.

He looked up as if sensing her focus. Their eyes locked, and the hope that the months away would have dulled the, ugh, *feelings* she had for him turned out to be just that: a hope. Nick Stavros still made her feel things. Want things. But what, exactly? She wasn't sure of the answer herself. Because even if she got it, knowing her, knowing her life, she'd just mess it up.

He turned away, breaking their eye contact. But not before she read the look that shadowed his almost too perfect, almost too handsome face, a look that was all too familiar to Teddy Cannon: disappointment. She wondered if he'd be able to put aside *his* feelings when it came to selecting students for the FBI track. Had she ruined her shot before she'd even stepped in the ring? She couldn't let that happen.

She returned her focus to Clint as he introduced a new instructor, Special Officer Joan Wessner, who would be leading their Secret Service training. Early thirties, with ruler-straight black hair and a sharp jawline. Everything about her read tightness and precision.

Just what I need, another stickler for the rules on my case.

Teddy noticed a slight stiffness in Wessner's gait as she leaned in to the mic, sharing a few words about the value of Secret Service work. Forget everything they'd seen in the movies and on TV, she explained. They weren't just goons in aviators, black suits, and earpieces, hovering in the background at press conferences. Whether the people they protected lived or died was a direct result of how well they performed their duty. On that somber note, the assembly ended.

As they left the auditorium, students relinquished their cell phones and other devices that connected them to the outside world. A grumble sounded among the new recruits, but Teddy and her friends understood that for security purposes, they had to be cut off from social media and other electronic communications. The temptation to post a selfie on Instagram was a risk that the Whitfield Institute couldn't take.

From there they went to an informal meet-and-greet in Harris Hall—a rare chance for upper and lower classes to mingle. Teddy glanced around the room and saw the group of star students who liked to call themselves the Alphas—Ben Tucker, Zac Rogers, Henry Cummings, Ava Laureau, Liz Lynch, and finally, Kate Atkins, Teddy's old nemesis.

They exchanged a cool nod. Even though she and Kate had reached an uneasy truce at the end of last semester, Teddy knew better than to let her guard down around a competitor. Kate Atkins would do anything she could to get ahead.

Clint's deep baritone broke through the chatter of students catching up about their summer vacations: "My office, Teddy. Ten minutes."

Teddy sighed. They'd all shown up late. Why was she always on the chopping block?

She dropped her duffel in the lobby of Harris Hall, then walked—slowly, stretching those ten minutes—back to Fort McDowell and trudged up the familiar staircase to Clint's office.

"Hey," she said, poking her head inside his open office door. "You wanted to see me?" She sent another zing to her mental shield, making sure the electric barrier that surrounded her mind was up in full force. She may have been exhausted, but she wasn't an idiot. Clint Corbett was a powerful telepath.

Clint shoved aside the papers he'd been working on. As Teddy stepped into the room, she couldn't help but check him over for traces of what had happened last year, when Clint had been shot by Brett Evans—a student who had betrayed them to join the Patriot Corps. She had used her newly learned telekinesis to slow time and alter the bullet's path, changing the trajectory from Clint's chest to his shoulder. He still looked like the former college linebacker she'd met all those months ago in the Bellagio, but his movements were more measured, as if his recovery was taking longer than he liked.

"How are you feeling?" she asked.

He raised his arm above his head, showing how far he could extend it. "I'm in PT three times a week. But I didn't call you in here to give you a report on my shoulder mobility. Why were you late?"

She slipped into the chair. It didn't feel great to be back in the so-called hot seat. Didn't feel great to be starting this year on the wrong foot, especially with Clint. Despite everything that had happened between them, despite the fact that she wasn't sure she could trust him, his approval still meant a lot to her. Though Teddy would rather run ten of Boyd's obstacle courses than admit it.

"It's kind of a long story," she said.

"I have time," Clint said.

She ran the moves in her head. Lie to him? Tell the truth? Neither was a great option, so she decided she'd do a little bit of both. She sent another pulse of energy to her shield and said, "We were following a lead. Hoping to find Molly. But, well, it didn't pan out."

"Like you followed a lead last year, Teddy?"

Yes, she'd screwed up before, but that was before. She made a face and didn't bother to reply.

After a beat, Clint turned and opened a drawer in the file cabinet behind him. He pulled out a thick folder. "I've been doing some research, too," he said. "I've managed to identify another member of the Patriot Corps, based on some incidents in the late nineties."

"What kind of incidents?" Teddy went through her mental Rolodex. There was the earthquake in Los Angeles that she was convinced had a paranormal cause. The Ukrainian assassination. The freak train derailment in Portugal. And then the bombing in New York . . .

"A series of vigilante bombings. One of the members of the Patriot Corps was captured on camera, exiting the building just before the bomb exploded. With this new lead, we have a clear directive for how to proceed with our investigation."

Teddy shifted forward in her seat, her heart beating erratically in her chest. This was a game changer. They had a name. A solid lead. Someone to track down. "Who?"

"Marysue Delaney."

She stared at him. Then laughed. Because at first her mind couldn't process what Clint was saying. And if she laughed, somehow she could turn his words into what she was sure they must be: a joke. "You . . . you can't be serious."

"I've confirmed it with other officials," Clint said. "It's definitive. I'm sorry."

He reached into the manila folder and withdrew a single black-and-white photo, placing it on the desk in front of her. This was an elaborate joke, Teddy knew.

But Clint wasn't smiling. Reluctantly, Teddy lifted the photo: a woman, dressed in a pale blouse and slim skirt, her dark hair caught in a ponytail, walking away from a high-rise office building. Her features were contorted, her body tense. Nonetheless, Teddy recognized her.

Teddy set the photograph down and allowed her gaze to wander Clint's office as her mind raced, frantically searching for explanations. All right, maybe this wasn't a joke. But it must be a misunderstanding. Teddy thought back to the vision she'd had of her mother running down the Sector Three corridor, so full of righteous fury. It was impossible to believe Marysue had become a willing participant in the PC. None of it made sense.

She looked at him. "Clint, you knew my mother. You were friends. You can't believe—"

He paused to tap his index finger against the photo. "Facts are stubborn things."

"It's not a fact, Clint. It's a photograph. We don't know the context. Maybe it was just a coincidence that she was there at all."

"A coincidence? Please."

"If you took a picture of Molly last year, you'd think she was guilty, too."

"Teddy." Clint's brow furrowed. "Molly *was* guilty. She got caught up in a bad situation. She tried to fix her mistakes, but . . ." He trailed off as if unable to finish the thought: they had all let her down in the end. "You're not being objective here," he said.

"I am being objective! The Patriot Corps must have done something to my mother, just like they did something to Molly. We're missing something here, Clint. I can sense it."

"You *sense* it?" he said, his tone just incredulous enough to set her teeth on edge. "With psychic insights? Are you simply projecting your wishes here? Or have you seen something you're not sharing?"

She'd seen something, all right, back in Sector Three. "You just have to trust me on this."

Clint waved that away. "I trust proof. I know this is hard for you to accept, but if your mother played a part in that bombing, she has to face the consequences of her actions."

Teddy said nothing.

The silence stretched to uncomfortable lengths. He studied her for a long moment, then sighed. "I wanted to do you this courtesy. We're investigating this lead. And we've got to do this right. We're all under scrutiny this year. You, after that stunt you pulled breaking in to the FBI offices last year. Me, due to my mishandling of Yates's case and his subsequent escape. I now have higher-ups questioning whether I'm qualified to teach law enforcement, let alone run this place."

The admission—that Clint's position as dean of Whitfield Institute had come under review after the discovery of his role in last year's Yates scandal—was news to her. But she couldn't say she was entirely surprised. Clint, Mr. By-the-Book himself, had broken his number one rule to put Yates in prison, psychically tampering with Yates's mind to coerce a confession. A move that was so far outside the policies he preached that she'd been stunned when she'd first learned of it. A move that proved how committed Clint was to putting members of the PC away. For good.

"Yates hasn't made contact, has he?" he asked.

She sent another burst of energy to her shield, watching the electricity climb higher in her mind's eye. "I thought he might reach out over the summer," she said, finding another way to hide the truth without lying. Her fingers brushed the necklace in her pocket. "He promised to help, but you know Yates."

"Right," he said. "I guess I'm not surprised that he used you, just like he uses everyone." Clint reached for the photograph of Marysue, tucked it back in the manila folder, and filed it away. "What matters is that we both have the same goal. Stopping the PC. Which means stopping Yates. Marysue will lead us to them. If you want to make amends for your actions last year, you'll be on board with this, recruit."

Teddy paused, considering her options. She could end this now. Report her meeting in Jackpot. Give Yates up. But Yates was the one person in the world who could help Teddy find her mother—and not because he wanted to put her in jail. As she considered which man to trust, Teddy stacked Clint's track record against Yates's. There was no question that her allegiances lay with Clint. But she couldn't let him get to Marysue first. She couldn't give up Derek Yates yet.

As though sensing her resistance, Clint said, "You got that, Teddy?"

She snapped her attention back to Clint as he rolled his stiff shoulder. "Got it. So, we done?" She stood, anxious to put an end to the conversation.

"Almost." Clint thumbed through another file on his desk. "I've been reviewing the plan for our tutorial sessions. Last year you told me about your dreams of a yellow house."

"The yellow house?" she said, voice cracking. She was a better liar than this. Maybe Pyro was right. She was losing her poker face. She cleared her throat and tried again. "What about it?"

"Astral travelers often have their first out-of-body experiences through altered states. Dreams, specifically, when their minds are relaxed. If those dreams felt different, it's not a stretch to assume that if you're able to extend your astral body for telekinesis, maybe you've also had OBEs during sleep."

"I think I would know if I was having an out-of-body experience," she said.

"You didn't know for years that you were psychic."

True.

Teddy mulled that over. Astral travel. First Yates and now Clint. Had Yates been right about her mother's necklace unlocking some sort of potential in her ability? Immediately, she released her grip on the stone and crossed her arms over her chest, conscious of keeping her hands as far from the necklace in her pocket as possible.

Maybe that was what had triggered her experience back at Sector Three. Which meant she couldn't have gone back to that memory without the necklace. *No*, she corrected herself, it wasn't a memory. If what Clint said was true, astral travel had taken her back in time.

"The point is," Clint continued, "it's worth exploring in our tutorials. Especially since your OBEs seem connected to your experiences with your mother. This year you'll be working with Dunn on psychometry—"

"I'm not a psychometrist," she protested. She only knew one psychometrist who had the ability to glean psychic information through touch: Jeremy Lee.

"I know. But all students will learn to use psychometry to hone their abilities. Another tool in your arsenal. It's especially useful for evidence investigation. I believe that if we find an object of Marysue's, it may be able to focus your travels. We may be able to find her."

The knowledge that she had a conduit to Marysue in her pocket filled Teddy with more hope than she'd felt in a long time. Maybe ever. She was about to embark on a dangerous game, though it was one she'd played before: keeping secrets from Clint while trying to stay one step ahead of Yates.

He dismissed her with a curt nod. "I'll see you at the end of the week for our first session."

"I'll be ready." She already was.

CHAPTER SEVEN

IF ANYONE HAD TOLD TEDDY CANNON A YEAR AGO that she would *willingly* sit on a Zen meditation lawn—actually meditating, mind you, not because she was trying to avoid someone to whom she owed money—she would have laughed out loud. But when she was confronted by the familiar sign (*Meditation Lawn: Please Remove Shoes*) after leaving Clint's office, Teddy kicked off her combat boots and sat cross-legged on the grass.

She took a deep breath and felt in her pocket for her mother's necklace. She wished it had come with operating instructions, or at least a warning, like Jillian's natural vetiver-patchouli essential oil: *not to be taken orally*. She tried to center herself, to pull up Dunn's meditation techniques. She could do this on her own. She'd done it a day ago in Sector Three.

But no matter how calm she willed her mind, and how hard she pushed to try to connect to the necklace, nothing happened. The sky began to darken, the wind picked up, and Teddy had to face the facts: she was still sitting barefoot and cross-legged on the grass and about to get rained on.

Teddy pulled on her boots and climbed the stairs to the third floor of Harris Hall. As second-years, Teddy and Jillian had been given a bigger room than the year before. It had the same austere pine furniture and cots as their previous quarters, but with two large windows and a sunny exposure, it was definitely a step up. If only the view was a little more inspiring than Alcatraz.

Jillian had already made her mark. Potted ivy, lavender, and sage lined the windowsills. A colorful quilt was draped over one of the beds, a framed vinyl album cover of the Grateful Dead hung by a dresser. Teddy's gaze settled on what lay beneath it: a photo of Jillian and Eli in an antique silver frame. She picked it up for a closer look. Eli and Jillian stood in front of an animal shelter. Jillian held a rangy-looking mutt. Eli held Jillian. They both beamed.

The door opened and Jillian entered, wrapped in a brightly patterned bathrobe, hair dripping wet from the shower.

Teddy put down the photograph. "How's it possible that you've already unpacked, decorated, and showered? I'm still wearing the same underwear from before we left for Jackpot," she said.

Jillian shrugged, set aside her shower caddy, and tugged a comb through her tangle of long blond curls. As she did, Teddy noticed the new earrings again, the bars glinting in her friend's ears. She'd messed up by forgetting Jillian's birthday.

Teddy was determined to make amends. She made her way to her side of the room, unzipped her duffel, and pulled out her sheets. "How about we hit the Cantina Friday night?" she said. "I hear since we made it through our first year, we can leave campus as we please." Jillian remained silent, so Teddy kept rambling. "Or would you rather venture to San Francisco? I owe you birthday drinks."

"Actually, I've already made plans to meet someone at the Cantina on Friday."

"Already? You've unpacked, decorated, showered, and made plans?" Teddy let out a laugh that sounded pathetic even to her ears. "Second-year meet-up I didn't know about?"

Jillian shook her head. "I'm meeting Eli. We have to go over some HEAT business that I didn't get to before I left for Jackpot."

"Eli's coming here? To the Cantina? Do you think that's a good idea?"

Jillian shrugged. "He thinks Whitfield is for law enforcement training, just like everyone else."

"Still," Teddy said. Though *technically*, it wasn't against the rules, the fact that Jillian had invited a nonpsychic to Angel Island put her on edge. If Eli found out what really happened at their super-secret psychic training facility . . . What would the consequences be for Jillian? Expulsion? Teddy couldn't lose someone else. "Don't you think it's a little risky?"

Jillian turned to look at her. "Listen, Teddy, if there's anything I've learned from being your friend, it's that some risks are worth it. I like this guy." She blushed. "Maybe even more than I should, considering how long I've known him."

That Teddy could understand. Hearts on the table. But there was something about Eli that Teddy didn't like. And it wasn't just his cargo shorts.

But she bit back her criticism and any mean-spirited comments about Eli's street style. "If you're happy, I'm happy too," she said. It was a lie. A big one. She hoped Jillian couldn't see through her poker face.

Jillian smiled. "Thanks, I am."

Teddy turned back to her duffel bag and watched as Jillian took out a notebook and a small manual about interpreting canine dreams. Jillian had always been Teddy's shoulder to lean on when she needed it. And Teddy needed her now. The possibility of Marysue's involvement in the darker aspects of the Patriot Corps remained something Teddy refused to accept.

"So," Teddy began, trying to change the subject, "I met with Clint today. He had a theory about my mom. He thinks she was an active participant in that New York bombing."

Jillian looked up from her notebook. "It's definitely a possibility, right?"

"Well, yeah. But . . ." Teddy took a breath. "He wants me to help track her down. Bring her to justice, like Yates."

"That makes sense, I guess. For Clint." Jillian glanced down at her work. "Hey, I've got to get this done. Can we talk later? I'm going to the library to see if there's a book on animal thought patterns and theories of consciousness."

What was Jillian saying? That Clint was right? Just whose side was she on, anyway?

Teddy looked away, busying herself with tucking in her sheets. She was angry, embarrassed. "Yeah, sure. Whatever."

Jillian grabbed her bag, and then she was gone. Teddy studied the door. She knew she and Jillian were going through a rough patch, but her friend's dismissal seemed plain cold.

Not wanting to be alone, Teddy wandered down the hall. She found Dara in her room, sitting cross-legged on her bed, a manila folder in front of her.

"Studying already?" Teddy said. "You trying to make me look bad?"

"Not studying," Dara said. "Well, not schoolwork, at least." She nodded to the corner of her plaid comforter. "Sit down." Teddy sat. Dara went on, "It's Molly's Whitfield file."

"Really?" Teddy leaned closer. She had pulled a similar stunt last year, with the help of her occasional nemesis Kate. Teddy had been trying to verify a story about an altercation between Molly and another student. But she'd merely looked at the paperwork, not taken it outright. "How'd you manage to sneak that from the file room?"

"I may have told the secretary in the main office that I had a death vision about her husband. Grabbed my head and groaned. She freaked and then ran out of the room to call him. Once the coast was clear, it was pretty easy to find the folder in the file room."

"Remind me never to get on your bad side."

Dara tucked a platinum braid behind her ear. Like Teddy's, her lobes were studded with multiple piercings. "I can't stop thinking about Molly," she said. "All summer long, I kept believing I saw her. I'd be walking down the street, and I'd see her turning the corner up ahead. In a coffee shop, I thought she was sitting at the table behind me. Like she was lurking at the edges of my vision, but when I turned to look, she'd just . . . vanish."

Teddy nodded, telling herself that was what a good friend would do.

"I asked a hacker friend in New Orleans who dabbles on the Darknet to put a feeler out. He's got his connections, but honestly, it's a long shot."

"It's always worth taking a shot," Teddy agreed, though in truth she had little faith that Molly would be found online. Yes, Molly was well-known in hacker circles, but under an alias. Or multiple. If someone with Molly's skill set wanted to be found, she would be. And if she didn't . . .

Dara took a deep breath, as though summoning her courage. "So I promised myself I'd do some digging when I got back to school. I'm not going to let her just disappear."

Teddy nodded at the file. "What does it say?"

"Haven't been able to bring myself to look yet."

Teddy opened the folder and flipped past several pages' worth of Molly's Whitfield transcripts. Nothing remarkable. That was followed by a page with the heading: *Molly Quinn—Known IP Addresses*. Beneath was a column of numbers. She showed the page to Dara. "What does this mean?"

"A way to track Molly's presence online," Dara said. "I'll pass that on to my contact in New Orleans." She folded the page and slipped it into her notebook. "What else?"

"Eversley's medical report from Molly's accident," Teddy said, turning to the next page. But before she could finish scanning it, Dara snatched it from her hand. "Hey, I was reading that," Teddy protested.

Dara ignored her. Her brows drew together as she skimmed the medical jargon. "This isn't about Molly's accident. Look at the dates. It starts from second semester last year. That was *before* Molly was injured in her fall."

She passed it back to Teddy, who scanned Eversley's summary:

Subject seems to have had temporary suppression of genetic expression (though not completely silenced). Markers still present in bloodwork. Further testing necessary to track. Subject reports altered mood, depression, fatigue, headaches, inflammation, trouble sleeping. Keep monitoring. Recommend discontinuing medication at this time until further trial research has been completed.

Teddy turned to the next page. Another entry:

Some ability returned, but not all. Still cannot determine what the cause of repression patterns—testing points to chemical intervention, but potentially paired with some sort of endoscopic surgery. Pituitary involved? Need to find way to examine—

"He was experimenting on her," Dara said.

"Testing. Monitoring," Teddy countered, not wanting Dara to get lost in the conspiracy theories she so loved. "After Molly came back from break. She was . . . different, we all noticed it. Jeremy hinted that maybe the PC had helped her curb her abilities."

"But Teddy," Dara said, "Eversley doesn't work for the PC."

"What else could this mean?"

"I don't know, but we owe it to Molly to find out. To find her."

They sat there for a long moment. Trying to understand what could have happened to their friend.

"Do you think the PC has her?" Teddy asked. Was Molly somewhere undergoing more experiments, like the ones her father had at Sector Three?

"I don't know." Dara pointed at the jewelry around Teddy's neck. "But if that thing really works, maybe it can help us find out."

Teddy's hand went to her throat, where she felt the cool stone of her mother's necklace. She hadn't even been conscious of slipping it on. She pulled it off over her head and tucked it back in her pocket. "Jeremy must be involved," Teddy said, recalling with a chill their toxic relationship.

"I never understood what she saw in him," Dara said.

"Kind of like Jillian and Eli."

Dara shook her head. "I don't personally understand that attraction, either. I tend to lean more toward those who eat less hemp." She closed the folder. "Distract me."

Teddy smiled. "Are you sure? After . . ." She trailed off, indicating the file.

"We're not going to find Molly tonight. But maybe I can prevent you from smothering Jillian with a handwoven tapestry while she sleeps."

Teddy took a deep, grateful breath and launched into the whole story, starting with the disturbing vision she'd had of her parents in Sector Three, and ending with Clint's promise to help her hone the ability to use an object as a conduit to astral travel.

"You know what the travel stuff reminds me of?" Dara said. "The Stargate Project."

"What's that? Another conspiracy?" Teddy asked.

"You never heard of it?"

"I don't go as deep into the inner recesses of Reddit conspiracy theory forums as you do."

Dara laughed. "This one's on Wikipedia. Government program in the eighties, designed to explore remote psychic viewing. Or traveling."

"I wonder why they stopped it."

"Probably didn't. Just took it deep underground."

"Literally underground," Teddy agreed, thinking about Sector Three.

"Or Whitfield," Dara said. She arched one pierced eyebrow. "How's that for a conspiracy theory?"

Teddy laughed. Then finally looked around the room, noticing the bright pink bedspread and plethora of scented candles. "Oh my God, I'm sorry. I didn't even ask who you're saddled with this year, now that Molly's—"

Just then the door opened and Ava Laureau entered, throwing a look of casual disgust at Teddy's presence. Teddy didn't recognize her at first, because Ava wore a gold face mask and had her hair in rollers.

"Beauty-sleep train is about to leave the station, Dara," Ava tsked. "You know this."

"It's ten already?" Teddy asked.

As Ava removed the K-Beauty situation from her face, Teddy stood and moved to the door. "Thanks," she said to Dara. "For listening."

She walked back to her room. Empty. Jillian was probably still in the library working on HEAT business. Teddy slumped on her bed, took the necklace out of her pocket, and studied it once more. If this was the key, she had to find the lock. Or maybe this was the lock and she was the key? Whatever. Metaphors were Clint's thing.

Teddy tried to center her breathing, concentrate her psychic energy. She willed that telltale heat to form in her palm, despite how awful the travel had been. She'd never experienced pain like that. She'd thought her lungs would burst, her head would explode. Not only had the physical experience been disorienting, the emotional toll had been alarming as well. She was willing to go through it all over again, however, if it brought answers. But no matter how hard she squeezed the stone in her hand, the pendant remained cold.

CHAPTER EIGHT

CLASSES STARTED PROMPTLY AT NINE O'CLOCK THE next morning after a healthy and hearty breakfast of vegan flourless blueberry oatcakes with non-dairy vanilla cream. The only thing that would have made it better would have been bacon, lots of bacon. Also if Jillian had somehow acknowledged Teddy instead of focusing all her attention on her canine dream diary.

After breakfast, Teddy walked with Dara to their first class, Psychometry. The familiar room beckoned at the end of the polished parquet hallway. Another thing that beckoned? Nick Stavros, who stood a few feet away from the classroom door.

"Hey," Teddy said, drawing to a stop beside Dara. "I'll meet you inside, okay?"

Dara hesitated outside Professor Dunn's classroom. Following Teddy's gaze, she spotted Nick. "Seriously, Teddy? Not again. I thought you were over it."

"I am over it," Teddy snapped back. "Over *him*. Not that there ever was—Look, never mind. Just go in without me, all right? I'll be there in a second."

She strode—okay, she hoped she strode; she was walking with as much confidence as she could muster—down the hallway toward Nick. She'd seen him at the assembly, but that had been at a distance. This was the first time they'd been up close and personal in months. He looked good. Tan and fit, his dark hair swept back. He'd probably just finished a run, she thought, remembering how he liked to take long, solitary laps around the island.

Last year, running had been her favorite way to clear her head, too. If she were being 100 percent honest with herself, it was also what she'd done to accidentally-on-purpose run into Nick. She blushed at the memory of her almost teenage-like crush.

"Teddy," Nick said, buttoning his jacket, his greeting cool but not unfriendly.

"Hey, Nick." She was surprised at how easy it felt, standing next to him again. She was even more surprised to find that the nervousness she usually felt around him was gone. Maybe her crush was, well, crushed. Too much had happened between them to ever go back to the way it was. Now there was only one thing she wanted, and it wasn't his arms around her waist, as nice as it was.

He looked over her shoulder at the other students filing into the classroom. "Something I can do for you?"

"Yeah," she said. "I just wanted to make sure we're okay. After, you know, everything that happened."

His expression gave nothing away, so she watched his eyes. She could just as easily have pushed into his head. But that would have been a violation of trust. She was beyond that now. She was an adult. She may have thought she needed to be with someone like Nick in order to level up into adulthood, but somehow, Teddy found, she was getting to that place all on her own. A flicker of something that might have been amusement flashed through the green depths of his eyes.

"Yeah," he finally said. "I know. And yeah, we're good."

"Good. I'm glad. Because—" She paused, cleared her throat. How was she supposed to say what she really wanted to tell him?

Don't hold what happened last year against me. I want you to hire me at the end of all this. All right, Cannon. Just out with it.

"I'm really hoping for a spot on the FBI track."

His face still gave nothing away, but Teddy could have sworn that the corner of his mouth ticked up. "And why's that?"

"Because I think that's the track I'm best suited for. Also—" She hesitated, considering her words.

Because everything else feels like a dead end or a hopeless riddle.

She needed access to things. Top-secret things. Redacted things. Anything and everything pertaining to the PC. Because a necklace wasn't a cache of information she could read. Because Yates and Clint weren't people she could control. But since she couldn't say that, she decided to go with as much of the truth as she could: "I need to find my birth parents. Find out what happened to them."

"And you think, as an FBI agent, you'll have access to all sorts of information."

She nodded.

"You realize," he said with a sigh, "that's entirely the wrong reason to become an FBI agent. The agency is bigger than anyone's personal life. Even yours."

That stung more than Teddy wanted to let on. He wasn't hearing this right. If she could explain . . . "I know that, Nick. I was just—"

"It's about serving your country. Any good FBI agent understands that. Maybe you will, too, at the end of this." He looked back over her shoulder. "I should get in there."

Before she could say another word, he moved past her and down the hall, then ducked into Professor Dunn's classroom.

Teddy stared after him, telling herself the conversation could have gone worse. She could have made a joke about their one-night stand. Could have mentioned breaking in to the FBI building last year. But in the end, Nick had shot her down.

She gathered her dignity and followed him inside only to find a classroom full of students staring at her and Sergeant Boyd—rather than Professor Dunn—standing at the lectern in front of the room.

Upon Teddy's entrance, Boyd paused dramatically, and her lips curved upward in that tight, poisonous sneer Teddy had spent her entire first year learning to dread. "How nice of you to join us, recruit."

Too bad she'd run away and joined Whitfield Institute rather than the circus. She'd take a lion and a tiger and twenty clowns over Boyd any day. She scrambled into a seat and waited for Whitfield's own version of the three-ring show to begin.

Pyro leaned forward from the chair behind her. "Dara said you were talking to Stavros? Really, Teddy?"

She hissed back, "None of your business."

Boyd's eyes narrowed. "Late *and* disruptive, Cannon? I'll see you in my office after class."

Teddy clenched her jaw. Wouldn't be Whitfield without Boyd on her. The allure of a fresh start sure had worn off fast.

"You have made it through your first year. But don't believe that your place here is safe," Boyd said, addressing the room. "Because you've made it, more will be expected of you—both in the classroom and in the field. This year, we start assessing you for placement on government service tracks."

"I heard a rumor that at the end of the third year, the top students get to pick their track," Kate interrupted.

"I'm getting there, Ms. Atkins. Yes and no," Boyd said. "You may request a specific posting, but there is only one way to influence that outcome." She paused dramatically. "And that is by your performance. Your drive. Your dedication. To that end, we will be evaluating you both in your classes and on your casework. Starting now."

Teddy watched as Boyd turned and seated herself between Nick and Joan Wessner, Whitfield's new Secret Service instructor. Teddy knew that as long as Boyd had a say, she'd never let Teddy pick her own track. Now Professor Amar Dunn ambled to the front of the room, late, as always. His hair was shoulder-length and wavy and wet—no doubt from surfing this morning—his Nirvana concert T-shirt tattered and worn—no doubt from actually attending that concert years earlier. Teddy had underestimated him initially. He looked like he belonged on a beach, not in a classroom. But the guy was a bona fide genius.

"Emotions," Dunn began, lightly tapping against his temple, "do not simply happen up here. Fear makes our palms sweat. Our face goes purple with rage. The sight of someone we love makes our heart leap. We gasp or even faint when shocked. Get goose bumps when spooked. And so on and so forth. In sum, emotions put our body through physiological changes. The more intense the emotion, the stronger our physical reaction. But it's even more than that—why do you think they call it a gut feeling? Because we sense it in our gut. We *feel* with both our body and our mind." Moving to the blackboard, Dunn lifted a piece of chalk and scribbled out a word.

"Psychometry," he said. "Who can tell me what that means?"

Ben Tucker's hand shot up. "The ability to use an inanimate object to gain information about the person or place associated with that object. Like with a photograph of a crime scene: sometimes looking at a picture will trigger a vision." He leaned back in his seat, preening with satisfaction.

"Thank you, Mr. Tucker," Dunn said. "That's certainly a start. But that's not exactly correct."

Teddy was surprised when Dara tentatively raised her hand. "While it's true that a photograph can bring on a vision, we have to also think of objects that don't have implicit narratives."

Teddy studied her friend. Was there more to Dara's new power than she'd shared? The death visions she'd been getting over the summer—could some have been triggered through this kind of psychometric connection?

Dara continued, "Like with an object. For example, from our case last year. Marlena's jewelry." It had been their first field case, and Jillian had performed psychometry when she'd used the murder victim's ring to connect with Marlena's spirit.

Dunn nodded. "As psychics, we can 'read' the energy of these objects, using an item to trigger a psychometric moment—but if you want to be technical . . ." He turned to the board. "Recent studies have shown that emotions are more than just chemical reactions in the brain. Instead, scientists in the field of psychoneuroimmunology are suggesting that emotions are molecules: short chains of amino acids and receptors that can be found throughout the body. Those gut feelings? Emotion molecules in your gut. Psychics have known for years than emotions are tangible and that your DNA leaves behind traces of emotional history to study. Science, it seems, is finally catching up."

Dara cleared her throat. "So that DNA remains on a piece of jewelry, like Marlena's ring."

Or a pendant, Teddy thought. *Like my mother's necklace.*

Dara continued, "What you're saying, Professor Dunn, is that if you consider emotions as entities and not abstractions, then maybe it's not the object itself that will tell us something but the traces of emotion imprinted on that object."

"Exactly."

"How does that help us get a read on an object?" Ben asked.

"Good question, Mr. Tucker. Objects become imbued with genetic material. So technically, what we're doing in psychometry when we touch an object is trying to pick up on those molecules and use them as a way to jump-start our abilities. It's a shortcut. These objects, through touch, may be a way to mitigate limitations to your powers, such as temporal and spatial distance."

Teddy knew Clint wanted her to develop this skill to travel with the necklace. Though Teddy wasn't sure how it would help with astral telepathy. But if psychometry was a shortcut into someone's head? If she could avoid the mental work of building a house? She'd save so much psychic energy.

Ava raised her hand. "When you say 'objects,' you're also talking about murder weapons, right?"

"Certainly," Dunn said, "but not exclusively. As Ms. Jones mentioned, any object significant to a specific event—or important to a person at that event—can be a highly effective psychometric tool." He began to walk up the aisle between the students. "There are psychics who specialize in psychometry, gleaning all sensory information from touch. But it's a skill almost all of us can hone and then employ to receive sensory information that relates to our abilities. Clairaudients will likely hear information when they touch an object. A clairvoyant will have a vision."

"Where does that leave me?" Pyro asked from behind Teddy. "Hard to imagine that controlling fire can relate to all this."

Dunn paused, considering the question. "Guess we'll have to find out." If anyone else had said it, Teddy would have assumed the words were a joke, but Dunn spoke with genuine curiosity. He shot a glance to the corner of the room, where Boyd, Wessner, and Nick watched. "As Sergeant Boyd mentioned, this year we begin evaluating you for government tracks. Obviously, psychometric skills are helpful with evidence work."

FBI. Her chance to prove herself to Nick.

"So, today," Dunn continued, "we're going to attempt to read objects. Learn to sense the human energy permeating the inanimate. I want you to think of your fingertips as magnets and those emotion molecules as metal. You need to draw them to you. Or, if we're thinking more touchy-feely, sense the part of the object that's charged with emotion and then tap in to it. That's how you need to focus your psychic energy. You'll know when it starts working."

"How?" Teddy asked.

"Heat," Pyro answered without missing a beat. "The object will get warm. I guess any stored energy, even psychic energy, can cause an exothermic reaction."

Just like the stone did.

Dunn lifted a black cloth bag and explained that each of them would place a personal possession in it, and then a student would draw an object to read. In order for the exercise to work, the owners had to remain anonymous. Dunn would wait outside with the bag as each student brought him an item.

One by one the students filed into the hall to give their object to Dunn. When it was Teddy's turn to deposit her item into the bag, she hesitated for a moment, holding the necklace in her fist. She wanted desperately to see if another psychic could provide insights into her mother's past. At the same time, she wasn't sure she wanted to risk exposing her mother's secrets.

"Ms. Cannon?" Dunn prompted.

Teddy dropped the pendant in the bag. She returned to the classroom, then watched Boyd, Nick, and Wessner leave the room one by one to deposit a personal item.

Dunn returned, swept his gaze over the room. "Who'd like to go first?"

Ava raised her hand. "As a medium, I've done object work before. So I should be a natural." She sneaked a smile in Nick's direction. Teddy rolled her eyes.

Dunn brought the bag to Ava. She stuck in her hand and retrieved a small American flag pin. Teddy wondered if it belonged to Nick or Boyd. But in truth, it could have belonged to anyone in the room. Maybe Kate, whose family served in the military.

"Remember," Dunn coached, "your fingers are magnets."

Ava nodded, focusing intensely on the task. She rubbed her hands together, then held the pin in her palms.

"Can you feel the energy?" Dunn asked.

"I can."

"Good. Tell us what you sense."

The class fell into a hush. She cocked her head one way and then the other, as if fine-tuning her reception. "Blood," she said. "Blood everywhere. A lot of it. Shock. Pain. It's happening fast. Too fast. It feels hot. I think it's a bullet wound."

"Any read on who the object may belong to?" Dunn guided.

Ava's eyes glazed over as if she were slipping into a trance. Her voice pitched low. "My partner's hit. Call for backup. It's her leg. Protect—"

In seconds, Wessner was up and across the room, grabbing the pin from Ava's hands and slipping it into her own pocket. "You can write down that she passed," Wessner said quietly to Dunn, then went back to her seat in the corner.

Ava smiled wide. Which struck Teddy as . . . wrong.

A stillness settled over the room. "Next?" Dunn said.

The class stayed silent. Not a lot of volunteers eager to follow Ava's performance.

Now or never, Cannon.

Teddy raised a hand.

Dunn brought the black bag and instructed Teddy to remove the first object she touched. She reached in and came out with a wooden bangle bracelet she immediately recognized as Jillian's.

She took a deep breath. *Like magnets,* Dunn had said. Teddy rolled her fingers against her thumbs, generating friction. She picked up the bracelet, closed her eyes, and tried to focus on sensing the Jillian-ness of the jewelry: her split-level in Jersey and her hamster, Fred, and her penchant for patchouli. Her summer with Eli. Eli, what was his deal, anyway? But . . . no. Teddy was supposed to be focusing on the emotion molecules.

She centered her thoughts and tried again. The wood began to warm beneath her fingertips. It was working! Even though she wasn't in the mood, Teddy felt happy. But there was something underneath. Nerves? Anxiety? She felt her heart speed up. And then, without having to do the work of picturing a house and building a bridge into

Jillian's mind, she found her astral self reach out, and all of a sudden, she was inside Jillian's head.

Immediately, Teddy could tell how visiting a memory was different from what she'd experienced when she'd traveled in Sector Three. In the bunker, she had visited the past. She'd been *there*, experiencing events in real time. Now, inside Jillian's thoughts, the edges of the scene were softer, blurrier. Time bounced, and she struggled to pin down the details of what unfolded in front of her.

Jillian and Eli were sitting in a small unfamiliar apartment, and she saw Eli holding a brochure for a company called Hyle Pharmaceuticals. Teddy could make out only snippets of the conversation: Eli telling Jillian that because of the cruel experiments they performed on animals, Hyle Pharmaceuticals was their next target. *We have to stop them. We'll do whatever it takes*, Eli said. Jillian nodded. *Whatever it takes.*

Startled, Teddy dropped the bracelet and looked at her friend. She knew Jillian was in deep, but *whatever it takes?* This didn't feel right.

"Well?" Dunn asked. "What did you see?"

Teddy turned to find everyone in the room watching her expectantly. "Uh . . . the object was Jillian's," she said, then concocted a quick lie. "A past memory with Fred, her pet hamster. From when she was sick."

Jillian tsked and shook her head. "She's not a pet, she's a friend."

"A hamster," Boyd said, shaking her head, clearly unimpressed. Dunn moved on to the next student.

Teddy flushed. Had she blown her chance for FBI track already? Should she have reported what she'd seen? It had been only a conversation, after all. It wasn't like she'd seen them doing anything wrong. But it did sound ominous. Teddy cast a look at Jillian, who avoided her eye. Teddy refocused her attention on the classroom. Her necklace was still in that bag. She cringed at the thought of someone like Kate pulling the pendant from the sack and identifying it as hers.

So she was both relieved and disappointed when Pyro was the one to draw her object out. Obviously, he recognized it as the necklace Yates had given her. But Pyro himself had said that his power probably wouldn't be useful in any psychometric practice. Teddy bit the inside of her lip, hoping that if he got any information about her mother, he would have the sense to lie in front of the class, as she had done for Jillian.

She didn't have to worry for long, because just moments after wrapping the necklace in his hands, he began to cough, then wiped his eyes. He dropped the necklace, cast a quick glance at Teddy, and then looked at Dunn. "Sorry," he said. "I think there was smoke—like a chimney fire? I'm not really sure."

A chime signaled the end of the lecture. "We'll continue this next time," Dunn called. "Keep fine-tuning your skills."

Teddy stood, hoping to catch Jillian so they could talk about her memory. But Jillian had already grabbed her things and ducked out of the room. Pyro caught up to her in the hall.

"If this is about Nick," she said, "I don't want to hear it."

"It's not." He grabbed her arm and steered her into an empty classroom. "I saw something."

He'd seen something when he held the necklace? She braced herself and said, "Tell me."

"Well, not saw, smelled." He hesitated, as though trying to find the precise words to convey his impression. "Smoke. And almonds."

"Almonds?" Not exactly the answer she expected to hear.

"I know you're not going to want to hear this, Teddy, but I smelled almonds. That means what I reacted to wasn't a regular fire. It was a bomb."

"I don't understand."

"C-4 is an explosive that smells like almonds. Whoever was wearing that necklace was directly involved in a bombing."

Teddy cocked her head, confused. Why did he think this information would be difficult for her? "Pyro, we were all just in Sector Three," she said. "My mother was there years ago. It exploded, remember?"

"That wasn't a C-4 bomb," Pyro said. "We don't know what exactly happened at Sector Three. But when I held that necklace? That was C-4. Your mother was involved in setting off an IED."

Teddy's stomach began to churn. Echoes of the conversation she'd had yesterday with Clint flooded her mind. The photo of Marysue striding past the New York City office building seconds before a bomb went off. And now Pyro was condemning her. Claiming that since Marysue's necklace had triggered the scent of C-4 in his mind, she was directly involved in setting off an IED. A huge leap. A smell wasn't conclusive. And even if they could prove that Marysue had been present at the bombing, no one knew *why* her mother had been there. What her role had been. And until she had those answers, Teddy wasn't going to stop digging.

Draw the emotions to you, Dunn had said. Teddy Cannon wasn't usually the type to do emotions. She preferred to hide behind the familiar defenses of snark and sarcasm. But at night, in those unguarded moments when she'd dreamed of the yellow house, she had felt love and loss, coupled with a strong dose of longing and regret. Maybe even a tinge of anger. Emotions that had frightened her as a small child, for they were hopelessly beyond her understanding. Maybe they still were. But they'd made a strong impression. Teddy felt like she knew her mother, understood her in a way that Pyro and Clint never could.

"I'm sorry, Teddy," Pyro said. "But you need to face the facts. Your mother's an active member of the PC."

"You're wrong," Teddy countered defiantly.

She turned and walked away. The woman she'd met in her dreams never would have willingly committed those crimes. And Teddy was going to prove it.

CHAPTER NINE

"FALL IN!" ROSEMARY BOYD CALLED.

Their first week as sophomores ended with a course in tactical training led by Boyd, the school's sadist in chief. She sent them on warm-up laps around the gym, followed by a turn on the brutal indoor obstacle course they had mastered last year. That meant vaulting over a goalpost barrier, scaling up a wall and rappelling down, scrambling under obstacles on their belly, traversing a wobbly beam without falling, swinging from a ten-foot-high monkey bar using hand-over-hand strength, and flying through the air on a rope. No matter how hard they worked or how well they did, Boyd berated them for getting soft and lazy over the summer.

When the course finally ended, Teddy headed for the locker room, drenched and smelling like the fermented tofu that had been on the menu for lunch. After washing away the evidence of Boyd's socially acceptable BDSM tendencies in a twenty-minute shower, Teddy threw on a pair of Whitfield-issued sweatpants and a clean tee and made her way to Harris Hall.

"Hey!" Dara called out to Teddy as she was leaving the gym. "Everyone's going to the Cantina after dinner to celebrate surviving the first week. You in?"

"Absolutely," Teddy called back.

Back in the dorm room, Teddy waited for Jillian, but she never showed up. So Teddy headed out to the Cantina with Pyro and Dara.

When they got there, they discovered that Jillian and Eli had beat them to it, snagging the best table on the deck, overlooking the beach.

"Should we respect their privacy?" Dara asked.

"Hell, no," Teddy said, and they scraped some chairs over and joined the two lovebirds, putting in a quick order for drinks.

"Why don't you have a seat," Jillian said sarcastically after Dara, Teddy, and Pyro had settled in. A waitress brought over a pitcher of margaritas with some chips and salsa. Teddy stirred her drink as she watched the setting sun turn the sky a blazing pink. A breeze cooled her skin. For a change, the music from the Cantina wasn't an annoying pop song. Instead, the soft rhythm of steel drums echoed around them. It was the perfect end to the day except for one thing.

Eli Nevin.

The presence of Jillian's cargo-shorts-wearing, cause-committed, conversation-monopolizing boyfriend meant they couldn't talk about anything that was happening at Whitfield. Except he wasn't wearing cargo shorts tonight. He was wearing *harem pants*. Could Jillian please take him shopping? And he didn't seem to be interested in discussing anything that didn't directly involve him.

"We're going to *stop* corporate animal testing once and for all," he said, concluding—please, God—his ten-minute rant. "Cruelty-free product development is the way of the future. Trust me."

"Dude, no one is doubting you," Dara said, sighing.

"Animals are *dying*," he continued, as though Dara hadn't spoken. "And for what? To help the profiteers skip to the front of the line with the FDA? So companies like Hyle Pharmaceuticals can get their over-priced drugs to market faster?"

At the mention of Hyle Pharmaceuticals, Teddy sat up straighter. The psychometric insight she'd gained when holding Jillian's bracelet leaped to the front of her thoughts. She hadn't had a chance to ask Jillian about what she'd seen. Granted, this wasn't the ideal place for it, but if she framed her words carefully . . .

"Jillian, how do you feel about what's happening at Hyle?"

"I think it's morally, ethically, and legally wrong. Animal rights are being stripped away, and for what?"

"Animal rights? Sure. I mean, no one wants—"

Jillian interrupted. "Fine, go ahead, minimize it. That's exactly what I'd expect from you, Teddy."

Teddy stared at her friend, stung by the contempt in her voice. "Wait. I only meant—"

"Animals are being *tortured*," she said. "Every day. While we sit here, drinking margaritas. We should be willing to do whatever it takes to protect them. I know I am."

"Whatever it takes?" Teddy said. The phrase she'd heard Jillian use in the memory. Despite the warmth of the evening, a cold chill shot down her spine. "Jillian, what does that even mean? What are you planning to do?"

"Like Eli said. Whatever it takes to stop animal testing." Jillian lifted her chin and squared her shoulders as if daring Teddy to challenge her. "That's what we're going to do."

Teddy shook her head, not quite believing what she was hearing. "Look, I get it. The protection of animals is important to you. But peaceful protests are one thing. Breaking the law is another."

"You're one to talk. After breaking in to the FBI building last year and stealing that—"

"Jillian!" Teddy interrupted, horrified that her friend would spill such a deep secret in front of Eli. As far as he knew, they were all a bunch of law enforcement recruits.

"I'm just saying you're being a bit hypocritical," Jillian said.

Pyro leaned forward and spoke directly to Eli: "Let me ask you something." Teddy knew from his tone that he'd had enough of the Jillian and Eli show. "You have any little kids in your life? A niece or nephew or something?"

"My brother has an eighteen-month-old daughter."

"What's her name?"

"Riley."

"Riley," Pyro repeated. "Cute. Now I want you to try to imagine how you might feel about animal testing if there were a new drug that could save Riley from a fatal disease, and a couple of lab rats had to be sacrificed to develop it. Would you be okay with that?"

Eli snorted in response. "There are ways to test drugs without torturing animals," he insisted. "That's why I started HEAT in the first place."

"I'm just saying it might be worth sacrificing a rodent or two if it meant saving someone's baby, you know?"

"That's a bit a species-ist," Jillian said to Pyro. "Who are we to decide which lives and dies?"

Pyro shrugged. "Guilty as charged. With the exception of a few politicians, I think most humans are superior to rats."

"A joke? You think this is funny?"

"Jillian, relax, Pyro was just—"

"They're testing their new drugs on dogs," Eli interrupted, "man's best friend, right? The one animal on the planet that has the greatest emotional connection to human beings. So much so that some owners claim their dogs have an actual sixth sense. Don't you think we have a duty to protect the creatures we share this earth with?"

Pyro drained his margarita and leaned back in his chair. "Whatever, man. Just keep talking. Seems to be what you're good at."

Teddy was aware of the other patrons in the Cantina laughing and having a good time while she flicked salt from the rim of her glass. Dara averted her gaze and toyed with the empty chip basket.

Jillian shoved back her chair and stood. "Don't we have to get to San Francisco?" she asked Eli. "The ferry will be here any minute."

Teddy was about to object when she remembered that they were second-years and allowed off the island without permission— provided they returned by curfew, which, on Friday, meant midnight.

Teddy wondered if she should remind Jillian. But her friend already looked so pissed that Teddy kept her mouth shut as Jillian and Eli said goodbye and headed off toward the ferry.

"That went well," Dara said wryly.

As Teddy watched them go, she couldn't help but think about another friend she'd failed: Molly. Jeremy had been there at every turn, taking her down an increasingly dark road toward *whatever-it-takesville*. She couldn't let Jillian follow that same path. "I should have stopped her," she said.

Dara took another sip of her drink. "She's a grown woman."

"She has such awful judgment when it comes to Eli, though. *He's* talking *her* into things that could ruin her career."

"She's got a right to make her own mistakes," Pyro said. Then he looked at Teddy. "Besides, how do you know what he's talking her into doing?"

Teddy slumped back, deflated. "It's just . . . I'm worried. When I held Jillian's bracelet, I saw her and Eli discussing Hyle Pharmaceuticals. They said they were going to do whatever it takes to stop animal testing."

Pyro raised an eyebrow. "You don't say."

"It's different," Teddy snapped, knowing Pyro was thinking of his own glimpse of Teddy's mother and the C-4 bomb. "Eli and Jillian were discussing an attack. We have more information, more context."

"An attack?" Dara prompted. "Did they say attack?"

"Well, no, but they said they'd do whatever it takes to stop animal testing."

"Which could mean organizing a boycott. Or writing letters. Or starting a Facebook page." Dara frowned. "We can't go around accusing people of crimes they haven't committed. We're getting into some real *Minority Report* shit if you open that can of worms."

Teddy pulled at the edge of the paper napkin under her drink. She watched the paper fibers dissolve in the condensation. "So what now?"

Dara blotted her mouth with a napkin and stood. "Nothing. I'm beat. Ava snores, and I need to get to sleep before she does. You coming?"

Before Teddy could reply, Pyro tucked his hand around her back. He found the bare slip of skin between her T-shirt and jeans, his fingers drawing lazy circles of heat. A gesture that belonged outside the lines of the friend zone they'd established. Another pass of his hand, and Teddy felt herself unwillingly relax into his touch. After the emotional toll of their first week at Whitfield, she didn't want to pull away. It felt good. Crazy good, considering she kind of wanted to both punch and jump the person who was touching her.

"I think I'll stay a little longer," she said.

Dara looked between the two of them. "Whatever, you two. Good night," she said, then walked off in the direction of the campus.

Teddy leaned in to Pyro; if they were going to do this, they needed rules. And they needed to clear the air. "Feel like heading down to the beach?" she said.

"Good idea."

He tossed a couple twenties on the table, then grabbed her hand and led her toward the pier. They took off their shoes and walked along the water's edge. Teddy, for once, let herself be led. The sand was cool beneath her feet, and the lap of gentle waves against the shore was the most soothing sound she could imagine. She'd suggested a walk on the beach so they could talk. But her good intentions faded as she felt that familiar attraction spark between them. Pyro moved closer. Her alarm bells sounded.

She ignored them.

The moment stretched. Her gaze locked on Pyro's. The question of a kiss rose between them. No, not a question. An inevitability.

That mysterious pull that seemed to always hover between them was even more present. When he leaned in to kiss her, Teddy gave herself permission to lace her hands around his neck. Soon it became one of those feels-too-good-to-stop moments, fueled by margaritas and overwhelming, why-fight-it chemistry. She pulled him closer. Granted, she might regret it in the morning, but right then, regret was not an emotion she struggled with.

She melted in to him. She traced her hands across his shoulders, then drew her palms down flat against his chest, thrilling at the erratic beat of his heart.

She was ready to lose herself, but Pyro misunderstood—perhaps thinking she meant to push him away—and drew back slightly, breaking their kiss.

"Teddy?" His dark eyes searched hers. He stepped away from her, his posture stiff. "It's about Dunn's class, isn't it? The stuff I picked up when I held your mother's necklace."

"What are you talking about?"

"You're pissed at me for telling you the truth about your mother."

What?

Her brain took a moment to catch up.

The truth? His version of it, more like.

Anger flashed through Teddy. Reining it in, she kept her tone firm and reasonable. Eventually, she'd prove him wrong, but this wasn't the time or the place for that discussion. "Look," she said, "I'm glad you told me. Don't ever hold anything back because you think I can't handle it, okay?"

He studied her. "You sure?"

"Yeah, I'm sure."

He seemed to accept her reply, but as she thought about what he had said, it was clear that whatever had been between them had cooled. That was what had felt so perfect about Pyro. The *not* thinking. Just allowing herself to be swept away. She turned and looked toward campus.

"We should head back."

"Already?"

She took a breath. "I'm sorry," she said. "It's just like I said in that diner in Jackpot. I don't think I can do this right now. There's just too much going on. I have to concentrate on what's important."

His expression tightened. "What's important. Right."

She registered his reaction when the words hit. And the realization that followed.

You're not important.

Not what she meant at all. But more explanations would only make it worse. They turned away from the water and began the uphill climb toward the campus in silence. At the lobby of her dorm, Pyro paused. "Eventually," he said, "you're going to realize that you can't do this alone. I know you think you're a hotshot poker player, but this time, you mucked the wrong card."

CHAPTER TEN

TEDDY WAITED FOR THE DOOR TO CLICK SHUT BEhind her, adding a strange sense of finality to Pyro's goodbye. He was telling her she'd screwed up. And a little nagging voice whispered that maybe he was right. From the first moment she'd met him, everything about Lucas Costa had screamed EASY SEXY FUN TIMES. But lately? Fun, sure. Sexy? Definitely. Easy? Hell, no. She liked Pyro. More than she wanted to admit. She liked to look at him, she liked to touch him, she liked that thing he did with his tongue . . . But she needed to get serious about her life. There was so much on the line. And the red-hot distraction that was Pyro would derail everything.

Teddy kicked off her boots, noticing that sand had gotten into her socks. She glanced at the empty bed on the other side of her room. If she could talk over this Pyro thing with Jillian, she'd feel so much better. But Jillian was now another problem that Teddy had to worry about. There were only so many things she could keep track of at once.

She flopped down on her bed, hugging her pillow to her chest. Did normal twentysomethings have to deal with all this crap? Or just people like psychics at places like Whitfield?

Whether it was from the margaritas or the sheer exhaustion, Teddy couldn't tell, but before she knew it—sandy feet and all—she was facedown on her bed, still wearing her jeans, sinking fast into a dark and dreamless sleep.

———

She woke to beeping. An incessant beeping. Not chanting. Not sage. Not talks about circadian rhythms. Definitely not naked yoga (which, though she'd acclimated to it, she didn't really enjoy). She reached out to swat away her alarm, causing the cheap plastic clock to crash to the floor. Teddy rubbed her eyes. She had a headache. She cracked one eye open. She couldn't see straight, but it wasn't because of a measly margarita; she was better than that. She just didn't want to face the day, not after her interactions with Pyro and Jillian.

Speaking of.

Teddy turned to look at the twin bed across the room. Her roommate's quilt was still tucked in. Teddy hadn't heard Jillian come in last night. And that was because she hadn't. The thought set Teddy on edge. Who would have guessed that her roommate would turn into such a rule breaker?

When they'd planned to break in to the FBI last year in order to procure the suppressed information needed to free Derek Yates, Jillian had been the one to point out the moral implication: *Either way, it's wrong*. At the time, Teddy hadn't been sure that Jillian would help. But now she would do whatever it took? Jillian had always been committed to animals, but this was different. This was about Eli.

Teddy shucked off her covers. She picked up the necklace on her nightstand, rubbed the stone in her palm, tried to generate heat, to connect to her mother. The stone stayed cold. Frustrated, she put the necklace in her nightstand drawer and slammed it shut. She needed to clear her head. A run would be just the thing. She threw on shorts and a tee, laced her sneakers, and headed out to the trail.

Afterward, showered and dressed, she made her way to Harris Hall for breakfast. The chef must have been in a good mood because there were eggs on the menu, not egg substitutes. Saturday mornings, sophomores had class until noon; then they were free for the rest of the weekend. Jillian hadn't made an appearance yet.

Dara was seated at a table there, however, deep in conversation with her roommate, Ava Laureau. Teddy heard raised voices all the way from the buffet but didn't expect the topic.

"Do not try to tell me that *The Next Generation* is the best iteration of the series. Have you seen *Deep Space Nine*? I mean, have you *really* watched it?" Dara said, anger at the edges of her voice.

"Of course I've seen all of *Deep Space Nine*." Ava flipped her hair. "Who do you think I am?"

"What's going on, Cannon?" came a voice from behind her. One that could belong only to Kate Atkins. Her tray was piled with eggs, gluten-free toast, and orange juice, as well as a glass of thick green sludge that Teddy really didn't want to know about.

Teddy nodded toward Ava and Dara as she walked over and took a seat next to the pair. "I think they've found common ground."

"Oh yeah?" Kate raised her eyebrows, then slipped into the chair beside her.

The discussion continued for a few more minutes, delving into the merits of Captains Picard versus Sisko, before Ava broke it off with an exaggerated groan. "If we're having this argument this early, I need coffee, or whatever chicory crap they serve here." She left the table.

"Care to explain?" Teddy said to Dara.

"What's to explain? She's a Trekkie." Dara pushed around her oatmeal. Chimes sounded, signaling the start of their first Secret Service class—and still no sign of Jillian.

Teddy, mindful that Kate was sitting next to her, said with all the casualness she could muster, "Seen Jillian this morning?"

Dara's eyebrows furrowed. "Nope, why?"

Dammit.

"No reason. Thought she came down to breakfast early." The second chime sounded, and they gathered their plates.

Dara and Kate turned toward the academic halls of Fort McDowell, but Teddy hung behind. Maybe Jillian was back in their room? What happened if a recruit missed class because she was freeing a bunch of animals from a lab in San Francisco?

"You coming, Cannon?" Kate said.

Teddy hesitated. "Going to grab some chicory. I'll be right there." She turned back to the buffet, pretending to busy herself with a bamboo cup. When she turned around, she almost ran smack into Pyro.

"Hey," he said.

"Hey," she said flatly, then looked over his shoulder for any sign of Jillian.

"What, am I boring you already?" His voice had an edge. Anger? Hurt? Either way, she didn't have time right now.

"Jillian didn't come home last night. And she's not back on campus."

"And you think this has something to do with the hippie?"

Teddy nodded.

Another chime. They'd be late if they didn't hightail it to the gymnasium. On the way, Teddy filled him in. Not only about Jillian but also about what she'd seen when she'd held Jillian's bracelet. How she didn't want Jillian to risk her standing at school for a guy like Eli—even if she believed in the cause.

They stopped at the gymnasium. Teddy could see the other second-years assembled on the bleachers. Wessner called from inside: "I start my classes on time, recruits!" Teddy took a deep breath. Another day at Whitfield was about to begin, with or without her roommate.

Even before the lecture started, Teddy could tell that she liked Joan Wessner. It wasn't her perfectly pleated wide-leg gray pants, or her crisp white starched blouse (standard G-man-wear or, in this case, G-woman). It was that she seemed to care. Teddy saw a seership textbook from last year resting beside Wessner's manual about Secret Service protocol. Many government workers—including Nick—were reluctant to work with psychics. But before them stood a government employee who wanted to learn more about psychics. Refreshing, to say the least.

Wessner scanned the room. "We're missing someone," she said. "Who?"

"My roommate," Teddy said. "Sick this morning. I—"

"Dropped her off at the infirmary," Pyro said. "With Nurse Bell. She won't make it to class."

Both Kate and Dara turned toward Teddy, obviously confused. Dara mouthed, *What are you talking about?*

"How unfortunate." Wessner frowned, her hand resting on the seership textbook. "I thought psychics didn't get sick. I was talking to Professor Dunn the other day, and he mentioned that your immune systems didn't function the same way as nonpsychics'."

Teddy took a moment to process Wessner's words. Due to her misdiagnosis of epilepsy, Teddy had spent most of her life thinking of herself as someone with a chronic illness. So it had never occurred to her that she was actually remarkably healthy. As she reflected on a childhood full of the usual flu shots and doctors' trips, she realized that she'd never had a cold she hadn't faked in order to get out of something.

Before she could respond, the door opened, and Jillian entered in a tumble of blond hair. "Sorry I'm late, I made—"

"A miraculous recovery!" Teddy said.

"Yeah, you really looked like crap this morning, Jillian," Pyro said. "Must have been a bad headache." Jillian gave him a hurt look, and he added, "No offense."

In truth, Jillian did look bad. Dark circles beneath her eyes, her face unusually pale. Gone were the signature fringe jacket and the vintage prints. Instead, she wore skinny jeans and a dark henley that looked like they'd come from Teddy's own wardrobe.

As the attention centered on her, Jillian froze. Teddy could see her trying to process these obvious clues and then, after literally mouthing, *Oh*, she coughed once. "Yeah, feeling a lot better now." She sat down in an empty chair next to Teddy.

Wessner looked down at her paper. "Ms. Blustein, I take it?"

"Yes, ma'am," Jillian said, and then whispered to Teddy, "I owe you one."

"Just tell me you didn't do anything stupid," Teddy said under her breath, "and we're even."

"It's not *stupid*." Jillian pressed her lips together and turned to face the front of the classroom.

Wessner began. "I want to tell you a little about myself before we learn the protocol of the best and most challenging job in the United States government." As she walked the length of the room, Teddy couldn't help but notice the way she leaned on her right side.

"I was raised Catholic," Wessner continued, "so the psychic stuff is new to me. But I'm here to learn, just like you. And I trust that as much as I make the effort to study and respect your craft, you, in turn, will respect mine." She scanned the room, stopping at Jillian.

From the back, Teddy heard someone scoff. "Walking beside a limo, guarding some political stiff in a parade, doesn't seem *that* hard," Zac Rogers said.

Wessner's gaze snapped to where Zac sat. "If that's all you think the Secret Service does, you're sorely mistaken, Mr.——"

"Rogers," he said.

"The Secret Service started as a counterfeiting agency. We still serve in that role. In addition to protecting high-level government dignitaries, the Service is involved in various areas of intelligence and investigation. Do not mistake me. This is the highest level of government service."

"It was just a joke," Zac grumbled.

"And we joke that our agents go to the FBI when they need a vacation. The type of training you will be doing in my class will test your mental, physical, and psychological strength. If you want to succeed, you have to forget every defense strategy you've been taught in your other tactical classes. In order to give your life to protect someone else, you'll have to overcome the most basic instincts of self-preservation." Wessner paused, shifting her weight to her good leg. "Ordinarily, when shots are fired, you assume a defensive stance. You seek cover. In this classroom, when shots are fired? There's no hesitation. You're not seeking cover. You are the cover."

Wessner's speech silenced everyone.

"And that brings me to my second point. If shots are fired, you've already lost. Think Lincoln, Kennedy. None of those shooters needed a second shot to get it right. Your job is to surveil and identify threats *before* anything happens. You may be psychics. But my agents would give any of you a run for your money."

Teddy glanced to the obstacle course on the other side of the gymnasium with fresh eyes. In Boyd's class, they'd assessed every hurdle to minimize impact and conserve energy—the exercises had been in survival, even for a team. What plans did Wessner have that changed that? To the left of the course, Teddy saw a massive tarp covering a lumpy pile. Whatever Wessner had in store, odds were it lay under there.

Wessner's next words proved that guess correct.

"Meet your clients," she said. She walked over to the course and pulled off the black tarp, revealing a pile of burlap dummies. They'd seen those dummies. Last year in Boyd's first obstacle course from hell. "These are your protectees for the morning. They'll be your charges as you make your way through the obstacle course." Wessner blew a whistle, and the doors opened. Several students Teddy didn't recognize walked in. "I've solicited the help of some underclassmen and some paintball guns. Your job will be to complete the course without your protectee getting shot. That means you do what you need to to get the job done. It's not elegant, but we like to call this tactic 'being a meat shield.' You're going to get as big and wide and tall as you can."

Liz's hand shot up. "What if you're, well, vertically challenged?" Her petite frame had worked to her advantage when she was a gymnast, but in this test, not so much.

Wessner raised an eyebrow. "I do not think that assassins trying to kill the president of the United States care how tall you are, Ms.——?"

"Cook."

"Get creative, Ms. Cook. Use your abilities." Wessner flipped through the papers in her hand. "Says here you were on the short list for Team USA in 2012. Seems like you'll figure it out."

As they left the bleachers and moved toward the course, the door opened again. Boyd, Nick, and Clint entered. Teddy had almost forgotten. They would be evaluated at every turn. Just what she needed: more pressure to get it right.

"I think I'm going to name mine Cannon," Kate said, hefting a dummy onto her back.

Teddy snorted. "Yeah, and mine is Atkins. We'll see who has the last laugh when they finish first."

"If you don't complete the course, you're out," Wessner said. "If your dummy gets shot, you're out. Today I'm not looking for technique. I'm not looking for pretty. I'm looking for who has the raw material. Who can use what they've got to make it to the end. Who can fight against their instincts to protect their target."

Teddy picked up a dummy, hoisted it onto her shoulders. She could barely make it across the vault solo. And with an extra hundred pounds? She looked over her shoulder and saw Jillian yawn and struggle to grab one of dummies under the arms. She'd obviously been up all night with Eli.

Beside her, Kate nodded toward Jillian. "Looks like someone has a future as a security guard if she keeps this up."

Teddy's heart sank. She wanted to help Jillian, but she needed to ace this thing. She was already on Clint's shit list, and the semester had barely started. Nick wouldn't be doing her any favors. Boyd hated her.

"On my whistle," Wessner said.

Here's nothing.

But really:

Here's everything.

The chance to look good in front of her instructors, the hope of getting FBI track, the opportunity to kick Kate Atkins's ass. And then all Teddy could think about was how to lug a hundred pounds through Boyd's wet-dream obstacle course without getting shot with paintballs, falling on her face, or dropping the damn dummy. She was ready.

CHAPTER ELEVEN

NONE OF THEM MADE IT THROUGH THE OBSTACLE course.

"Failures. All of you," Wessner pronounced.

It had been optimistic, to say the least, when Teddy had dreamed of smoking Kate Atkins. Hauling a dummy though that hellscape had proved insanely difficult. Teddy had held out long enough to make it across the vault about three seconds after Kate hurled herself over. And Zac had eaten his words about the Secret Service when Wessner had personally shot both him and his dummy with a paintball halfway through the course.

The rigor of Secret Service training, on top of their military tactics, seership, and other casework, increased the second-year course load dramatically. So much that Teddy hadn't considered what loomed ahead on Monday afternoon until it arrived: her first tutorial with Clint.

Last year, they'd met to work on her telepathy and telekinesis. This year, they would be studying astral travel. She wanted to use the necklace to visit her mother's past. She wanted to know the truth, but deep down, she was a little afraid. Okay, maybe not afraid. Hesitant? Reluctant? A tiny bit nervous?

But she needed to learn how to master this skill. Which meant making Clint think she was fully on board with whatever plan he had to find Marysue. No—make that *capture* Marysue. So as she hiked the stairs to Clint's office in Fort McDowell, she did what she had to do. She put her mental shields up. And her wall? Supercharged.

She gave a sharp rap on his door and stepped inside. Her eyes went to the chalkboard behind his desk—a creaky relic in a wooden frame that looked like it was from the seventies. On it, he had drawn some sort of crazy diagram filled with multiple lines, x's, and o's. It looked like a hallucinogenic football play.

"Am I trying out for Whitfield's first psychic football squad?" Teddy said, pointing to the chalkboard. "Because I'm not really into organized sports."

Clint pressed his lips together in what Teddy knew was an effort to suppress a smile.

She yearned for things to be the way they had been last year— when she had played eager screwup and he her willing mentor. But too much had happened between them to ever go back to that.

"Have a seat," he said.

She dropped her backpack and slipped into the chair opposite him.

Clint took a deep breath. "This is serious, Teddy. Astral travel is dangerous. You could get hurt. Alter history. Trap yourself on the astral plane forever."

Teddy let that sink in. She'd had no clue what she was doing in Sector Three. What if her accidental trip had trapped her in that particular time loop—watching her father's torture, her mother's desperate panic—for eternity? She shuddered.

"Travel happens when your astral self separates from your physical self. Just like in your telekinesis. But instead of extending only one part of your body, you're going to detach completely. We'll begin by working on foundations. Then we'll work on moving through space—how to project your astral self onto different points in the present time line. Afterward, we can think about looking toward the past. As the diagram explains."

He stood at the chalkboard, pointing to the x's and o's, though

Teddy wasn't sure what each letter was supposed to represent. Was she an *x*? Or an *o*? Whatever letter, Clint was basically telling her that she could teleport.

"It's important to remember the astral principle that time isn't linear but simultaneous. Then you can travel anywhere you want. It's not about going backward or forward. Just about switching lanes." Clint flipped the board over. "Traveling in the present is the easiest. You're not projecting yourself through time. Just space. We call this remote viewing. It's the most common skill. Remote viewers use their astral bodies to see locations thousands of miles away."

Teddy's thoughts flickered to Stargate, the top-secret government program Dara had mentioned. She watched as Clint drew a circle on the board, which Teddy assumed was a representation of her. Underneath, he wrote the word *present*.

"The past is trickier," he said. "Events are fixed. But to be able to sift through time to find exactly the right moment? It can be like finding a needle in a haystack." *Past* went in the bottom left corner of the board. "And traveling to the future? As you know from last year, psychics can have visions of multiple futures, some that never come to pass. So visiting a future event will be the most challenging of all." At the top right of the chalkboard, Clint wrote the word *future*. "My hope for you, Teddy, as someone with astral abilities? Is that you can master them all." He drew a diagonal slash across the board, connecting past, present, and future.

"So," Teddy said. "No big deal."

"I know it seems like a lot, but we'll do it in stages. Our first goal is to work on present travel. As I mentioned, that's the simplest." He tossed aside the chalk and resumed his seat. "On that topic, I wanted to talk about your yellow-house dreams from last year."

She tensed. "What about them?"

"Was your mother there?"

Teddy recalled the warmth she'd felt the first time she'd walked up the steps of the cottage. The cheerful green door, the smell of dinner cooking. She'd felt her mother's presence. "Sometimes." She looked at Clint. "Why, can people see me when I travel?"

"No. But there's evidence suggesting that other astral travelers can see or at least sense each other's presence."

Her mother had noticed her in Sector Three. But in the yellow house, Teddy had never even seen her mother. Yet Teddy had always felt an intuition, like Marysue was right there waiting for her just around the corner.

Clint didn't have to push into Teddy's head to read her thoughts. "I think you were traveling in those dreams. To the past or the present or even the future, I'm not sure. Only you know what you saw, what you felt. But in altered states—like through dreams, meditation, or certain drugs—it becomes easier to separate your astral body and to visit other locations and time lines."

The dreams had felt real. Maybe that was why they'd had such a deep impact on her over the years. Before she'd ever set foot in the house in Jackpot, she'd recognized it. She'd known every hallway, every room. Because she'd been there. Her astral travel had taken her there.

Clint continued. "It's fortunate that you're studying psychometry this year with Professor Dunn. There may be a shortcut for us here. Not that I'm a fan of shortcuts, but there's an astral theory about a phenomenon called Pilgrim's Tunnels."

"What, does it take you back to the first Thanksgiving?" Teddy asked. "Can we reveal the holidays as a crock made up by Hallmark?"

C'mon. Laugh. If you laugh, I can convince myself there's a chance you're not going to punish my mother at the end of all this.

Clint narrowed his eyes. "No. It's named after a famous traveler named Robert Pilgrim. They're vortexes—tunnels through time and space that let you travel without doing the meditative work of separating your bodies—"

"Tunnels?" Teddy said, her heart rate picking up. That was what it had felt like back in the bunker, like she was being forced through a tunnel. But Clint was saying her body had stayed in the present Sector Three, and only her astral self had ventured through time.

"Tunnels, yes. With the help of an object related to the event or person you're trying to locate, the psychometric connection creates a vortex or a tunnel. We're working on finding an object of Marysue's, but Pilgrim theorized that this shortcut would be possible even without an object, if the traveler was connected to the event or person. Especially if the connection was genetic. And since you mentioned your dreams . . ." Clint trailed off.

Teddy fought the urge to reach into her pocket and touch her mother's pendant. "When do we start?"

"In a minute," he said. "I want to caution you about travel, especially to the past. Because there are rules you must adhere to. First, you can't change what's happened."

Unbidden, Teddy's eyes settled on the screw that sat on Clint's desk. The one from Sector Three. The one that Clint kept to remind himself of what had happened, what he'd lost.

"What's done is done, Teddy. What's in the past stays there."

"I've seen *The Butterfly Effect*," Teddy said. "Even though I wish I hadn't. Not Ashton Kutcher's greatest work."

Clint crossed his arms. Gave her The Look.

"All right. I get it, don't touch anything."

"Don't be flip about this. Your astral body, just like in your telekinesis, is able to interact with the physical world. So sure, it may seem like a joke to move"—Clint looked down at his desk—"a screw. But who knows what the ramifications might be? It's called the butterfly effect for a reason. Even the smallest event, like the landing of a butterfly, can result in world-altering repercussions for the future."

"Understood."

"I hope so. Any change you make to the past, even if it's accidental, could result in a future you're not a part of and erase the fact that you ever existed, leaving you with no physical body to come back to. You'd be trapped in the astral plane forever."

Teddy rubbed her forehead. This was a lot. She thought of her impromptu OBE in Sector Three. She hadn't touched anything, but still. Teddy knew herself. If she'd done something . . . She ran her finger over her arm. Remembered the shattered glass. "You said that my astral body can touch physical objects. That means I can get hurt while traveling."

Clint nodded. "If you're wounded while traveling, your physical body will be wounded. And if you die while traveling, the entirety of your consciousness—who you are—will cease to exist. Doctors may be able to heal your physical body, but what's left would be an empty shell."

Teddy shivered.

"Are you with me, Teddy? Knowing all the risks?"

She wasn't with him, not like he thought. But he didn't have to know that. She sent another burst of energy to her mental shield and nodded. "I'm ready."

"Good." His impassive features rarely gave anything away, but she didn't miss the flash of relief that crossed his face. In that instant, she realized that Clint needed her, just like Yates did. She stored that bit of knowledge away. When people were desperate, Teddy Cannon could use it to her advantage.

Clint gestured to the couch in the corner of his office. "Today I'd like to guide you through some meditation in order to work on detaching your astral body completely from your physical body." He turned on a CD player. New age music filled the room—hand cymbals, a flowing creek, a flute. So like Jillian, and so unlike Clint. Teddy settled on the couch and tried to relax as he began to recite the guided meditation, telling her to be conscious of her breathing, counting to four so she would slow down her inhalations and exhalations. But she couldn't. She felt his anxious stare like a weight upon her mind.

Teddy felt utterly relieved when a knock on Clint's door interrupted them. "I'm sorry. I should have put a sign up," he said.

The door opened and there stood Nick, who looked from Clint to Teddy. "Apologies, I didn't realize I was interrupting."

"It's fine." Teddy swung her legs over the side of the couch and sat up. She was grateful for a reprieve. "Only the possibility of me traveling through time and space and being trapped forever in another vortex."

Nick furrowed his brow. "I can come back—"

"What is it, Nick?" Clint asked.

"You know that break-in Boyd asked me to look into?" He paused, shot a significant glance at Teddy. "I just received some information."

Clint nodded at Teddy. She got the memo. Time to go. "I was just leaving." She stood and grabbed her backpack.

She made a hasty exit and closed the door behind her but lingered for just a moment, curious about this mysterious break-in that had captured Boyd's attention. She assumed it was something that had happened on campus. Another break-in at the lab, maybe. Was Jeremy back? Some news of Molly? But as they spoke, the low rumble of Clint's voice produced two words with distinct clarity.

Hyle Pharmaceuticals.

CHAPTER TWELVE

TEDDY FROZE OUTSIDE CLINT'S OFFICE. IF SHE COULD pull off astral travel, she'd be behind that door in a heartbeat. A break-in at Hyle Pharmaceuticals. The likelihood that her friend and said friend's alternative-pants-wearing activist boyfriend were involved? One hundred percent. Whitfield dining hall organically cleared, USDA-certified, no additives, preservatives, or artificial flavors required, Grade-A definitely.

Teddy rubbed her forehead. That was why Jillian had pulled that all-nighter on Friday in San Francisco. It all added up now: missing curfew, her dark clothing, her reluctance to account for her whereabouts. The chance that Nick would discover Jillian's involvement was practically guaranteed. He was an FBI agent, after all. No way would two amateurs be able to break in to a pharmaceutical lab without leaving some evidence behind. Knowing Jillian, she had probably cuddled half the dogs in the lab, leaving her DNA on every surface possible.

Oh, Jillian. What have you done?

Even though Teddy wanted to hear more, she had to get back to the dorm to warn Jillian. Right after giving her a talking-to for her recklessness. Being an activist was one thing. But this was breaking and entering. It was exactly the kind of illegal activity that could get Jillian kicked out of Whitfield. Teddy couldn't let that happen. She'd already lost Molly. She wouldn't lose another friend.

By the time Teddy reached her room, she'd worked herself into a state of high anxiety. If she didn't take a breath and calm down, she'd end up ripping Jillian a new aura instead of getting the information she needed to understand what was happening in Clint's office. *Be there for her*, Teddy coached herself. *That's what friends do.* She thought back to last year, when Jillian had done that for her.

Inside their room, she found Jillian lying down with a damp washcloth on her forehead. Teddy stopped in the doorway. Obviously Jillian hadn't slept well (if she'd slept at all) in the last couple of days. As she entered, Jillian removed the washcloth and glanced up: her usually bright eyes were dull.

Teddy took a deep breath and tried to channel her roommate's cheerier disposition. "Hey there. You okay?"

Jillian didn't respond.

"Look, we need to talk about whatever's going on with you and Eli."

Jillian blinked once and resumed her very important task of studying the water stains on the ceiling.

Teddy took a step closer to Jillian's bed. Maybe a joke would lighten the mood, bring her out of her funk. "If it'll make you feel better, I can chant. I can sage this whole place down. But I'm drawing the line at anything involving nudity."

Jillian blinked again. That was when Teddy ran out of patience. "I just came from Clint's office," she said. "They know about the break-in at Hyle Pharmaceuticals."

Finally, after a silence that lasted too long for comfort, Jillian drew in a ragged breath and said, "You have no idea what they're doing to the animals in that lab. Testing some kind of new drug on them. There was this one black Lab. Sadie. She must have been, like, twelve years old. Oh, Teddy, it was horrible."

Teddy wanted to yell at her for being so stupid that she'd gotten caught, but the middle of a sob story about a furry pharmaceutical test subject wasn't the best moment.

"What happened?" she asked instead.

"After HEAT found out what was going on in the lab, we came up with a plan to break in and set the animals free."

Whatever it takes.

Finally, Teddy knew exactly what that meant—days too late to do anything about it.

Jillian continued, "I told Eli I knew about secured facilities. That I'd had some experience getting in and out without detection. But the whole thing was a disaster."

She seemed relieved to be confiding in Teddy. But with each new detail of the botched mission, Teddy felt worse. Jillian, plus animals in danger, multiplied by Eli, equaled bad decisions—ones driven by emotion, not by logic.

"Why didn't you talk to me before you did anything?" Teddy asked.

"I wanted to. But you were so rude to Eli the other night. You didn't care at all about the animals. None of you did. How could I expect you to understand why we had to break in and stop it?"

"So this is all my fault?"

"This isn't about you, Teddy." Jillian reached for a crumpled tissue and dabbed at her cheeks, then leaned back against her pillow. "The point is, we weren't doing any harm. We just wanted to free those poor dogs. We didn't get far, anyway. A security guard spotted us, so we ran."

"You were seen? Jesus, Jillian." Teddy ran a hand through her hair. "If you get kicked out of Whitfield, then what? You won't be able to help anyone, human or animal. You really want to risk everything you've worked so hard for? Is Eli worth it?"

Jillian's eyes flashed. "Yes, as a matter of fact, he is. But I didn't do it for Eli. I did it for the animals. Someone needed to take action on their behalf. And even though we didn't release them, at least we have proof of Hyle's misdoings." She stood abruptly, went to her desk to shuffle through her papers, then tossed a lab report on Teddy's lap. "There, read it for yourself."

Teddy ignored it. She didn't need to open the report to read the writing on the wall: Jillian Blustein was about to be expelled from Whitfield for breaking in to a secure lab. And not for the first time.

"Listen, when Clint asks you about the lab, can you say that it was Eli's idea? That you had no idea what he'd planned until it was too late?"

"I knew what I was getting into."

"I understand that, but—"

"Forget it, Teddy. I'm not throwing Eli under the bus."

Teddy couldn't believe it. Even when Jillian's ass was on the line, she was still worried about Eli. Teddy switched tactics and tried again. "Look, Nick and Clint must know that someone from school is involved with the break-in, otherwise, why would they be looking into it? Boyd *ordered* the investigation. After what happened last year, that means there'll be serious consequences."

Jillian went quiet, her eyes now dry. Teddy waited for Jillian to soften again so she could continue. That was what had always happened before. But this time Jillian spoke first. "Yeah," she said. "Well, whose fault it that?"

Ouch.

Before Teddy could think of a reply, Dara appeared at the door. "Hey," she said. "Boyd is looking for you."

"Me?" Teddy asked. Force of habit, because Boyd was perennially pissed at her.

"Not you," Dara said. "Boyd's in Clint's office with Nick. They want to see Jillian right away. And they don't look happy."

Teddy waited in the room for Jillian to return. After two hours had passed, Teddy wandered to Clint's office to see if the interrogation was still under way, harboring the vague, absurdly unlikely idea that she might be able to help. But no. Clint's office was locked, and the lights were off. Nor was Jillian at the dining hall, the gym, or the library. Fighting back images of her friend being strong-armed onto a ferry and escorted off the island, Teddy made her way down to the docks. No sign of Jillian there, either. Her concern mounting, Teddy turned to hike back to main campus.

When she was back at the door of her room, before she could insert her key, Jillian's high-pitched giggle echoed into the hall. Teddy's concern turned to anger. She'd spent hours walking around campus looking for her roommate, and she'd been in their room playing carefree schoolgirl?

A second later, the door swung open, revealing Pyro. In her room. With Jillian.

But one glance past him let her know there was nothing funny going on. At least not *that* kind of funny.

Jillian stood on her bed, waving two silk scarves in the air. "And when you talk to a cow," she was telling Dara, "you can't put up with any bull. Get it?"

"Yeah, Jillian." Dara sighed. "I get it."

Pyro grimaced at Teddy. "She might have gone a little overboard with the tequila."

"You think?" Teddy reached for the bottle. Break-ins and now contraband. She wondered if she knew Jillian at all.

Dara frowned at Teddy. "What happened to you?"

"Oh, nothing much. I just spent the last two hours wandering around like a complete idiot, looking for Jillian."

"You did?" Jillian trilled, bouncing on the bed. She gave a puzzled frown. "Why? I've been here."

Teddy turned to Pyro. "Where'd you get tequila?"

"One of the security guards owed me a favor. So he didn't check my bag on the way up from the Cantina." Pyro poured Teddy a shot.

She downed it, then brought up her glass for another. Screw the rules. She was pissed, she was tired, and since she'd skipped dinner looking for her ungrateful friend, who hadn't even had the courtesy to come back to their room after the meeting and tell her what had happened, she was hungry. Might as well add irritated as hell to the list while she was at it.

"Well?" Teddy said. "What happened with Boyd?"

"Probation," Jillian said, as if it were a death sentence. "For three whole months. I'm basically under house arrest for the rest of the semester. I can't leave the island. And that means I can't see Eli."

Teddy's mood immediately brightened. For maybe the first time in history, Teddy Cannon actually agreed with Rosemary Boyd. It looked like her roommate was about to undergo a mandatory little Eli Nevin detox. A punishment worthy of a celebration.

Jillian sank down on the mattress. "Boyd wanted to kick me out of school, but Clint wouldn't let her. He said that since the security guard showed up before we released the animals, there was no actual crime committed—well, except for B and E." She paused, giggled. "Nick kept calling it B and E. Do you know what that stands for, Pyro?"

"Breaking and entering."

"Right! *Not* bacon and eggs. Or business and economics. Breaking and entering. That's what Eli and I did. Along with probation, I have to write a letter saying I understand the seriousness of my actions."

So Clint had stood up for Jillian. Teddy made a mental note to thank him in their next session. She watched as Jillian flopped back on her pillow, arms splayed. "The room is so dizzy right now." She gave two heavy blinks and closed her eyes. A minute later, she was snoring.

Teddy grabbed the bottle and moved across the room. She settled on the floor, letting Dara sprawl on her bed while Pyro slid into her chair and propped his feet on her desk.

"You may joke that I'm a conspiracy theorist, but what I can't figure out," Dara said, "is what all this has to do with Whitfield Institute."

Teddy looked at her. "Meaning?"

"Why would Boyd order an investigation before they even knew students were involved? They must've just put it together that Jillian broke in. Otherwise Clint would have called her into his office much earlier."

Teddy shrugged. "FBI protocol?"

"From Boyd? She's military. It's not a government lab. Or is it?" Dara said.

"Not sure. I just know that it was a seriously reckless move on Jillian's part," Teddy said.

They sat in silence until Pyro broke it: "When Jillian wakes up tomorrow with a killer hangover, I guess I can't make any 'Who Let the Dogs Out' jokes."

"Yeah, no." As much as she wanted to laugh, Teddy couldn't. "Jillian never used to be like this. It wouldn't have happened if she hadn't met Eli over the summer."

Dara let out a breath. "Well, to be fair, her picker's not great. Remember Brett?"

Teddy frowned at the reminder of Brett Evans, Jillian's love interest last year, a third-year recruit turned PC member. The same Brett Evans who'd shot and almost killed Clint.

"I just get this sense that he's using her." Teddy shrugged. "She doesn't see it that way, obviously."

Dara gave a sorrowful shake of her head. "They never do. Not till it's over."

"I don't know," Pyro put in. "Eli is kind of annoying, but maybe he's got a point."

Teddy turned. "What the hell? You're actually defending the guy?"

"Give me a break. It's just—why dogs?"

"Dogs?"

"We had four German shepherds in our K9 unit. Brave, loyal, smart, playful, the whole bit. It pisses me off to imagine them stuck in a cage somewhere. Don't most labs test their products on mice or rats or whatever? Why is Hyle using dogs?"

Good question. Teddy rummaged through the papers piled near her desk until she found what she was looking for.

"What's that?" Dara asked.

"Something Jillian snatched from the pharmaceutical lab."

"You've been holding out on me. You know I love an illicit report. Gimme."

Teddy swiped her hand away. "I'm reading this."

Dara rolled onto her side and peered over her shoulder. "Waste of time. You don't understand science talk. Admit it."

It was true. Under the daunting heading "Experimentation on Gene Mutation, Expression, and Function in Canine Subjects" loomed a dense paragraph with terms like *adenovirus* and *delivery systems* and *cranial pressure alleviation*. A drug identified as X-498. Teddy couldn't make heads or tails of it. Pun intended.

Her thoughts drifted back to Eli's diatribe at the Cantina Friday night. *Some owners claim their dogs have an actual sixth sense.* Coincidence? Maybe. But Teddy wasn't a big believer in coincidence. She kept reading. Finally, something caught her eye. A name. One she recognized.

Why was the Whitfield Institute so concerned with a break-in at a private lab before it knew that one of its students had been involved?

Printed in bold black type in the byline was the answer: By Dr. David Eversley, MD.

The school doctor at the Whitfield Institute for Law Enforcement Training and Development.

CHAPTER THIRTEEN

WHEN TEDDY HAD ARRIVED AT WHITFIELD LAST YEAR, Dr. Eversley had taken a sample of her blood and explained the founder's intentions to research the scientific origins of psychic expression. Yates had cautioned her about a place that used students as a subject pool. How could she not have seen that Eversley's research would eventually lead here? As much as Teddy hated to admit it, Yates had been right . . . again.

The morning after she read the Hyle Pharmaceuticals report, Teddy stood before Clint's office door with Pyro, Jillian, and Dara at her side. None of them had slept much the night before. They'd spent hours poring over the report, trying to decipher the scientific jargon. Then they'd combed through Molly's file, looking for connections. When their discussion had become heated enough to rouse Jillian from her drunken slumber, they'd filled her in and gone around the issue a second time. But no matter how many hours they spent, they couldn't come to a consensus on what the report meant. Each time, their conversation ended on the same line from Eversley's note in Molly's file: *Patient is excellent candidate for Hyle Pharmaceuticals X-498 clinical trial. Recommend once animal testing is cleared.*

They needed more information. There was only one place to get it.

Teddy took a deep breath and pushed the power to eleven on the electricity that made up her mental shield. Readied herself for what was likely to be an ugly, confrontational meeting.

Pyro placed a reassuring hand on her back. "We're ready," he said. "Let's do this."

Teddy gave him a decisive nod, then lifted her fist and rapped on Clint's office door.

"One second," he called.

Teddy didn't wait. She twisted the handle and stepped inside. Her friends followed.

Clint set down the pen he'd been holding and leaned back in his chair. "Well," he drawled, "looks like you four have something on your mind."

Teddy bit her tongue. A year ago, when they'd first started working together, she'd liked Clint. But now there were too many secrets and half-truths between them. It wasn't that they were on different sides of the table. They were playing different games.

"Well?" he prompted. "Anyone going to tell me what's going on here?"

Teddy passed him the Hyle Pharmaceuticals report, along with Eversely's recommendation that Molly undergo treatment. Teddy had vowed to remain cool and collected, to get the facts regarding Hyle Pharmaceuticals, Molly Quinn, and Dr. Eversley. But as she regarded Clint, she felt her carefully practiced, rational questions evaporating. There was only one phrase that could do this moment justice.

"What the hell, Clint?"

He frowned at the paperwork. "What is this?"

"You tell us."

Clint lifted the pages. A full ten minutes later, he set the paperwork down. His deep voice cut through the suffocating silence. "What I want to know is how you four came into possession of what is clearly a proprietary internal memo belonging to Hyle Pharmaceuticals. As well as a student's classified file."

"*That's* your takeaway?" Teddy's agitation rocketed. "We're not going to play that game. How we got it doesn't matter. What matters is what those papers say."

"Clint, those animals are sick," Jillian said. "What they're doing to them is horrible."

"And Eversley wanted to do that to Molly," Dara interrupted. "Tell us straight, Clint. Does Hyle plan to experiment on psychics?"

"So what happens now that Molly's not here?" Teddy demanded. "Let me guess: they start testing on us. Dose our water, sprinkle it in our granola. You promised this wasn't going to turn into Sector Three."

Clint angled himself to face her. "And I meant it. You have my word."

"Your word. Yeah."

Clint looked offended. "Now wait a minute."

"No. We're not going to wait, Clint. Not this time." Teddy leaned closer. "We want answers. Eversely signed the report. Which means Whitfield Institute is somehow involved. Which is why you and Boyd and Nick handled the break-in. My guess is you wanted to keep it quiet. So what is the exact connection between this school and Hyle Pharmaceuticals?"

Clint set the paperwork on his desk carefully and deliberately, as though they'd handed him something that might explode if not handled with utmost care, rather than a student file and a lab report. He looked between them. "Sit down," he said. "All of you."

Teddy hesitated. Although she hadn't consciously decided to loom over his desk, she didn't want to give up that slight physical advantage. Sensing, however, that they weren't going to get any answers from Clint until they complied, the Misfits each pulled a chair into a loose semicircle in front of his desk and grudgingly sat down.

Clint paused. Squared the bottom of the sheets to the edge of his desk. Raised his gaze and looked at each of them in turn. "Item number one. All of you are aware that Molly Quinn found her gift of empathy a tremendous burden. She *voluntarily* underwent treatment at this institute to alleviate some of the unwanted effects of her psychic ability. When the time was right for her, she voluntarily left this campus. We did not hold her against her will, nor did we ever subject her to a treatment she didn't want. If you look at the bottom of her medical files, you'll see her signature of consent."

That was something. Though Jeremy had implied that the PC had overseen Molly's treatment. Was there another connection they had missed?

"Item number two. Until Jillian and her boyfriend broke in to the lab in San Francisco, Hyle was just a name to me, a Bay Area company that specialized in drug research and development. But you're right. There is a connection to Whitfield Institute. After some investigation, I've learned that Hollis Whitfield is the majority shareholder of Hyle Pharmaceuticals."

Teddy blinked. Wondered for a moment if she'd heard him correctly. Hollis Whitfield, founder of Whitfield Institute, the majority shareholder of Hyle Pharmaceuticals. The implications were horrifying. "How can you be so calm about this?" she demanded.

"Calm?" Clint said. "I'm not calm, Teddy. The truth is, I find it deeply upsetting. But I'm trying to remain objective. Like any good investigator would."

"Right," she scoffed. "Objective. Like you're objective about Yates? About my mother? Were they innocent until proven guilty?"

Clint's face darkened. "That's different."

"How?"

"Because their guilt has been demonstrated beyond a reasonable doubt—whether you want to accept that or not. But we don't have all the facts in this case."

Tense silence filled the room. Clint studied them, his expression inscrutable. After a long beat, he said, "After Jillian's incident, I started looking into Hyle Pharmaceuticals. When I discovered Hollis Whitfield's relationship to the company, I went to him and expressed my concerns. He explained that he'd brought Eversley over to Hyle to work on a specific project because Eversley is one of the best neuroscientists in the world. Hollis wanted his consultation and expertise. That's all. He assured me that there is no crossover between this institute and the drug they're developing."

"And you believe him?" Pyro scoffed.

"Yes."

Dara shook her head. "This memo talks about a gene therapy. Gene therapies cure mutations by replacing them with healthy genes. He wants to *cure* psychicness." As she paused, letting that sink in, Teddy's thoughts flashed to Molly and whatever treatment she had believed would cure her. It hadn't worked. It had changed her. Taken away the very essence of what had made her Molly.

Pyro's thoughts must have been traveling a similar path, for he said, "You can't believe drugs help. Otherwise you wouldn't work at a place like this."

"Exactly," Clint said. "Stop and actually think about that. Carry that logic one step further. Why would Hollis Whitfield, someone who's given millions of dollars to fund an institute for the express purpose of training psychics, want to cure psychicness?"

Pyro folded his arms across his chest, unmoved. "We need to shut Hyle down."

"On what grounds? C'mon, Lucas." Clint released an exasperated breath. "You were a cop. You know the rules as well as I do. Hyle hasn't broken any laws. Until they do, our hands are tied. We wait, we watch, we monitor the situation. Until then, nothing is happening on this campus. And if I thought for one moment that Hollis Whitfield planned to use students for experiments, I never would have signed on to be a part of it. *Never.* You're getting ahead of yourselves."

"But—" Jillian protested.

He held up a hand to stop her. "Yes, Jillian. The process has affected the lives of some animals. Which many drug companies routinely do. Safely and legally."

Teddy looked away. Despite Clint's reassurances, her fears hadn't been allayed in the slightest. Judging by her friends' skeptical expressions, the same was true for them.

"And though I appreciate your concerns, what troubles me," Clint continued, "is that you four have once again taken it upon yourselves to compromise your standing at this institution by bending the rules. By stealing student files. Breaking in to Hyle to satisfy your own personal agenda. Understand that any more of this behavior will not be tolerated. Continue only if you wish to forfeit your place at Whitfield. Am I making myself clear?"

Clint waited until they'd all mumbled their agreement, then shoved back his chair and stood, indicating their interview was at an end. They stood and silently filed out of his office. Teddy was last in line. When she moved to close the door behind her, Clint raised a hand to stop her. She motioned for her friends to go on, then stepped back inside.

"Your astral travel," he said without preamble. "Are you making any progress with the techniques we went over?"

Teddy shrugged. "I've been practicing, but I'm still having trouble."

Clint's eyes narrowed. "Then work on it, recruit. Don't just shrug it off. I thought I made it clear what the stakes are for both of us if we fail to bring down the PC."

Teddy blinked. "Understood," she clipped out. "Anything else?"

"No. Now go get to work."

"Yes, sir." With that, she turned and left Clint standing in the doorway of his office.

"Everything all right?" Pyro asked.

Not even close. They'd gone to Clint for answers, but he'd stonewalled them with promises that he was monitoring Hyle. But that didn't mean she intended to let the matter drop. The images of her father at Sector Three were too fresh in her mind. Logically, she understood what she'd seen had happened decades ago. Her father was gone. Even if she could master her astral travel enough to go back and release him from his leather bindings, free him from Sector Three, Teddy understood that her actions would set off a chain of events, whatever they were, that would change the future. Butterfly effect and all. Though she was a rule breaker, a rebel, even Teddy Cannon knew there were certain rules you didn't mess with. But the pain she'd seen. What those government officials had done to him . . .

And what if it was going to happen once more, at Hyle Pharmaceuticals? She felt the weight of her mother's crystal around her neck. Had Marysue somehow influenced the direction of her OBE, sending her back to that particular place and time as a warning? If so, Teddy wouldn't let her mother down, either. She couldn't alter the past, but she could damn well stop it from happening again. If Clint wouldn't give them the information they needed, she knew someone who would.

That night, before joining her friends for dinner, she went down to the Cantina and bought a postcard. A nice one that said: *Wish You Were Here!*

CHAPTER FOURTEEN

FOR THE NEXT THREE DAYS, TEDDY WALKED DOWN to the pier to watch tourists exit the ferry. Laughing and good-humored, they duckwalked down the plank, their gaits thrown off by the rocking of the boat. Tonight, a spectacular sunset lit the sky rose and orange behind them. These were the smart ones, she thought. The tourists who knew to skip San Francisco in the summer, when the sky was cold and damp and leaden with fog. The best time to visit was in the fall, when the crowds were gone, the air was warm, and the off-season rates meant everything was cheaper.

She waited until the last passenger exited the ferry, then turned around to make the trek back to campus. She spotted Pyro standing a few yards away, watching her. She went to join him. "Hey," she said. "What's up?"

He looked past her, scanning the group of new arrivals. Then his gaze returned to Teddy. "Disappointed?"

"What do you mean?"

"You sent for him, didn't you?" Before she could deny it, he took in her running clothes, and one corner of his mouth quirked up. "You're not exactly known for taking long jogs before dinner just for the fun of it. You've been coming down here the past three days, checking to see if Yates got your message."

She didn't bother to deny it. Yes, she'd sent the message. A Hail

Mary, to use one of Clint's football analogies. "And you don't approve."

"If I didn't, would it stop you?"

"Pyro—"

"He's a con, Teddy. I know how cons work. He was just buying time when he gave you that mailing address, giving you what you wanted so he could manipulate you."

Yates wasn't a liar. He'd already proved that, but Pyro still wasn't convinced. Frustrated, Teddy turned and studied the shoreline. She and Pyro kept reaching the same stalemate. Whether the subject was Marysue's guilt or Yates's motivations, they constantly found opposite ground. There had to be a way to make him understand.

She tugged a hand through her hair. "Do you remember when I passed out back in Sector Three?"

"Yeah. Why?"

"I didn't actually pass out."

"But we saw you—"

"Not in the normal sense, anyway. I had an astral travel experience. I went back in time to when my parents were there. I was in the lab when my father was being experimented on. Tortured, more accurately. I saw it happening."

"Why the hell didn't you say anything?"

She paused, considering how to express what it was that she wanted to say: *Because how could you have understood when I barely do?* Instead, she shrugged.

He caught her by the wrist and pulled her up against him, her back pressed up against his chest. Wrapped his arms around her and rested his chin lightly atop her head. She eased back against him. He felt strong and solid. They stood like that for a long moment, watching the sun sink into the bay.

"I'm glad you told me," he said. "Is there anything I can do?"

"Yeah, there is."

"What?"

"You can try to understand why I can't let this thing with Hyle Pharmaceuticals go. Not after I saw what they did in that lab to my father. I won't let it happen again."

"Clint swears it's not happening."

"And if Clint's wrong?"

She reached into her pocket, felt for her mother's necklace. The answers were out there, answers she desperately needed but didn't know how to access. Even with her mother's pendant. It was like getting a computer for Christmas and then hearing: *Surprise! No internet.*

"What if Yates is the only one who can help me?" she said. She didn't know what other options she had. She wasn't about to break in to Hyle Pharmaceuticals. Not worth getting kicked out of Whitfield, and she had no doubt Clint would make good on his threat. Other than pursue Eversley directly (which she doubted would bring results), she seemed to be back at square one.

"Hey, Teddy."

"Yeah?"

"Screw Yates." His signature smirk returned. "You've got me."

Pyro and Teddy walked back to her dorm room. Teddy sat on the edge of her mattress. Jillian would be out of the room until well after nine, at a tutorial with Ava and Professor Dunn for mediumship. Teddy patted the space next to her and said, "Okay. We've got the room to ourselves for the next two hours. Let's do it."

Pyro leaned against her closet door, folded his arms over his chest, and regarded her through narrowed eyes. "You've got to be kidding. I can't keep up with all this 'Are we or aren't we?' business."

She threw a pillow at him. "Not that." As much as *that* would be really freaking great right now. She wanted to feel outside of herself.

Wanted not to think. Wanted that great big shattering release. But traveling, in a way, would accomplish the same thing. Or *almost* the same thing, if she could finally manage it.

"What do you need me to do?" he asked.

"Clint has me working on meditations. I suck at them."

Pyro sat on the bed next to her as she explained how the process worked. Before she could effectively direct her astral travel, she needed to let go of all interfering thoughts. Jillian could fall into a deep meditative state in an instant. So could most of her classmates. Teddy, however, constantly struggled to calm her mind. She hated letting her guard down, hated feeling vulnerable and exposed. She hoped, however, that guided meditations—with someone she could trust—would help.

Pyro kicked off his shoes and lay down on her bed, holding one arm open to invite her to join him. Teddy stretched out against him, resting her cheek on his chest. Her head rose slightly with every breath he took.

"Ready?" he asked.

"Yes." She clearly and firmly set her goal: separate from her body and direct her consciousness through space. She felt safe and secure. Relaxed.

"Feel the air enter your lungs," Pyro began, his voice low and steady in her ear. He counted to four to set a gentle rhythm for her breaths, then guided her through Professor Dunn's meditation techniques step-by-step, encouraging her to let go of stress, to silence her thoughts.

Teddy felt the tension seep from her body. She forgot about Sector Three and her father and mother. Yates. Molly. While usually, she waited for Clint to signal a movement from one phase of the exercise to the next, now she lost track of time, content to simply be in this moment—weightless.

Then, in a quicksilver instant, everything changed. Her lungs constricted, cutting off her air supply. She felt sharp, piercing pain in her chest. She opened her mouth to alert Pyro that something was wrong but found that she couldn't speak. She felt herself drop, plummeting downward, as though the bed beneath her had been snatched away. It felt like the gravity that bound her to the earth had ceased to exist. She blinked and discovered that she was still in her dorm room—but no longer on her bed.

Rather, her *body* was on her bed, lying against Pyro, but *she*, her astral self, was floating above, watching.

She hung there, suspended and amazed, until stark terror shot through her. Maybe she'd done it wrong and was dead. Clint had warned her how serious astral travel was, but she hadn't listened. Blinding despair engulfed her. She'd never be able to rejoin her body. The fear hit her like a sucker punch to the chest. Her breath caught, and the room dimmed as she spun.

"All right, Teddy. Time to wake up."

She blinked and tried to focus. It was like she was seeing Pyro doubled—from above and below—before he finally swam into focus as a single living being. Then she slammed back into her physical body. The sensation stung like a full-body belly flop from ten feet above a pool.

Teddy dragged in a ragged breath as relief poured through her. Slowly, she came into awareness of her body. Felt the tingling in her limbs as blood began to flow more rapidly through her arms and legs. Felt a lock of hair brush against her cheek. She wasn't dead. She'd separated her astral self from her physical body and projected herself on the current time line, a first step in astral travel. Until her terror had knocked her out of it, she'd been in a full-fledged OBE.

She'd done it. Deliberately and with intention. She wanted to laugh. Cry. Both. At once. While eating Ben & Jerry's and riding a motorcycle, drinking a fifth of Jack Daniel's, winning the lottery and having the best sex of her entire life.

Speaking of that last part: Teddy wrapped her arms around Pyro's chest and gave him a squeeze. "I did it."

He tilted his chin to look down at her. "Really? It looked to me like you were just taking a nap." She was scanning the ceiling, lost in thought. Her expression must have reflected her amazement, for he shook his head and said, "I can't even imagine. Where'd you go?"

"Not far. Just floating above the bed, watching us."

"Sounds kinky." His lips curled into a suggestive smile.

Teddy smiled back. "Stop it."

"Stop what? You're the one who admitted you like watching us together in bed."

She rolled onto her side, bringing them nose to nose. Her legs tangled with his. Their breath mingled. "Why can't you be good?" she asked.

"Because if I were good, you wouldn't want me."

"You sure?"

"Yeah." He sighed. "Pretty sure."

He toyed with the hem of her T-shirt. With his gaze locked on hers, he traced the skin above her low-slung jeans. She felt herself slip back into the relaxed state she'd been in moments earlier. Pyro made her feel like this. Pyro made her feel good. All of her earlier resistance and rationalization, her determination to remain strictly friends, seemed silly in retrospect. There was something about the two of them that worked.

She felt the heat of his body through her clothes, drew in the familiar scent of his skin. She ran her hand over his chest, felt his heat level start to burn through the thin material of his T-shirt.

Instead of reaching for her, he leaned back, putting a little distance between them. "Hold on, Teddy."

She blinked and pulled back. Frowned. "I thought you wanted—"

He gave a harsh laugh. "You know I do. But . . ."

"But what?"

"I thought about what you said back in that diner in Jackson. You're right. We can't go back to random hookups. Not anymore." He paused, seemed to gather his courage. "We've got too much to lose now. Or at least I do. I don't want to screw it up by screwing around."

She studied him in stunned silence. She and Pyro didn't do this. They teased and they flirted. They messed around. They didn't talk about their feelings. It was exhilarating and terrifying at the same time. The cowardly way out would be to reply with a joke. She had a number of them already on the tip of her tongue. There was a time when Teddy would have done that. But not now.

"I don't want to lose you, either," she admitted. She watched as something that looked like relief spread across his face. "The other night on the beach, you said something about me mucking the wrong card?"

Pyro smiled and slid her toward him. "You must have heard me wrong. I probably said something else. Some other activity that rhymes with *muck*?"

"No, you were right. I did muck the wrong card."

He slid his lips over hers, but Teddy turned slightly. "Wait. Just one more thing."

Pyro groaned. "Please tell me it's not another meditation. Because I'm anything but Zen right now."

He dragged a palm up her thigh. She had to swallow before she could speak. Even then, her voice came out all breathy and warm.

"If you set the fire alarm off again, I'm going to mucking kill you."

CHAPTER FIFTEEN

SEPTEMBER SLID INTO OCTOBER. BETWEEN SESSIONS with her professors and "sessions" with Pyro (one particularly memorable one in a deserted office near the gun range), Teddy found herself wrapped back into the daily life of being a Whitfield student. Still, she found her thoughts continually triangulating between her mother, the Hyle report, and Molly. Not that she was able to do much about any of it.

Jillian and Dara hadn't appreciated having to promise to stay out of Hyle Pharmaceuticals's business (but for different reasons). Nevertheless, they kept their word to stay on track, as did Teddy and Pyro. Teddy's mother's necklace remained tucked in her drawer. A temptation kept out of reach (unlike a certain steamy pyrokinetic) until she mastered travel without the object. And she was getting better. With Clint's guidance, she was able to astral-travel to different locations on campus, but only short distances and only for seconds at a time.

What didn't pass quickly? Rosemary Boyd's torturous training exercises. At that moment, Teddy Cannon found herself finishing the second round of a muscle-melting three-minute plank. She promised herself she wouldn't drop before Kate Atkins did. No sir, no ma'am, not in this lifetime. Not in the next lifetime, either, whether she reincarnated as a human or one of Jillian's pet hamsters.

Teddy shifted her weight on her palms, careful not to press too hard on the knuckle of her right index finger. It had been over a month since she'd astral-traveled to Sector Three, but that damn cut wouldn't heal. It seemed that every training exercise or activity required this finger, whether it was at the gun range or writing reports for casework or tackling the obstacle course. And each time she rebandaged the wound, the image of her father strapped to that metal chair came back to her. If anything Hyle developed came close to what she'd witnessed at Sector Three, she was determined to stomp in there and kick some serious pharmaceutical ass, regardless of what she'd promised Clint.

"Tighten your glutes! Engage your core!" Boyd yelled.

If my core were any more engaged, it would be registered for china at Bed Bath & Beyond.

Sweat slid down her arms. Teddy watched a droplet's journey down her wrist and onto the squishy blue mat that had absorbed the literal blood, sweat, and tears of every recruit who passed through Boyd's obstacle course.

Who in her right mind holds a plank for three minutes? And how, pray tell, does it come in handy in crime fighting?

Teddy shot another glance across the room to where Kate held her perfect alignment. Teddy shifted her hands and felt the scab on her finger tighten, then saw the telltale bloom of red through the Band-Aid.

Crap. Not again.

"All right, recruits. Fall out!" Boyd blew her whistle. Kate's knees dropped to the mat. Teddy's hit a second later. "Good improvement, Cannon."

Not exactly high praise, but she'd take what she could get from Boyd. In truth, she had improved in the last month. And not just on Boyd's sadistic course. She was gaining momentum in all her classes. Dedication with a laser-like focus had that kind of effect on a girl.

On the mat beside her, Dara groaned and rolled over. "Lunch?" she asked. "I hear they're serving lentil burgers."

"Ugh." But Teddy was starving, so she gathered up her things. She caught a glimpse of Boyd in a classic bullying pose, fists perched on hips and face screwed up in anger, lecturing Jillian.

One recruit whose dedication to success was seriously lacking? That would be Ms. Jillian Blustein. Still on probation, Jillian hadn't seen Eli in weeks. Teddy had hoped that Eli Nevin would be "out of sight, out of mind," but instead, he was all Jillian could talk about. Without the ability to go off-island or communicate via traditional means, she'd taken to sending messages via a pigeon she'd befriended and named Burt. But Burt, according to Jillian, had Alzheimer's and did not make a great carrier pigeon, because Eli had not written back.

Or Burt is just a bird, Teddy wanted to suggest. *Or Eli Nevin proved to be an environmentalist asshole who was only interested in using you.*

Teddy watched as Jillian's face turned red. Watched as Boyd walked away and Jillian wiped her eyes and then hurried out of the gymnasium to the bathroom at the end of the corridor.

Teddy waved Dara off and moved to follow her roommate. The bathroom was empty save for the last stall, which was shut. The sound of ragged breathing and desperate sniffles emanated from behind the stall door.

"Jillian? It's me. Are you okay?"

A sharp gasp, then, "Go away."

"C'mon, Jillian. I just want to talk."

"Go away."

As with her travel, the friend thing was getting easier. Even if it meant dealing with messy emotions from animal mediums overly invested in guys who wore bad pants. "I'm not going anywhere. You need a friend right now, and whether you like it or not, you've got me. So get your weepy, Eli-missing, naked-yoga-doing, animal-chatting self out here."

Teddy waited. She heard a snort, though whether it was of laughter or despair, she couldn't say. A second later, the door swung open and Jillian emerged. She looked almost cartoonlike in her misery. Blotchy skin, runny nose, eyes red and brimming with tears, blond curls matted with sweat from Boyd's butt-busting workout.

Then that six-foot-tall mess threw herself into Teddy's arms. Teddy staggered from the impact. "Oh, Teddy," Jillian said.

What followed was a gasping, shuddering, heart-wrenching account of two lovers separated by a cruel, unfeeling world. Teddy gritted her teeth and listened, forcing sympathetic noises at what she hoped were appropriate intervals. She didn't want to be having this conversation right now. She was hungry and due at the rifle range in thirty minutes. But she felt like she was still on friend probation, so maybe she owed Jillian at least this much.

After what felt like forever, there came a moment of silence, and Teddy belatedly realized that Jillian was staring at her expectantly, waiting for her to speak. Did she want her to say something nice about Eli? Comfort her? Teddy paused, searching for the right words. "Oh, um . . . yeah, it's totally unfair that you two can't be together. I know he really likes you."

"Thanks." Jillian wiped her eyes. "He is amazing and his dogs are amazing and he smells amazing and he makes amazing tea, and between you and me, he is really, really amazing in bed."

"You've mentioned that before. Again, I really don't need to know these things."

"It's totally healthy to have a good sex life. Root chakra."

"Jillian, I don't want to know about Eli's root . . . chakra."

"And that's why I'm sneaking off campus tonight. I have to see him."

Teddy blinked, certain she'd missed something. "What? No. Jillian, you can't do that. You can't even *think* about doing that. You're on probation. If you're caught sneaking off campus, you'll get kicked out of school."

Jillian brought up her chin. "I don't care. I have to see him."

Teddy narrowed her eyes. She'd been kind. She'd been empathetic.

She'd let Jillian cry on her shoulder. Enough already. "Don't be an idiot, Jillian. You're not going to throw away everything you've worked for just to spend a night with Eli."

Jillian reared back. "A minute ago, you agreed it wasn't fair that we were separated. Now what? It's okay as long as I don't act on it? You're such a hypocrite."

"What are you talking about?"

"You know exactly what I'm talking about. It's always the same with you. You're the one who's allowed to break the rules. But as soon as someone else wants to step out of line, they're in the wrong. Don't tell me that sneaking off with Pyro at all hours isn't rule breaking, because you know it is, we all signed the code of ethics."

Teddy was struck by two things. First, that Jillian had noticed Teddy and Pyro were back together. Well, not *together* together, but something. She'd thought she and Pyro had been discreet about it. Apparently not. And if Jillian knew, then Dara did, too, and how many other people? The revelation was distressing on several levels. So she focused on the second part of Jillian's attack, which was essentially that Teddy was a selfish jerk who cared only about herself. Definitely easier to tackle.

"I'm just trying to help."

Jillian's lip began to quiver again. "It's just"—she took a shaky breath—"it's not fair."

"Look, this won't last forever. Your probation ends soon. And then you can see him whenever you want."

"He hasn't written back. I don't even know if he's getting my messages. Burt—"

Yeah, Teddy knew all about Burt.

"—so can you go see him for me, Teddy? Please?"

Wait a second.

"Me? What good would that do?"

"Take this note. And since I can't go to him, ask him to come here."

"Eli isn't allowed on campus. You know that."

Jillian chewed her lip. "It's almost Halloween. He could come to the Cantina! Then I'll just happen to wander down, and Eli will just happen to be there—in costume, so nobody will even know it's him—voilà! Problem solved!"

If even a modicum of this planning had gone into their Hyle break-in . . .

But Jillian was looking at her, her face so full of hope and longing that Teddy didn't have the heart to say no. Even if she knew this was the worst plan ever.

"What do you think Eli is going to be for Halloween?" Teddy asked.

Boy, was she going to regret this.

After dinner, she found herself sneaking on the ferry, risking getting into trouble herself, in order to see a guy she didn't like so she could deliver a message she didn't approve of.

Friendship. Guess you have to suck it up sometimes.

As a second-year, Teddy could go off campus after hours, but she'd hoped that her first trip off-island to San Francisco would be for something fun—a concert, a drag show, a hamburger. Instead, she was on her way to the Mission District to track down Jillian's boyfriend.

Eli lived in a walk-up on one of the last ungentrified streets in the area. The front door to his building was unlocked; she figured the landlord wasn't too concerned with security risks. Or safety. The stoop was cracked, and the right-side hand railing seemed to be held on with a single screw and a half-assed prayer.

As someone who had dropped out of college and moved into the apartment above her parents' garage, Teddy didn't think she was one to judge anyone's lifestyle. But she did. She judged him. She loved judging Eli Nevin. He was one judgeable little son of a bitch. There was just something about him that set all of her hairs on end. Gut feeling or not, he wasn't right for Jillian.

Nevertheless, she jogged up the stairs to his apartment, eager to deliver Jillian's message and head back to campus.

She reached for the knob on Eli's door only to have it swing open at her touch. The apartment was dark, no noise from within. No music or TV. No dogs barking, which seemed unusual, considering. Eli must have taken the dogs out for a walk and hadn't bothered to lock the doors behind him. Which seemed either completely careless or ridiculously trusting. Both explanations pissed Teddy off.

But in case she was wrong: "Hey, Eli," she called, as she let herself in. "It's me, Teddy. I've got a message from Jillian. You around?"

No answer. Teddy reached for the light switch by the door and flicked it on. Tried it again. Tried a third time. Nothing. Which led her to concoct a totally different scenario: a fuse had blown in his crappy apartment, which meant Eli had probably gone to find the building super, which meant Teddy would be forced to wait in the dark for him to return.

Jillian had damn well better appreciate what I'm doing, because—

Something caught Teddy's attention. She froze, trying to identify it. Not a noise, precisely. Not a movement. Something else. Something there in the darkness, just beyond her grasp.

She focused hard and caught it. A buzz of energy, hovering on the edge of her perception.

She wasn't alone.

Someone else was in the apartment. Goose bumps shot up her spine. She focused hard, reaching out her consciousness through the small rooms and narrow hallway to find out who.

Before she could discern more, two figures emerged from the hallway. Too dark to make out any distinguishing characteristics. Teddy could identify only that one of them was large. As in almost twice her size. And then the mountain of a man started rushing toward her.

Teddy didn't think. Didn't make a conscious decision. Just allowed Boyd's training to take over and operated on muscle memory. She ducked low and pivoted, using her opponent's oncoming force against him. Simultaneously making herself a smaller target and driving her shoulder upward into his solar plexus. A deep grunt of pain told her she'd succeeded on that front, at least temporarily.

Next she launched herself toward the smaller of the pair. Aimed her elbow at what she hoped was the man's throat. She missed. A glancing blow. But Teddy recovered in time to grab a fistful of surprisingly longish hair and jerk the assailant backward. She was rewarded with a sharp cry of distress. The lights flickered on. Teddy blinked. The blond hair she'd grabbed belonged to a woman.

The second of shocked inaction cost her. The man, back on his feet, slammed Teddy hard enough to cause her to release her grip on the woman. He sent Teddy crashing into Eli's coffee table. Her head whipped back against the hard mahogany, so hard that the edges of her vision began to blur. The man loomed over her, fist raised.

"Enough!" the woman yelled.

Teddy blinked and shook her head, fighting to stay conscious as her assailants rushed out the door.

How many times can a psychic get hit in the head before she incurs irrevocable damage?

After what felt like hours later, a tongue in Teddy's ear roused her. It wasn't the good kind of tongue-in-ear action. Because the tongue belonged to a giant horse masquerading as a dog.

From down the hall, Teddy heard Eli's voice call out: "Mitzy! Where did you go? You're not supposed to take off without me!" That was followed by the sound of heavy footfalls, frantic yaps, and tiny claws scratching hardwood. Eli, returning home. With a groan,

Teddy rolled over onto her knees and attempted to stand but wasn't fast enough to avoid Mitzy's tongue and another wet kiss.

"I see you've met Mitzy," Eli said. The giant black pack animal's name was Mitzy. Figured. "And this is Percival. Percy, for short." Eli gestured to a tiny brown-and-white Chihuahua by his feet. He looked around the room and frowned. "Teddy? What the hell did you do to my apartment?"

"What did *I* do?" Teddy rose, swayed slightly, and looked around. Mayhem. And not just boy-man-in-his-twenties apartment mayhem. Now that the lights were back on, she could see. Drawers overturned, cushions ripped apart, cabinet contents waterfalling onto the floor. If Pyro had been there, he would have used his cop lingo and said the place had been tossed.

"You think *I* did this?"

Eli tilted his head. Considered that. "Oh. You mean there was another break-in?"

"And I walked right in the middle of— Wait a minute. What the hell do you mean, *another* break-in? How often does this happen?"

Eli shrugged. He unhooked the dogs' leashes, slipped off his jacket, hung the gear by the front door. "This isn't the first time."

"Are you kidding me? You put up with this on a routine basis?"

"No, not routine. Of course not. But it's happened before. Never like this, though." He gazed around the room, shook his head. Then he went into the kitchen, lit a flame under the kettle, and rooted through the mess for a packet of tea. She followed on his heels. He wore a faded gray *Save the Rhinos* T-shirt and a pair of low-slung jeans, which would have been normal if they hadn't been bright yellow.

"Eli, did it ever occur to you to move somewhere else?"

"It's an economically disadvantaged neighborhood, Teddy. People get desperate, you know? I try not to judge." Eli reached in the cabinet for a mug. It cracked in half when he touched it. As though someone had gone through the compartment with a stick, intent on reducing the crockery to shards. He stared at the broken handle. "My favorite mug," he said. "I got it in Colombia when I took part in a protest to demand higher wages for laborers harvesting coffee beans."

Of course he did. Teddy watched as he struggled to maintain his composure. After a long beat, he said, "You know, maybe you're right. I mean, it's one thing to come in and take what you need. This is, like, very disrespectful. It actually pisses me off."

About time.

But none of this was Eli's fault. "What'd they take?" she said instead.

"Good question." Eli left the kitchen and began roaming the apartment. "Not drugs. I had a wisdom tooth pulled last week, my oxycodone prescription is still on my nightstand. My laptop's right here, and they didn't touch my wallet. Not that I carry much cash. But still, forty bucks is forty bucks, right?"

Odd. Obviously the pair had been in the apartment long enough to render it a total disaster. Which meant they'd seen the drugs, the cash, the computer. But they hadn't touched any of it. Which meant they'd been looking for something else. But what—

"Damn, they knocked over my files."

"What files?"

"All my HEAT stuff. Our protest calendar, meeting schedule, email chain, future blog entries. I spent the whole morning organizing it, and now it's a total mess." He bent down to straighten the paperwork. "Why are you here, anyway? Is Jillian okay?"

"What? Oh yeah. She's fine." Teddy related Jillian's message about Halloween, then turned down his offer to stick around for a cup of tea. She didn't want to miss the last ferry back to campus. As she turned to go, she paused at the door. Examined it for signs of damage and found none. Both the lock and the doorframe were in perfect condition. "Eli, was your door locked when you left?"

"Yeah. I always lock it. Even when I'm just going out for a minute. Habit, I guess. Why?"

"What about the lights? You having any problem with them?"

"No. They work fine." He reached for the switch and demonstrated, flipping the overhead light on and off.

"Huh." Teddy paused. "Hey, when you and Jillian broke in to Hyle Pharmaceuticals—"

He stiffened. "What are you talking about? We didn't—"

"Relax, Eli. I know all about it. I know you took that report, too."

"Yeah, I guess. But we only took it so we could prove that Hyle's practices are morally and ethically corrupt, and that the company deserves to be held accountable."

"I don't care, Eli. I just need to know—" Teddy stopped herself, drew in a calming breath. "I mean, I understand why you guys broke in. How concerned you were about the lab animals. I get it, really. But did you take any other documents? Lift any sample drugs, touch anything else when you were there?"

"No. Nothing. Why?"

Relief poured through Teddy. The intruders hadn't been looking for stuff from Hyle. She forced what she hoped was a reassuring smile. "No reason. Just asking."

"You sure?"

"I'm sure. Just . . . be careful, all right?"

"Of course. Is everything okay, Teddy?"

"Sure," she lied. "Everything's fine. Especially if you read that note from Jillian. So we'll be seeing you soon, I guess."

CHAPTER SIXTEEN

TEDDY HOPPED OFF THE MUNI BUS TEN MINUTES BE-
fore the day's last ferry to Angel Island was scheduled to leave the pier.
Feeling jittery, she jostled her way through crowds of tourists, wishing
she had time to grab a cup of coffee. Not that coffee would help—her
thoughts were racing, and she needed something to take the edge off.
What she really wanted was a shot of Jack Daniel's followed by a Jack
Daniel's chaser, but since there weren't any bars in the family-friendly
vicinity of Pier 39, coffee would have to do.

She paid for a cup and made her way toward the boarding dock.
Her midair collision with Eli's coffee table hadn't been great for her
shoulder—or her spine or head, for that matter. Once the initial jolt
of adrenaline had worn off, her body began throbbing as though she
had been pummeled with a baseball bat. Or taken the brunt end of
one of Boyd's training exercises. But none of that mattered. What
mattered was—

"Theodora."

Teddy spun around and came face-to-face with Derek Yates.

Her first response was fury. Directed at herself. She had an entire
year of Whitfield Institute training under her belt and absolutely no
excuse for being caught unaware. Yes, the blow to the head had left her
a little dizzy, but that didn't matter. She'd left a *crime scene* and entered
a crowded public space, and she'd let her attention wander? Any one

of her instructors would have been all over her ass for the carelessness.

Her second response was also fury. Directed at Yates. "What the hell kind of game are you playing?" she demanded.

"I would hope you'd be better prepared than to allow someone to startle you in a crowd, Theodora. Particularly another psychic. And when you're on a secret mission, playing messenger for our two little lovebirds."

"How did you know about Jillian and Eli?" Teddy asked. She wondered, was it possible that Yates had sent those two goons? "What were you looking for?"

"Looking for?" His gaze hardened, and his mouth drew into a tight, pinched line. He cast a furtive glance around the open-air pier, then directed her to a secluded spot between two tourist shops carrying nearly identical merchandise: city maps, snow globes, tiny toy replicas of streetcars, Alcatraz Island T-shirts and ball caps. The shops were closed, the interior lights dimmed. Sheltering awnings offered both shadow and privacy. "Tell me what happened," he said.

He looked better than he had the last time she'd seen him, back in Sector Three, but that wasn't saying much. His dark eyes still had that wary, hunted look. Ready to flee or attack at the slightest provocation. The phrase Teddy once used to describe him still applied: lone wolf. And that told her everything. Yates was an escaped felon. He lived alone, traveled alone, acted alone. Always. If he'd wanted something in Eli's apartment, he would have broken in and searched for it himself. He wouldn't have hired anyone to do it for him.

"*Now*, Theodora. We don't have much time."

"No. Answer my questions first. What are you doing here?"

"You sent me a postcard, remember? I assumed something had happened."

She allowed herself a brief moment of victory. Pyro had been wrong. She'd sent that card, and Derek Yates had come running.

Well, more like he'd walked at a comfortable pace. She'd mailed the card a month ago. But he was here nonetheless.

"Talk, Theodora. What's happening?"

"A man and a woman broke in to Eli's apartment. Tore the place apart looking for something."

"You thought that I had something to do with it."

"Initially. But—"

"Why?"

For the same reason that, minutes earlier, Yates had scolded her. *I would hope you'd be better prepared than to allow someone to startle you in a crowd, Theodora. Particularly another psychic.* She knew exactly what he meant. The energy surrounding a psychic was different—subtle but recognizable. She'd felt it—like an electrical current hanging in the air—the moment she'd blundered into Eli's apartment. A warning she'd disregarded completely. She said as much to Yates.

"Psychics?" he repeated sharply. "These two were psychic. You're certain of that?"

Ninety, maybe ninety-five-percent certain. But Yates wasn't a bookie looking for odds. So she gave him the best answer she could. "Yes."

"They weren't with me, Theodora. I can assure you of that."

She believed him.

"What were they after?" he asked.

She told him about the lab report Jillian and Eli had lifted. "I assume it has something to do with that. One of the scientists who works at Whitfield Institute also works at Hyle. Dr. Eversley. He's developing something called X-498, a gene therapy developed to affect psychics."

"I see." A heavy pause, then, "Hyle Pharmaceuticals. You're aware that Hollis Whitfield is a majority stockholder."

"Yes. We discovered it a month ago. That's why I contacted you. But when I—"

"The attack," he interrupted. "What did your assailants look like? Details, Theodora."

The entire encounter had lasted, what? Three seconds, maybe four? Most of it entirely in the dark. A large man and a blond woman. But faces, heights, weights, ages? All a blur. She gave him impressions instead. "A large man. Really large. He moved awkwardly—quick but lumbering. And a woman, average size, white-blond hair."

Yates opened his mouth as though to reply, then changed his mind and shook his head, dismissing whatever he had been about to say. For the first time, she saw a flicker of fear enter his gaze.

"Who are they?" she demanded.

He shook off her question. "Now I understand why the situation in Jackpot has changed."

"Changed? What does that mean? The base isn't guarded now?"

"No. The base remains heavily guarded—even more so since our visit. They're bringing supplies and construction materials into Sector Three."

"So what's different?"

"The people I've been monitoring are no longer overseeing the work. They're here in San Francisco."

The ferry whistle blew, indicating that boarding was under way. Teddy shot an anxious glance at the pier. Fine if she got away with sneaking off-island. A total shit storm if she missed the last ferry back and her absence was noticed.

"You shared the Hyle report with Clint?" Yates asked.

"Of course."

"Let me guess," he said, not bothering to hide the contempt in his voice. "He assured you he has the situation under control. That there's nothing to worry about." Yates stepped away from her. Studied the ferry as though considering boarding it himself. "Clint doesn't understand. He doesn't have the full picture. We must stop whatever's happening at Hyle. I have to tell him face-to-face."

Teddy laughed. She couldn't help it. "Are you insane? If Clint knew that you were here, that I was talking to you—" She stopped abruptly.

Caught her breath. "He's determined to put you back in prison. He's pretty much made that his life's work. Finding and arresting you . . . and Marysue."

"Is that so?" A ghost of a smile touched Yates's lips. "It may be hard for you to believe, but we weren't always enemies. For a while, we were actually friends." He shook his head. "Perhaps that's impossible for you to imagine."

Actually, it wasn't. Last year, Yates had given Teddy a photo of himself with Clint and her birth parents. The four of them relaxed and happy, their arms wrapped around one another in an expression of affection and unity. The way she felt about Pyro, Jillian, and Dara. They were like family now. What could possibly occur that would drive them to hunt one another down?

"Explain it to me," she said. "Tell me what happened. Earlier, you said you came to San Francisco because *they* were here. Who are they?"

"I'm sorry, Theodora. That's a secret I can't burden you with yet."

A blast of the horn signaled the ferry's final boarding call. It was her last chance to get back to campus before curfew. The engine rumbled and fired to life. Teddy shouted to the crewman to wait. Yates kept pace with her as she strode toward the ferry.

"Your astral travel, Theodora. That's the key. You must master that skill. If what you've told me is true, our time is running out."

They reached the boarding plank. Teddy hesitated, one foot on the plank, one foot on the pier. "Astral travel? I don't understand—"

"On or off!" shouted the impatient crewman. "We've got a schedule to keep."

She turned back to Yates. "How do I find you?"

"You don't. I'll find you." He reached into the backpack he carried and removed a yellowed manila envelope, smudged and glossy with the patina of age. He passed it to her. "Don't worry. I'm not leaving you empty-handed. Study this. Then you'll understand the part you'll play."

"On or off!" the crewman shouted.

Teddy walked up the boarding plank. She turned at the rail, intending to call out another question to Yates, but he had disappeared once again into the crowd.

Pyro looked at the envelope. Picked it up and gave it a shake. "That's all he gave you? You sure?"

"Of course I'm sure," Teddy snapped. "That's it. One photo."

It was late, well after midnight. She, Pyro, Jillian, and Dara were gathered in her dorm room. They sat with their heads bent over the photo. Like the envelope that held it, the photo was worn with age, the corners rubbed round, the image faded. She watched as Dara lifted it, tilting it so the light reflected off the glossy surface.

The photo showed an unsmiling man in his early forties standing beside a storage building made of cinder blocks. Dark hair, dark eyes, medium build. Coarse, heavy eyebrows that formed a near-unibrow as he scowled into the distance. Barren desert stretched for miles in the background. The photo was slightly grainy. Likely a surveillance shot.

Dara said, "Whoever he was, he passed over. Shortly after that photo was taken. It happened fast. Like one second he was there, the next second he was gone."

Teddy nodded, accepting Dara's psychic read without question. In the weeks that had followed Professor Dunn's introductory lecture on psychometry, there had been two stars in his class. Ava, the medium. And Dara, whose death visions had transmuted into an ability to touch an object or study a photo and know whether the person in question had crossed over.

"How?" Teddy pressed. "Who is he?"

"I don't know. But I'm picking up a lot of shock. Disbelief. Horror. An accident, maybe." Dara shrugged and set the photo down. "I'm sorry, Teddy, but that's all I'm getting."

"Right before Yates gave me the photo, he said astral travel was the key. What did he mean? The key to what?"

Pyro grunted. "Typical Yates. More riddles than answers."

No.

That wasn't true. Yates hadn't been trying to frustrate her with riddles. He was under the misguided impression that by withholding names and information, he was somehow protecting her. He was doing what he felt was right. The way he'd abandoned them in Sector Three but stuck around to make sure they got out okay.

Jillian paced about the room. "What about Eli? Are you sure he wasn't hurt?"

"He's fine," Teddy reassured her for what felt like the twentieth time in as many minutes. "He wasn't even there when they broke in."

"Teddy *was* there when they broke in," Pyro reminded them. "Alone. What if they'd been armed? What if she'd been hurt?"

"But I wasn't," Teddy said.

"You could have been. This thing is getting out of control." Pyro stood. Nodded as though he'd come to a decision. "At this point, the only thing to do is pass that photo on to Clint."

"Give it to Clint?" Teddy studied him in disbelief. "And how am I going to explain where the photo came from?"

"Simple. You tell him the truth."

"The truth? Tell Clint I went off campus and had a meeting with Yates? Are you kidding me? Do you want me to get kicked out of school?"

Pyro's eyes flashed with anger. "You've forgotten I was a cop, Teddy. Don't think for a minute you can pull that crap on me."

"What the hell does that mean?"

"It means you're twisting the truth around to suit your own agenda. Here's the truth: you went off campus to pass a message from Jillian to Eli. Bad, but not bad enough to get you kicked out of school. Yates surprised you at the pier and passed you the photo. End of story. So you face Clint in the morning, give him the photo, confess the whole thing."

"I can't."

"Can't or won't?"

She felt her teeth clench. She relaxed her jaw, forced a reply. "Won't."

Because if she did what Pyro suggested, Clint would make it impossible for her to ever see Yates again. And at the moment, Yates was her only source for information. For what had happened in the past and what was happening in the present, both. She couldn't afford to shut that down.

"This isn't a game anymore. You could get hurt."

"What if Yates is right?" she said. "You all saw Sector Three. What if something like that is happening again? Don't we want all the information we can get, regardless of the source?"

"Regardless of the source? I think you've forgotten something. Yates was PC. And like it or not, so was your mother. She probably still is. If you want to pretend that doesn't matter, that's up to you. But don't ask the three of us to play along."

Shaken, she glanced at Dara and Jillian for support. Instead of meeting her eyes, they were busy studying the patterns in the carpet.

Only Pyro met her gaze. Normally, she associated Pyro with sexy, smoldering heat. Sometimes she forgot he'd had a career in law enforcement before joining Whitfield Institute. At the moment, however, the cool detachment with which he regarded her said he was all cop. Maybe always had been.

And that was the problem. Pyro, like Clint, viewed the world in black and white. Teddy loved all the opportunities the gray spaces afforded.

He studied her, his expression showing no sign of softening. "There's no in between here, Teddy. You're either with Yates or you're against him. I think it's pretty clear what you've decided."

CHAPTER SEVENTEEN

IN THE WEEKS THAT FOLLOWED HER ARGUMENT WITH Pyro, two things happened. Well, one thing happened—their class-work became more demanding—and the other thing didn't. Teddy wanted it to happen, but with each passing day, it seemed about as likely to occur as a date with Ryan Gosling or winning the lottery or discovering that, yes, subsisting on ice cream and hamburgers for the rest of her adult life could be healthful. Specifically, she was waiting for an apology from Pyro. Or some acknowledgment that he understood where she was coming from. Instead, they exchanged cursory words only when the situation demanded it.

Twice Teddy came close to turning over the photo to Clint. Twice she decided against it. Not yet. Not until she knew more. Then she'd involve Clint. In the meantime, she'd taken to carrying Yates's photo with her, tucked in the same pocket as the photo of her parents that he'd given her last year. Also in her pocket was her mother's necklace. For the past month, it had remained stashed in the drawer of her bedside table. No longer. She needed every token with her now—for luck, for courage, for *something*.

She stepped into Professor Dunn's classroom. Since their first lecture on the subject of psychometry, Dunn had continued to expand on the process of using touch to garner psychic information. He'd outlined the physics and the metaphysics involved, explained the science behind the associative link that psychometric objects provided to psychics, and given them multiple theoretical approaches to the topic.

Today, however, they were going to put those theories to the test. They'd either prove they were capable of using their psychic training to solve an actual case, or they'd fail. This was black or white, too. There was no in between.

Dunn, dressed in a Ramones tee, stood at the lectern beside a towering pile of banker's boxes. "Today," he said, "we start work on your midterm assignment. You'll be expected to use your newly honed psychometric ability to garner information on a cold case. You'll be working in teams of two, which I will be assigning."

Teddy suppressed a groan. If she had to partner with Kate, or Ava, or worse, Pyro . . . she didn't even want to think about it.

Dunn continued. "I'll be looking for proof of your work, detailed outlines of how you arrived at your evidence and what methodology was used, along with an essay explaining your reasoning and citing at least two scientific sources from the texts we've discussed."

At this, Teddy groaned aloud, as did the rest of the class. If someone had told her learning to be a kick-ass psychic crime fighter meant taking science classes . . .

"Atkins, you'll be with . . ."

As Dunn scanned his list, Teddy silently said a prayer to whoever was presiding over the astral plane.

"Costa."

Thank you, whoever you are, Lady Spirit Mother Empress Holy One Above.

"Cannon . . ." Dunn said, making eye contact with Teddy. "Cummings."

Cummings. Henry Cummings. Golfing, my-daddy-is-richer-than-your-daddy, meet-me-at-the-club-later Henry Cummings?

Teddy knew he was a clairvoyant with a preppy pedigree, and an Alpha, but she didn't know much else about him. Other than he annoyed the hell out of her. But he wasn't Pyro. At least he had that much going for him. She ventured a glance in Henry's direction, noting his look of horror. Jerk. At least she'd had the courtesy to hide her dislike. She straightened in her seat. The end of November couldn't come soon enough.

"You'll have the rest of class to go over your cases," Dunn explained. "By the close of this session, I'll be collecting an initial psychometric impression that will go toward your final grade. Cases have been preassigned, taking your abilities and interests into account." He moved through the classroom, handing out boxes. Once he reached Teddy's desk, he hesitated. Then he set down a dusty brown box with the name *Polson* scrawled on the side.

Dunn looked at the clock. "Time starts now."

Henry swung his head, signaling that she should come to him.

Nuh-uh, buddy, that's not how this is going to work.

She gestured to her desk, indicating that she was the one who had the files.

Henry sighed and stood up. He brushed off the chair beside her and sat down. "If we're going to work together," he announced, "we should begin by setting some ground rules."

"Ground rules?"

"Listen, we both know you have a certain reputation. Let me say it right up front. No tricks, no sneaking around, no crazy stunts. You seem to get into trouble a lot, which is something I'd rather not do, if possible." He crossed his arms over his neatly pressed Whitfield polo shirt—who ironed a cotton polo?—and stared at her.

Teddy felt her temperature rise. Did this freckle-faced frat boy just tell her she had a *reputation*? There was only one allowable response. She opened her mouth to snarl a reply but caught herself just in time. Wessner was in the audience. Test number one, she surmised: her ability to work with an obnoxious colleague without immediately resorting to verbal or physical abuse, no matter how badly said colleague had it coming.

"Look," she said, "let's just get to work, all right?" She elbowed the banker's box toward him. Inside was a thick stack of manila folders, along with several sealed bags of evidence. "How does Dunn expect us to go through all of this in"—Teddy glanced at the clock—"an hour?"

"He doesn't expect that. He asked for a psychometric impression." Henry pulled open one of the evidence bags. "Learn to follow instructions, Cannon. We just have to read the objects."

Teddy frowned. In order to use her abilities, she first needed a sense of the case. She dug through the files until she found what she was looking for: a case summary. She opened it, and her heart skipped a beat. Stamped at the top was the FBI logo, followed by the words *Classified Material*. She hadn't been given any old cold case. She'd been given an FBI cold case. She bit her lip to stop an idiotic grin from spreading across her face. Granted, it was from 1995, and the file had been heavily redacted, but still.

"John Polson," she read aloud, scanning the portions of the report that hadn't been blacked out. "Suspected small-arms dealer. Dealt mainly in semiautomatic assault rifles. Under FBI surveillance for providing weapons to drug cartels operating here in the U.S. Looks like most of his contacts were in the Southwest, just across the border."

"Nice guy."

"Transported the weapons himself," she continued. "He flew an ultralight. Kept it low, was able to avoid radar detection."

"An ultralight?"

"A one-person plane. Apparently, the plane crashed shortly after takeoff from a private airstrip in Nevada."

"Good riddance," Henry said, rolling his eyes. "Tell me why we care what happened to this guy?"

Excellent question. What about this particular case merited the investigation of psychics over two decades later? Teddy didn't have an answer, but she was thinking hard. Probably not the arms-running connection; that case against Polson was watertight. That meant FBI investigators had questions about the murder and subsequent crash— which happened to take place at an airstrip about seventy miles outside of Jackpot.

Which stopped Teddy in her tracks. She cast a look at Clint and Nick. Had she been assigned the case because it had something to do with her mother? The PC? If so, Dunn and Wessner were playing things pretty cool. A minute ago, they'd been watching her and Henry, seeing how they'd react to each other. But now they stood off to one side of the room, engaged in casual conversation, paying her absolutely no attention.

"Anyway," she continued, "the autopsy revealed that death was by gunshot wound, not the plane crash."

"Suicide."

"No," Teddy said, continuing to read, "he was shot in the back of the skull with a small-caliber revolver. The trajectory of the bullet's path ruled out suicide. But no weapon matching the gunshot wound was found in the cockpit or anywhere near the crash site. They didn't find another body, either. Just Polson."

"The plot thickens." Henry ripped open an evidence bag and spilled out the contents. "Let's get to work."

He sorted the evidence. A bit of charred leather—something that once was a pilot seat, or a briefcase, or a shoe. Too small to know just by looking at it. A gold wristwatch, the glass face shattered. A hundred-dollar bill, smudged with ash. A scrap of heavy cloth, also smudged with ash. Assorted metal debris. And last of all, an assortment of shell casings, all of them high-caliber, twisted and misshapen from exposure to intense heat. The kind of heat generated by an explosion. None of which fit the weapon Polson had been shot with.

Teddy scanned the items, then shot a glance at Henry. "You're clairvoyant, right?" Kate was claircognizant, which meant she was able to divine knowledge without any clear source, but Teddy had never teamed up with someone whose psychic gift was the ability to see glimpses of the future.

Henry nodded. "Yeah, but I'm developing my ability to see the past as well. Given how old this stuff is, that's definitely going to be a challenge."

"Right."

Henry gave a small, nervous cough. "All right, then. Let's get started."

"Wait." Teddy tapped the stack of files. "Shouldn't we read more about the case?"

"Later. Initial psychometric impressions, remember? That's all Dunn wants today." At her hesitation, he removed an envelope from one of the files and tossed it toward her. "There are some photos here, if you need to give them a look. Personally, I prefer not to taint my mind with any images except the ones I intuit psychically."

She resisted the urge to roll her eyes. *Yeah, I get it, you're so much better than me. Very subtle.*

She watched as he reached for one of the mangled shell casings and wrapped his fist around it. Then he settled back in his chair with his eyes closed. Following his lead, Teddy picked up the scrap of leather, clutched it tightly, and closed her eyes.

Nothing but her own rapid breathing and random unconnected thoughts skittering around her brain. A monkey playing pinball had more self-control. Teddy opened her eyes to say as much but stopped herself. Henry was already deep in trance. A quick glance around the room confirmed that the rest of her classmates were as well.

Dammit.

She looked at the clock. She didn't have time to joke around. Her future rested on her ability to get some sort of read on these objects. When five more minutes had passed without any psychic glimpses, Teddy begrudgingly reached for the envelope of photos. Just to put her mind in the right place, she rationalized. She shuffled through images of the crash site, the cache of confiscated weapons.

And then she reached a surveillance photo of a man standing beside the ultralight.

Teddy reeled in shock as her heart slammed against her chest. The photo slipped from her fingers. She quickly picked it up again and studied the man's face. Dark hair, dark eyes, medium build. Unibrow scowl. The man from the photo Yates had given her. She was absolutely sure of it. She'd spent hours staring at that face.

Her mind raced. Somehow Yates had influenced which case she'd been given. But how? Then she thought of how simple it had been for Dara to trick the woman who monitored the file room into stepping away, allowing Dara to sneak in and grab Molly's file. Yates could have easily performed a similar maneuver, mentally influencing one of the civilian staff who traveled on and off the island to switch the file boxes around, ensuring that Teddy got the Polson case. After all, this was a man who'd manipulated prison guards at San Quentin. Who'd knocked out the sentries at Sector Three with a hard stare. Switching a couple of file boxes would have been child's play for him.

Teddy examined the photo with new urgency. She retraced the furtive conversation she'd had with Yates. She'd told him about the two psychics breaking in to Eli's apartment. The gene therapy that Whitfield and Eversley were developing at Hyle Pharmaceuticals. In response, Yates had passed her the photograph. He'd told her that astral travel was the key, and then he'd said, *Study this. Then you'll understand what you'll need to do.*

With a renewed sense of purpose, she tightened her grip on the leather scrap and felt for the necklace in her pocket. She focused her thoughts. John Polson's plane had crashed in the Nevada desert shortly after takeoff.

Show me what happened.

Still nothing. She took another breath. Wondered what Yates knew.

If this case did have something to do with her mother, Teddy wasn't sure she wanted to know what had happened. But no, she'd asked for this. No turning back now. She closed her eyes and tried to center her energy, expelling the hesitation hovering at the edges of her thoughts.

Show me.

To her astonishment, a subtle warmth started to tingle at the center of her palm. But it wasn't the hand squeezing the leather scrap. It was the hand in her pocket, the one wrapped around the necklace.

She sank into bottomless blackness, as if someone had turned off every light in the world. Panic seized her as recognition set in. She was about to enter a full-fledged OBE. She hurtled down that small, invisible tunnel.

Not here. Not now.

Information hit Teddy's senses all at once. Sights, sounds, smells. And the smell was . . . rank. Probably coming from the garbage piled on the sidewalk less than a foot away. She squinted and gazed upward. Midday. Blinding light and horns blaring. Traffic. She looked up to see buildings—skyscrapers, their mirrored surfaces reflecting the enormity of the city.

Her astral travel had brought her to New York City.

She squinted into the sun, clocked the street sign above her. Broadway and Forty-Seventh Street. It didn't make sense. Polson's plane had exploded in the Nevada desert. But rather than generating a psychometric impression from Polson's scrap of leather, Marysue's necklace had catapulted her here. Teddy walked to a corner, looked through the glass of a *Village Voice* newspaper box. The date on the front page: October 27, 1998.

Why is that date so familiar?

She pivoted to avoid a collision with a pedestrian but grazed him in the shoulder and felt like she'd stuck her hand out a car window on a highway. The pedestrian recoiled briefly, offering a confused glance in

Teddy's direction before walking off. It wasn't like bodies meeting on the physical plane—but the man clearly had felt *something*.

She remembered Clint's lesson. Only travelers could identify other travelers. And this man wasn't one.

Teddy looked around. A yellow cab pulled to the curb; the ad on top of the taxi was for Blockbuster Video, trumpeting the release to VHS of the hit movie *Titanic*. Down the block, she saw a man pushing against the current of the crowd, head tucked low, brown leather briefcase in hand. Hair neatly parted, suit neatly pressed. Derek Yates.

For a second, Teddy felt frozen in place, but then she remembered he couldn't see her. He wasn't a traveler. She began to weave her way toward him. What was Yates doing in New York in 1998? She watched as he stopped at a bench on the corner. She followed his gaze. A man on a pay phone hung up his call. Nodded. He was similarly dressed in a suit, but large and bulky in the shoulders. The kind of guy she wouldn't want to see coming toward her in an alley. Out of place among the midtown commuters.

Something was happening. She rubbed the necklace in her pocket. New York City. October 1998.

It had something to do with Dara. A warning, maybe? She tried to flip through her mental Rolodex of Dara's proclamations. The surveillance photo, that she remembered. The first of Dara's warnings about the past—that had happened back in their apartment in San Francisco, over the summer. She had stumbled against a cabinet. By Dara's feet, a newspaper. *The New York Times*. October 27, 1998.

The PC bombing.

Fighting a sense of paralyzing dread, Teddy turned to look up at the building in front of her. She had to do something to stop it, but what? Alert the authorities. Set off a fire alarm to clear the building occupants. But no. She couldn't alter the past under any circumstances. Those were rules she couldn't break. When she turned back to the bench, Yates was gone. All she saw was the back of a woman dressed in a black wool coat, dark hair twisted in a tight bun, the leather brief-case Yates had carried now in her hand. In one of the building's glass panels, Teddy could make out the woman's warped reflection.

Marysue Delaney.

Teddy watched in horror as her mother stepped toward the build-ing, breezed through a revolving door, then disappeared inside. Teddy tried to convince herself that what she was seeing wasn't real. Wasn't true. Her mother *couldn't* be part of the bombing. There must be some explanation, something she wasn't seeing. Her brain spun through ra-tionalizations, trying to bridge the gaps to make the events before her something different from what they appeared to be. But she couldn't. She clenched her fists, willing her OBE to end.

It didn't.

Marysue exited the building and walked away from Teddy, heading uptown. As Teddy watched, the mirrored panels swelled as though the building itself had exhaled. The dark glass shattered. Teddy caught the faint whiff of almonds in the wind, and she was sure it wasn't from the Nuts 4 Nuts guy on the corner. The explosion knocked her off her feet, propelling her backward onto the rough concrete sidewalk.

CHAPTER EIGHTEEN

TEDDY WOKE TO SOMEONE TUGGING ON HER FOOT. Not gentle tugs, either. Pulling like the person was intent on removing her ankle from her leg. She parted her lips and croaked, "Hey, knock it off."

"Settle down, young lady," a brisk voice replied. "There'll be no dirty shoes in my beds."

Teddy began to object that her shoes weren't dirty, but she caught herself. That wasn't really the point. The point was, where was she, and how did she get there? Another fierce tug accompanied by a grunt, and her combat boot slipped from her foot and thudded to the floor, where it joined its partner. Teddy flexed her newly liberated toes. At least that felt good. As for the rest of her . . .

The back of her head hurt like a mother. Wincing, she ran her hand over a lump the size of a golf ball. Her eyelids felt glued shut. Just prying them open required all the strength she could manage. Ignoring the protests of her aching body, she slowly leveraged herself into a sitting position. She was lying in bed, fully clothed.

She blinked as the figure hovering at the foot of her bed slowly swam into focus. The woman was dressed in nurse's whites. A halo of strawberry blond curls framed her face. Nurse Bell.

"How you gave yourself a concussion falling from a chair, I'll never know," Nurse Bell said.

Teddy was in the infirmary. A glance around the room confirmed it. She scanned her memory, looking for an explanation as to how she got there. She didn't remember falling from a chair. She'd been in Dunn's class, working with Henry on their project. One she hadn't completed because her mother's necklace had launched her back in time to New York City.

Marysue. The C-4. The explosion.

Her throat swelled shut and tears welled. She furiously blinked them back. She wouldn't allow herself to be weak. Not after what she'd seen.

Clint, Pyro, Dara, and Jillian had been right all along. The truth settled on her like a physical weight. In Teddy's mind, Marysue had always been on the edges, maybe standing watch, clearing the way—not the person responsible for the attack. Her mother had been the one to actually carry the bomb inside the building.

Teddy had to tell someone where she'd been. She threw back her sheet and tried to stand but couldn't. Her legs gave way and she collapsed back onto the bed, feeling like she'd been flattened by a semi.

Nurse Bell clucked her tongue and lifted Teddy's wrist to check her pulse.

"How long do I have to stay here?" Teddy grit out.

"You need a little rest," Bell pronounced. She deposited a can of ginger ale and a few packets of saltine crackers on Teddy's bedside tray.

Teddy choked back a morbid laugh. As if saltines and ginger ale could fix her problem.

Nurse Bell frowned. "Your eyes are unfocused. Is the room spinning?"

"A little."

"In that case, Dr. Eversley should clear you, just to be on the safe side. Not like you kids get sick much, anyway. Might as well enjoy the rest."

Eversley? No thanks. The morning had been rough enough. Teddy didn't plan to stick around and allow herself to become one of Eversley's test subjects.

Nurse Bell turned away and paused with her hand on the privacy curtain that sectioned off Teddy's bed from the rest of the room. "Open or closed?"

"Open."

Easier to escape that way.

Bell nodded and consulted her watch. "I'll be back to check on you in precisely thirty minutes. I expect to find you here. Do *not* make me come looking for you. I have two students with broken bones and one with food poisoning. I don't have time for foolishness."

With that, she thrust back the curtain to reveal the adjoining bed, which, to Teddy's surprise, was occupied. A young guy lay flat on his back, his eyes closed, a compress settled over the upper half of his face. He wore a white cotton tee and torn, faded jeans. His feet were bare.

He didn't move or indicate in any way that he was aware of Teddy's presence. But the moment the door closed behind Bell, he said, "So. Nurse Ratched's confining you here against your will, too, huh?"

"Looks like it," she replied, sparing him another quick glance. She didn't think she knew him, but it was hard to tell with the compress covering half his face. Maybe a first-year recruit. It didn't matter. She wasn't in the mood for talking. Her mind was too occupied with the events she'd seen. Yates. Her mother.

The bombing of the office building in New York City, fall 1998. She remembered the newspaper clippings she'd amassed over the summer. Twenty people had been killed, among them eight suspected members of Al-Qaeda who had targeted U.S. embassies in Kenya and Tanzania. The other twelve fatalities had been innocent victims in the wrong place at the wrong time. But that was how the PC worked. Collateral damage was acceptable so long as the job got done.

She cursed Clint. He may have taught her about Pilgrim's Tunnels, but he hadn't taught her how to protect herself, mentally, physically, or emotionally. Spontaneous astral travel was causing more than a couple of bumps and bruises. And there was something else that troubled her. Something she couldn't quite put her finger on.

"I'm Miles," he said.

She sighed, reluctantly drawing herself out of her grim thoughts. "Teddy."

"Teddy?" he said. "As in bear?"

She snapped her head in his direction, causing the room to spin again. She hadn't heard that joke since probably third grade. "As in call me that again and I'm putting those boots back on to kick your ass."

He laughed. "Easy, Rambo. I'm just really bad with names. I do a word-association thing to help me remember. Habit." He removed the compress and rolled onto his side to face her.

He was cute. And he obviously liked old Sylvester Stallone movies. He was long and lean. Olive skinned with dark blue eyes and shaggy dark blond hair. She was caught off guard by how good-looking he was, and she instantly felt bad for noticing. "What are you in for?"

"Just the mother of all migraines," he said. "They tell me it's not fatal—though sometimes it's so bad I almost wish it was, you know?"

Teddy didn't know. But that definitely put her own aches and pains in perspective. As difficult as astral travel was, she couldn't imagine pain so intense that death would seem like a release. "That's awful. Have you always had them?"

Miles shook his head. "It's my new medication. One of the side effects, I guess. But it's brutal."

Teddy murmured sympathetically, even as she wondered why a recruit was on any medication at all. Symptoms of psychic power were often misdiagnosed and "cured" with everything from homeopathic remedies to full-strength antipsychotics. When she'd first arrived at Whitfield, she'd gone cold turkey, ditching the epilepsy medicine she'd been prescribed for years. But she knew better than to ask Miles what he was on or why he was taking medication. She'd hated it when people had given her the third degree about her condition. It wasn't anyone else's business.

Eager for a change of topic, she glanced out the window. She spotted Hollis Whitfield standing outside the clinic, deep in conversation with Dr. Eversley. Teddy went cold. They looked serious—agitated, even. Teddy wondered if they were talking about Hyle Pharmaceuticals. She leveraged herself out of bed and went to the window. If only she could hear what they were saying.

"What is it?" Miles asked.

Teddy turned to see him grab a pair of glasses from the bedside table and slip them on. Vintage round wire frames. Impossible for anyone except John Lennon to pull off. And Miles, apparently.

He stood and moved across the room with small, cautious steps, as though not quite convinced that his legs would carry him. He stopped beside her and peered out the window at Whitfield and Eversley. "*Those* guys? You in trouble or something?"

"Not at the moment, but give me time." Turning, she gave him a vague warning: "You're new around here, so I'll give you a tip—stay away from both of them."

He frowned. "Why?"

"Well, the one in the lab coat, that's Dr. Eversley. Nurse Ratched's boss. He seems like he's got our best interests at heart, being a doctor and all, but I'm not so sure."

"And the other guy?"

Right. Whitfield. What did Teddy really know? Not enough to justify scaring some green recruit. "That's Hollis Whitfield, our commander in chief. He's the money behind everything. He generally keeps a pretty low profile, like he's watching it all play out from the shadows. I dunno, something about him just gives me the creeps."

"Geez, you make him sound like a movie villain."

Hey, if he thought this was a joke, fine. No one could say she hadn't warned him. "Maybe," she allowed with a shrug. "All I know is that he's richer than God. And sometimes you put money and power together and . . . no checks, no balances, no accountability. Just because you're rich doesn't mean you can do whatever you want."

Miles opened his mouth to reply, then went pale. His knees buckled, and Teddy was certain if she hadn't caught his elbow, he would have collapsed to the floor. She helped him back to his bed where he sat down, holding the edge of the mattress for support.

"You all right?" she asked. Stupid question. Obviously, he wasn't.

"Just need to breathe for a second," he said.

Teddy watched his chest rise as he drew in deep lungfuls of air and then slowly exhaled. She recognized the pattern and remembered that the breathing techniques they'd learned from Dunn could also be incredibly effective in managing pain. After a few minutes, he was once again able to stand, brushing her off when she moved to help him.

"I'm fine," he said with a note of frustration. "Actually, I'm going to see if I can find the dear nurse and ask about my medication. I missed my last dose, which is probably why this happened."

"Maybe I should go with—" Teddy started. If she accompanied him, maybe she could find a way to casually eavesdrop on Whitfield and Eversley.

But Miles shook off the offer. "I don't want you to get in trouble because of me. You have orders to stay in bed. I don't. I'll be fine."

Damn.

In that case, could he hurry up and go already? Because there was only one other way to catch what they were saying. From the window, Teddy watched Eversley pull a piece of paper out of his briefcase and show it to Whitfield.

Miles bent to pick up his sneakers. "I'll see you around, Teddy." He hesitated at the door, gripping its frame a moment for balance. "See, I told you I wouldn't forget your name."

She couldn't help but smile, despite everything. "Nice to meet you, Miles."

With that, he nodded and left. Which meant that Teddy could get to work. Traveling so soon after her ill-fated trip to New York seemed a pretty stupid idea. Add a possible concussion on top of that? But then Teddy Cannon wasn't known for thinking things through. She was more of a ready, fire, aim type of girl.

Besides, thanks to Clint's tutorials, this was well within her new skill set. She didn't need to move through time, just space. Even banged up and bruised as she was, she could do it. She returned to her bed and lay down. Determined exactly where she wanted to go, pictured herself standing there, then braced herself for the agonizing tug as her astral body separated from her physical one.

The world went black. Gasping, Teddy opened her eyes, welcoming the weightless feeling, to find herself outside the clinic, standing mere inches away from Eversley and Whitfield. Neither man indicated the slightest awareness that she was there.

"But there are side effects. Serious side effects," Eversley said, his tone anxious, impatient. "We should delay production. It's too risky."

"No," Whitfield returned sharply. "No delay. We move forward. If you can't do it, I'll find someone who can."

"I cannot recommend against that strongly enough."

"We have a test subject. We have the drug. We proceed."

Heated discussion followed, too full of medical jargon for Teddy to properly grasp what Eversley was saying. Neither Whitfield nor Eversley had mentioned Hyle Pharmaceuticals or X-498 specifically, but that didn't stop her from speculating. Had they begun testing the new genetic drug on human subjects? No one she knew would willingly volunteer to have their powers curtailed. Well, no one except Molly. Molly, who had fought so desperately not to feel anything in order to feel normal. Molly, who had vanished from the hospital last year. Could she be Hyle's human test subject? Teddy's mind reeled. She needed Dara. Dara would understand what they were saying, how it all connected.

From the doorway to the clinic, a voice broke Teddy's concentration, pulling her back to her sickbed and to her physical body.

"How you feeling, recruit?"

Clint Corbett loomed. Maybe not the *last* person she wanted to see, but damn near the end of the list.

"Just peachy." She leaned back against her pillow and stared out the window, willing him to take the hint and leave. He didn't.

"I heard you passed out in Dunn's class. Just hit the floor. What happened?"

Professor Dunn's class. *Shit.* The conversation between Whitfield and Eversley had driven everything else from her mind, to the point where she had almost forgotten why she was in the infirmary in the first place.

He pulled up a chair and sat down next to her bed. Waited for her to speak.

"I had an OBE," she said. "I astral-traveled to the site of the explosion. Was right there when the bomb went off."

"I'm not sure I understand. You mean the case Dunn assigned you? I thought—"

"No, that case was about a plane crash." She shook her head impatiently. "I'm talking about the bombing, Clint. I was there. I saw it."

Clint frowned. "Teddy, I'm not following."

"The New York City bombing. October 1998. You showed me the photo of my mother passing the building just before the bomb went off, remember?"

Clint's expression of surprise slowly morphed into one of skepticism. "Just like that? Just by thinking about an explosion?"

"How would I know? You're the expert here. You tell me how it works."

"Want to tell me why you're so pissed off right now?"

The silence stretched. Teddy knew she wasn't being reasonable. "Because you knew, Clint. That's why. You knew that photo of my mother would trigger something. And you wanted me to know my mother was guilty. Well, I saw her take the bomb into that building. You won. Happy?"

Maybe her OBE had something to do with the photo, though she suspected it had a lot more to do with Marysue's pendant, which had warmed in her hand just before she'd launched into her astral travel. But she wasn't about to open *that* door.

Finally, Clint spoke. "You're right. I did—I do—want you to find Marysue, but not to torture you, Teddy. I need to stop the PC. That's what this is about. Nothing else matters."

"That's exactly the problem. *Nothing* else matters to you. Nothing. Not finding Molly or shutting down Hyle Pharmaceuticals. Everyone's accusing me of having tunnel vision. Of living in the past. But it looks like we both have the same problem."

He shifted on his feet. "It's a problem worth solving. I thought that was your goal, too. Finding the PC. In fact, I heard you were more than a little fixated over the summer."

She rubbed the back of her head, where the knot throbbed. "Yeah, maybe a little."

"So what's the problem?"

She paused, drew in a shaky breath. "The problem is, we're on different sides. You're chasing Marysue down because you want her locked away with the rest of the PC. I just want answers." That wasn't the whole truth. She wanted answers. But she also wanted her mom.

"But when presented with answers, you seem reluctant to accept them," Clint pointed out. "You saw for yourself this time, and still . . ."

Maybe it was because she didn't want to accept the simplest answer, Occam's razor and all that: Marysue was a member of the PC; she'd meant to bomb that building; she'd acted with intention. Accepting this explanation meant accepting that the mother she thought she knew was just a dream.

And if Teddy Cannon was going to stay on track, the track that meant she fought for what was good, what was right, the track that kept her at Whitfield School for Psychics, that was something she couldn't accept. At least not until she understood Marysue's intention. If she could fit this piece into the puzzle that was her existence as a psychic, she'd feel complete.

Clint crossed his arms over his chest. Gave her a hard stare. "Your mother is PC."

"Because I refuse to believe that's *all* she is. And forcing me to witness her crimes in some sort of astral trial isn't going to change that. Not until I know *why* she did what she did."

"I'm not trying to force you, Teddy, I'm trying to help you."

"How is this helping?"

"I—"

"Miss Cannon?" Nurse Bell interrupted from the doorway. "How are we doing?"

"I'm fine." Teddy cast a glare at Clint. "Or I would be."

"Has the spinning stopped?"

No.

"Yes," Teddy said.

"In that case, you may return to your dorm room to rest. Come back tomorrow and I'll check on you."

"Thanks."

Clint stepped back from her bed. He looked as though he wanted to take her arm, to help her stand, to say more, but refrained from doing anything at all. Good deduction on his part. She'd had enough of Clint Corbett's help. Enough of his help to last a whole lifetime. In fact, several, considering she could now technically travel to different time lines.

So Teddy grabbed her boots and got the hell out of there.

CHAPTER NINETEEN

WHILE THE ANSWERS SHE NEEDED REMAINED OUT OF reach, Teddy's only alternative was to apply herself to her studies so that she came out first in her class. Though a long game, the coveted FBI track would give her access to information that otherwise eluded her. So she worked on her astral travel. Attempted to master her psychometric skills. Threw herself into Boyd's obstacle courses with everything she had. Meditated the hell out of the Zen garden. Ate vegan. Teddy Cannon wasn't patient. But she was stubborn. She had resolve. She could do it.

At the moment, however, her resolve was being sorely tested. She sat in a musty corner of the Whitfield library, staring not at the pile of casework in front of her but at Henry Cummings. To say he was a distraction would be an understatement. Gone was the ironed polo shirt. Instead, he was wearing mesh. And sequins.

"Stop looking at me like that," Henry said, gaze trained on the paper in front of him.

Teddy tried to suppress a smile but utterly failed. "I mean, how could I not look at you. You're so . . . sparkly."

Henry put his folder down. "I am dressed as America's sweetheart, Olympic medalist Adam Rippon. Who, I would wager, based on how he always seemed to know exactly which moves the judges wanted to see and in what order they wanted to see them, is probably psychic."

"I didn't say anything." Teddy shuffled through the box at her feet. "It's Halloween. We're supposed to be having fun tonight."

"We might both be having a lot more fun if we could figure out this case."

They'd spent hours in seership and their case studies class working through the logistics of John Polson's death. Though they'd combed the reports and summaries, neither had experienced any psychic breakthroughs. The ballistics report continued to stump Teddy. The bullet used to kill Polson didn't match any weapon carried on the plane.

Sloppy police work, she figured. But when she'd requested to see the bullet for herself, the local Tacoma PD had returned empty-handed. After Dunn had sent the request through the chain of command, the evidence baggie? Suspiciously missing. And as much as she wanted to blame the Alpha currently masquerading as America's sweetheart for their failure, it wasn't like she'd done any better.

Her classmates, despite also having complex assignments, had one thing they didn't: witnesses. No one had been in the plane with John Polson. No one had seen the aircraft go down. The member of the Tacoma PD who'd worked the case was now deceased.

"If we could interview someone connected to the case, we'd have an easier go. Instead, we can only rely on our psychic abilities to gather new information. Which leaves us in the same place we started—i.e., with absolutely nothing."

"So we take a break," Henry said.

"No. We keep working."

"You think that sitting here while everyone else is partying is going to make a difference in cracking a twenty-year-old case? Newsflash, Teddy. He's dead. He'll still be dead in the morning."

Teddy knew that Henry had a point. But schoolwork provided cover. As she grappled with the frustration of having only pieces of Marysue's story—pieces that created a picture she couldn't accept— staying busy was the one thing that kept her sane.

"What are you supposed to be, anyway, a depressed person?"

Teddy was wearing her usual outfit. Jeans, combat boots, white tee. "Ha-ha, very funny." She turned back to the paperwork.

"I hear there's going to be a sundae bar."

"What?"

"A sundae bar," he repeated. "At the Halloween party. With actual ice cream."

Teddy rubbed her head. She knew she really was depressed when the idea of ice cream—*real* ice cream, not the fat-free Tofutti crap they usually served here—didn't excite her.

"And I have a date," he said. "Believe it or not, some of us have lives outside of classes."

She sighed. "Fine, okay. I give up. Go on your date. Eat ice cream."

"Hallclujah," he responded, leaving Teddy alone to her thoughts.

Yeah, he was an Alpha. But there was something Teddy liked about Henry Cummings, even in a see-through skater suit.

She returned her attention to the files. Whereas with Marysue's case, Teddy had been presented an answer she didn't want to accept, the Polson case seemed to have no answers at all. She'd received no psychometric reads on any of the objects. No psychic clues from any of the FBI reports. There had to be something important she was missing. She sighed and shuffled through the reports. Supposedly, they'd been given these cases based on their skill sets. Her telepathy hadn't yielded any results. Neither would telekinesis. How could either skill help, she thought grumpily, when everyone connected to the case was long gone—

It hit her with the force of ten paintball guns targeting her at once. The answer practically stung. Not telepathy. Not telekinesis. Astral travel. A skill so new to her and so unmanageable that she hadn't even considered it.

The bullet to the back of Polson's skull, when Polson had been flying the ultralight alone. The fact that no corresponding weapon had been recovered from the cockpit or the crash site. No human remains except Polson's had been found. It all pointed to one thing.

An astral traveler had murdered Polson sometime after takeoff.

It would be hard, near impossible, to project oneself into a moving object. But an experienced astral traveler could do it, Teddy guessed. And that same astral traveler could carry an object—say, a gun— leaving behind Polson's body and ballistic clues but no trace of the weapon.

Teddy's stomach plunged as Yates's words took on a new and sinister meaning. *Study this, and you'll know what you need to do.* She'd been hoping he would help her get to the bottom of what was happening at Hyle Pharmaceuticals. Or maybe give her a warning regarding the pair of psychics who had broken in to Eli's apartment. Was he suggesting she use her newfound skill to act as a time-traveling assassin? That didn't sound like a warning. It sounded like a PC recruitment pitch.

Suddenly chilled, she glanced around the dimly lit room. She saw menacing shadows where there hadn't been any before. Sitting by herself in the vast, empty library quickly lost its appeal. She should have left with Henry. She gathered her books and files and turned to go.

She stood and spun around—and walked directly into a man. She lurched back, expecting—despite herself—to see the goon from Eli's apartment. But it was Pyro. He caught her by the arms to steady her, then let her go. Dara and Jillian stood behind him. It didn't require special insight to see that they were on their way to the party. Dara, in a green jacket and wide circle glasses, could be none other than nineties sardonic-comic queen Daria Morgendorffer. Jillian rocked a Haight-Ashbury, peace-loving flower-child getup—a look that wasn't much of a stretch from her normal wardrobe. Pyro was too cool for a costume and just wore his usual jeans and dark T-shirt. His only concession to Halloween was black eyeliner. He looked hot. Not that she cared one way or another, she told herself. And then spent the next thirty seconds trying to convince herself that was true.

Dara flicked a glance over Teddy's attire and deadpanned, "I see I'm the only one who made an effort this year."

"I let you put makeup on me, Jones," Pyro said. "That required effort on both our parts." He leveled a look at Teddy, then looked away.

"So," Dara said. "You coming or what?"

Pyro arched a brow as if daring her to say no. A cocky expression. A look hinting that maybe he was getting as tired of their ongoing drama as she was. Maybe tonight they could figure out a way to move past it. So, yeah, for a lot of reasons, she was happy to ditch her solitary stint at the library and head out with her friends.

When they arrived at Harris Hall, she noted that the dining staff had decided to go with a "Stephen King" theme. In the corner, a bunch of first-years went at a giant piñata of Pennywise. Teddy scanned the crowd, wondering if she'd catch a glimpse of Miles, the guy from the infirmary. Just to check in and see how he was doing. No luck. Half the students were in costume, so it wasn't like she would be able to recognize him anyway.

They gorged on the sundae bar, then joined the catcalling when it was time to judge the costume contest. (Henry lost to a fourth-year clairaudient dressed as a mime, which struck Teddy as grossly unfair—a classic case of popularity triumphing over originality and style.)

After a bit, the music slowed, and Pyro suggested the two of them move onto the dance floor. Which sounded like a great idea to Teddy.

"No," Jillian cut in, bouncing on her toes with excitement. "She can't. It's nine o'clock, so it's time for Teddy to take me to the Cantina for drinks. She forgot my birthday this summer, so she promised we'd do something special to make up for it. Remember, Teddy?"

"I did?"

"Tonight?" Pyro frowned. "Why head off campus when there's an actual party here?"

Jillian shot Teddy a look. "Because it's *Halloween*. Remember, Teddy?"

What—Oh. Eli. The message.

Not only had she promised Jillian, she'd helped engineer the illicit get-together. No backing out now. Brushing off Pyro and Dara's offer to accompany them, they made promises to return to the party after a quick round of drinks and headed out.

The Cantina was packed. They'd barely made it through the door when a superhero sporting a red and silver suit, with a mask covering the upper half of his face, caught Jillian around the waist and pulled her into his embrace. After some serious PDA—which went on *waaaay* too long for Teddy's comfort—Eli led them to a table he'd secured earlier.

"Everything all right now, Eli?" Teddy asked.

"Perfect," he replied, his eyes not leaving Jillian, who beamed back at him.

There was nothing as obnoxious as a couple in the throes of mad, all-consuming love. "I was talking about the break-in," she clarified. "Has anything else happened?"

Eli reluctantly turned his man-bunned head in her direction. "Oh, that." He waved his hand dismissively. "Nah. I got the super to install a heavy-duty dead bolt on my door, so it's cool. Nobody's broken in since."

She enjoyed a moment of relief, and even toyed with the idea of ordering a drink, but the waitstaff was swamped, and she didn't want it badly enough to claw her way through the crowd at the bar. Instead, she watched Eli and Jillian gush over each other as though they'd been parted for years rather than weeks. If one night of eco-friendly canoodling would put a smile back on her roommate's face (and maybe stop her moping around long enough to get her ass back in gear and pay attention to her studies), so be it.

But there was only so much Teddy could take. "I'm heading back."

Jillian tore her gaze away from Eli. "Oh. Don't you want to stay for a drink?"

"Nah, I'm good." She hesitated. Glanced around the bar. Everything seemed okay, but . . . "Listen, you guys. Lay low, okay? Just to be safe."

"What do you mean?" Eli asked.

"I mean, just tone down the HEAT stuff until we're sure whoever broke in to your apartment isn't coming back."

Eli gave her a condescending smile. "Risk equals reward, Teddy. If any social justice movement worried about the consequences of their actions—"

"Just chill for a couple of weeks, Eli. Then you can go back to fixing the world."

Jillian squeezed his hand. "Please, Eli? Teddy's right. I want to make sure you're safe."

Teddy swore she could actually *see* Eli's ego inflate. "I guess I could do that," he said.

Good enough. Teddy left the Cantina and hiked back to campus. She slipped back into Harris Hall and found the party in full swing. She scanned the room for her friends. Her gaze landed on Pyro. Teddy felt a smile curve her lips. If he took just one step toward her, she was certain they could finally put their stupid argument behind them. Instead, Pyro turned to say something to Clint. Clint nodded, glanced at Teddy, and stepped away.

"What was that about?" she asked when she reached Pyro's side.

He ignored her question, asking one of his own. "How's Eli?"

She felt her eyes widen in surprise. "How did you—"

"Give me a break."

"And you told Clint?"

His gaze darkened. "Of course not. When he saw you two leave, he figured it out on his own. Jillian's not exactly subtle. And Clint's not stupid." He pursed his lips, shook his head. "The things you civilians think you can get away with."

"And you cops got it all figured out, huh?"

"Pretty much, yeah."

"What's going to happen to Jillian?" she asked. "Is Clint going to expel her for leaving campus without permission?"

"No. She was smart. She didn't actually leave campus. Technically, it's not a probation violation. As long as Jillian shows up to class tomorrow on time, I think he'll let it slide."

"You're kidding. I thought—"

"That Clint was an asshole? Who didn't understand that Jillian made a stupid mistake, following her heart rather than her head, but didn't mean to do any harm? Who, in fact, was probably trying to protect her?" He cocked his head.

Teddy felt her cheeks heat. Yeah, that was exactly what she thought.

He stretched one arm past her shoulder, bracing himself on the wall behind her. Leaned closer. "You're confused about cops, Teddy. With a few really shitty exceptions, we aren't the bad guys."

She liked having Pyro close again. She liked the sound of his voice, the heat of his gaze, and the smell of his skin. Liked talking things over with him. Liked the sexy way the eyeliner framed his dark eyes. She'd missed him, she realized. Maybe as much as Jillian had missed Eli. She could let it slide, what he had said about her mother.

"So I'm thinking," she ventured slowly, "I've got my room to myself tonight."

"You must be psychic," he said. "I was just thinking that same thing."

CHAPTER TWENTY

EARLY NOVEMBER PASSED IN A BLUR. TEDDY AND HENRY turned in their casework and received high marks from Dunn. No word came from Yates, which was kind of a relief, as it allowed Teddy to focus on her courses.

With only two days until Thanksgiving break, Teddy went on an extra-long jog to get one last look at the island before she headed back to Vegas to see her family. By the time she finished and took a quick shower, she was running late and had to make a mad dash across campus to reach Wessner's class on time.

She'd barely slipped into her seat when Wessner instructed everyone to take out their notebooks. Wessner tucked her straight hair behind her ears and wrote *Ordnance Bombs* on the whiteboard in precise letters. Next to it, she wrote *IEDs*, then drew a vertical line separating the two. She turned to face the class. "Who can tell me what an IED is?"

"Improvised explosive device," Pyro called out.

Teddy couldn't help but smile. Dunn's psychometry class had been a struggle for Pyro. But bombs were definitely in his wheelhouse, and this was a unit he'd been looking forward to exploring.

Wessner continued, "Can anyone tell me what an ordnance bomb is?"

Kate Atkins's hand shot up. "Ordnance refers to anything that originates from the military. So an ordnance bomb is professional—military-grade."

"Very good." Wessner turned to write the answers on the appropriate sides of the whiteboard. Under *Ordnance Bombs*, she wrote *Military*, and in the *IED* column, she wrote *Terrorists*.

Wessner turned on the smartboard projector and took the class through a series of PowerPoint slides showing materials used to make IEDs, including fuses, timers, dynamite, plastic explosives, drain cleaner, rust remover, pool sanitizer, and model engine fuel. Bombs were a sexy topic, and Teddy noticed that she and Pyro weren't the only enraptured students. Everyone was glued to the images.

Teddy looked back at the screen, waiting to see a picture of C-4, the chemical used in the bomb her mother had detonated in New York in 1998. But it wasn't listed there.

When Wessner turned to the class and asked if there were any questions, Teddy raised her hand. "What about C-4?" she asked after Wessner called on her. "Isn't that sometimes used in IEDs?"

"C-4 is a military-grade plastic explosive," Wessner explained. "So you'd rarely see it in an improvised explosive. It's simply not easily available to the public."

Teddy met Pyro's eyes, and a look passed between them. She knew they were connecting the same dots. If C-4 wasn't readily available to the public, did the Patriot Corps have some kind of hidden source within the military—a connection with access to powerful explosives?

Wessner moved on to protocol, explaining that Secret Service agents had specific rules to follow in the event that a suspected explosive device was found in a public setting. "Who can tell me the first thing an agent would be expected to do?" she asked.

Once again, Kate's hand shot up. Wessner ignored her and glanced around the room. Liz Cook said, "Um . . . first I would determine if it was really a bomb?"

"You sure you'd want to waste those precious seconds?"

Liz just shrugged. Meanwhile, Kate's hand went even straighter and higher. Teddy worried she might dislocate a shoulder. She felt a warm glow of satisfaction when Wessner ignored her once again. "Mr. Costa?" she inquired.

"Evacuate," he said. "Get everyone the hell out of the area as quickly as possible."

"That's correct," Wessner said. "Your first instinct must always be to clear the area. Don't forget that." She paused and gazed significantly around the room, driving the point home.

"But today," she continued, "I want to talk about defusing a bomb. A step you take only if there's no way to evacuate, no time to get the bomb squad called in."

She clicked to an image of a simple homemade bomb. She broke down the graphic, distinguishing it by weapon type, delivery mechanism, and trigger mechanism. Then she explained how to recognize the main components and how to handle them. Which, in a word, was *carefully*.

"Once you do that, you have to sever the wire connecting the detonator to the rest of the device. That will render it inert. Sounds simple enough, right?"

The remark drew a few uneasy titters throughout the room.

She continued, "The problem, of course, is that IEDs don't come with instruction manuals, and when there are multiple wires, tilt sensors, and even fake detonators, it takes a trained eye to determine which one to cut. Now, pay attention, because a mistake here can result in catastrophic loss of life, including your protectee and other innocent civilians."

Teddy couldn't help noticing that the agent's life wasn't part of the equation. Meat shields, indeed.

The rest of the lecture focused on detonator connections as Wessner took them through a series of slides showing at least sixty different homemade bombs. With each graphic, she explained how to figure out which wire was the one that could disconnect the detonator from the explosive. Teddy—along with everyone else in the room—took copious notes. It was dizzying and far too much to remember. She glanced over at Kate's desk and saw twice as many notes that were at least four times neater, complete with diagrams. It looked like a textbook. Who took notes like that? Sheesh. The woman was a machine.

"We're going to have a hands-on exercise where you will work to disarm a simulated IED. There's a special incentive to finish the exercise first. The winning team will get real-world field experience providing protection to some VIPs—our own Hollis Whitfield and his grandson, who are hosting a party at their home in Tiburon. They will need a protection detail at the event, as an animal rights group has recently targeted them with threats and harassment."

Teddy went cold and then hot. Animal rights group? HEAT, of course. *Eli*. He'd promised her that he'd back off Whitfield and Hyle Pharmaceuticals. It was bad enough that he had broken into a lab.

But maybe Wessner was exaggerating. Maybe it was Hyle Pharmaceuticals that had received the threats, not Whitfield himself. Teddy chewed her lip and decided that if Whitfield was in danger, he would be requesting professional protection, not trainees.

To test her theory, she raised her hand and asked, "Why us? Why not actual law enforcement?"

"Mr. Whitfield has refused official protection," Wessner said. "As many public figures are apt to do, unfortunately."

"Why?"

"First, he doesn't deem the threat credible. He doesn't believe harassment will escalate into violence. Second, he doesn't want to draw negative publicity to his business, or attract further attention to the group that is harassing him. We reached a compromise. Dean Corbett convinced him to allow students to act as a protection detail the day of the event, as a fieldwork exercise."

Teddy turned toward where Jillian was sitting and tried to catch her eye. But her friend's head was down. There was no way Teddy could discern what—if anything—her roommate knew about this. Not without invading her thoughts telepathically, that is. She resolved to find out later and refocused her attention on the lecture.

"You'll work in teams of two," Wessner said, and began to pair people with the student sitting next to them. That meant Pyro was working with Jillian. And Teddy and Kate were working together. Okay, not a love match. But if she wanted to win this damned thing, Kate was the teammate to have.

Wessner walked around the room, carefully setting a simulated IED in front of each team. The one Teddy and Kate faced looked like two metal canisters with an old-style cell phone affixed to the top with black electrical tape. The phone, which was clearly the detonating device, had three wires leading from it—they were all blue.

Wessner gave each team one wire cutter. "This isn't a movie. This isn't which color wire to cut. You think someone building a bomb is going to color-code for your convenience? They *want* the bomb to go off. Your job is to make sure it doesn't." She set a timer in front of the room and said, "Begin."

The room fell into a hush of teams whispering. After a few moments, Dara and Ben's voices began to rise.

"Not that one, you idiot," Dara said.

"Trust me," Ben said. "I got this."

Teddy tried to ignore them; she and Kate inspected the wires on their bomb as carefully as possible. Suddenly, Dara cried out, and Teddy looked over to see her covered in red paint. Ben was also splattered. Wessner had rigged the bombs with paint to simulate blood.

Ava erupted in a fit of laughter, and Teddy wondered if her high school class had voted her Least Likely to Grow Up. Wessner frowned. "Not funny, Ms. Laureau. That could have been the blood of innocent bystanders."

"Concentrate, dammit," Kate whispered to Teddy. "We can't afford to make a mistake here. We need to disconnect the power source and remove the blasting caps."

Teddy turned her attention back to their bomb and tried to tune out the other paint-splatter explosions erupting throughout the classroom. Recalling Wessner's demonstration slides, Teddy followed the line of a blue wire that connected directly to the phone battery.

"That's a dummy wire," Kate said. "A trick."

"Are you sure?" Teddy said.

"Of course I'm sure."

"But how?"

"Because I know." Kate shook her head as if Teddy were insufferably stupid. "Wessner didn't say we couldn't use our psychic powers to figure this out. And I'm claircognizant, remember? I just *know* which one it is. It's the one on the left." With that, Kate handed Teddy the wire cutters.

"You want *me* to cut it?" Teddy said. "Why not you?"

"I'm the one who figured out which wire it is. You have to do something valuable on this team."

Teddy let out a sigh and hoped Kate wasn't sabotaging her. She took the tool, opened the blades over the wire on the left, closed her eyes, and prayed. Then she squeezed.

She heard the distinct snip of the wire breaking and then . . . nothing. No bang. No paint. "Congratulations, Cannon and Atkins," Wessner said. "You're the winners of the challenge. That means you ladies will provide the security detail for Whitfield's Thanksgiving party."

Wait, what?

Wessner hadn't said anything about the party being on *Thanksgiving*. What about her mother's turkey? Aunt Vicky's green bean casserole? What about goopy cranberry sauce and marshmallowy sweet potatoes and pecan pie for dessert? What about her chance to escape all the pressures of school and enjoy the company of her family? Gone.

It had all disappeared faster than her father's famous oyster stuffing.

Teddy was permitted to use Whitfield Institute's front office phone to call her parents and tell them she wouldn't be home for the holiday. She dreaded making the call. Knowing them, they probably had a list of things they wanted to do together to celebrate.

"Hey, Teddy, want some advice?"

She glanced at Dara, who'd accompanied her to the front office. One look at her unsympathetic expression—the kind that told Teddy she was about to deliver some tough love—and she had her answer. "No."

"Get over yourself," Dara continued, as if she hadn't heard. "You're studying for a career in law enforcement. Among special perks like getting shot at, writing reports in triplicate, and surrounding ourselves with lowlife criminals, we rarely get to spend the holidays with our families. The job comes first."

"Thanks. Very helpful."

Teddy went inside, shutting the office door in Dara's face as she did.

As it turned out, it was good advice. Once Teddy explained where she'd be and why, her parents were more than just understanding—they were proud. Which meant that Teddy felt a little bit proud, too. She ended the call by promising to fly home for a visit as soon as her schedule permitted.

When she stepped out of the office, Dara was waiting for her. "Well? How'd it go?"

"Actually," she replied, "not bad."

Dara fell into step beside her as they headed back to the dorms. "Hey, why don't Pyro and I stick around campus this weekend so you don't have to eat tofurkey all by your lonesome?"

Teddy pulled herself together and forced a smile. Just because she was stuck on campus didn't mean she wanted her friends to hang around. They had friends and family waiting at home, too. "Nah, I'm good."

"You sure?"

"Absolutely. Besides, I've got my good buddy Kate Atkins to keep me company. What could possibly go wrong?"

CHAPTER TWENTY-ONE

TEDDY DUCKED JUST IN TIME TO AVOID BEING WHACKED in the head by the thick manila envelope sailing across her dorm room. Kate's scornful voice followed. "What the hell, Cannon? You didn't even bother to open the dossier I left for you to review. That intel came from Wessner, you know."

Teddy rolled her eyes. It was a party, after all, not a protest. She didn't need a dossier to tell her what she'd find at Whitfield's home: a bunch of über-wealthy friends and family members, dressed in ridiculously formal clothing, when everybody knew elastic waists were the *only* way to go on Thanksgiving. Including Whitfield's grandson, likely a horrifically spoiled thirteen-year-old kid with an Xbox controller semipermanently affixed to his hand.

The truth was, Teddy *had* given the dossier a cursory glance. There was a note about HEAT, which had recently pressured Hyle to shut down its lab through a lengthy petition. She and Kate had only Wessner's word to go on about the threat, because there was nothing specific in the file about who had made it and what he or she had said.

The thing that interested her about Whitfield was his connection to Dr. Eversley. And Eversley wasn't on the guest list included in the dossier. Nor were any of the board members of Hyle Pharmaceuticals. Which meant this was going to be a boring social event. Teddy's only hope of gaining any meaningful insight on what was happening at Hyle would be if she left the party to snoop through Whitfield's personal papers. An action she hadn't entirely ruled out.

She gave her hair a final comb-through, then stood and cast a longing glance at her combat boots, which lay sprawled on the floor near her closet.

"You're kidding, right?" Kate's voice dripped sarcasm. "Would it hurt you to *try* to be a little professional?"

A second eye roll was too much even for Teddy, so she simply slipped her feet into Dara's navy pumps. As Teddy's wardrobe lacked anything that might be considered professional, Dara had outfitted her for the occasion: a navy silk blouse and matching navy dress pants, a skinny silver belt cinched around her waist. Glitzy enough for the party, but something she could move fast in if she had to. As they weren't authorized to carry weapons, she didn't have to worry about concealing a holster.

She wondered if Kate had gotten the memo. Kate had gone for a fifties-style G-man look. She sported a pair of black pants and a jacket bulky enough to conceal a pair of AK-15s. Her hair was knotted in a severe bun at the nape of her neck. If Kate harbored any intention of heading into the city after the party—the idea had certainly crossed Teddy's mind—that outfit wasn't doing her any favors.

Thirty minutes later, the boat Hollis Whitfield had hired to ferry guests to his Tiburon home gently bumped against the pier to his private beach. From there, a chauffeur-driven Range Rover conveyed Teddy and Kate up a steep wooded slope to a house that looked as if it had been carved into the hillside. They walked up to an enormous deck offering panoramic views of the city, the Golden Gate Bridge, and Teddy's own home away from home, Angel Island—though it was strangely disquieting to see it from this perspective. Viewed from afar, it looked so small and self-contained, yet when she was at Whitfield Institute, it comprised her entire world.

Teddy turned to enter the mansion. Kate caught her arm. "Let's sync up first. What channel?"

Teddy shrugged. "Lucky seven works for me."

Last year, Professor Dunn had taught them all the techniques necessary to engage in two-way auditory telepathy. They began by imagining walkie-talkies tuned to the same frequency. They visualized the number of the channel, then synced their breathing. Teddy and Kate had been telepathic partners on different occasions in their first year at Whitfield. Teddy found it easy to reconnect with her. Within seconds, the rhythm of Kate's breathing came through: steady and regular beats, as constant as a metronome. Then her voice: *You ready, Cannon?*

Born that way.

Let's just get through this, all right? Don't screw up.

Kate strode past her and went inside. Teddy loitered on the deck for a few minutes longer, enjoying the view, then followed. The rooms were architectural marvels of stark simplicity, meant to dazzle guests with their enormous windows, incomprehensible modern art, and sleek metal furniture that looked painful to sit on. All very impressive and, to Teddy's mind, at least, entirely unoriginal. She'd hoped Hollis Whitfield's home would reveal *something* about him. But this place was as personal as a bank lobby.

She snagged a couple of hors d'oeuvres from a passing waiter and turned her attention to the guests. Maybe sixty or so in attendance, plus a few familiar faces from Whitfield Institute. Teddy spotted Hollis Whitfield, naturally, but also Joan Wessner, Sergeant Rosemary Boyd, and Clint Corbett. So much for her plan to disappear for a bit and rifle through Whitfield's stuff.

Everyone was relaxed and at ease, mingling and chatting, a cocktail or glass of wine in hand. Wine. Now, there was an idea . . .

Don't even think about it, Cannon. We're on duty, remember?

Why don't you go find a pole to salute, Atkins?

Speaking of saluting, Teddy was surprised at the number of military personnel milling among the guests. But then maybe Hollis was doing some patriotic thing, inviting servicemen and -women stationed away from their families to enjoy Thanksgiving with—

Her thoughts slammed to a halt as her gaze locked on a tall man with erect bearing and dark eyes, his silver hair trimmed in a military-style buzz cut. He wore an army Class A uniform, a crowded array of medals pinned to his chest.

General Maddux. Teddy recognized him instantly, though they'd met only once, and very briefly: almost a year ago, a New Year's party at Jeremy's parents' house. Older but definitely not elderly. The kind of guy who looked at ease among these privileged people. The kind of guy who radiated power, discipline, and order. Sergeant Boyd's dream date.

Kate, who came from a family of career military officers, was already fawning over the guy. Teddy's gut reaction? Stomach-tightening, heart-pounding stress. Their eyes met, and Teddy instantly averted her gaze. She had absolutely no interest in engaging in small talk or playing the haven't-we-met-before game.

Teddy turned toward a young, good-looking guy. Judging by his flat, almost pained expression, he definitely wasn't enjoying himself. Something about him was vaguely familiar, though she couldn't quite place him. He was tall and lean, wearing a conservative suit and polished wing tips. His hair was swept back from his face, his mouth was pinched, and his eyes, well, she couldn't see his eyes behind his vintage eyeglasses . . . Miles. The guy she'd met at the infirmary.

What the hell is he doing here?

Miles Whitfield, Kate informed her. *As in Hollis Whitfield's grandson. If you'd bothered to read the dossier, you'd know that.*

Miles was Whitfield's grandson? And not a student? No wonder she hadn't seen him around campus. Of course, she couldn't blame herself for assuming that a young guy in Whitfield's infirmary was a student. A natural mistake.

Teddy wondered if Miles Whitfield knew that his grandfather funded a school for psychics. She made a mental note to remember that he was *not* a student. And unless she learned otherwise, she had to assume he didn't.

Next time, do your homework, Cannon.

Teddy ignored Kate's smug condescension and made a beeline for Miles. "Hey," she said, smiling brightly. "You've got to quit following me around. It's getting embarrassing."

He turned slowly, almost mechanically, toward her. No wonder she hadn't recognized him immediately. Nothing about him reminded her of the young, flirty guy she'd crushed on at the infirmary. His eyes were hollow, his skin pallid, and his expression not just blank but stripped. As though every ounce of his personality had been drained away.

She gently placed her hand on his arm. "Hey, Miles. It's Teddy—as in bear. We met at the infirmary a few weeks ago, remember?"

He blinked heavily, then forced his lips into a weak semblance of a smile. "Hey, Teddy. Sure I remember you." His voice sounded strained. He cleared his throat. "Couldn't get enough of me, huh?"

Teddy smiled, gamely continuing the charade that he was just fine. "Whitfield's grandson?"

He shrugged, slightly sheepish. "A guy's got to have a little fun now and then."

"Hey, I get it," she said, and was pretty sure she did. As the heir to an unfathomable fortune, he probably had a hard time figuring out if people liked him or his money. Better to keep it under wraps when you first met someone.

"What are you doing here, anyway?" he asked.

"I'm on duty."

"Duty?"

"You know, general surveillance. Keeping an eye on things. Making sure there isn't any trouble."

"Why would there be trouble?"

Stupid slip of the tongue on her part. Teddy studied his face, trying to determine if he was challenging her for information or truly ignorant of HEAT's harassment of his grandfather, not to mention that he was currently surrounded by several powerful psychics who would protect him at all costs. She decided it was the latter.

"There won't be," she said. She gestured to the bankers and billionaires, the women in pearls. "But you never know. Any minute now, this crowd could get rough." She expected him to smile. But the easygoing guy she'd met at the infirmary was gone.

"Right." He looked around the room. "All the ass-kissing, the fawning over my grandfather." Teddy said nothing. It was hard to think of an appropriate response. He shook his head. "Sorry. I didn't mean to sound so harsh. Not feeling great today."

"How are those migraines, Miles? Have you found any relief?"

"Relief?" He lightly brushed his temple with one hand. "No. But I think I've learned to manage them better. At least that's what Dr. Eversley says."

"Maybe Dr. Eversley's wrong," Teddy said before she could stop herself. "Maybe you shouldn't be taking your medication at all if it's causing such horrible side effects."

"He says I need it."

Teddy chewed her bottom lip, hesitating. This was dangerous territory. Miles's medical issues were none of her business. On top of that, Wessner had repeatedly lectured them that the only way for a Secret Service agent to do her job was to remain impersonal and detached. Emotional involvement with the subject invariably led to serious errors in judgment.

But whatever Miles was taking was obviously *hurting* him. She couldn't just shrug that off. Particularly not if Eversley was the one prescribing the medication.

"You know," she said, "before I came to Whitfield, I was misdiagnosed with epilepsy. For years I was treated with the wrong medication and lived with debilitating side effects. Seizures, mood swings, memory gaps—it was awful. I put up with it until I found out what was really wrong with me." Or right with her, Teddy supposed, depending on where one came down on the "gift" of psychic ability. She wondered what, if anything, he knew about her world.

Miles frowned at her. "What are you saying?"

She took a deep breath, gathering her courage. "Maybe you shouldn't be seeing Eversley. Or not *just* Eversley. Maybe a different doctor would give you a different diagnosis, or change your medication—"

"But my grandfather thinks Dr. Eversley is brilliant."

"Yes, but a second opinion—"

"Miles! There you are!"

Teddy looked up to see an attractive, immaculately groomed woman in her early sixties. "Do forgive the interruption, but there are some friends of your grandfather's here whom you simply must meet. I'll have you back to your friend in two shakes, I promise!" With that, she led Miles into the crowd.

Teddy watched him go, sighing. Perfect. She'd said just enough to confuse Miles, but not enough to prompt him into taking action. She scanned the room for suspicious characters and, spying none, moved to the bar. If she couldn't have a real drink, a tonic and lime would have to do. She waited as the bartender transferred a new set of clean glasses to the drink station behind the bar. Then he turned around.

And it was a "he" she recognized.

"Eli!" she gasped.

But Eli had no reaction to seeing her. He looked right through her, as though he'd never met her before.

Teddy's eyes narrowed as alarm bells went off in her head. For months Eli had said that HEAT would use whatever means necessary to stop Whitfield and Hyle Pharmaceuticals from experimenting on animals. They had pressured Hyle to shut down its lab peacefully. And she was supposed to believe it was just a coincidence that he was here at Whitfield's home?

She wasn't buying it.

She watched him circle the perimeter of the room, picking up abandoned plates and empty glasses. He moved with smooth efficiency, as though he'd done the job for years. Dressed in starched black pants, white shirt, and black bow tie, he didn't look like himself. Teddy reconsidered her initial suspicion. While Jillian hadn't specifically mentioned what Eli did for money, he paid the rent somehow. But if he was working a job, why would he pretend not to know her?

She was about to alert Kate when an empty wineglass fumbled from his grasp, rolling beneath the table where the punch bowl sat. Eli made a show of ducking under the table to retrieve it, only to come up empty-handed.

Probably nothing. But odd. Maybe the glass had broken, and Eli had gone in search of a dustpan.

Teddy approached the table to confirm.

She lifted the tablecloth and peeked beneath it.

There was no glass. Broken or otherwise.

Instead: a blinking light and a mass of wires. A single word screamed through her mind:

Bomb.

CHAPTER TWENTY-TWO

BOMB.

It couldn't be real. It couldn't be happening. Someone else, someone more qualified, was bound to step in. But she had no idea where Clint and the rest of the school staff were.

This was on her.

She remembered what Wessner had taught them, and those instructions became the only thing in Teddy's universe.

Evacuate. Clear the room.

"Bomb," Teddy said, at first loud enough only for her own ears to pick up. She cleared her throat and shoved the words out again. "Bomb! Clear the room!"

Teddy? Kate's voice. Thank God. They were still synced.

IED. Help me. Now.

IED? You sure? How—

Thirty seconds! Teddy's gaze fixed on the tiny red numbers at the top of the IED. *Twenty-nine!*

"Bomb!" Teddy shouted again. "Clear the room! Everyone out! Move!"

Whitfield's guests turned toward her, their faces mirroring the same incomprehension she'd felt seconds earlier. Then understanding dawned. The cry was picked up and repeated by people in her immediate vicinity. Panicked, they started pushing toward the nearest exit, which happened to be the French doors that opened onto the balcony.

Wrong way, Teddy realized, watching as they slammed up against the doors. In commercial spaces, fire regulations mandated that doors open outward, so a room could be evacuated quickly in the event of an emergency. But there were no such regulations for private spaces. Whitfield's architects had designed the interior so that the French doors opened into the room. A feature that made the doors impossible to open with so many people pushed up against them.

She saw Miles standing motionless in the middle of the crowd, clutching his forehead in pain. She saw Clint making his way toward her, but he was blocked by General Maddux, who was trying to move in the opposite direction.

Teddy looked where the general was attempting to flee: a hallway that led to the dining room. The hallway had been blocked by a folding panel designed to screen guests from staff as they set the table and arranged the dinner buffet. It was the perfect escape route, but no one else had seen it.

"This way!" Teddy screamed, trying to direct the crowd's attention to the exit. She had wasted another precious second debating whether she should focus on evacuating the room or disabling the IED.

Then Boyd was at her side, and Teddy's decision was made for her. The sergeant knocked over the partition, grabbed a guest by the arm, and shoved the woman through the newly clear hallway. She reached for another guest to repeat the maneuver. It was working, but not fast enough. No way would the room be cleared before the bomb detonated. Wessner's instructions rang in her head once again.

If escape isn't possible, defuse the bomb.

Teddy ripped her attention away from Boyd. She whirled around and squatted in front of the low table. Flipped up the linen tablecloth. Saw a block of what looked like gray modeling clay. Caught the faint smell of something familiar. Sweet and nutty. C-4.

She remembered enough of Wessner's lecture to know that when triggered by another blast—say, the blast of a detonator—the explosive power of that lump of C-4 would reduce Whitfield's living room to rubble.

The trick was to disable the detonator without setting it off. Teddy scanned the device. She identified a pressure cooker valve, laced with a spiderweb of gray wires running into the back of an attached digital clock. Textbook IED. She watched the red numbers blink from fifteen seconds to fourteen.

She bit down hard on her bottom lip. On the surface, her task was simple. Disable the blasting cap. Disconnect the wire that would trigger the detonator. But there were too many wires. They were twisted together in a complicated knot that made guesswork impossible. One wrong move—

Kate knocked against her shoulder as she dropped to her knees beside Teddy.

Kate! There are a bazillion wires here. Which one do we pull?

Let me think!

There's no time.

I don't have a read, Teddy. Not yet. Give me a second.

Eleven seconds. Ten.

Kate! Now!

The upper left! Disconnect the upper-left wire!

Her hand shaking, Teddy reached for the IED. But just as her fingers brushed the wire, Clint slammed against her. He grabbed her with one hand, Kate with the other, and dragged them away from the table.

Teddy fought against him. "I've got to disconnect it!" she said. But Clint didn't hear her. He was in linebacker mode, intent on protecting them from the bomb.

He knocked her and Kate to the ground, shielding them from the forthcoming blast. Teddy struggled beneath him but was pinned by his weight. Trapped, she peered across the room, desperately watched the timer blink.

Six seconds. Five.

Miles, perhaps unaware where the danger lay, moved away from the panicked crowd and stepped closer to the bomb. He'd be the IED's first victim. Her assignment was to protect him. And there was nothing she could do. Wessner's voice echoed in her head: *Failures. All of you.*

But then her training kicked in. Another voice in her head. Her own.

You've got this. You've stopped bullets. You can do what no one else in this room can: buy time.

Teddy conjured up the image of the film deck in her mind, felt the metal reels turning in her hand.

Slowly, slowly. Slow everything down. I am a being of a simultaneous universe.

Three seconds left.

She saw Whitfield's white hair fluttering ever so gently back and forth as Boyd shoved him toward the hallway. She saw a single bead of sweat pooling on Miles's upper lip. Even Clint's voice— *"Everyone down! Now!"*—sounded like a record played at modified speed.

Teddy focused on extending her astral hand toward the upper-left wire. Traced it down inside the casing of the clock, past its internal mechanisms. She plucked the wire from the power source where it was attached.

And then the film reels she'd been mentally manipulating spun out of her control. The accumulated seconds returned with a vengeance. Allowing her one second to know that she and Kate had failed. She watched in horror as the IED lit up like a Vegas slot machine. She heard Kate gasp. Not the upper left. Kate had chosen the wrong wire.

Teddy closed her eyes and braced for the explosion, wondering what the end would feel like.

CHAPTER TWENTY-THREE

SHE FELT A BLAST OF AIR, A SHOCK WAVE OF POWER-ful energy, and then . . . nothing. No brilliant light. No searing heat. No ear-splitting explosion. No agonizing pain. Nothing. Nothing but Clint's smothering weight pinning her to the floor.

Teddy opened her eyes and looked at the IED. The C-4 was a misshapen mass of grayish putty; the timer and wires were scorched black. The detonator had fired. The blasting cap had gone off. But there hadn't been an explosion.

Teddy? Kate's voice. *What the hell just happened?*

Clint rolled over, and Teddy immediately scrambled out from beneath him. She scurried on her hands and knees toward the IED. Totally inert. Just a lump of C-4, disconnected from the triggered detonator and blasting cap. It didn't make sense.

She heard a groan and saw Miles huddled on the floor, rocking back and forth and holding his head in his hands.

"Miles, are you all right?"

No answer. His skin was waxen, his eyes were closed. His arms and legs tremored. Teddy, more than anyone, would recognize the signs of a seizure, even if she had been misdiagnosed as a child.

"Hey!" Teddy shouted. "A doctor! I need a doctor over here!"

She'd anticipated someone would rush to her aid. But panic had narrowed her vision. She'd been aware only that Miles needed help. As she looked up to repeat her shout—louder this time—she was forced to acknowledge the pandemonium sweeping across the room.

None of the guests were aware that the IED had been neutralized. Chaos reigned, though at least there were fewer people to contend with. Boyd and Wessner had succeeded in turning the tide of fleeing guests away from the French doors and were funneling them through the dining room hallway and out the front door.

Teddy saw one woman whose face had been shoved so forcefully against the French doors that a pane had shattered; her forehead and cheek were bleeding. A man cradled what was likely a broken wrist. An elderly woman sprawled unconscious on the floor, her husband bent beside her.

Miles gave another groan. Before Teddy could react, Hollis Whitfield was kneeling at her side. So was Kate. "Let's get him off the floor," Whitfield said.

Teddy caught her lip, uncertain. "Shouldn't we wait for a doctor?"

"Not necessary," Whitfield said. His brow was furrowed, but his voice was firm. "He's had these episodes before. He'll be just fine. Won't you, Miles?"

"Already fine," Miles said out, struggling to stand.

On one hand, the most prudent move was to wait for a doctor to check him over. But Teddy had her own long and painful history of dealing with illness. She remembered all too clearly her desperate desire for privacy after such a turn. So she simply watched as Whitfield lifted Miles to his feet and together they moved gingerly down the hall.

Teddy's next thought was of Eli.

She sprang up and ran into the kitchen. Empty. The back door was flung wide open—likely the exit that the catering staff had taken. She was about to leave when the sound of running water caught her ear. She was sure Eli would have fled by now, so she was shocked to find him standing at the sink in a small pantry, washing a wineglass. Scrubbing and rinsing the same glass over and over.

"Eli?"

No response.

Teddy took him by the elbow and turned him to face her. For the first time that night, she looked directly into his eyes. They were distant and unfocused. Pupils too large. Teddy recognized the look. The cops last year in the Vegas casino. Molly in the obstacle course. The security guards at Sector Three. No wonder he hadn't recognized her earlier that evening.

Eli was being mentally influenced. Someone had psychically manipulated him into setting off the IED.

Yates.

But just because Yates was capable didn't mean he'd done it. Teddy had surveilled the party upon arrival but had seen no sign of Yates. She hadn't noticed anyone suspicious among the guests.

If not Yates, who? And why?

Teddy needed answers. Fast. She grabbed Eli by the shoulders and shook him. It was brutish but effective. Eli's eyes came into focus, and his expression sharpened. "Teddy? What are you doing here?" He blinked and looked around, as if taking in his surroundings for the first time. "Hey. Where'd everyone go?"

"Clear!" Kate called into the kitchen. "Wessner's cleared the IED!"

Eli's baffled gaze slowly moved from Kate to Teddy. "Wait a minute, what?"

"There was a bomb—a bomb scare—but it's over now."

"A *bomb*? Holy shit. But—"

"Listen," Teddy said. "The authorities are going to blame HEAT. And you."

"Me? Are you crazy? I would never resort to violence. That's not what HEAT does. Jillian knows that. Just ask her!"

"What were you thinking, threatening Hollis Whitfield?"

"Threatening Hollis Whitfield?" He continued to stare at her, looking baffled. "What the hell are you talking about? You asked me to back off, Teddy, and I have."

"Eli, I know what happened. You threatened—"

"I haven't threatened anybody. Neither has HEAT. I swear."

Teddy's eyes narrowed. No jury would believe it was a coincidence that a bomb was planted at a social gathering of the Hyle Pharmaceuticals board just days after HEAT had pressured Hyle to shut down its lab. Particularly when witnesses could place HEAT's leader near the scene. Maybe that was what *someone else* was counting on: whoever had engineered the IED had covered their tracks by setting up Eli Nevin as the fall guy.

She watched horrified understanding dawn on Eli's face as he reached the same conclusion. "Someone else did this, Teddy. It wasn't me."

Teddy wasn't a fan of Eli's. Never had been, probably never would be. But she did believe him. And she was certain he'd been mentally influenced into triggering the detonator on the IED. She wasn't going to stand by and see him arrested and thrown in prison for something he didn't do.

"Go," she urged. "Do not talk to anybody. And don't go back to your apartment. It may not be safe. Do you have someplace else you can stay?"

"A friend of mine runs a rescue shelter in Mendocino. I could crash there."

"Good. Go. I'll find you as soon as it's safe."

For once, Eli didn't ask any questions. He turned and ran out the door.

Teddy moved to the window and looked for signs of Yates, recognizing the futility even as she scanned the sloping backyard. If Yates had been involved, he would be long gone.

"Who was that?" Kate asked.

"What? Oh. Catering staff. He doesn't know anything."

Not a lie, but not the whole truth, either.

It was then that Wessner stepped into the kitchen, preventing Kate from asking any more questions. "All right, heroes," she said. "Come with me."

Teddy and Kate reported to Whitfield's home office. Boyd, Clint, and Wessner stationed themselves on one side of the room, while Whitfield perched on the edge of a massive oak desk. Pictures of Miles as a young kid, always by himself, were scattered over the walls of the room's dark paneling. Holding a place of honor over the mantel was a framed photograph of a handsome young marine in full dress uniform, an array of medals pinned to his chest. The resemblance was strong enough for Teddy to peg him as a relative.

Before she could examine the photo further, Whitfield asked her to recap how she and Kate had identified and disarmed the IED.

Teddy hesitated. How had she and Kate disarmed an IED packed with enough explosive power to blow the side off the building? The old punch line sprang to her lips: *carefully*.

But since she suspected humor wouldn't be appreciated, she replied, "Training, sir."

"I need you to be a little more specific than that."

General Maddux stepped forward. He stood a little too close, in Teddy's opinion. One of those men who instinctively attempted to intimidate everyone they met. The worst. "We'd all like you to be a little more specific. What branch of law enforcement are you with?"

"These two are students at my institute," Whitfield said, gesturing to her and Kate.

"Students?" Maddux repeated. "Yet they were able to disarm a sensitive IED? How is that possible?"

"The truth is," Teddy said, "I'm not sure we did disarm it."

Wessner looked at her. "Your modesty is unnecessary, Teddy. Obviously, you two figured out how to separate the detonator from the

C-4. I personally examined the device. The blasting cap exploded. Had it not been disarmed, none of us would be standing here now."

Teddy looked at Kate, who simply shrugged. "You're right, ma'am. But I'm not being modest. The truth is, I cut the wrong wire. That IED did not explode when it should have."

"Explain," Wessner clipped out.

Again Teddy hesitated, looking at Maddux.

Clint cleared his throat. "If you'll excuse us, General. It appears my recruits need to discuss sensitive information. Information that is restricted to staff and recruits of the Whitfield Institute."

"I'm a general in the United States Army. That should give me adequate clearance."

Clint met his eyes. "With all due respect, sir, it doesn't."

The two men locked gazes, sizing each other up. At length, Maddux broke the silence. "And you are?"

"Clint Corbett. Dean of students at Whitfield Institute."

"Given the chaos that we all just endured, Dean Corbett, might I suggest you're a bit over your head? I am offering my assistance. I think you would be wise to take it."

"I have the situation—"

"General Maddux and I have been friends for decades," Whitfield interrupted. "We can trust him. Furthermore, he has expertise in the field of military ordnance that may be of use. The faster we bring closure to this matter and shut down any unnecessary publicity, the better. It's bad enough that HEAT pressured Hyle into shutting down our lab. We cannot condone their escalating tactics." He stood and paced in front of his desk. "We're damned lucky someone wasn't killed today."

"What escalating tactics?" Maddux asked.

At Whitfield's nod, Wessner briefed the general on HEAT. Whitfield confessed that he had received another threat that very morning—though Wessner didn't specify who had made the threat and what he or she had said. Whitfield didn't elaborate, either. And Teddy didn't share what she now believed to be true: HEAT hadn't made a threat that morning.

The general frowned. "You knew about this threat, and yet you put yourself and your guests in jeopardy by using students for protection?"

Whitfield flushed. "Obviously, I had no way of knowing this would happen. There have been other . . . disruptions, but they've been only nuisances. There was no reason to suspect today would be any different."

But there was a reason, Teddy thought. *HEAT didn't make the most recent threats. Someone else did.* There was no way to say that without disclosing her conversation with Eli.

Whitfield drew himself up. "It doesn't matter," he continued. "I will not be bullied or intimidated. The work undertaken at Hyle Pharmaceuticals is too important to be shut down."

"What work?" Teddy said before she could stop herself. "Miles could have been killed today. He was standing right beside the IED. What's so important that you would risk his life?"

Whitfield paled. He seemed to consider Teddy's words. "Miles was beside the IED . . ." He moved around his desk, collapsed into his chair. "Tell me exactly what happened."

Teddy shot another glance at Maddux, which Whitfield dismissed with an impatient roll of his wrist. "Go on."

She looked at Clint, who reluctantly nodded, giving her permission to speak. Not like they had much of a choice. Hollis Whitfield was, after all, the founder of Whitfield Institute, a school for psychics. Ultimately, the decision of whom to include in the inner circle rested with him.

She told them that she and Kate had communicated telepathically. That Kate had used claircognizance to choose the wire. Teddy explained how she'd slowed time and disconnected the wire from the power source astrally. She told them that, despite their best efforts to disable the IED, she had seen the device light up, ready to explode, but somehow it hadn't.

Maddux took this all in. A sour look on his face. Then he shook his head. "I don't like what I'm hearing."

"What do you mean?" Whitfield asked.

"I thought you were preparing students for a career in service to their country. Law enforcement, military, CIA. That sort of thing. Not filling their heads with useless pseudoscience mumbo jumbo."

Clint bristled. "Whether or not you understand our methods, General, seems beside the point. These students disabled an IED psychically."

Maddux held up a hand to silence him. He looked directly at Whitfield. "I'm ashamed to admit the military has made similar mistakes in the past, Hollis. As have other branches of the government. Training soldiers to use so-called extrasensory perception. Naturally, none of it went anywhere. A huge waste of money, time, and effort. What you need is someone who can get to the facts, not stir up nonsense." He paused, made a point of glaring at Clint. Then he turned to Teddy. "You were right there. On duty. Did you see who planted the IED?"

Teddy felt all eyes on her and made sure her mental shield was firmly in place. "No, sir."

"Any suspects?"

Yates and a lineup of various PC members flashed through her head: the large man, the blond woman . . . Marysue. "No, sir."

He asked Kate the same questions. She glanced to Teddy before shaking her head.

"I believe my point is proved." Maddux swung around to nod at Whitfield. "A roomful of people and no suspects. Hollis, your recruits would benefit from training in how to conduct an actual investigation, rather than whatever useless rubbish they've been taught. If you'll allow me, I'll get some of my men to focus on this HEAT organization, bring them in, and get answers."

"Absolutely not," Clint said. "We'll handle this in-house, the way we've always done."

Whitfield's jaw moved as he thought, as though he were literally chewing over possible responses and outcomes. At length, he nodded at Clint. "We keep it in-house. But I want results, Clint. Not excuses and delays."

The last bit, a direct slap at Clint, was undoubtedly for the general's benefit. But Clint took the verbal jab without objection. He'd won—for now, at least—and wasn't going to complain. "Understood."

Teddy and Kate were dismissed. Kate, who'd been fawning over the general earlier that evening, looked shaken. She mumbled something about patrolling the estate to see if she could come up with anything they'd missed.

Teddy stopped her. "Kate."

"Yeah?"

"That guy's an asshole. Don't listen to him."

Kate looked past Teddy into the trampled remains of the living room: overturned tables and chairs, spilled food, draperies hanging askew. Judging from her distant expression, Teddy guessed she wasn't seeing any of it.

"You know that's what I want to do, right? Go into service. I can trace my family's military ties all the way back to the Revolutionary War. But how am I supposed to serve if everyone I meet thinks what I can do is bullshit?"

"Look, not everyone is as closed-minded as that guy."

Kate sighed. "You don't know how it works, Teddy. Maddux is a legend. If he thinks what we do is bullshit, so will everyone else."

The admission of doubt was rare for Kate. Teddy thought for a moment before replying. "Then quit now," she said. "Or suck it up and prove that two-star idiot wrong. Show how good you are. If anyone can do it, you can."

"Right. Like it's that easy."

"I didn't say it would be easy. I said you can do it. It hurts like hell for me to admit it, but you're good at this." She paused. "Not as good as me, but hey, what do you expect?"

"I'll go toe-to-toe with you any day, Cannon." A smile flickered briefly across Kate's lips. Then she paused, cocked her head. "Now tell me: Who was that guy in the kitchen?"

"I don't know who you're talking about."

"Sure, Cannon. Sure." With that, Kate turned and strode away.

Teddy stood for a moment, thinking, when a moan came from down the hall. Another victim of the rush toward the French doors? She followed the sound into a stately wood-paneled library and found Miles lying on a leather couch. His glasses rested on a side table. He had his hands pressed over his eyes, and the overhead lights were out.

"Miles? Can I get you anything?"

"Need my medication," he mumbled.

He directed her to a black velvet pouch tucked in a drawer in a small end table. She walked it over to him and helped him to a seated position. Miles unbuttoned his pants and lowered them to his knees, exposing his boxers. He seemed almost oblivious to the fact that Teddy was there. He pulled a wrapped medical syringe from the bag, ripped it open with his teeth. Without bothering to clean the area with one of the alcohol swabs included in the kit, he jabbed the needle into his thigh and pressed the plunger. His head fell against the sofa and his eyes began to close.

"Morphine?" Teddy asked.

"I wish."

"What did you just take?"

"That new drug I told you about. Some kind of blocker. It's supposed to help level my moods, prevent blackouts and seizures."

"Is it safe? I thought it gave you those horrible migraines."

"Trade-offs," he said.

"But—"

"Don't," he said. He opened his eyes. "Don't even think about telling me what to do. You have no idea what my life was like without this stuff. What it's like to lose control. What it's like to feel . . . crazy."

Teddy stared back. "Try me. I told you before that I was misdiagnosed as epileptic. Tell me exactly what I don't understand. Living on edge, never knowing what will happen next? The humiliation of waking up on the floor to a roomful of pitying stares? Not being able to trust your own body? Going to dozens of doctors to fix it, living with the constant hope of a cure that never comes? Is that what I don't understand?"

She expected Miles to turn away. Instead, he reached for her hand. Then his face relaxed, and he drifted to sleep without bothering to pull up his pants.

Teddy watched him for a moment, then reached for the syringe and checked the label. Xantal. Manufactured by none other than Hyle Pharmaceuticals. Must be nice to have a rich grandfather who could custom-make you a cure.

Kate walked into the room and froze. Saw Teddy holding the needle, Miles unconscious with his pants bunched around his knees. "Whoa. Oh. Um. Sorry to interrupt."

Teddy blushed. "It's not what it looks like."

"I don't even know what it looks like. Anyway, the boat is leaving."

Miles turned over in his sleep, nestling deeper into the couch. Teddy put the empty syringe on the desk and followed Kate out of the room.

CHAPTER TWENTY-FOUR

MONDAY MORNING FOLLOWING THANKSGIVING BREAK brought the return of Whitfield Institute's student population. Which meant classes resumed, intense physical training continued, exploding shells echoed from the firing range, and the scent of vegan lasagna wafted from the cafeteria. Everything was back to normal. With one notable exception.

"Hey! Look. That's *her*!"

Two first-year recruits nearly stumbled over themselves as they craned their necks to watch Teddy trek from her dorm to the academic buildings.

Word had spread about what had happened at Hollis Whitfield's party, making Teddy a bona fide hero. *Her.* A hero. Absurd. If Teddy Cannon ever achieved any sort of notoriety, it was for screwing up. This lavish, undeserved praise made her skin crawl. The IED could have just as easily exploded in her face. Instead of calling her a hero, everyone would be reminiscing at her memorial service about her witty sense of humor, peculiar eating habits, and unusual choice of footwear.

Worse, she had lied by omission to Clint by not telling him Eli had been mentally manipulated into setting off the IED. Clint was already on edge, his mood foul. One word and he'd have Eli jailed and Jillian expelled. God only knew what he'd do to Teddy for encouraging Eli to slip away from the party. The criminal charge of aiding and abetting came to mind.

She spotted Dara moving through the commons and doubled her pace to reach her.

"Well, look who's here," Dara drawled. "Ms. Hero herself. You and Kate sure have—"

"I need to talk to you," Teddy blurted. "It's important."

Dara studied her face for a beat, then said, "C'mon, let's go back to my room."

Once they were there, Dara seated herself on her bed, back pressed up against the headboard and ankles crossed. She looked at Teddy. "Go. What's on your mind?"

Teddy hesitated, looking for a place to sit down before she launched into what she wanted to say. Ava wasn't there, so Teddy could have sat on her bed, but the fluffy pink comforter, along with the messy sheets and pillows, screamed private, personal space. Ditto Ava's desk chair, which was littered with strewn clothing and undergarments. In the end Teddy sank onto the floor, back pressed up against the closet door and legs stretched out in front of her as she filled Dara in on what had happened at Hollis Whitfield's home.

"*Eli?*" Dara said. "Jillian's Eli? He planted that bomb? I can't believe it."

"Well, that's the thing—"

"I mean, I know he drives us crazy with his batshit commitment to his causes. But planting a *bomb?* Deliberately hurting and maybe even killing people?" Dara let out a breath. Shook her head. "Does Jillian know?"

"I haven't seen Jillian since before break, so I haven't had a chance to tell her."

"You will tell her, right? I mean, she has to know." Dara's eyes suddenly went wide. "Oh my God. You don't think Jillian had anything to do with it, do you?"

"No. I don't think Eli did, either."

"Wait a minute. What? You told me you saw him fiddle with the IED just before it went live."

"I did. But I also saw him in the kitchen after we stopped the explosion. His eyes had that dazed, I'm-knocking-but-nobody's-home look we're so familiar with."

Dara drew in a sharp breath. "You think somebody mentally influenced him into setting that bomb?"

Teddy gave a single nod.

"Who?"

"I don't know. Maybe Yates. Maybe that pair of psychics who broke in to Eli's apartment a few weeks ago. Maybe someone else."

"Jesus. Was I the only one who wasn't at this party?" Dara shook her head. Then, "Did you tell Clint? Wessner?"

"Not a word. I told Eli to get the hell out of there. If someone was using him, I didn't want him to get into trouble. He's hiding out with a buddy in Mendocino. I figured I'd wait until it was clear, then go see him and find out what happened."

"Did you?"

"I couldn't. Didn't have a chance, I swear. Every time I tried to get off campus, I ran into Clint. I'm starting to think that wasn't a coincidence."

"What about Yates? Has he been in touch?"

Teddy shook her head. Not since he'd slipped her the Polson file. In typical Yates fashion, he'd dumped that mess in her lap and then slipped away, leaving her with far more questions than answers.

Dara sighed and leaned her head against the headboard. Tilted up her chin to study the ceiling. "All right," she said. "We find Jillian, tell her everything that went down. Ask her if she spoke to Eli about Whitfield's party. Ask her if she knew anything about the bomb."

"And then?"

"Then we need to get our asses out to Mendocino to see Eli. Figure out what's going on."

Finally. A plan. As Teddy stood, she felt the burden she'd been carrying for days slowly lift from her shoulders, almost as though it had been a physical weight.

She and Dara filled Pyro in over lunch. All they had to do next was speak to Jillian.

Except she never showed up. Not for morning yoga, not for psychometry with Dunn, not for fitness with Boyd.

Fighting an escalating sense of panic, Teddy, Dara, and Pyro grabbed the four o'clock ferry to Tiburon, then rented a car and shot north on 101 toward Mendocino.

CHAPTER TWENTY-FIVE

TEDDY, PYRO, AND DARA FOLLOWED A LONG DIRT driveway to a dilapidated two-story farmhouse. Tucked beside it was an enormous red barn with a chain-link enclosure. At least a dozen dogs of assorted breeds—or no breed at all—romped and played. When the three of them stepped out of the car, the dogs erupted in a chorus of howls.

They'd found the place. Or at least they hoped they had. A quick scan of the phone book in the local Laundromat had shown Matt's Mutts of Mendocino as the only animal rescue in the area.

They skirted the barn and went directly to the house. Pyro rapped on the door. It was a cop knock, firm and no-nonsense, that meant important business. The kind of knock that would bring someone around.

Except it didn't. Only the sound of excited barking greeted them. One was a high-pitched yip, the other deep and throaty.

Mitzy and Percy.

If Eli was inside, he didn't respond. Which was probably a smart defensive move on Eli's part but a hassle for them.

Dara reached for the doorknob. Locked.

Pyro said, "Step back. I'll get it."

Teddy placed her hand on his arm to stop him. Pyro's method would damage the mechanism, and she didn't want that. Too obvious a tell. She had no idea whom they were up against. Until she did, they had to be careful. Better they find Eli and leave no evidence that they'd been there.

"Let me," she said, fishing a bobby pin from her pocket. It was a flimsy lock, after all.

She heard the faint clicking sound she was after and pushed the door open.

They were met by the jubilant tail wagging and sloppy licks of Mitzy and Percy, who crowded through the doorway to greet them. Teddy shoved the dogs back and stepped inside. They moved quickly through the house, searching for Eli. He wasn't there.

But Jillian was.

She sat huddled on a bed in an upstairs room, her knees drawn up. Eli's beloved Greenpeace T-shirt was clutched in her hands. She turned to face Teddy, Pyro, and Dara. "He's gone," she said, her voice so weak and trembling that Teddy could barely make it out.

"Gone?" Teddy echoed, immediately imagining the worst. "As in—"

"No," Dara interrupted, cutting her off. She shot Teddy a dire look that telegraphed, *He's not dead, you idiot, so don't go there.*

Pyro moved to the bed. The mattress groaned as he sat down beside Jillian. "Hey. We were pretty worried when you didn't show up for classes. Next time let us know what's going on, okay?"

Jillian turned her tear-streaked face toward him. "Okay." She took a deep, shuddering breath, then said, "Something's happened to Eli. We were supposed to meet here the Friday after Thanksgiving, but he didn't show up. He wouldn't do that. He wouldn't forget about me. He just wouldn't. Something's happened to him. I know it."

"Jillian," Teddy said, "I saw Eli on Thanksgiving Day at Hollis Whitfield's home."

"You did?" Jillian's face immediately brightened. She shot forward on the bed, eagerly leaning toward Teddy. "Was he all right? Did he say anything about me? Did he—"

"Something did happen. We need to talk to you about it." With that, Teddy launched into a retelling of the events at the party, ending with the dazed and disoriented state in which she'd found Eli after the IED had failed to detonate.

"But he wouldn't do that!" Jillian protested. "Eli would never hurt anybody. He would never set off a bomb in a roomful of people. Oh my God, has he been arrested? Is that why he's not here?"

"Jillian, you're not hearing us," Dara said gently. "We think someone mentally influenced Eli to set off that bomb. He may be in trouble. That's why we need to find him. *Now*."

Jillian's tears started anew. "Don't you think I've been trying to find him? But Mitzy doesn't know where he is, and neither does Percy, and neither does Tabby, and neither—"

"Let me see Eli's shirt," Teddy interrupted, before Jillian went on to list the entire Eli Nevin menagerie.

Thank goodness for Professor Dunn's teaching. Although psychometry wasn't Teddy's forte, she hoped her work this semester would pay off. Eli's shirt should act as a psychic shortcut, allowing her astral self direct access to Eli's astral self. The method had worked in the classroom, and it had worked with her mother's necklace. Now she just had to test it in a real-time, real-world application.

She wrapped the thin cotton around her hands. The T-shirt had been worn so often that the fabric was threadbare in spots, the Greenpeace logo cracked and peeling. The scent of Eli's skin—or at least the scent of his organic aftershave—came through loud and clear.

Teddy sat at the foot of the bed and closed her eyes. Pictured Eli wearing the shirt, lecturing them all about the dangers of global warming. Eli wrapping his arm around Jillian's waist and nuzzling her neck. Eli tossing Mitzy a vegan dog treat.

Eli.

Teddy freeze-framed an image in her mind as her astral self reached out to Eli. First and most important: *Where are you?*

Darkness and silence answered her. Either Eli didn't know, or he didn't want to say, or she had failed to make a connection. Impossible to know which.

Teddy swallowed her frustration and tried again. Recalling her suspicion that Yates could have mentally influenced Eli at the party, she telepathically asked: *What did Yates tell you to do?*

Images swirled before her, a dizzying kaleidoscope of color and motion as Eli's memories shuffled. When they stopped, she spotted Eli standing at a farmers' market at the Marina Green on an unseasonably warm San Francisco day. Teddy had a sense that this was a recent memory, weeks or maybe days old. Eli was deep in conversation with a man of average height and build. The man's back was to Teddy, but something about the way he held himself was familiar. Teddy edged her astral self closer to listen in. The voice she heard sent shivers down her spine.

It's time for action, Eli. Time to make a difference, to enact change. You don't achieve anything with markers and poster boards. Use HEAT. Do whatever it takes to shut down Hyle Pharmaceuticals. You cannot allow X-498 to go into production.

Yates.

Teddy gasped, breaking her connection. Goose bumps broke out on her skin as a trickle of sweat raced down her spine. She blinked, once again back in a Mendocino farmhouse with her friends.

"Did you reach Eli?" Jillian asked anxiously. "Did you find him? Where is he?"

"No, I couldn't find him." Teddy shook her head, loath to let her friend down, but she didn't have a choice. "I did confirm that Yates was behind the plan to use HEAT to shut down Hyle Pharmaceuticals. He planted the idea in Eli's mind."

Dara asked, "Was he the one who mentally influenced Eli to set off the IED?"

"I don't know." The phrase *whatever it takes* rang in her ears. "But yeah. Probably." She should have known. She had given Yates an inch, and he had taken a mile.

"Why?" Pyro asked. "What's he after?"

"It's never clear what Yates wants, is it?" Teddy asked. "But it has something to do with the drug in the Hyle memo: X-498. He wanted Eli to use HEAT to stop it from going into production."

"Right. So if we can't find Eli, we find Yates," Pyro said. "Obviously, they've been connected from the start."

Teddy started to object, but stopped. Yes, Eli and Yates were connected. He had given Eli that note back in the summer. But she wasn't sure how long Yates had been influencing Eli. Was their meet-cute engineered by Yates and not by fate? Or had Yates simply seen an opportunity in HEAT and twisted it for his own ends? A chicken-or-egg question if there ever was one.

Jillian, as if wondering the same thing, turned to Teddy.

"You okay?" Teddy asked.

Jillian gave a brave nod, but Teddy knew better than to believe her. No, she wasn't okay. She wouldn't be okay until she knew Eli was safe.

That responsibility fell squarely on Teddy's shoulders. She was the one who'd opened the door and let Yates into their lives. Now it was up to her to contain him.

Dara stood and gestured to Mitzy and Percy. "Jillian, leave these beasts here. They'll be in good hands. Write your friend who runs this doggy zoo a note. Let him know that if Eli does show up, he should get in touch with you immediately. You're coming with us."

"Shouldn't I wait here, just in case?"

"No," Teddy said. "No more waiting. Not for Eli, and definitely not for Yates."

Derek Yates had finally gone too far. No more allowing him to string her out on promises that he'd help her find Marysue. They'd passed the point of playing games and keeping secrets. He'd used Eli for his own ends, then thrown him away, hurting Jillian in the process. If that IED at Whitfield's party had exploded, dozens of people would have died.

Her gaze met Pyro's, and she gave a tight nod. There was only one person besides Teddy who'd been zealously tracking Yates. One person who'd been trying to uncover more about whatever was happening at Hyle Pharmaceuticals.

It was time to talk to Clint Corbett. No more half-truths and evasions. It was time for them to all be on the same side of the table.

CHAPTER TWENTY-SIX

BY EARLY EVENING, THEY WERE BACK ON CAMPUS. They'd skipped dinner, but Teddy wasn't hungry. Apparently, neither was Pyro, Dara, or Jillian, for there were no requests to swing by the dining hall. They walked directly toward Fort McDowell and climbed the flights of stairs that led to Clint's office.

Teddy sounded a quick rap on the weathered oak door. At Clint's call to enter, she stepped inside. Her friends followed behind her.

"I was wondering when you four would show up." He gave the clock that hung above his door a pointed stare, then tossed aside the magazine he'd been reading. "You realize I could indefinitely suspend all of you right now for any number of infractions." His gaze moved to Jillian. "Particularly you, Jillian. In light of your recent probation and what happened over the weekend with HEAT."

Her face red and teary, Jillian drew a shuddering breath and said, "I think Eli's in trouble."

"You're damned right he's in trouble. Breaking in to Hyle's lab was one thing, but—"

"No," Dara interrupted, "not that kind of trouble."

Pyro pulled out a chair and sat down. "You need to hear this, Clint. All of it."

Clint frowned. He scanned them in turn, then his eyes fixed on Teddy.

"I think it might be best if I started from the beginning," she said.

She took a deep breath, lowered all of her mental defenses, then launched into a history of the incidents she'd been hiding from Clint. Starting from Yates's note at the Cantina last year: how they'd spent their summer researching, and the cryptic message he'd sent them containing the coordinates for the yellow house. How they'd met him in Jackpot the day before school started. How they'd visited Sector Three. How Yates had promised to help Teddy find her mother if she kept silent about his whereabouts.

She told him about the break-in at Eli's apartment. How what Yates wanted from her was somehow connected to the Polson case. How she'd seen a mentally influenced Eli trigger the IED at Whitfield's party, then she'd let him escape. Finally, exhausted, she told him that when she'd held Eli's shirt in her hands hours ago, Yates's true intent had been revealed.

"Yates is using Eli. Using HEAT to disrupt what's happening at Hyle Pharmaceuticals. It's all connected to that drug we read about in the Hyle report. X-498. He told Eli to do whatever it takes to see its production stopped."

Clint sat for a long time. He shook his head and muttered, "He wants the drug for himself. This is why I wanted to stop him in the first place. Keep him behind bars."

And Yates had been behind bars. Until Teddy had intervened and helped engineer his escape from San Quentin. A tsunami-sized wave of guilt washed over her. Clint could do as he saw fit. Punish her. Arrest her. Kick her out of school for good. She knew FBI track would never be hers now, but at least she wasn't hiding anything anymore.

Pyro began to say something, but Clint waved him off. "Give me a minute," he said. He stood and moved to the window, deep in thought. Finally, he turned back to face them. "Since you first brought Hyle Pharmaceuticals to my attention, I've been looking into what's been happening there. No one has had access to a pool of psychic individuals to study before—"

"Not since Sector Three," Teddy interrupted.

Clint's eyes met hers. "Right. Not since Sector Three."

Dara said, "And then Whitfield Institute opened. So we are lab rats."

"Research was never meant to be experimentation," Clint said. "Although maybe I was idealistic to believe that. But getting back to Yates and his focus on Hyle Pharmaceuticals. The report that Eli lifted outlines specific aspects of the psychic genetic code. They unlocked the code. They found their way in. That's how they were able to develop a drug that represses psychic power."

"But that drug doesn't work," Jillian objected. "I saw what it did to those poor dogs."

"You're right. The drug isn't ready yet for human testing. But that isn't the point."

"What is the point?" Teddy asked.

Clint scrubbed his hands over his face. "Ever wonder why you don't get sick? The psychic immune system works differently than the nonpsychic. Usually, gene therapies are delivered with a nonthreatening virus, something that's injected into the bloodstream that carries the healthy genes."

"Right," Dara said, "but why would Yates want a drug that represses psychic—" She stopped abruptly. "Oh, shit. I get it. Hyle solved the problem."

"What do you mean?" Teddy said. What wasn't she following?

Clint continued his explanation. "Psychic immune systems don't recognize the typical viruses used in gene therapy. Hyle tried to circumvent the problem by creating an artificial virus, one that would deliver genes to suppress psychic ability."

Teddy shivered. "You mean like a supervirus?"

Clint nodded. "Hyle has jumped some serious steps in terms of psychic genetics research. Think about it—what if this virus carries other genes? Psychic genes?"

"Yates could make his own army of psychic soldiers."

"Exactly."

Dara drew in a sharp breath. Teddy couldn't help thinking of the blood samples that Jeremy had stolen from the infirmary last year. Her own DNA could be used against her.

"So we force Whitfield to shut down Hyle for good," Teddy said. "Now. Tell him how dangerous this shit is."

"Do you think I haven't tried? He won't do it. He says the research is too important to shut down. He's added extra security to the lab. I'll keep pushing him, but so far, he won't budge."

"Where does this leave us?" Teddy asked Clint. "I mean, what do we do? How do we stop Yates?"

"We use his own scheme against him." He looked at Teddy. "How did Yates plan on helping you find your mother?"

Teddy took a steadying breath. She'd known this moment was coming. Dreaded it. But she had no choice but to lay all her cards on the table. She pulled the ametrine necklace from her pocket and set it on Clint's desk.

"Oh," he said. "That explains it."

"Explains what?"

Clint resumed his seat behind his desk. "Do you remember that afternoon following Professor Dunn's class when you ended up in the infirmary? You had an astral travel experience and accused me of triggering the episode. But I knew it didn't work that way. Simply showing you a photo of Marysue in the vicinity of a PC bombing shouldn't have sent you spiraling back in time." He pointed to the pendant. "I didn't trigger the event. Your mother's pendant did."

Teddy nodded. She'd known that at the time, of course. But she'd been pissed off. Wanted to blame someone. Clint had been an easy target. "I'm sorry. I shouldn't have—"

"You said that also happened to you at Sector Three."

"Yes, but—"

"When there is a large energy event, objects that were present then often become imprinted with the memory of the event."

"So my mom's necklace has PTSD?"

"Something like that." He flashed a smile, then sobered. "But there may be more to it. I think Marysue might have been using that necklace as a conduit to send you messages. Warning you about the dangers of medical experimentation by showing you exactly what happened to your father at Sector Three. I think she also tried to warn you about what's happening at Hyle."

That part didn't make sense. Teddy frowned. "By showing me a bombing that happened in New York in 1998? How could the two possibly be connected?"

"There's only one way to find out. Go back in, Teddy. See what she wants you to know."

Teddy instinctively recoiled. She didn't want to go back in time. She couldn't watch that building explode again, knowing that people inside would die horrible, senseless deaths. She cast a panicked glance at Dara, suddenly understanding what her friend been talking about earlier that summer. A death warning was fine. Using a psychic skill to help someone avoid imminent danger was one thing. But to simply stand by and watch people die with no way to save them? Unbearable.

Pyro stood. "You can't expect her to just—"

Teddy's heart skipped. There he was, as always, standing up for her. Nick never did that, not really. But she looked at Clint. "I'll do it."

Clint dismissed Pyro, Dara, and Jillian. He dragged a sturdy wooden chair across the room and plopped it in the middle of his office.

"Sit," he said. "My instinct is—has always been—to protect you. But I can't shield you from everything. I can't shield you from the truth. You need to see what happened, and how, and then we can figure out why and stop it from happening again."

Once Teddy was seated, Clint turned his attention to the pendant. Picked it up. "I remember when your father gave this necklace to your mother," he said, a small, sad smile on his face. "It was well before you were born, before I left the base for good. Richard was actually nervous. He wondered if it was too grand a gesture. But he wanted her to know how he felt."

Teddy felt her eyes welling up. She hadn't been prepared to hear something so personal about her father. He had become nothing more than a character in a story. A man who had been driven insane, who had turned violent, shot up a base, and died. But now she was faced with another man. A man who loved a woman so much that he gave her a giant stone that screamed *Be mine forever.*

"Your mother wore it every day. Like a wedding band."

"Why are you telling me this?" she asked, wiping her tears on her sleeve.

"Empathy. It's a psychic's most important tool. People are complicated. They do good and bad things. We all do, including your parents. Remember that when you see whatever you're about to see."

Teddy nodded. She told him about the excruciating pain and discomfort that came during the transition when she traveled. Clint nodded. Now that he knew about the necklace, he said, he could give her new tools for traveling that should alleviate most of the discomfort. He reminded her of the dangers of travel. She couldn't try to change the past. And any injury would be carried back to the present.

He put his hand on the stiff wooden chair. "Ready?"

"Yes."

"Your feet planted on the ground, your posture fluid and upright, your head high and chin aligned with your chest. You are connected to the earth and the sky, to the universe."

Teddy relaxed her body and followed his instructions.

"Close your eyes and take hold of the stone." He placed the necklace in Teddy's hands. She wrapped the delicate silver chain around her palm and curled her fist around the stone. She felt the warmth of Clint's calloused hands braced over hers.

"In the past, you were dragged behind the stone, a wild horse you were barely holding on to. This time, I want you to command it to take you somewhere. Feel the warmth of the necklace in your hands and demand it take you where you want to go."

The stone began to heat in her hands, a subtle glowing warmth that grew steadily stronger. *Take me to New York City*, Teddy commanded firmly, directing her astral self to be taken to a specific place at a specific moment. *October 27, 1998. Show me what Marysue wants me to see.*

This time, she was in control. No fishhook grabbing and jerking her away. The pressure on her chest was immense but bearable. She plunged into the Pilgrim's Tunnel as though surfing an intense wave—one wrong move and the whole thing could collapse on top of her. She clung on, rocketing forward, until she emerged on the other side.

She was there.

New York City. Cars and trucks and pedestrians swarming all around her. A ceaseless stream of movement and noise. People carrying on with their day, oblivious as to what was about to happen.

Battling a surge of helpless anxiety, she watched the now familiar scene: Yates placing the leather briefcase under the bench, signaling to the burly man on the pay phone that the device was ready. She caught the faint smell of something familiar. Sweet and nutty. C-4.

Teddy had learned in Wessner's class that bomb makers often had a signature, a way of doing things. Whoever made this bomb had made the IED she'd discovered at Whitfield's party. She was certain of it. Teddy fought an urge to grab the briefcase and run. It all seemed so pointless, her being there, if she couldn't stop the bomb. Just then, Marysue lifted the briefcase and carried it into the office building.

Teddy raced after her, this time following her mother inside the building. She knew she shouldn't be in there. If the bomb went off and she was within range, she could suffer horrible and real consequences. But still she felt compelled to follow. She rounded the corner and saw her mother pause, leaning against the shiny lobby wall. Was she having second thoughts? Maybe she wasn't the one who'd done the bombing after all? Then her mother steeled herself and turned toward the elevator, but not before reaching out and pulling the fire alarm.

The loud, repetitive bleat of the alarm drove people into the lobby. In the ensuing swarm of fleeing office workers, Marysue slipped from view. Teddy followed the stream of the building's occupants—who looked alternately confused, bemused, or annoyed—out of the building and into the street. A few lit cigarettes, and others peeled away to grab a cup of coffee. Their lives saved by Marysue's action. Teddy had missed the fire alarm going off the first time she'd been there. She wondered now what else she'd missed.

She hunkered low, bracing herself. When the explosion came, it was every bit as staggering as she remembered. The shattering of dark glass and the propulsive shock of the blast nearly knocked her off her feet. But she had to see what happened next.

Even as prepared as she'd been, she nearly missed Marysue in the resultant chaos, the screaming terror that filled the street in the aftermath of the bombing.

Her dark coat flapping behind her, Marysue raced away. Teddy followed. Her mother made it one block, then two. She reached a pay phone and ducked inside, pulling the clear glass door shut behind her. Teddy saw tears streaming down her cheeks.

The pay phone began to ring.

Marysue took a deep shuddering breath, then lifted the receiver. "Colonel," she said. "Target hit. Confirmed kill."

Teddy expected her to hang up. Instead, her knuckles white, Marysue clung to the receiver, listening. A look of anguish overtook her features. "*No*. You said this was the last one. You promised you'd let me go."

The door to the pay phone was slammed open by the same large, menacing man Yates had signaled earlier. Teddy gaped in stunned surprise, helpless to do anything but watch as he wrapped one thick, beefy arm around Marysue's waist and the other around her face. He pressed a white cloth over her mouth and nose. The sharp, cloyingly sweet scent of diethyl ether burned Teddy's nostrils. She watched, her heart thudding in fear, as Marysue bucked against him, struggling to break free, then went limp in his arms.

If only the butterfly effect hadn't loomed so large and portentous. Butterflies were stupid insects, if you asked Teddy. It took everything she had to keep herself from charging in to save Marysue from whatever the hell had happened to her.

A black sedan skidded to a stop at the curb. An attractive woman with white-blond hair stepped out of the vehicle. She flung open the rear passenger door. "Stanton, over here!"

Stanton dragged Marysue's limp body to the sedan and stuffed her inside. "Drive, Nilsson." He leveraged himself into the back seat and slammed the door while the blonde jumped behind the wheel. The car peeled off.

Teddy wanted to throw herself in front of the vehicle. And it wasn't just Wessner's Secret Service training that made this urge so strong. It was something else. She wanted to save her mother. But there was nothing she could do. She felt like she was being ripped in two. Just like when she traveled, a thousand tiny hooks tearing her apart. She wanted to go but knew she should stay. The sedan sped off and disappeared into the heavy stream of midmorning traffic, and Teddy wanted to be with her.

But she couldn't.

She was alone. Her mother was gone.

No.

Instantly, she felt like she'd made a mistake. She should have followed her mother. Her mother, who hadn't really wanted to hurt anyone. Clint had been wrong. She began to run, fighting against the measure of time itself. If she could get to the car, then what? She felt something grasp her middle. The wind was knocked from her lungs.

No. No.

She could fight this. She wasn't ready to leave yet. The world tilted sideways, spun out of her grasp, then righted itself. When she opened her eyes, her heart was racing as though she'd just completed a 5K.

"You're okay, Teddy. You're here in my office." Clint's voice.

"She didn't—she didn't want to do it." Her guilt at not being able to help her mother was tempered by a sense of relief. Her mother hadn't wanted to hurt anyone. Marysue was being forced to work for the PC. That was why she had set off the fire alarm to warn as many people as possible before the bomb went off. And the people who'd abducted Marysue? The very same pair who'd broken in to Eli's apartment.

She felt Clint's huge, strong hand on top of hers. She looked up into his eyes. "You were right, Clint. My mother was trying to tell me something."

"What?"

"Who's behind this. Identifying the PC members we're tracking. Exactly what you've wanted all along. You're right that she'd lead us to them. The man we're after is named Stanton. The woman is named Nilsson. They broke in to Eli's apartment. They're responsible for the IED at Whitfield's party. And I can give you detailed descriptions of both."

CHAPTER TWENTY-SEVEN

TEDDY KNEW HOW LAW ENFORCEMENT WORKED. THE wheels of justice tended to grind rather than spin. But that hadn't prepared her for days that would drag into weeks without a sighting, let alone an apprehension, of Yates, Stanton, or Nilsson. Nick, on Clint's request, posted an APB. Local authorities were given background and descriptions. Highways and public transportation throughout the Bay Area were monitored. Teddy knew it was a long shot. They were trained professionals, masters in the art of disappearance, and now they'd vanished completely.

So had Eli, even though half the teachers at Whitfield were looking for him. General Maddux was looking, too: he had discovered the connection and named Eli as a prime suspect.

Although she tried to focus on her studies, Teddy's mind was so clouded with worry that she didn't see Wessner walking down the corridor toward her. They nearly collided. Teddy stopped short and mumbled an apology. But as she turned to leave, Wessner stopped her: "Just a minute, Miss Cannon. As it happens, I wanted to speak to you anyway. I have another assignment for you."

Wessner looked at Teddy expectantly. Clearly, she was waiting for some kind of reaction about getting a special assignment, so Teddy plastered a smile on her face. "Oh? What's that?"

"Whitfield's grandson, Miles, is vacationing at the family's ski lodge in Lake Tahoe. We think it would be wise for him to have security."

An upscale ski resort. Most people would be thrilled. But Teddy and snow didn't get along. Still, a temporary change of scenery might be good. And Tahoe was only a couple of hours away. If something did happen, she could be back on campus almost immediately.

"And everyone involved thought that was a good idea?" she asked.

"Well," Wessner said, "you must have made some impression on Miles, because he requested you specifically."

Teddy hadn't seen Miles since Whitfield's party. So he remembered the brief conversation they'd had in his grandfather's study. He'd been so out of it at the time, she hadn't thought he would. "Sure, I'm happy to help."

"I'm glad you're so agreeable, Teddy. Because the assignment is over Christmas break."

"Christmas?"

Another holiday ruined.

"Is that okay?"

Teddy exhaled. Having to miss another trip to see her parents seemed ridiculously unfair. Only this time, a part of her was also the tiniest bit relieved. She didn't want her parents to worry about her. And the only way to accomplish that was to put on an act that everything was fine at school. She wasn't convinced she could pull off that farce for the entire two-week break. "Fine," she said.

"Good. I'll send you a dossier. Whitfield has made it clear that he doesn't want Miles to feel like his vacation is being ruined by a security detail. He made a special request for a laid-back approach—not the usual Secret Service protocol—more like a vigilant friend."

"Got it." Teddy thought for a moment, then said, "Anything going on with HEAT?"

Wessner hesitated. "Hollis Whitfield received two untraceable phone messages making vague remarks about what would happen if Hyle continued testing on animals."

Teddy's brow tightened. What on earth was Yates up to? "Why wasn't I—"

"We don't know who engineered those threats. They could have been made by fringe elements of Eli's original group. Likely, it's completely unconnected to recent events."

Teddy nodded, reluctantly backing down. She had to quit jumping at every possible lead. Just because she expected to see a monster lurking in the shadows didn't mean it was really there. "And Miles? What does he know about this?" She paused to swirl her hand around, indicating their surroundings. "About us?"

"He knows what the general public knows—that Whitfield is a law enforcement institute."

Teddy couldn't see how that was possible, given how close Miles seemed to his grandfather. But she'd continue to keep the Big Secret. "Will I get a partner?"

"Fortunately, Dara Jones is available. I think her particular set of skills could be useful here. I hope you agree."

Teddy smiled. "Pretty sure we can make that work."

Teddy stood in her dorm room, staring at the open suitcase on her bed. Her wardrobe wasn't cutting it. Her heaviest sweaters were cotton-wool blends, hardly appropriate for the ski slopes of Lake Tahoe. She stole a glance at the stack of sweaters piled in Jillian's closet. Heavy wool: East Coast sweaters. Exactly what someone who was headed to Tahoe for a couple of days might want to wear.

Jillian sat across from her, simultaneously watching Teddy and chewing nervously on her cuticle. Thinking about Eli, no doubt.

"Aren't you taking those home with you?" Teddy asked, dropping a hint she hoped was loud enough to be heard over the din of Jillian's anxiety.

"Home? I can't go home. What if Eli needs me?"

Teddy sat next to her and gave her arm a squeeze. "You know Clint and Nick are both looking for him."

Jillian nodded. "I just wish there was something I could do."

Teddy didn't know quite what to say to that. She searched her mental files of Comforting Friend Remarks, because she really did want to help. But all she could come up with was, "It'll be all right."

Jillian caught her lower lip between her teeth and looked away. They attended an institute that prepared them for careers in law enforcement. Which meant they were familiar with missing persons stats. On any given day in the United States, nearly ninety thousand people were counted as missing. More than half of them were adults. Some of them vanished deliberately. To evade creditors. To ditch the burden of a bad relationship, family pressures, or problems at work. To escape the threat of facing criminal charges on everything from tax evasion to felony murder.

But not all of those ninety thousand people vanished deliberately. Some of them were taken. And in cases like those, the first twenty-four hours were the most critical. The longer it took for a case to be solved, the less likely it was that the case would result in a positive outcome.

They were on day twenty-nine with Eli.

Dara had expressed to Teddy that she was convinced Molly's disappearance and Eli's disappearance were inextricably wound—but she wouldn't say why. If the PC was involved, she was likely correct. Not that this was something either of them intended to share with Jillian. Jillian was holding it together by a thin enough thread as it was.

"You know, it wasn't an act," Jillian said.

"What wasn't?"

"What Eli and I had. *Have*. I don't care how much Yates influenced him. What we feel for each other is real."

"I know," Teddy said, and she meant it.

The worry relaxed from Jillian's forehead. Then something

occurred to her, and her eyes lit up as if someone had ignited a spar-kler. "Hey!" she said. "You don't have anything warm to wear in Tahoe. You should borrow some of my sweaters!"

Now, why didn't I think of that?

They set about choosing sweaters. Teddy was particularly fond of a deep red V-neck that was more sexy than practical, and she folded it neatly into her suitcase. At Jillian's insistence, she tried on a knobby gray turtleneck and had just pulled it on over her head when Pyro appeared at the door.

"What's going on?" he asked.

"Teddy's going to Lake Tahoe!" Jillian chirped.

"Oh yeah?" Pyro looked surprised, and Teddy felt a pang of guilt for not having mentioned the trip to him sooner. But they'd all been so preoccupied with everything that had been happening, there just hadn't been time. "What's in Lake Tahoe?"

"Wessner gave me an assignment," she said, and then added, "It was kind of last-minute."

"Oh?"

"She needed someone to watch over Miles, make sure he stays safe after what happened at Thanksgiving. Miles asked for me."

"You and Miles, huh?" He shrugged it off as if it were nothing. Pyro was as cool as he was hot, but he couldn't hide the flash of hurt that flickered across his face, and Teddy caught the whole thing. Once again, she was guilty of letting everything else take priority over Pyro. When she got back, she'd have a little making up to do.

"Me, Miles, and Dara," she said, emphasis on Dara. She stepped past Pyro and caught his hand, taking him with her into the hallway. Once outside of Jillian's view, she wrapped her arms around his neck and pulled him closer. "Jillian lent me her sweaters. Now it's your turn."

"You want my sweaters?"

"Nope. But I was hoping you might give me something to help keep me warm."

That smirk. One day, she might get tired of it. But she sincerely doubted it. Especially when one of those smirks preceded a deep, smoldering kiss.

Almost before Teddy could catch her breath, Dara showed up at the door, dragging a wheeled suitcase behind her.

"Knock it off, you two," she said. "We don't have time for any fire alarms. Teddy and I have a plane to catch."

CHAPTER TWENTY-EIGHT

THE PLANE WAS PRIVATE, AS IT TURNED OUT. *SO THIS is what it's like to be rich,* Teddy thought as the car service delivered them to Whitfield's seventeen-room rustic lodge on the pristine slopes of Lake Tahoe's North Shore.

"Jeez, where's the gift shop?" Dara said, as they stood gaping at the sprawling residence.

The door was unlocked and they went inside, where they were welcomed by the toasty warmth of a blazing fire. A soaring evergreen decked out with lights and holiday ornaments stood to one side of the room. Across from it was the massive stone hearth, which also twinkled with holiday decor. Teddy pulled off her hat and looked around. Except for the fireplace, the entryway was all knotty pine, from the paneled walls to the sweeping vaulted ceiling with its massive roof beams. It opened up to the back of the house, which was lined with windows, offering an expansive view of the crystal blue lake. Teddy gazed over the magnificent alpine-like vista and had one thought: *casinos.*

True, the view was spectacular. The house was spectacular. And she knew that anybody in her right mind would be swept away by the grandeur. But Teddy couldn't help it. The border between California and Nevada bisected Tahoe, which meant that her home state was on the opposite shore. While people on this side of the lake strapped on skis and filled their lungs with rushing air, people on the other side sat in front of slot machines, roulette wheels, and—her pulse rocketed at the thought, she couldn't help it—poker tables. She could almost feel the waxy cards slip between her fingers.

Not that I'll get to play, she thought, deliberately tamping down her excitement. She and Dara were there on assignment, not to mess around.

"Hey, you made it!" Miles said, emerging from an arched doorway on the right.

He seemed to be in a good mood. No, a great mood. As if he were delighted to see them. Or maybe to see *her*. It was hard to tell. In any case, he appeared to have recovered since the last time she'd seen him. He'd been nearly catatonic at Whitfield's Thanksgiving party. Now he was all smiles.

"Nice little cabin in the woods you got here," she said.

Miles adjusted his glasses. "You like it?"

"Guess it'll do," Dara said. "If the Motel 6 is booked."

Miles laughed, and Teddy introduced him to Dara. "Dara . . . Dara . . ." he said, as if searching for something in his mind. Teddy remembered how he'd told her he was bad at names and surmised that he was groping for a pneumonic. "Dara, my darling," he finally said.

Dara furrowed her brow in response. "Um, no."

"Don't mind him," Teddy said. "He just needs a way to remember your name."

"In that case, don't worry about it," she said. "I'll answer to anything, though *goddess* works best."

Miles gave them a tour of the house and showed them to their rooms. Once they'd settled in, Teddy suggested they take a pre-dinner walk around the grounds. A not so subtle way to accomplish Wessner's first rule of protective surveillance: know your territory. Check for potential threats and hazards, as well as means of escape.

That meant putting on one of Jillian's sweaters, which she layered over a turtleneck and topped with a red fleece jacket. She shoved a pair of gloves in one pocket, just in case.

Dara studied her. "You realize it's like forty degrees out, right?"

"You think I need another layer?"

Dara rolled her eyes.

"Hey, give me a break. I'm a Vegas girl. We grab our mittens when the temperature drops below Wayne Newton's age."

Miles waited for them on the back deck. He opened the gate, and they walked down a steep flight of stairs to a path that meandered along the shore of the lake.

As they walked, Miles kept his hands in his pockets, fiddling with something that made a jangling noise.

"This is a little weird for me," he said. "Having bodyguards."

"Because we're women?" Dara said.

Miles laughed. "I'd rather have you and Teddy than some hulking goons. It's just that I don't feel like I'm in any danger. I mean, look around." He indicated the entire vista, including the lake to their right.

Teddy did look around. In fact, she'd been looking since the moment she stepped out on the deck. And he was right—there was nothing menacing in any direction. "It's beautiful," she agreed, then, "How have you been feeling? Those migraines . . ."

"I never seem to get them when I'm here."

"Even on the medication?" She was being nosy. But she knew Eversley was involved in whatever he was being prescribed, and she couldn't help worrying that he was being overmedicated.

"Yeah, I guess so. It's just that my moods get out of whack sometimes. Or I get these black holes in my memory. The meds seem to help. When I go off them, I can have . . . outbursts. I'm trying to control it. But if it happens, please don't take it personally."

Teddy nodded. "Thanks for letting us know."

Clearly embarrassed, he gave them an apologetic shrug and attempted a smile. "It's a choice, you know? The migraines or the moods. I'd rather not deal with either one, but that option isn't on the table."

He led them farther along the shoreline, obviously uncomfortable with the topic. Teddy got the hint and dropped it. They strolled in silence for a while, until Dara remarked that the setting reminded her of a date she'd once gone on with a girl she'd been crushing on for months. It had ended disastrously when she'd tried to impress the girl with a little impromptu rock climbing. She'd fallen and broken her ankle, and the girl had to carry her back to their car. That story led to another. Eventually, they turned giddy and started recounting their worst-ever dates. (*Really, Miles? A girl who insisted on showing you a dozen Instagram photos of her horse with face filters, and you still pretended you were interested?*)

They stopped at a large jutting rock that offered a breathtaking view of the sunset. The moment would have been completely serene if Miles hadn't continued to jangle whatever was in his pocket. A nervous habit, Teddy supposed, but one that was starting to grate on her nerves.

Apparently, Dara felt the same way. She extended her hand, palm up. "All right, Miles. Give it up. What are you fiddling with?"

"What? Oh. Sorry." He reached in his pocket and pulled out a set of worn metal dog tags on a key chain. The name Whitfield, Julian C., was etched on them. "My dad's," he said.

Teddy thought of the photograph she'd seen in Whitfield's office. The handsome marine with an array of medals pinned to his chest. "Is he still—"

"No. He died years ago on a tour of duty in Afghanistan."

She and Dara murmured their sympathy, but Miles shook it off. "I was eight at the time, and he'd been on tour for most of my childhood, so I don't really remember him. You'd think I could just let it go, right?" Frowning, he ran his thumb over his father's name. "Problem is, I still really don't know how he died, and that drives me crazy."

Dara's brow furrowed. "Didn't anyone tell you?"

"Well, yeah. Officially, he died from an explosion. I dug around online and found an article about the incident. A bomb killed twenty-two people and wounded fourteen. And I always thought that meant he was a hero, dying that way. But I overhead my grandfather talking one time, and it turns out that's not true. He said my father made some kind of terrible mistake and set the bomb off. Then my father took his own life. That's why my grandfather is so worried about my blackouts and mood swings. He thinks my dad lost it. He's afraid it could be hereditary."

"Oh, Miles," Teddy said.

"Anyway, that's what led me to my grandfather. I didn't even know what was happening. One day I was at my father's funeral in tight shoes and stiff pants, and the next I was being moved into my grandfather's house in Tiburon."

"What happened to your mom?" Dara asked.

Miles shrugged. "She told my grandfather she was sick of raising me on my own—that she'd basically been a widow her whole marriage, and she'd had enough. I can't blame my mom. I was a difficult kid."

Teddy let out a breath. "Me too," she said. Her birth father had also died. And her birth mother had abandoned her. *But maybe not by choice*, a small voice inside Teddy said as she thought about the memory of Marysue being pulled into the car.

Their eyes met. The twilight shadows lengthened. A cool breeze rushed past them, rustling the trees. Then the moment passed. She pulled her jacket zipper up to her neck. Miles shoved the dog tags back in his pocket. "It's hard, you know. I want to move forward. I just have so many questions about my past."

Teddy knew that feeling, too. It was a unique kind of pain, being unable to connect with your own history. "Would you like me to help you find out?" she asked.

Dara's head snapped up. She shot Teddy a look.

"How would you do that?" he asked.

Good question. It was way outside the boundary of protocol. That, and while the dog tags would be a powerful psychometric tool, as they were an object of daily use, she wouldn't be able to use them for telepathy, as she'd done with Eli's Greenpeace shirt. She couldn't scan the memory of a dead person. No, this would require astral projection. And she had done that only with her mother's necklace. Still, she was eager to try. The only problem was that she couldn't tell Miles any of this.

Teddy pursed her lips. "The internet," she said. "I'm a pretty good sleuth, and I might even be able to access some FBI files." It was a little white lie. She didn't have any kind of security clearance with the Bureau. "I'll just need—"

"These," Miles said, and pressed the dog tags into her palm. "With my father's name, rank, and serial number."

"I'll try my best," she said, and thrust them deep into the pocket of her fleece jacket. Their mood far more somber than it had been when they'd left, they headed back to the house.

Ten minutes in, they encountered a paved road. Just as Teddy stepped out to cross, a pickup truck swerved around the bend, music blaring and tires skidding. The guy didn't touch his brakes. Just laid down on his horn, causing Teddy to jump back and sprawl on her ass in a mass of pine needles and slushy snow.

Miles leaped forward. "Son of a bitch!" he shouted after the driver.

The driver thrust his hand out the window in a single-finger salute.

Just then a branch split from a towering pine and came crashing down, landing squarely on the truck's hood. Missed the windshield by inches. The driver slammed his brakes, hit a patch of ice, and went into a 360-degree spin. For one heart-stopping second, it looked like the truck was about to veer off the road and careen down the side of the mountain. It didn't. Instead, the passenger door smashed up against a protective highway railing, bringing the vehicle to a crashing, wheezing stop.

White-faced, the driver stumbled out and inspected the damage.

"You all right?" Dara shouted.

He didn't answer. Just shoved the branch off his hood, climbed back in, and limped off in his wrecked truck, going a fraction of his previous speed.

"You okay, Teddy?" Miles asked, bending to help her up.

"What just happened?" She looked at the fallen branch, then at the truck's slowly receding taillights.

"I don't know." Miles looked as shocked as she felt. "But it looks like that asshole got a taste of instant karma."

All Teddy could think about was how her charge had stood feet from danger while, once again, she had sprawled on the ground.

After dinner, Teddy sat cross-legged in the middle of the guest room's plush bed, staring at the dog tags in her hand. She breathed slowly, trying to get herself into a relaxed state, preparing for the painful tug of separation.

"You're going through with it?" Dara asked.

"I'm going to try," Teddy said. "It would probably be more helpful if you did it."

Dara shook her head. "No, ma'am, that's way above my pay grade."

The thought of traveling to a war zone didn't appeal to her, either. But Miles deserved to know what had happened to his father. And if she could help *someone* find closure, she was going to do it. She wrapped her hand around the cold metal. *Take me to Afghanistan*, she commanded, as Clint had taught her. *Take me to Miles's father. Take me to the day he died.*

Nothing happened. She slowed her breathing even more. Repeated her commands. Rubbed at the dog tags. She tried again and again, trying to pull her astral self from her body. But it was no use, and at last, she gave up. Marysue's necklace, it seemed, was her only conduit across time and space. Frustrated, Teddy threw the key chain toward the desk.

"I have to do everything around here, don't I?" Dara snatched it out of the air with a one-handed catch. She wrapped her fingers around the dog tags and closed her eyes.

Teddy waited for several long, pulsing moments. When Dara finally opened her eyes, she looked stricken.

"What is it?" Teddy said. "What did you see?"

"A lot of death. Dozens of men. A few women. An explosion. A lot of it's fuzzy, but there's one thing I can tell you for sure." She paused to hold up the tags. "Whoever was wearing these tags didn't kill himself. He died trying to save the others. And Teddy?"

"What?"

"I think he was psychic."

CHAPTER TWENTY-NINE

THE NEXT MORNING WAS CLEAR BUT COLD. AT BREAK-
fast, Teddy looked out the window and saw a picture postcard of win-
ter beauty, complete with delicately pointed icicles hanging from the
house's eaves. Pretty from the warmth of the kitchen nook, but she
had no desire to venture outside on such a frigid day.

Until Miles stepped into the kitchen and announced that he was
heading into Tahoe City to do some last-minute Christmas shopping.
"Anybody want to come?" he asked.

It wasn't a matter of *want to*. It was a matter of *have to*. No matter how much the three of them were acting like friends, they weren't.
Teddy and Dara were his security detail. The two of them shared a look.
Teddy didn't need to sync up with Dara to know her thoughts. Her head
tilt seemed to say, *You do it—you said you wanted to talk to him, anyway.*

Right. Miles's father, the highly decorated marine, had been psychic, at least according to Dara. It made sense. Why else would Hollis
Whitfield be interested in founding a school for psychics? The disturbing part was that he'd never told Miles. Of course, Teddy couldn't
be the one to tell him—not without exposing herself, the school, everything. But she could tell Miles some of it. She owed him that much,
at least. She went upstairs to bundle up.

A short while later, she and Miles headed out to his Land Rover.
Miles wore a down coat and had an olive-green canvas satchel slung
across his body.

"My meds," he said with a shrug when he saw Teddy looking at it. "Just in case." He tossed her the car keys. "You mind driving?"

"Sounds good to me." She gave him back the key chain with his father's dog tags, as if they were making an even exchange.

She pulled out of the driveway and onto the tree-lined roadway. When Teddy was younger, the car had been where she and her mom had their most serious heart-to-hearts, and where she'd broached difficult subjects. Like the time she'd cut school in eighth grade and thought she could get away with it, or the trouble she had gotten into at Stanford just before they kicked her out. Teddy recently saw an article advising parents to use car rides for exactly these kind of talks, since it could be easier to cover tough emotional terrain when you weren't eye-to-eye. She doubted her mother had read any studies on this—she just had good instincts.

"So?" Miles asked after she turned onto Highway 28. "Did you find anything out?"

And there it was.

"Actually, I have some good news," she said. "You were right about your father. He didn't commit suicide. He actually died saving his fellow soldiers. A bomber entered the base. Your father stopped him."

The last part was deductive reasoning, stitching together Dara's vision with an archived *Wall Street Journal* article and some internet forums Teddy had burrowed into.

Miles went quiet. He stared out the window as he absorbed the news. She watched his jaw tighten. Saw the cords in his neck stretch. Teddy wanted to reach out to him but resisted the impulse. The moment felt intensely private, and she wasn't sure her touch would be welcome. She waited, giving him time.

He slammed the dashboard with his hand, hitting it so hard that Teddy's own hand stung in response. "I knew it. I just knew it."

"I think you can feel proud of him," she said. Teddy wondered if she could have done what Miles's father had. Sacrificed herself for so many.

"Anything else I should know?"

Of course there was. But there was so little she could actually tell.

Another long pause before Miles asked, "Was all this on the internet? Could you send me a link?"

Teddy let out a breath. She had been expecting this question and was prepared with a plausible lie. "Sorry. A lot of it came from confidential files."

They drove in silence, and Teddy watched the landscape start to repopulate as they got closer to town. When she couldn't bear it any longer, she started asking him stupid questions about Tahoe—what his favorite stores were, where he liked to eat. She could tell he was distracted, but he played along, directing Teddy to a parking space on Lake Boulevard, where they got out of the car. She pulled her knitted hat over her ears and turned her collar up against the chill. He hesitated beside the car. She sensed him processing the news, storing it someplace stoic. He wasn't ready to move forward yet. But he could pretend for now.

He pulled off his glasses to wipe the lenses, and she was struck again by the deep blue of his irises. He really was attractive, there was no denying it. How bright he seemed to shine sometimes. It caught her off guard.

He transferred his attention to Teddy. Before putting his glasses back on, he held her gaze. The timing was all wrong. Maybe if things were different. She was his security detail. And there was Pyro, and she wasn't ready to throw away whatever they had.

"I promised my grandfather I'd pick up a gift for his assistant," he said, pointing toward the street and releasing her from his gaze. He led her toward a high-end jewelry boutique. "Then we'll grab a bite somewhere." When they reached the store, he said, "You know, you don't have to stick to me like glue. I know my grandfather worries, but I'm capable of handling myself."

"Of course."

"What I'm saying is, if you want to run your own errands and meet me back here, that's fine."

Miles didn't want her breathing down his neck. He wasn't a child, and he didn't need a babysitter. She got it. Teddy glanced around, taking in the bright holiday decor and Tudor-style storefronts. No threats that she could see. Just upscale shoppers and drivers in expensive SUVs jockeying for parking spaces, caught up in the last-minute rush for gifts.

"Sure," she said. "We can do that."

But when he went into the store, Teddy didn't feel right abandoning her charge. She was on the job; no matter what Miles said, she was supposed to watch him. She peered in the window to make sure everything looked okay. The store had a guard positioned by the door. There were three employees, and three customers besides Miles, all of them focused intently on the shiny merchandise. Miles scanned the displays for several minutes before asking a saleswoman to show him something. He took off his satchel and laid it on the counter as he inspected a man's watch.

It all looked perfectly benign. Teddy turned her back on the store and surveilled the street like a bona fide Secret Service agent. After a few minutes of just standing there, she was so cold that she thought she might fulfill her mother's prophecy of making a face that would freeze that way forever. She pulled her scarf up around her face and breathed into it. A chic woman wearing an expensive black wool hat and matching coat strode past her into the store.

Teddy glanced across the street to where a line of massive icicles hung from an awning. To Teddy, they looked like missiles ready to launch. But shoppers passed beneath them with indifference, so she shrugged off her concern.

Until she saw a male figure in the shadows beneath them. Yates? No, she decided. It couldn't be. He was too large. But maybe his heavy coat was playing tricks with her perception. Then the man quickly turned down a side street.

Teddy's pulse shot up. If it was Yates, she couldn't let him get away.

First, though, she glanced back into the jewelry store to make sure Miles was okay. He was still studying watches. Only now, to Teddy's astonishment, the woman in the black hat was inching closer to his satchel. She laid a gloved hand on it and slid it beneath her coat in one swift, practiced motion. *A thief.*

Teddy glanced back to where she had seen the male figure only seconds ago. Gone. In the jewelry store, the woman was moving toward the door. Teddy burst inside and ran at the woman, grabbing her arm. The woman released an outraged cry and pulled back. Just as Teddy tightened her grip, a massive weight crashed against her side and knocked her to the floor. The security guard, tackling *her* rather than the would-be thief. Teddy watched in helpless frustration as the woman slipped out of the store.

"What the hell?" Miles said, pulling the guard off her.

"Your satchel," Teddy gasped, drawing herself up. "She tried to steal it."

Miles's eyes went dark with fury as he looked from his satchel, which now lay on the floor near Teddy, to the door. Teddy followed his gaze as he clocked the woman dashing across the street toward an alleyway between stores, where a car was waiting for her. Just as she approached it, a massive icicle—two feet long and as pointed as a dagger—broke free from the awning and sliced through the air. The woman was just quick enough to avoid it. It crashed to the pavement, missing her by a whisper.

Teddy shot out of the store and stared after her, shock rendering her temporarily frozen. Their tussle had knocked the woman's hat from her head. She had white-blond hair.

"That woman was batshit crazy," Miles said, coming out to stand beside her.

"I'm not so sure," Teddy countered. The car vanished around the corner before she could track the plate.

"Why would someone want to steal a canvas bag when they could make off with a twenty-thousand-dollar watch just as easily?"

She turned to look at him. His eyes were bright, and he was breathing hard from the excitement. But there was something else. Something Teddy recognized. A peculiar buzz of energy stirring the air around him. Whatever he had in that bag was more valuable than any Rolex. "Let me see it," she said.

He shrugged, unfastened the buckles, and flipped open the satchel. "Nothing to see. Just my medication. Which reminds me." Miles paused, rubbing his head. "I should take another dose soon."

Inside were three wrapped syringes. Teddy pulled one of them out and studied the wrapper. Saw the Hyle Pharmaceuticals logo. The drug name Xantal was next to the words NOT FOR RESALE. And under that, layered between scientific gobbledygook in print so fine Teddy would have missed it entirely had she not been looking for it, was the in-house name of the drug.

X-498.

The drug that Hyle Pharmaceuticals had engineered for psychic experimentation.

Miles Whitfield was the test subject.

Horror raced through her as the pieces came together. Miles had some kind of telekinetic power. Something he couldn't control and wasn't even aware of. That accounted for the violent mood swings, the migraines, the gaps in his memory. That was why the tree branch had snapped when he was angry. Why the icicle had fallen and nearly killed the blond woman.

Like Teddy throughout her childhood, Miles was having his psychic powers repressed by drugs. Only, in his case, it was intentional.

She steered Miles back to the car. "We're going," she said. She started the car and cranked up the heat, but nothing could ease the chill that ran through her.

"Wait, I have to—" he started. "And you just got tackled by a giant. Are you okay?"

Teddy swallowed. What could she tell him? All of it, she supposed. About himself. About the school. About his grandfather's involvement. But that was a huge step. And before she went there, she needed answers.

"You're going to have to trust me," she said. "I'll tell you everything, I promise. But for now, don't take any more of those injections. And whatever you do, don't let anyone get hold of them." She'd never thought she'd feed anyone—let alone someone she liked—the kind of crap she was always hearing from Clint and Yates. But here she was, giving Miles just enough information to keep him in line.

CHAPTER THIRTY

ONCE THEY WERE BACK AT THE HOUSE, TEDDY WENT straight to Dara's guest suite.

"Good, you're back," Dara said. She'd been sitting at a desk, a laptop borrowed from Hollis Whitfield open beside her, but the moment Teddy entered the room, she spun around to face her. When Teddy opened her mouth to fill her in on what had happened in the shopping district, Dara stopped her.

"Me first," she said. "I put in a call to Clint. Talked to him about Hollis Whitfield's son. Long story short, Clint thinks the guy was probably an ergokinetic."

"Ergokinetic?"

"Yeah. Someone who has the ability to manipulate energy. Like hold it in, store it, then release it. It's a rare psychic skill and, according to Clint, almost impossible to manage. Most ergokinetics are unstable—his word, not mine. The fact that they have so much raw power coursing through them at all times makes them prone to dramatic mood swings and violent fits of temper."

Teddy nodded. "How does the ability manifest?"

"That's where it gets dangerous. Ergokinetics are naturally drawn to ordnance work. Obviously, the preferred way to deal with a bomb is to disarm it. But say you can't. You get there too late or you trigger a land mine. An ergokinetic can *absorb* a bomb's energy. Save the lives of everyone around him."

Teddy thought about the stunning array of medals pinned to Julian Whitfield's chest.

"The problem is," Dara continued, "ergokinetics can't do it for long. There's only so much energy they can absorb. Ultimately, they burn out. Or if they absorb a charge large enough? Or don't know how to properly release it? The energy gets to be too much, and they can't control it. Then . . ." She paused. "Energy only has one place to go." Her mouth twisted in a grim line.

"Let me get this straight," Teddy said. She kept hoping Dara would interrupt again, just so she didn't have to say the next part. But this time, Dara kept quiet. "You think that Julian Whitfield turned into a human bomb."

Dara nodded.

Teddy sank into a chair. Slipped off her coat and hat and tossed them aside. "Well," she said, "I have news for you, too. Miles is the Hyle test subject."

Dara's jaw dropped. Her eyes grew wide. Teddy was glad her friend was sitting down. If she hadn't been, she might have toppled over. "Holy shit." Dara thought for a moment. Her eyes shot back and forth, silently calculating. "Miles inherited his father's ability, didn't he?"

Teddy ran through recent events: the tree branch yesterday, the icicle this morning. Miles must have absorbed the energy of the IED at Whitfield's party. He'd been releasing bursts of it ever since—but only when provoked. "But I don't think Miles is aware what he's doing."

Dara slumped back against her chair as though Teddy had shoved her. "Holy shit," she repeated.

Whitfield knew, Teddy thought, doing a little calculating of her own. That's why he paled when he'd learned how close Miles had been to the bomb, especially when Teddy and Kate had puzzled over why the device hadn't exploded. Miles had saved their lives, at a cost to his own.

Dara shook her head as though to clear it. "Whitfield developed X-498 to repress Miles's ergokinetic ability. That's what this is about."

"Xantal," Teddy corrected. But yeah, that was essentially correct. "We've got to talk to him, get him to shut down production. Now."

"You're in luck. The house manager knocked on my door a couple hours ago. Apparently, Hollis himself is on his way. He decided he wanted to spend Christmas Eve here. He might even be here already."

Some luck. Teddy would have preferred to postpone the confrontation, as well as her report of the afternoon's events. Give herself a little time to think things through. But if Hollis Whitfield was there, she had no excuse to put it off. She rose and moved to the door. "Miles went to his room to lie down. Keep an eye on him, will you? I'll be back."

"Teddy," Dara said, hesitation in her voice. "Are you sure about this? If his ability is as unpredictable as Clint believes—if Whitfield is doing all this because of what happened to Miles's dad—maybe Miles really needs the medication."

"Shouldn't that be up to Miles?"

Their eyes met. *What if the drug had been available to Molly?* Dara said, "Think about it. Whatever Eversley—or the PC—was up to, they didn't have this kind of study . . ."

She trailed off, looking miserable, and Teddy understood. Molly was constantly on Dara's mind. Teddy suspected that she ran through every scenario again and again, wondering what she could have done differently to help their friend. "Dara, this isn't about Molly."

"Point is, let's not rush into anything with Miles. Once he knows, there's no going back."

Teddy hesitated at the doorway. She ran her hand along the exquisite wooden paneling. Lovely but cold. She'd heard that wood was supposed to feel warm. It didn't, not here. Something about this house filled her with a vague sense of icy dread. Despite the grandeur, she'd felt this way ever since she stepped inside the lodge. She couldn't blame the blanket of snow that coated the grounds or a draft that slipped beneath the doors. This was something else. A dull foreboding, constant as a toothache, that left her perpetually chilled.

Teddy said, "Nilsson and Stanton showed up in Tahoe today. Nilsson made a grab for the Xantal. Didn't get it," she clarified at Dara's gasp, "but somehow they knew where to find it. Whether or not they're working with Yates, I don't know. But they knew Miles carried it on him. So this can't wait. None of it can. Whitfield needs to know what's going on."

She turned and made her way downstairs. Whitfield's chef was in the kitchen. As she passed the dining room, Teddy heard the clatter of pots and pans, the sizzle of something cooking. The aroma of onions and garlic wafted from the kitchen. It smelled delicious and absolutely unappetizing at the same time. For once, Teddy had no desire to eat.

She found Whitfield in his study, seated in a thronelike wingback chair upholstered in perfectly distressed leather. A fire blazed in the hearth. The picture of regal contentment. At her knock, he glanced up from the book he'd been reading. "Miss Cannon. Come in." He set aside his book and gestured to a bottle of Scotch with an exotic label. "Can I offer you a drink? Or are you officially on duty?"

"Yes, but either way, I'd pass, sir," she said. She didn't want to drink with this man.

He indicated the chair opposite him. "I assume everything's all right?" he said once she was seated.

"Actually, no. It's not."

Displeasure flashed across Whitfield's patrician features. The look was tinged with maybe a hint of superiority, as though Teddy were a valet reporting that his car had been scratched. "If you're unhappy with your room, Miss Cannon, I'll ask my housekeeper—"

"I'm talking about what you're doing to Miles. I'm talking about Xantal."

Whitfield put down his glass. Carefully. Took a moment to square the edge of the bottle to the edge of the tray. Once satisfied with the arrangement of objects on the side table, he returned his attention to Teddy. "What do you know?"

"I know you created a supervirus and then a drug to suppress psychic expression." She waited for several pulsing moments as he took that in.

Finally, he said, "And how did you find that out?"

Teddy couldn't control her anger, but she didn't want to. "You're experimenting with a medication that would destroy people like me—the very people your school is supposed to be educating—and your concern is how I found out?"

He pressed his lips together. "I'm asking because you're focusing on only a very small part of the picture."

"You're medicating Miles without his consent! How can you rationalize—"

"Ms. Cannon," he said, "I understand you're upset."

Upset? He had to be kidding. She was furious. Betrayed. "I—"

"You need to listen to me," he interrupted. "I'm not trying to hurt Miles or anyone else. I believe in the power of psychics to do so much good for our world. That's why I founded the school. But you have to understand. My son, Julian, was a powerful psychic. Incredibly powerful. But he couldn't control his gift. His gift was bigger than he was, and it eventually destroyed him."

"Miles isn't his father."

"He has the same ability. A highly dangerous one. Not just to him but to others. I'm doing my best to protect him from that. To protect us all from that."

He stood and moved to the fireplace. He braced one hand on the mantel, lifted a poker, and stirred the logs. Directing his gaze toward the flames rather than her, he said, "After my son was killed, I devoted myself to helping psychics learn to control their powers and harness them for the greater good. But I always knew that there were some psychics, like Julian, who would never be able to perform that role. So I founded Hyle. Funded the research and development of Xantal. It's groundbreaking therapy. One that can alleviate a burden from those who can't protect themselves. It could be Miles's only chance at a long and healthy life. His only chance at not being a force of destruction. Can't you see I'm doing the *right* thing? Can't you see I'm acting in his interest and not against it?"

Teddy rubbed her forehead. She understood. But didn't Miles deserve to know? Didn't he deserve a chance to see if he could master his powers? "Even if I did agree with you, it wouldn't be fair not to at least let him decide for himself. Besides the interpersonal family drama, which I'm not about to get into, can't you see that what you've opened is a veritable Pandora's box in terms of psychic genetics? If this research falls into the wrong hands, HEAT would be the least of your concerns—"

Whitfield's cell phone rang, interrupting Teddy's thought. He checked caller ID, then looked at Teddy. "I am willing to take that risk. If you'll excuse me, I have to take this. And I demand privacy."

She stepped into the hall but lingered outside his door. She would grudgingly accept that their conversation had been interrupted, but she was unwilling to consider it over. Not until they'd discussed what had happened that afternoon. If the PC was after Xantal, Whitfield needed to be made aware of *that* threat.

Moments later—was it her imagination?—she thought she caught the words "demonstrators" and "Hyle Pharmaceuticals" from the other side of the door.

Teddy froze. The combination of protesters and Hyle Pharmaceuticals meant only one thing: HEAT was active once again. Coupled with Nilsson and Stanton's appearance in town, it was all too coincidental. If she'd learned anything from training, it was that coincidences were never just coincidences, not when so many threads of a case suddenly came together.

She didn't waste any time debating whether to use her astral projection to slip inside Whitfield's study and hear what was going on. Lives were at stake. She needed to know.

With Pyro and Clint's coaching, Teddy had perfected the art of meditating into a near-instant state of relaxation. She planted her feet firmly on the ground, slowly breathed in and out. Straightened her spine, brought her head high, aligned her chin with her chest. Relaxed her body, zoned out of her current surroundings, and eased into an otherworldly state of being, mentally connecting it to the earth and sky, bringing herself into the oneness of the universe.

Then she released her astral body from her physical one. And there it was—that jerk—a terrible, dark, agonizing pull. Followed almost immediately by lightness.

Her astral body was inside Whitfield's office, floating over his mahogany desk as he sat, his fist curled around the old telephone receiver. From her vantage point, she could see that Whitfield's seemingly thick white hair was starting to thin at the crown.

"What do you mean, you can't clear them from the property?" he demanded. "They're protesters, a bunch of wannabes." A pause as he listened to whatever was being said on the other end. "I don't care if the media is there. They're on private property. Call the police. Do something. That's what I'm paying you for." Another pause. "You sure it was him? That Nevin character? And you caught him on our security camera?" A note of victory crept into Whitfield's voice. "Have him arrested. He almost killed my grandson."

Eli Nevin was *alive*. Shock coursed through Teddy. She struggled to decide whether she was deeply relieved or furious that his disappearing act had put Jillian through a solid month of hell. Both, really.

"If you can't handle it, I'll handle it myself," Whitfield barked into the receiver. "Get the plane ready." With that, he slammed down the phone.

The noise startled Teddy's astral body, and it went crashing back into her physical one. Her knees nearly gave out, but she recovered enough to remain standing.

Whitfield flung open the door to his office and stepped out. Gave Teddy a cursory glance as he strode past her. "Pack your things. Tell your friend and Miles, too. The jet will be ready in thirty minutes. We'll have Christmas in San Francisco." With that, he walked away.

This was the first time in a long time that Teddy had felt some sympathy for Clint. How, truly, can you protect someone from himself?

She didn't have an answer when she knocked on Miles's door. "Almost ready?" she called.

"Just about. Come in."

She opened the door and saw Miles throwing his things into a suitcase. She looked around and didn't see any sign of his satchel or the syringes. She hesitated in his doorway.

"Everything okay?" he asked.

"I was just wondering about your medication."

"What about it?"

"Are you taking it with you?"

"Why do you care?"

"Miles, I just want to make sure it's someplace secure—"

"But you're still going to keep me in the dark."

Teddy stepped inside the room and shut the door behind her. "For a little while longer, yes."

"First some crazy woman tries to steal it from me, and now you come in here all concerned about 'securing' it." He turned and pulled something out from under the pillows on his bed. When he turned back to her, he was holding the canvas bag. "I've been injecting this shit into my body. Don't you think I deserve to know what the hell is going on?"

"Of course you do," Teddy said, and she meant it.

"Then tell me!"

She wanted to. She'd been medicated for so many years; learning the truth about who she was and who her parents had been had liberated her. She opened her mouth, wondering what small bits of truth would satisfy him. But it was impossible to give him any piece of it without unraveling the fiction of his happy life and exposing secrets that she had promised to keep. The silence stretched.

"Fine," he said, and turned his back to her. In one quick movement, he pulled one of the wrapped syringes from the bag, ripped off the paper with his teeth. "I think I need another dose."

"Miles, don't."

He dropped his pants and stood there in his boxers, holding the syringe next to his thigh. "And why not? The drug levels my moods, calms me down. Give me one reason why I shouldn't take it." He pressed the needle against his flesh, ready to plunge it.

"Because it's not designed to treat a mood disorder." She exhaled, hoping that would satisfy him for now.

His expression was dark, unappeased. "Then what's it for?"

For a moment, she considered letting him do it. After all, he had taken it before. But she couldn't. She either had to tell him or let him inject himself with a drug that Hyle was developing to suppress psychic expression.

She tried to remember how Clint had first told her. He was direct, she recalled. Straightforward. "There's no simple way to put this," she said, "so I'll just say it. You, Miles Whitfield, are psychic. And that drug was designed to repress your power."

Miles stared at her. "Psychic? I'm not psychic."

"Specifically," Teddy continued, "you're ergokinetic. Why do you think the bomb exploded but didn't hurt anyone at your grandfather's party? You absorbed the energy. Why do you think that tree branch crashed in the woods, landing squarely on the hood of the reckless driver? The icicle that nearly impaled the thief? You channeled the energy. You're psychic, Miles. Like me."

Miles dropped the needle as his face went white in shock. Teddy slumped back against the door. She'd done it—told him the truth. There was no going back now. And so, with only ten minutes before they had to catch a plane to San Francisco and head to Hyle Pharmaceuticals, Teddy told him as much of the truth as she could: about his father, his grandfather, the Whitfield Institute, and her own psychic abilities.

"Miles!" his grandfather called from downstairs. "We have to leave. The plane is ready."

"Just a minute," he called, and then said to Teddy, "You actually believe I have psychic powers?"

Teddy remembered how hard it had been for her to accept this fundamental truth about herself. Miles was definitely an ergokinetic. No other explanation fit.

She studied his face and felt like she was looking straight into her own past.

"Yes, Miles. I really do."

CHAPTER THIRTY-ONE

AS FAR AS STRETCH LIMOS WERE CONCERNED, THE one that picked them up at the airport was relatively sedate. More like something a politician would ride in than the kind of glitzy, blinged-out monstrosities that cruised the Vegas Strip. Still, Dara was impressed. "Never been in one of these," she whispered to Teddy. "Too bad this isn't the time to poke my head through the sunroof and wave around a bottle of champagne."

Later, maybe. Definitely not now. Teddy and Dara sat with their backs to the driver, and Whitfield and Miles faced them. There was a small bar lined with top-shelf Scotch, vodka, and gin, but Teddy knew no one was in the mood to drink. No one was in the mood to talk, either.

She glanced around the vehicle's interior. She didn't need to read minds to follow the paths everyone's thoughts had traveled. Whitfield was anxious about the disruption at Hyle. Miles was furiously brooding over the fact that not only had his grandfather hidden the truth from him for years, he had also medicated him without consent. Dara was wondering if the stretch limo had a sick sound system. Teddy was sorting through the events of the last few months. Though she knew it all intersected somewhere—Hyle Pharmaceuticals, the PC, Whitfield Institute—the Venn diagram connecting them felt too narrow to wedge open with words. So they traveled in uncomfortable silence until they reached the laboratory.

The corporate headquarters occupied a four-story building located on a one-way street in South San Francisco. A building so plain and unremarkable, Teddy would have passed by without a second glance had it not been for the police car idling in front, blue lights flashing, monitoring a group of roughly fifty protesters who swarmed around the entrance.

Whitfield cursed under his breath, his body stiffening. He cracked his window, perhaps to get a better look at the scene, and the crowd's muffled chants amplified: "Cruella! De Vil! How many animals did you kill?"

"Why the hell aren't the police doing anything to get rid of these idiots?" he growled.

"It's called the First Amendment," Miles said. "They have a right to protest against something they feel is wrong." He leveled his grandfather with a dark glare. "We all should have that right. *Informed* protest." Only Teddy could name the emotion behind his words: betrayal.

Whitfield frowned but didn't pursue the comment. He directed his driver to pull around to the side entrance.

Teddy scanned the crowd for Eli. She couldn't spot him in the jostling mass of people but knew he had to be there. She'd overheard Whitfield confirm it. Besides, this was a HEAT event, and HEAT was Eli's baby.

As the limo slowed, Dara leaned toward Whitfield. "Sir, you and I will jump out and move inside at the count of three. Do not look at the protesters, keep your eyes on the door." Teddy started to slide over to join them, but Dara shook her off. "I'll cover Whitfield, you stay with Miles. He's your charge until we're released from duty." She turned back to Whitfield. "One, two, three."

Dara threw open the door and hustled Whitfield into the side door. Teddy watched, impressed at her friend's professionalism. She might just make one hell of a Secret Service agent.

Miles stared after his grandfather. Teddy saw his jaw tighten. Watched the cords in his neck stretch. He flexed his knee up and down, clenched and unclenched his fist. "All these years. I was actually grateful to him for taking me in after my dad died." He gave the canvas satchel resting at his feet a pointed glare. "And what has he been doing? Lying to me."

Teddy immediately regretted having told Miles the truth. Her timing had been awful. If she'd only waited until they reached Tiburon, Whitfield could have explained his reasoning. Explained that he'd been trying to protect Miles, not hurt him. But the more time Miles had to brood over what Whitfield had done, the more furious he became. Teddy did not want to see his ergokinetic energy released here. Not within this pulsing mass of people. The odds of someone getting hurt were too high.

She saw her greatest fear: a buzz of energy hovering just on the edge of her perception. She had come to recognize it as the stirrings of psychic power. "Listen to me, Miles. You have to stay calm. Those breathing exercises you learned for managing pain? Do them now. Don't let your anger—"

We must speak, Theodora.

Yates. A chill raced up Teddy's spine. She shored up her protective psychic walls.

Miles asked, "What? What is it?"

Teddy held up a finger. She twisted around and tapped the partition. The driver slid it open and met her eyes in the rearview mirror. "Swing around and make a slow pass by the front gate," she instructed.

The driver inched the car forward. Teddy peered through the tinted window, searching the faces of the protesters. Mostly early-twentysomethings waving signs. Loads of scraggly beards, ripped jeans, and backpacks with patches of hackneyed wisdom sewn on.

Then her gaze stumbled over a slim man standing by himself on the eastern side of the building, away from the swarm of protesters. Deliberately removed from the crowd. Closely shorn hair, dark gaze. A posture that suggested confidence and control.

Derek Yates.

Teddy swung around to face Miles. "Wait here," she said firmly. "Do not get out of this car." She turned to the driver. "Let me out, lock the doors, and drive back around to the side entrance. Do not let anyone in this car except Dara, me, or Hollis Whitfield. Understood?" She was barking orders and it felt good. Anger was her charge.

Teddy flung open the door and stepped onto the asphalt. She was on fire, flushed. The noise around her was nearly deafening.

"Hey, hey, ho, ho! Animal testing has got to go!"

She shouldered through the crowd of protesters and made her way over to Yates.

Teddy was sick of this man. Sick of his witty banter, his half-truths and manipulations. Everything. She needed him gone. Out of her life and back in prison, where he belonged.

That hurts, Theodora.

She was so angry she had momentarily allowed her mental defenses to slip. She shored them up once more before he could reenter her thoughts. "No, you don't. You aren't going to mentally influence me, Yates. You don't get to use me the way you used Eli. In fact, you don't get to talk to me anymore. Consider this our final goodbye." Teddy was yelling now, but it didn't matter. The din of the crowd was all around them, blanketing their words. They were in a private cocoon.

"You don't understand, Theodora. I need you alive. That's why I risked coming here today."

She released a bark of laughter. She couldn't help it. "Protecting me? Who the hell do you think was bent over that little IED you set up at Whitfield's party? If that had gone off, my face would've been splattered over the walls." That last part was a test. If she could catch him in a lie . . .

Impatience entered his tone. "Did you study the Polson case? Have you gained control of your astral travel?" A pause as he finally caught up, then, "IED? What IED?"

She took a deep breath, reined in her anger. How could he have not known about the IED? But there was only one thing she needed from Yates now. "Where's Eli? Whitfield's security team caught him on their surveillance camera earlier, so I know he's here somewhere. What have you done with him?"

"Theodora, listen to me. I need to know—"

"Where's Eli? And don't tell me you didn't plant that suggestion for him to interrupt the production of Xantal."

"Xantal?"

She gave an impatient wave of her hand. "X-498. Xantal. They're the same thing." She threw Yates's words back in his face. " 'Do whatever it takes to shut down Hyle Pharmaceuticals.' I know you influenced Eli, so don't bother to deny it. That's what you said: *whatever it takes*. Including planting an IED. Isn't that right?"

Yates looked away from her as though distracted. No, not distracted. Deeply concerned. "What else, Theodora?"

"What do you mean, what else? You—"

"I need to know what else has been happening."

She opened her mouth to spew an ugly retort, intent on walking away. Before she could get the words out, she felt something like an ice cream brain freeze but a thousand times worse. Yates had neutralized her mental defenses with an ease that was terrifying. Grimacing, she doubled over, her hands at her temples.

"I'm sorry to do it this way, Theodora, but I have to know."

Teddy's eyes widened in dismay as the pressure increased and the memories replayed in her mind's eye. Eli, mentally influenced at the party. His subsequent disappearance. The IED. Miles's ergokinetic ability. The attempted theft of Xantal by Nilsson and Stanton.

At last Yates released her from his psychic grip. She staggered backward. Nauseated. Dizzy. Furious.

Yates looked at her. "We may be too late after all."

Teddy couldn't begin to guess what he meant. She couldn't even figure out whose side he was on. She only knew she couldn't let him get away. She lunged for him. The crowd swarmed closer, converging on them. Teddy was jostled, pushed, and shoved, carried away from Yates by a stream of shouting, chanting people.

A HEAT protester whipped off her own shirt and poured what looked like blood from a water jug all over her head. Then she swung her long hair around and splattered the crowd with the red substance. Teddy felt some of it go in her mouth. A sweet, syrupy flavor. The crowd erupted in cheers, raising their signs and their fists.

Teddy struggled to break free of the pulsing throb of bodies. When she finally burst from the crowd, Yates was gone.

She caught her breath. She scanned the vicinity for a clue to the direction he'd taken. Not north, not south. Her gaze skidded to a stop at the eastern side of the building. Whitfield's limo. The passenger door was hanging open.

She was in a full sprint by the time she reached the car.

Empty.

No sign of Miles or the driver. As she took a step back, the glint from an object resting in the gutter caught her eye. Her heart drumming wildly in her throat, she reached down to pick it up.

Miles's glasses. The left lens cracked, the wire frames bent.

Teddy ran to the side entrance and pounded on it. A security guard buzzed her into the service entrance foyer. He took one look at her and reached for his gun.

"Wait. She's with us!" The guard holstered his gun as Dara reached out to touch Teddy's cheek. "Oh my God, you're bleeding."

"Corn syrup and red food coloring," Teddy gasped. "Is Miles here?"

"Miles? I thought he was with you. In the car."

Teddy looked at the security guard. "Did anyone come through this door?"

"Just Mr. Whitfield's driver. He needed to use the bathroom. Dude looked all spaced out. I thought he was going to be sick."

Spaced out. Teddy knew what that meant. He'd been mentally influenced into leaving the vehicle. It was Yates, it had to be. Meaning Miles had been left alone, completely unprotected. With four syringes of his medication tucked away in his canvas messenger bag.

She turned to Dara. "Miles is gone. And so is the Xantal."

CHAPTER THIRTY-TWO

LEAVING DARA ON DUTY TO ACCOMPANY WHITFIELD to his home in Tiburon, Teddy caught the first ferry back to campus. The nearly empty vessel slugged its way through the bay's choppy currents, battling unusually rough water and fog so dense her hand disappeared when she held it in front of her. She stood at the bow, welcoming the cool sting of salt water and the rough jostling of the boat.

Miles was gone. It had been *her* job to protect him. If Yates hadn't distracted her, he'd be safe right now. Home with his grandfather in Tiburon, getting ready to celebrate Christmas. Instead, he was gone. No, worse than that. *Gone* implied that he'd taken off for a little while but would soon return.

Although Hollis Whitfield had said it wasn't unusual for Miles to take off in a sulk when he was irritated, Teddy's professional instinct told her that wasn't the case now. Whoever had taken Miles had also succeeded in grabbing the Xantal. Which meant it was very likely that Miles was in danger. She absently twisted his glasses in her hands, mentally willing the ferry to move faster. She had to talk to Clint. To Wessner.

When the ferry bumped up against the pier, Teddy leaped onto the dock without waiting for the crew to lower the gangplank. She raced up the path that led to campus, checked through the security gates, then barreled straight toward the faculty wing.

Teddy had envisioned her role as that of town crier. Raising the alarm and rousing the troops. Spinning everyone within earshot into immediate and urgent action. But heavy silence echoed through the halls. Clint didn't answer her urgent rapping at his office door. Neither did Wessner.

Her pulse began to thrum heavily in her ears. *Christmas break.*

No classes, no students, no instructors. Surely someone had been left behind to keep an eye on things. Fighting a rising sense of panic, she turned and headed toward the faculty living quarters. She pounded on Clint's residence door, but it was the door across the hall that flew open.

"Teddy?"

She spun around. Nick Stavros. He studied her with a puzzled frown. "What are you doing here? I thought you'd been assigned Whitfield's detail."

Teddy's relief at having found someone to talk to was so acute that her knees nearly buckled. Her words tumbled out in a long, almost incoherent stream. "Nick, I screwed up. I was supposed to be protecting Miles, but there were so many protesters, and when I saw Yates in the crowd—"

"Whoa." He held up his palms. "Hold on." He widened the door to his suite, beckoning her inside with a tilt of his head. "Come in."

Teddy nodded and brushed past him. But the moment she stepped inside, she abruptly stopped. Everything looked exactly as it had a year ago, when she had invented a pretense to sneak into his room to secretly copy his laptop files. The memory struck her with such mortifying clarity—how she'd come on to Nick, turned their physical attraction into something she could manipulate to achieve her own ends—that for a moment her sense of shame was so great, it drove all thoughts of Miles from her mind.

"Sit down," he said.

Teddy nodded, recalling what had brought her there in the first place. She had bigger issues to deal with at the moment. She scanned the room, considering her options. The sofa, across which was spread a newspaper he must have been reading when she'd interrupted him, or a club chair set at a right angle to the sofa. She lowered herself into the chair and watched as Nick moved to the suite's tiny kitchen, removed a glass from a cabinet, and filled it with tap water.

"Here." He passed her the glass. She hadn't realized she was thirsty, but to her surprise, she downed it in one long gulp. He took the empty glass, set it on the coffee table, then seated himself on the sofa. "All right. Give me a full report. What happened?"

A full report.

Exactly the words Teddy needed to hear. A not so subtle reminder that she was a recruit and was expected to act like it. She collected her thoughts and walked him through the day's events.

"Did Yates directly threaten Miles in any way?" Nick asked when she'd finished.

"Well, no, not specifically." She replayed their conversation in her mind. "But Nick, it was *Yates.* You can't imagine his presence there was just a coincidence."

Nick leaned back and stretched one arm over the back of the sofa. Looked thoughtful. "I don't know what his presence meant, but we shouldn't assume he had anything to do with Miles's disappearance."

"How can you say that?"

"Teddy, think. If Yates did want to grab Miles, why would he make his presence known to you?"

"He wanted to distract me. Get me to leave Miles unprotected. An obvious ploy, but I fell for it."

"Maybe."

"You don't sound convinced."

"I'm not saying there's not a connection to Miles's disappearance. But let's not assume the worst. Miles might have wandered away on his own. You said he was agitated, upset at his grandfather. Maybe he saw the protesters, a group he'd been sympathetic to in the past, and just wanted to get away."

"And his glasses?"

"Knocked off as he jostled through the crowd." Nick shook his head. "You heard no gunshot or cry for help. Saw no signs of a struggle or foul play. So we call it a disappearance, think about where he might have gone, and take it from there."

"The Xantal?"

"We should assume Miles has it with him."

"But—"

"Less than twenty-four hours ago, that woman, Nilsson, made a grab for the Xantal. She showed no interest at all in harming Miles. What would have happened to change that?"

Teddy stood abruptly, moved to the window, and looked down. The view was of the courtyard, though it was too dark and foggy to see much of it. All she could make out was the dim glow of solar accent lights illuminating the rocky footpaths below. Even though she couldn't see the courtyard, she knew it was there. Just as she couldn't prove Miles was in danger, but she felt it deep inside.

Turning, she said, "What about Eli? That has to be connected, doesn't it? Eli disappears, shows up at this HEAT protest, and now Miles is gone?"

He frowned. "They don't have to be connected, but they could be. I'll concede that."

"I would feel a hell of a lot better if I knew where Miles was right now."

"I would too."

He drew the knuckle of his index finger along his bottom lip, a habit she'd forgotten he had, but one that sent her spiraling back a year in time as effectively as any Pilgrim's Tunnel. She'd once found that particular gesture so sexy. But now, watching him, she felt nothing at all. She hadn't necessarily wanted a relationship with Nick—she could see now how unsuited they were for each other—but she had sabotaged any chance they might have had with an ease that shocked her. Just the way she had tried to push Pyro away, nearly sabotaging any chance they might have had. Fortunately, she hadn't succeeded. She suddenly missed him with an intensity that surprised her.

Although her thoughts had temporarily wandered, Nick's stayed straight on track. "You said Dara stayed with Hollis Whitfield?"

"Yes."

"So I'll get Dara on the phone, tell her to have Hollis give her a list of Miles's friends, places he liked to hang out. We'll start looking there. While she pulls that together, I'll contact Clint and Wessner, bring them up to speed, check out Clint's most recent intel on Yates."

Teddy nodded. It sounded like a good plan. "What should I do?"

"Assuming we don't find Miles within the next couple of hours, what's the first thing Clint and Wessner will want to see once they're back on campus?"

Teddy sighed. "A written report."

"Exactly. So get on it."

Back in her room, Teddy could think of nothing she wanted to do less than paperwork. But at least it kept her busy. She toyed with Miles's glasses as she waited for the knock on her door, for Nick to tell her that Miles had been found unharmed.

It didn't come.

A little after two in the morning, she undressed and climbed beneath the covers, but sleep eluded her. No matter how desperately she tried to redirect her thoughts, they kept drifting back to Miles. Where was he? Was he frightened, injured? She'd let him down in so many ways, and not just professionally. She focused on the shadows flitting across the ceiling until she finally drifted into a light, troubled sleep.

CHAPTER THIRTY-THREE

TEDDY WOKE ON CHRISTMAS MORNING TO FIND A note slipped beneath her door. A slim white sheet with Clint's name printed on the top, two words scribbled beneath it: *My office*.

Despite the cursory nature of the summons, relief bloomed within her. Clint was back. She threw on her clothes, dragged her fingers through her hair, and shot out the door, heading straight to the administrative wing. Her mind raced ahead of her steps. Nick must have reached Clint last night and explained the situation. Now Clint was here, ready to help find Miles. Maybe he already had. Maybe Miles was safe, having spent the night with a friend, and Clint had returned to campus to reprimand Teddy for her failure to keep Miles under surveillance. Which would be fine. She'd accept whatever punishment Clint doled out as long as Miles was safe.

She reached his office, knocked, and threw open the door. One look at Clint promptly disabused her of any hope that Miles had been found. Clint's jaw was set, his posture stiff. Dara was already there, her expression every bit as grim as Clint's. To their left stood Pyro and Jillian. Teddy fought an instinct to launch herself into Pyro's arms for a reassuring hug.

Clint gestured her into a chair. "Dara's already given me her version of events," he said. "Now I want yours. Take it from the top and fill me in."

Teddy held nothing back, relating everything from Miles's mood swings to the fact that he'd been prescribed Xantal. She concluded with her suspicion that Yates had been involved in Miles's disappearance. Intellectually, she understood Nick's arguments to the contrary, but on a gut level, she wasn't buying it. They continued to retrace the events leading up to Miles's disappearance until a knock on the door interrupted them.

Agent Wessner stuck her head inside. "There's been a development."

Teddy tensed. Wessner's voice was as carefully neutral as her expression, but that in itself was a giveaway. Wessner wouldn't go out of her way to hide good news. And she certainly wouldn't be so scrupulous about avoiding Teddy's gaze. Which meant whatever she had to share was at the very least troubling. And at worst, well . . .

"If you will all follow me to the conference room." Wessner turned without another word, leaving them to follow.

Teddy rose from her chair, her shaky legs barely supporting her. She didn't dare meet the eyes of her friends—she couldn't face the blame she might find there. Teddy had been the one assigned to protect Miles. If something had happened to him because she'd screwed up, she'd carry that with her the rest of her life.

As they stepped into the conference room, Teddy was surprised to see four people already seated at a large mahogany table: Hollis Whitfield, Nick Stavros, Kate Atkins, and General Maddux. Teddy's gaze went to Hollis Whitfield. He appeared to have aged decades in the hours since she'd seen him last. The patrician self-assurance was gone. His eyes were red-rimmed, his skin ashen.

Wessner waited for the newcomers to be seated, then moved to the head of the table. On the wall behind her was a flat-screen television. She lifted a slim black remote and announced, "Approximately thirty minutes ago, we received a video from a group identifying themselves as members of HEAT." She pointed the remote at the television, then hesitated and looked at Whitfield. "Hollis," she said, her voice softening, "you've already seen this. If you'd rather wait outside while we—"

"No." Whitfield fixed his eyes on the screen. "Play it."

Wessner opened her mouth as if to object, then seemed to change her mind. She gave a curt nod and pushed a button. Nothing but static fuzz until the screen slowly went dark, reduced to a glowing pinprick of light. A digital blink and a single image swam into focus.

Miles. Unconscious and strapped to a metal chair. His head against his chest. Bleeding from the temple and chin. His lower lip split, his left eye swollen and bruised.

Teddy heard a soft cry of distress, and it took her a full second to realize the sound had slipped through her own lips. She clamped her jaw and stared at the screen, refusing to allow herself even the momentary relief of looking away. She was responsible for this. She had to *see it*.

Initially, the camera's focus had been tight on Miles. Now the view broadened slightly as the angle widened to reveal a vast, dimly lit space. Cement floor and metal walls. Lofty ceilings and industrial lighting, scraps of sheet metal haphazardly piled in one corner. Teddy had the general impression of a warehouse. No windows, or windows that had been partially blacked out. Either way, impossible to tell whether the video had been shot at night or during the day.

She took all that in, then her gaze narrowed on the black-clothed figure who stood behind Miles. Although the person could be seen only from the neck down, the shape of the body strongly suggested male. As Teddy watched, he raised his hand and pushed the barrel of a snub-nosed, semiautomatic pistol against a spot just above Miles's right ear.

Then he began to speak. "Hollis Whitfield and members of the Hyle Pharmaceuticals board."

"*No!*" Jillian gasped.

Eli Nevin. Teddy had recognized his voice the moment he began to speak. Judging from Jillian's anguished reaction, she had as well. It sounded like Eli, but there was something off . . . Teddy cut a quick, puzzled glance at Pyro and Dara, then returned her attention to the video as Eli continued speaking.

"HEAT's demands are simple," he said. "One: Hyle must permanently shut down production of Xantal. Two: All lab animals must be removed from testing facilities and placed in no-kill shelters. Three: Hollis Whitfield must atone for his sins by resigning from all board positions, publicly and privately held. You have twenty-four hours. Should you choose not to comply with our demands within that time, Miles Whitfield will be executed."

The screen went black. Wessner pressed a button to shut it off.

Pyro, Dara, and Teddy all began speaking at once. Clint silenced them, then looked directly at Wessner. "What do you know?"

"We've identified the speaker as Eli Nevin, leader of the organization known as HEAT."

"No!" Jillian cried. "It can't be! Eli would *never*—"

"That's *enough*." Maddux slammed his palm on the slick mahogany table. He leaned toward Jillian, his eyes blazing. "It's bad enough that Hollis has to go through this," he gritted out. "I will not allow you to defend the man who's threatening his grandson's life. Is that understood?"

Clint looked as if he wanted to say something to Maddux but demurred. It was clear that the general was in charge now, even within Whitfield Institute's walls.

Jillian shrank back in her chair, her arms wrapped around herself, her blue eyes brimming with tears. "I don't understand." Her voice was little more than a ragged whisper. "Eli would never hurt anyone or anything."

"Is it true you were romantically involved with Nevin?" Maddux pressed.

"Well, yes, but—"

"And the two of you broke in to Hyle Pharmaceuticals in September of this year?"

Jillian nodded as silent tears streamed down her cheeks. "For the animals—"

"Where is he?"

"I . . . I don't know."

"*Where is he?*"

"I don't know!" Jillian wailed. "I just know Eli wouldn't do this!"

"I'm afraid that's no longer an issue for debate," Wessner said. "Ms. Atkins has identified the voice of the man in the video as belonging to the same Eli Nevin who is wanted in conjunction with the bombing that took place at Hollis Whitfield's home on Thanksgiving Day."

Nick said, "Surveillance footage shows that Eli Nevin was also present at yesterday's HEAT protest at Hyle Pharmaceuticals." His gaze met Teddy's, then slipped away. "The same event where Miles was last seen."

"Yates," Teddy blurted out. "He's the one behind this, not HEAT, not Eli. Yates is mentally influencing Eli."

Maddux leaned forward. "What is she talking about?"

"Teddy, we've been through this—" Nick began, but Maddux cut him off.

"Derek Yates?" he snapped, swinging around to glare at Teddy. "The man you helped escape from prison last year? I've read your files, Ms. Cannon. You seem to be at the center of trouble everywhere you go."

Teddy shook her head. "Please listen." Fighting a rising sense of panic, she swallowed hard and started again. "Mr. Whitfield, I saw Eli at your party after the bomb was disarmed. I saw Eli's eyes—I know what mental influence looks like."

"Why the hell didn't you report it at the time?" Maddux shot back.

She turned to Clint. "Clint, *listen*. Yates was influencing him to read that—"

"We have less than twenty-four hours to save Miles's life," Maddux interrupted. "I will not allow a single moment of time to be wasted on wild conjectures that lead us nowhere. We have a suspect. We have motive."

"It's not wild conjecture. I know—" Teddy started.

"I believe her," Clint said.

"She knows *nothing*," Maddux finished savagely. "The only fact we have firmly in hand is that *you* were the one who was supposed to be protecting Miles when he was taken." He let that sink in, then pointed to the TV. "We have the tape. Eli Nevin has been positively identified. HEAT has claimed responsibility. All the evidence we need in order to proceed is right there."

"He's right," said Whitfield. "That group . . ." His voice gave out, and he hung his head in a posture of utter defeat. "I should have taken their protests seriously. If anything happens to Miles . . ."

Clint leaned across the table, his expression that of a man tasked with delivering unpleasant but necessary news. "Hollis, have you considered agreeing to their demands?"

Whitfield stared at him, aghast. "Agree? You're suggesting I give them what they want?"

"I'm suggesting we should at least discuss it."

Whitfield brought up his chin. "No. There's no discussion. I can't do that."

"Surely nothing is worth your grandson's life," Dara put in. "Miles is worth a thousand times more than any profit Xantal might one day make."

"Money?" Whitfield recoiled as though he'd been slapped. "You think this is about money? I'm sure you all know by now what happened to my son. I can't let that happen to my grandson."

"And," Maddux interjected, "we do not yield to terrorists. We have no reason to trust that Miles would be safe even if we did comply with their demands."

"In that case, we'll find him," Pyro promised. "We'll bring him home. This is what we've been trained to do."

"What you've been trained to do," Maddux scoffed. "Where's Eli Nevin? You've been looking for him for weeks, haven't you? And you still haven't found him."

Clint leaned across the table. "Wait just a damned a minute—"

"*Stop.*" Hollis Whitfield rose to his feet. "Both of you, that's enough. We have less than twenty-four hours to find Miles. We can't waste time infighting. I'm putting General Maddux in charge of this investigation."

Clint rose to his feet, challenging Whitfield directly. "Hollis, you're not thinking clearly. With all due respect, this is way outside the general's line of expertise. If we want to find Miles, we put together a combined task force. Me, Agent Stavros, and Agent Wessner, along with my recruits—"

"I'm sorry, Clint." Whitfield moved to the door. "But I put my faith in all of you once, and now Miles's life is in danger." He shook his head. "I can't risk it again. I expect you to follow the general's leadership and find my grandson." With that, he turned and left.

A deathly silence hung across the room. After a minute, Maddux rose. To his credit, he didn't gloat. He simply sent everyone out to await his orders, with the exception of Jillian, who was directed to remain in the conference room for further interrogation.

CHAPTER THIRTY-FOUR

TEDDY FOLLOWED THE OTHERS INTO THE HALL, TOO shaken to think, let alone move. She felt completely blindsided. Clint always knew what to do. But instead of depending on him, Whitfield had put Maddux in charge. Maddux, a hostile, unknown quantity who didn't trust psychics. A factor in the equation that she hadn't anticipated.

She put a hand to her temple, as though physically attempting to put her thoughts in order. But she couldn't shake off the shock of seeing Miles in that video. Or maybe she was just in shock, period. Everything felt foggy, like she was stuck underwater.

"Teddy, you with us?" Pyro tucked his fingers beneath her chin, tilted her face to meet his eyes. "We need to figure out what we're going to do."

Wasn't that obvious? She blinked, looked at him. "We need to find Miles."

Dara shivered. "Let's get the hell out of here."

Pyro caught Teddy's elbow and steered her out of Fort McDowell and toward the dorms. Once he reached her room, he opened the door and ushered Teddy and Dara inside.

Teddy sat down, nearly paralyzed by guilt. She was responsible for the disastrous chain of events that had taken so many: Molly. Eli. And now Miles. Miles, whom she was supposed to be protecting. If she hadn't allowed herself to be distracted by Yates in the first place, Miles would be okay. If she hadn't been obsessed with tracking Yates down all summer, none of this would have happened.

No, she thought. She wouldn't allow herself to wallow. She couldn't afford to waste time. They had less than twenty-four hours to find Miles. As her resolve hardened, the fog that had enveloped her slowly faded away. She needed to think. She couldn't slow time to stop this from happening. Couldn't peek into someone's head to get the answers. She had to put together the pieces and take action. Fast.

Almost immediately, she grasped an advantage she and her friends had that Maddux lacked. It wasn't that they were psychic—though she assumed that would help. It was that she knew who had taken Miles. Maddux was wrong. It wasn't HEAT, and it wasn't Eli Nevin.

Derek Yates.

Yates must have masterminded the whole thing, lying to Teddy as necessary. And he wasn't a lone wolf. Not any longer. He must have reunited with Nilsson and Stanton. Four people besides him, maybe more. They needed food, shelter, access to video equipment, a soundproof room to detain Eli and Miles. That meant he'd taken up residence somewhere.

All they had to do was find him.

The door opened, accompanied by a muted sob. Footsteps. And then Jillian appeared. "They think," she said, struggling to catch her breath between sobs, "that Eli did it. They think he's behind all of it. I told them he's been missing. I told them he wouldn't hurt anyone. Even if the surveillance camera did show him at the protest, it doesn't mean anything, right?"

"It does mean something, Jillian."

Jillian turned her tear-streaked face toward Teddy.

"It means someone's been manipulating Eli from the very start, setting him up, with exactly this outcome in mind."

Dara shot her a dark look for her bluntness, then reached out to comfort Jillian.

"So we find him," Teddy continued ruthlessly, speaking as much to herself as to Jillian, "make sure Eli's okay, make sure Miles is okay. Make sure something like this never happens again."

Teddy reached for the pair of wire glasses resting on her nightstand. Wrapped her fingers around the slim gold wire. Part of her wanted to believe that Miles had left a clue for her. A way for her to find him. Dunn had taught her psychometry. Wessner had taught her to put the life of her protectee above her own. Boyd had taught them that failure was not an option. Time to put those lessons to the test.

They chose to work from Professor Dunn's classroom, hoping that location would bring their psychometry lessons more forcefully to mind. Teddy, Dara, Jillian, and Pyro arranged their desks in a loose circle, facing one another. In the oak grain of her desk, Teddy noted that a previous recruit had carved a heart around *LK+NE 4EVER*. She guessed defacing school property never got old. But nothing was 4ever. Nothing was absolute. Even time. Any psychic worth her salt knew that.

"All right," Dara said. "Who goes first?"

Teddy didn't want it to be Dara. If Dara had a death warning or a death vision . . .

Pyro reached for the glasses, taking the choice away from them all. He held them in his hand, closed his eyes, and slipped into a meditative state. "Chemicals," he said. "Something flammable, but I can't place it. Ammonia, maybe? I see a color, too. Red. But not blood. Also heat. Like a long, shimmering wave of heat." He opened his eyes and looked at Teddy and Dara. "Does that make sense? Was there anything like that at the protest?"

Teddy caught her bottom lip, thinking. "I don't remember any chemicals. No ammonia. But at the protest, a woman splashed me with corn syrup that had been dyed to look like blood." Pyro was on track, though the information he'd garnered was useless in finding Miles. Unless the chemicals meant something to Dara?

Dara shook her head. "Sorry. I was in the lobby with Whitfield. No chemicals there. All I saw was a chubby security guard." She looked at Pyro. "But let's not write it off. If you were right about the fake blood, there's a good chance you're right about the chemicals. Maybe a warehouse where cleaning products are stored, like a janitorial supply closet?"

"Good," Teddy encouraged. "We're getting somewhere."

Dara passed Teddy Miles's glasses. She hesitated before taking them. Marysue's necklace had been the only object she'd used successfully for astral travel. She had tried and failed with Miles's father's dog tags. But it was worth another shot. There was so much at stake.

Taking a breath, she tried to sink into a meditative state. After the meeting with General Maddux, she'd felt cloudy, confused—emotions swirling around her, as if she were caught in a riptide. She needed to change that energy. Create a new visual. She imagined herself under the surface of the water, falling deep within herself, looking up at a clear marbled surface from cold, quiet depths, willing the feeling of panic into one of calm concentration. When her mind settled, she directed her thoughts to the object in her hand. *Where's Miles? Please.*

But the glasses stayed cold.

Clint had instructed her not to ask but demand. She took another breath, recentered her thoughts. *Show me what happened to Miles. Take me back to the protest at Hyle Pharmaceuticals. December 24, 2018.*

The metal of the glasses in her hand buzzed with life, buzzed with *Miles*. She could feel him there somehow, his hand in hers. And then she felt the dreaded familiar pull, the compression of every cell in her body, and she was through a Pilgrim's Tunnel, emerging outside the headquarters of Hyle Pharmaceuticals.

It had worked.

Teddy stumbled as she twisted to avoid a protester. In her peripheral vision, she watched as the limo pulled up, as Whitfield, Dara, and past-Teddy walked into the building. She knew Yates was already there, but she suppressed her instinct to search for him in the crowd. She'd been talking to him at the time Miles had been taken, so he must not have been working alone. She kept her focus on Whitfield's limo. And there they were, the same couple she'd seen before. In Eli's apartment, and then in New York City, pulling Marysue from the phone booth. Nilsson and Stanton—now grabbing Miles, who was wearing his canvas satchel strapped across his chest, from the back of the limo and pushing him through the crowd.

Teddy felt her grip on time slipping. The pressure was back, the intense pull that would send her ricocheting back to present time. She filled her lungs with air and centered her thoughts, determined not to pass out.

She came back to herself, gasping.

"Here." Pyro practically shoved a glass of water at her. "Deep breaths. What did you see?"

"Miles. With Nilsson and Stanton." She took a sip as she gathered her thoughts. "So we were right. Eli didn't do it. The PC has him—and they have the Xantal."

The Misfits sat in silence for a moment, absorbing the news. They all knew what had to come next but wanted to put it off as long as possible. Teddy studied the glasses in her hand.

"It's better if we know," Dara said at last.

Teddy nodded. Reminded herself that no matter what Dara saw, they'd stopped death before. With Molly. There was a chance that they could stop it this time as well.

She handed the glasses to Dara, reluctant to let go of them, not only for what Dara might reveal but also to hand over what she had left of Miles. She'd known him only a short time, but she felt inextricably bound to him. He was cute, of course. But the similarities in their pasts made her feel for him in a way she couldn't explain.

Teddy watched as Dara's eyes rolled back in her head and her fingers tightened around the metal frames. Her mouth formed a tight line, then her lips parted with a sharp gasp. She dropped the glasses as though they were on fire.

She took a moment to compose herself. "Miles is still alive," she said. "So is Eli."

Pyro said, "But you saw something. Something bad."

Dara nodded. "I felt as though I was floating, flying . . . I don't know how else to describe it. Just *aloft*. Then there was an explosion—everything lit up, searing hot." Frowning, she caught her bottom lip and turned to Pyro. "Maybe something to do with your chemicals?"

"Sounds like it." He moved to pick up the glasses again.

"Wait," Teddy said. "Was this a past vision or a death warning?"

"That's the problem. I'm not sure. I think it was a death warning. I got a glimpse of Miles and Eli. They're hurt but still alive. But something about where they're being held was familiar." Dara clutched the glasses in her hand, closed her eyes again. "I recognized the place, like I'd been there before. But there's this feeling in my chest. This dread." She shivered and opened her eyes. "Like everything's telling me not to go."

Pyro leaned back in his chair. "Okay. So here's what we have. Yates was at the demonstration. So were Nilsson and Stanton. They may or may not have been working together—"

"Oh, they're working together," Teddy interrupted.

"Maybe," Pyro said. "Perhaps Yates distracted Teddy while the PC took Miles. We know that Eli and Miles are alive and being held someplace where volatile chemicals might also be stored." He lifted his chin toward Dara. "There may also be an airfield nearby. That means they need space, which rules out the city and immediate vicinity." He looked around the room. "Anything else?"

"Earlier, you mentioned heat," Teddy said. "Was that a reference to an explosion as well?"

Pyro thought about it, shook his head. "No. Just a feeling that it was hot. Like temperature."

"Where does that leave us?" Dara said. "We've all tried our hands at this psychometric business, and we're no closer to finding them than when we started."

"Not everyone has tried yet," Teddy said, looking to Jillian.

Jillian released a stuttery sigh. "I'm better with animals than humans. And my powers haven't helped locate anyone before."

Dara handed the glasses to Jillian. "For Eli, remember?"

Jillian took the metal frames. Closed her eyes. Brow furrowed in concentration, she began to mutter, and cluck, and tweet . . . animal sounds? "Gophers, moles, coyotes. Desert tortoise. A greater sage grouse . . . A greater sage grouse." She opened her eyes. Beamed at them all. "It's familiar because we've been there before."

The Misfits looked at one another, wondering who would speak first. Teddy knew each of them had a very good idea where they would be headed next. And she was sure none of them wanted to return.

Someone had to break the silence. "Pack your bags," Teddy said. "We're going to Jackpot."

CHAPTER THIRTY-FIVE

TEDDY AND HER FRIENDS RAN ACROSS CAMPUS. THEY couldn't waste time taking the ferry into the city and then driving to Jackpot. Minutes mattered. They needed to get there fast. Teddy knew of only one person who would believe that Miles was being held on an officially retired base that was once the site of a top-secret military experiment gone awry. Someone who had been there himself.

As they ran toward Clint Corbett's office, Teddy spotted someone running right toward them.

"Teddy! I was just coming to find you." Henry Cummings, pink faced and out of breath.

"No time, man," Pyro said, pushing past him.

"It's—Wait—" Henry turned and ran alongside them like a lapdog nipping at their heels. Teddy saw something in his face that gave her pause. She stopped her dash and turned toward him. Her friends stopped with her. They created a small circle, all bending to clutch their knees and catch their breath.

"Talk," Teddy said, her chest burning.

"You know I'm clairvoyant, right?" Henry said.

"Yes, Henry, we know," Dara said. "Very exciting. If you don't mind—"

Teddy held up her hand. She wanted to hear this. Alpha status notwithstanding, Henry wasn't a bad guy. If he had ventured onto campus on Christmas Day to track her down, it had to be important.

Henry's heavy breathing finally slowed. "I'm not sure what it means, but I saw something. Or more like I have a message for you, Teddy."

"Dude, enough of the dramatics," Dara said. "Spit it out. We're on a clock, here."

Henry shook his head. "I'm just having trouble explaining it, okay?" He turned to Teddy. "A bomb. You're supposed to let it—I don't know how to say this. But you're not supposed to stop it. You have to let it explode."

Teddy blinked. "What does that mean, Henry? When? Where? What bomb? Who's triggering it? What does it look like? How does this help?" With a finger, she poked Henry's chest at each question. She knew she was losing control of herself. But bombs had become a tense subject for her as of late. And so had ambiguity.

"I'm sorry, that's all I have," Henry said simply.

"You are one shitty oracle," Dara said.

They left him standing where he was and raced on. They found Clint behind his desk. Nick was there, too.

"What is it?" Clint asked, coming to his feet the moment they burst into his office.

"We know where Miles is," Teddy said.

The roar of the helicopter's blades was louder than Teddy could have imagined. Even with the required headgear on, she was nearly deafened by the rapid thumping of the rotors. Fortunately, it had taken far less convincing to get Clint and Nick on board than she'd thought it would. After she filled them in, Clint sprang into action, offering up use of a school helicopter. He told them he wasn't sure Whitfield would provide consent quickly enough, so he went with "fly first and answer questions later."

Jackpot was a little over 550 miles as the crow flew, and a helicopter traveled at about 160 miles per hour. That would get them to the base in about three and half hours. Clint would accompany them to Jackpot, while Nick would inform Whitfield and Maddux of their plan. If they were going to an active base, they would need a general like Maddux to give them clearance. Nick would also see about getting a Jackpot FBI team mobilized to meet them there.

And just like that, they were high above the vast desert, on their way to save Miles and Eli. They were floating, flying in a helicopter, just as Dara had envisioned. But did that mean the searing explosion she'd foreseen was coming next? Teddy was reminded how she'd heard hidden words in the repetitive drone of the air conditioner in her freshman-year dorm: *Study, study, study* or *Vodka, vodka, vodka.* Now, as the helicopter's blades whirled above her head, she was hearing something else. Something that sounded very much like *Beware, beware, beware.*

Teddy looked around at her friends on the flight. Pyro, Jillian, Dara, and Clint. She found it hard to believe that she had known them just over a year. There was no one she would rather go to war with.

Clint sent her a reassuring nod. He seemed to be enjoying himself. Despite the dire circumstances, it probably felt good to be out of the classroom and back in the heat of things. Pun intended.

A tinny voice crackled into her headset. "Sir, we do not have military clearance to land on the base," the chopper pilot said. "We risk being fired upon if we enter the airspace. I can return to our point of origin, or I can let you off outside of the base's regulated airspace."

Without hesitation, Clint pointed at the desert floor.

———

Teddy watched the helicopter tip and bank away, peeling off into the high blue sky. Clint had ordered the pilot to refuel and return to this spot within the hour. He'd tried to call Whitfield and Nick to see if they'd gotten Maddux to clear their visit to the base, but his phone didn't have reception out here in the desert.

"Now what?" Jillian asked.

"Now we test all the endurance training we put you through this year," Clint said.

By the time they reached the main road, a thick film of sweat coated every inch of Teddy's body. Sand stung her eyes. Her throat was so parched she couldn't swallow. The desert heat was winning this battle, and it was a bloodbath. Nothing Boyd had thrown her way had prepared for this.

Jillian tried to flag down the occasional passing motorist, but no one came close to stopping. "What is wrong with people?"

Maybe it wasn't the people driving by, Teddy thought. Maybe, given the Misfits' current motley state, people were more inclined to lock their doors as they passed rather than pull over and offer them a ride.

"We'll never be able to walk all the way to Sector Three," Dara said.

"Wait a minute," Jillian said. "What's Pyro doing?"

Teddy turned and saw Pyro rolling tumbleweeds and other debris into the road. Soon there was a large pile. With a flick of his finger, Pyro set it ablaze, blocking the road just as a giant semi was approaching.

"Good thinking, recruit," Clint said.

The driver leaned out the window. "Accident?" he asked. "You folks all right?"

"Just need a little help," Clint said, stepping forward. Almost instantly, the driver's eyes glazed over. Teddy watched, impressed by how quickly he could mentally influence someone. He was as powerful as Yates, though she rarely saw him exercise that power. She remembered the day they'd met in the Bellagio all those months ago. The way he had effortlessly shoved Sergei off her tail.

They climbed into the cab. Pyro drove, heavy-footed at first, sputtering and stalling until he got the hang of the semi's steering shaft. Whereas Yates would have left the driver by the side of the road, Clint signaled to drop him off at a casino in Jackpot. He handed the man a crisp hundred-dollar bill and instructed him to play nickel slots until they returned. The casino doors had barely closed when they took off again.

Pyro headed west on Main Street, leaving the town of Jackpot behind. He steered the truck onto the familiar dirt road, the truck shaking and bouncing with every divot and pothole.

"There it is!" he shouted.

The base looked much more active than it had at the end of summer. This time there was a proper checkpoint with a large metal gate guarding the entrance. Pyro pulled forward, then slowed to a stop. A soldier jumped out of his booth and approached the window. "State your business."

"We have clearance for a visit," Pyro said. "From the Whitfield Institute."

"Who cleared you?"

"General Maddux."

The soldier stiffened. He looked at Pyro for a long moment and then headed back to the booth.

Worry gnawed at Teddy as she watched the guard lift a clipboard and flip through the pages. Picked up a phone to make a call. Nick should have reached Maddux by now. Surely they'd had time to alert the base.

"Something's wrong," Pyro muttered.

Clint's gaze fixed on the guard. "Stay calm, Lucas. When he comes back, I'll just kindly suggest he open the gate."

But Teddy suddenly knew that this man wouldn't be coming back to speak with them. She could see his back tense and his hand tighten around the receiver while his other hand dipped toward his automatic weapon.

"Back up! Back up!" Teddy shouted just as two more soldiers ran out, weapons raised.

Pyro threw the truck into reverse, flying down the long driveway.

Surprisingly, no military vehicles gave chase as Pyro sped away from the base. He pulled to a stop, dust floating all around them.

"Now what?" Dara asked.

"We go somewhere we have phone reception. I need to get in touch with Nick or Maddux. We are clearly not welcome on that base," Clint said.

"No! We can't wait for that!" Jillian cried. "We're running out of time!"

Teddy knew she was right. They couldn't wait for backup. For more phone calls and clearance. There was no time left. She turned to Pyro and put her hand on his arm. He looked at her for a long moment and then nodded. "It's go time," he said, and turned the truck around.

Pyro revved the engine, slammed the gas pedal to the floor. They were driving eighty miles per hour when they smashed through the security gate. The guards scattered, and the metal crumpled like aluminum against the semi's grille. Pyro let out a loud whoop. Teddy heard Clint laugh, a rare sound if there ever was one. She felt exhilarated and ready for anything as she pointed Pyro toward Sector Three.

Until a tall woman with white-blond hair stepped into the path of the truck. Nilsson. She calmly held up her right hand.

It was as if the truck hit an invisible brick wall. How had she managed it?

The front of the cab crushed into itself, and the back of the truck somersaulted overhead. Teddy felt the entire world turning upside down and inside out. Time slowed, but Teddy wasn't controlling it this time. She saw a flash of metal, her mother's necklace, somehow thrown from her pocket. She reached for it, her hands curling around it, as if moving through mud.

Then everything went black.

CHAPTER THIRTY-SIX

TEDDY SNAPPED HER EYES OPEN IN PANIC—THE KIND that came only when you overslept the morning before a big interview, or maybe a court appearance, only to realize you'd spent the previous night drinking vodka tonics like a sorority girl on the eve of her twenty-first birthday. She felt as though gravity had somehow shifted, pinning her limbs to the ground while at the same time propelling her brain through outer space. Groggy and faintly nauseated, she forced her eyes open and took in her surroundings. She was lying on the concrete floor of an unfamiliar room. Above her were white institutional tiles, rows of blinding fluorescent lights. The room was large but windowless, with just one desk in the corner. Behind it, a black leather armchair facing away from her. On the opposite side of the desk were two smaller tan swivel chairs.

Teddy took a deep breath and forced herself to focus. The last thing she remembered was sitting in the truck with Clint and her friends. That was where her memory stopped. Ignoring her body's protests, she eased herself upright. More troubling was that she couldn't remember getting here. If she was actually in a *here*. Was she in a memory? Had she traveled? Fighting an escalating sense of panic, she tried to ground herself. Yes, that was why she felt simultaneously light-headed and bruised. She was outside her body. But where had she left it?

A light, almost imperceptible *swish* coming from the corner desk caught her attention. The brush of a heel against the floor or an elbow against an armrest. A sound so soft she'd almost missed it. Teddy's thoughts snapped to attention as the sound's meaning was made instantly clear: someone was in the room with her. Her gaze shot to the black leather armchair. Whoever was seated there must have sensed she'd awakened, because the chair slowly swiveled in Teddy's direction as if it held some sort of villain in a cheesy Bond movie.

Except it wasn't a villain.

Her mother looked young, maybe mid-to-late twenties. She was dressed in the same square-shouldered jacket she'd worn in New York City in 1998.

Whatever had happened in the truck had caused Teddy to travel to the past.

At long last, she was face-to-face with her birth mother. Marysue's gaze moved from Teddy to the room's only door, which looked like military-grade metal and remained securely shut. Marysue's lips parted as if she were about to speak. But she quickly collected herself. She sat up straighter. She *knew* Teddy was there. Was that even possible? Or was Teddy just projecting her desperate long-held desire onto the situation? No. Clint had told her that travelers could see one another. Teddy allowed herself to study her mother.

Their eyes locked.

Teddy swallowed against a fist-sized lump in her throat, unable to speak. When she was younger, she'd imagined this moment many times over. But as she'd grown, the emotions that surrounded the reunion had shifted. Joy, anger, pain, hate . . . and now relief. She'd spent months obsessively tracking Marysue. And now she was looking at the woman who had become so central to Teddy's purpose. So central to the mystery of—well, everything.

To this Marysue, Teddy was a stranger. Some random twenty-five-year-old with dark hair and weird clothes.

But a twenty-five-year-old who looked very much like her. Maybe, just maybe, that would be enough for her birth mother to connect the dots.

Please. Recognize me.

Marysue's eyes sharpened. "What in the hell do you think you're doing here?"

Teddy swallowed. Maybe she *did* know Teddy. Granted, she hadn't expected such a cold greeting from her mother, but . . .

"I—I'm not sure."

"You aren't supposed to be here. Who sent you?"

Teddy stood up and took a step toward her mother. "No one! I . . ."

Marysue looked confused. "Then why are you here?"

"Look, I'm not sure, either." Teddy felt like she was in trouble. But she couldn't tell if it was for crossing some sort of mother-daughter time-traveler boundary or for coming up against a PC agent. She cleared her throat, deciding to proceed on neutral territory. "I've been waiting to talk to you."

Marysue's brow furrowed. "You've been tracking me?"

"Yes, but not like you think, I—"

Marysue stood. From her pocket she pulled out a knife—small but dangerous. "What am I supposed to think? You appeared out of thin air into a locked room. I know you're a traveler."

Teddy's head dropped. Marysue's reaction wasn't because she knew Teddy as her daughter. Just a psychic who shared her ability. One who had shown up at a questionable moment.

Teddy struggled to find her next words. She wanted to tell her mother who she was, but for once, she found herself speechless.

Marysue stared solemnly at Teddy, eyes bright, muscles taut. "I don't know why you're here, but you shouldn't be. They'll find out. If they don't already know. And it's too late to help, if that's why you're here."

But it wasn't too late. Couldn't be. Otherwise, why would Teddy be here? Bracing herself, she took a deep breath and moved forward.

She'd moved doors, moved time, moved across the country to re-start her life, but that step felt like the boldest, bravest thing she'd ever done. With that step, she decided she would tell Marysue what she needed to know to change the time line in the present. Together they would prevent the PC from growing stronger in the past. Molly would never disappear. Miles would never be kidnapped. It was the only way Teddy could save the people she cared about. Butterfly effect be damned. Surely this was a workaround. This was why she'd been propelled back. And after, once she'd found the words to explain everything to Marysue, she would say: *You can trust me, because I'm Theodora. Teddy. I'm your daughter.*

But before she could speak, before she could utter those longed-for words, the metal door burst open, and a man and woman dressed in combat fatigues entered the room. In a blink of an eye, the knife disappeared up Marysue's sleeve. The small weapon was useless against these two powerful psychics—Stanton and Nilsson. Teddy recognized them both. Younger but still dangerous.

Teddy tensed, but they looked right past her, unable to see her, and surrounded Marysue.

Stanton said, "The colonel's not happy with you."

"I'm not happy with the colonel," Marysue said. In one lithe movement, she slid the desk drawer shut.

Stanton seemed momentarily taken aback by her defiance. He took a step closer to her—a not so subtle threat. Nilsson walked around the desk. She seated herself in the armchair that Marysue had vacated, lounging against the black leather as if it were a throne. A smug smile curved her lips. "At what point did you assume your feelings were important to anyone?"

Marysue glared at her. "We had a deal. This was supposed to be my last mission, and then I was done. I'd be allowed to be with"—a short breath, as though she didn't want to say any more but couldn't help it—"we had a deal."

Nilsson's pale brows rose fractionally. "Come now. Did you really think he would ever let you go? Daughter or no."

Marysue's eyes blazed. And time, for Teddy, stood still. And not because she made it. Marysue had become a member of the PC *for* Teddy. To *save* Teddy. She'd been the reason her mother had blown up buildings? Killed people? Nausea curled through her stomach, and Teddy was sure that in her body, years and miles away, the physical response echoed tenfold. *She'd* been the reason for everything.

"I'm done," Marysue said. "Whether the colonel keeps his word or not, I'm leaving." Marysue made to move to the door, but as soon as she tried to open it, Stanton lunged forward and stretched his arm over her head, slamming one beefy palm against the door to hold it shut. Apparently, the move was not unexpected. Marysue twisted around, and Teddy caught the flash of a steel blade in her right hand. Marysue drew her arm back, clearly intent on driving Stanton away from the door.

Absolutely the wrong move. Boyd would have gone apoplectic if she'd seen it. Teddy knew against an opponent like Stanton—who was a foot taller and likely two hundred pounds heavier—a knife to the thigh would have been most effective. Marysue didn't know how to wield her weapon. Part of Teddy was happy, since her mother wasn't a killing machine; the other part was very nervous for what was about to unfold.

Stanton did exactly what Teddy predicted he would: caught Marysue's slender wrist and squeezed hard. Marysue gave a cry of pain and dropped the blade. It clattered uselessly to the floor.

He shoved Marysue against the door. His face pink with unspent rage, he lifted her until her toes were dangling off the floor and terror flooded her eyes.

Teddy shot forward. She didn't think, didn't plan, just reacted. She lunged for the knife, intent on driving it into Stanton's left kidney. She gripped the knife and drew it back and screamed, throat raw.

"Don't you dare hurt my mother!" she said, and prepared to drive the blade through Stanton's flesh. Something burned hot in her pocket. Seared. The necklace.

Teddy saw Marysue's eyes go wide with realization, then heard her yell: "No!" before Teddy was propelled back with such force that she felt like she'd tumble through the astral plane forever.

Teddy couldn't breathe. Her lungs felt like they'd collapsed. If she couldn't breathe—

But she coughed. Once, twice.

Stop. Open your eyes. Breathe.

Some voice deep within her guided her back into her physical body. A moment ago, she'd been about to change the course of history forever. She had been in the same room with Marysue, the same time line. And Teddy had choked.

Now she was waking up unconscious in another room without knowing how the hell she'd gotten here. On some kind of a gurney, with her wrists in restraints. It hurt like a bitch. She was definitely on earth. Otherwise, her body wouldn't feel like she'd been hit by a Mack truck. Mack truck, her friends—

Teddy scanned the room. Above her was the white-tiled ceiling with its rows of fluorescent lights. Only now, instead of the lone desk and chairs, there was a row of hospital beds. Floor-to-ceiling medicinal cabinets occupied the far-right wall.

She turned her head to the left and saw someone in the bed next to hers.

Miles. He lay utterly still, his long limbs neatly arrayed beneath a white cotton sheet. His eyes closed, his lips shut. His skin so pale it looked almost waxen. A fine sheen of perspiration plastered his hair to his forehead. No movement at all—not even the slight rise and fall of his chest to indicate breathing. Teddy's heart slammed against her ribs.

Everything within her screamed. "Miles," she yelled, her voice hoarse with pain, dehydration, desperation, Teddy didn't know. "Miles, wake up."

He didn't stir.

Please, don't let him be dead.

"He's not—yet," a cool female voice said.

Teddy pulled her mental shields up with whatever energy she had left. The door slammed, and Teddy saw Nilsson. Twenty years older but the same cold eyes. The same woman who had—for Teddy, just moments ago—informed her mother that she was sentenced to serve the PC forever.

Teddy fought an urge to propel every psychic attack she could in Nilsson's direction. But she had to be smart. She had to save her energy. She also had to quell the desire to find out more about her mother, to know what had happened that day and why. She pushed aside her fury.

"What have you done to Miles? What have you done to my friends?" she demanded.

Nilsson shook her head, then—with the same languid confidence from all those years ago—walked to a cabinet and withdrew a pair of blue rubber gloves. "Don't worry, Ms. Cannon," she said, as she snapped on the gloves. "Miles Whitfield is alive for now. Unfortunately, I can't say the same for that other young man, Eli Nevin. Pity. He proved very useful to the cause."

Teddy's breath caught. She stared hard at Nilsson, searching for any signs of a bluff.

If Eli was dead, it would be Teddy's fault. She'd seen how dangerous the situation was, but she'd let it play out. She'd used Eli as a pawn to draw out the PC. Hadn't involved Clint or asked for help until it was too late. Then another thought struck her: *Jillian.* If Eli was dead, how would Jillian bear it? It would destroy her. Teddy yanked against her restraints, desperate to free herself and do something, anything.

Nilsson continued, "Even if we'd planted it, it couldn't have worked better. Eli was an easy target for mental influence. And he had a connection to you. After we identified that he had it in for Hyle Pharmaceuticals, he made a convenient tool. And HEAT? We couldn't have asked for a better cover."

"You manipulated Eli from the start," Teddy said, furious at herself for not having looked to other members of the PC instead of Yates. She'd been blind in her hurt over his manipulation, and she'd failed to see other forces at work. "You blamed the bombing on HEAT when the PC was behind it the whole time."

Nilsson stepped closer and tilted her head to study Teddy. She hadn't confirmed or denied anything. She didn't have to. "When I saw you last year, I was struck by how much you resemble your mother."

"Last year?" Teddy scanned her memory for when she might have crossed paths with Nilsson before their brief encounter in Tahoe. Then, in a flash, it hit her, a memory from the deep recesses in her brain, quicksilver and fleeting, just like Nilsson's hair. Every time she tried to catch the memory, it dissipated. "A hospital."

Nilsson's eyes flickered. "I'm impressed you remember that. But I know your mind is strong. Stronger than your friend's. Usually, I make people forget. That's what I can do. I block powers. Get in your mind so—"

The more she talked, the more came back to Teddy, not from memory but from logic. If Nilsson was at a hospital, that meant . . . her friend. *Molly.* "Where is she?" she demanded. "What have you done with her?"

But Nilsson continued, ignoring Teddy, "And I thought maybe this young woman could be an asset, like her mother. Maybe we can persuade her to work for us."

As if on cue, Stanton entered the room, accompanied by Jeremy Lee. Teddy stared at her former classmate and understood for the first time how it was possible to be sickened by the sight of someone.

"Teddy. I would say good to see you, but you look terrible." He spoke with chilling casualness, as if they had run into each other after a few months off for summer vacation. As if her situation—strapped to a bed with restraining cuffs—were normal.

She wanted to tell him to go throw himself off a bridge. But Teddy was desperate. If Teddy knew Jeremy at all, she knew he cared for Molly. That could be a way to appeal to him for help. "Jeremy. Please. It's not too late. Molly tried to help me. She would have wanted you to help, too. Please."

The mention of Molly made him pause.

"They've done something to her. We have to stop them," Teddy said.

"I—" Jeremy started.

"Enough," Nilsson said sharply. "We have work to do." She opened the cabinet, took out an empty syringe and a small vial of yellow liquid. She poked the syringe through the stopper and drew back the plunger.

Teddy's heart slammed against her ribs and started beating at triple its normal tempo. It wasn't Xantal. Xantal was clear. What was in the syringe, and what did Nilsson plan to do with it?

Nilsson walked straight to Miles and laid her other hand gently on his chest. Teddy yanked desperately against her restraints. "Don't touch him!"

Nilsson smiled. "If you would like to save your friends, you have one more chance to reconsider. Join us, save your friend. It's an entry deal we like to make here. You know, kind of like an email signup for fifteen percent off your first order."

The same choice Marysue had faced. Join the PC or lose someone she loved. But her mother had been terrified and alone. Out of options. That wasn't entirely true for Teddy. Even though they weren't with her, Teddy knew that her friends wouldn't want her to make this choice. Teddy could—and would—think of some other way. She looked Nilsson straight in the eye. "Go to hell."

Nilsson flicked the syringe with her forefinger.

Teddy mustered the last of her courage, one more try, one last ounce of begging: "If you hurt Miles, his grandfather will never rest until you are caught. Everyone at the Whitfield Institute knows we're here. The FBI does, too. And the U.S. military. In fact, General Maddux will be here any minute with the force of a real army. When he finds out the PC is using a military base, there will be hell to pay. I promise you."

Nilsson laughed. With her hand still on Miles, she glanced at Jeremy. "I thought you said she was smart. The general will be so disappointed."

The general.

What?

Jeremy shrugged and turned away. He pushed open the door. "Sir. She's ready to see you."

Black boots, polished to a sheen. His barrel chest blocked much of her vision. But she didn't have to look up to know that General Maddux had walked into the room.

Teddy scanned the three individuals standing before her. Jeremy, Nilsson, and Maddux stood shoulder to shoulder. She blinked as she attempted to process what she saw. Then the ugly reality sank in.

General Maddux was the leader of the Patriot Corps.

CHAPTER THIRTY-SEVEN

TEDDY'S UTTER SHOCK TOOK ABOUT .03 SECONDS TO turn into seething rage. The leader of the Patriot Corps had been under their noses the entire time. The man responsible for her father's death. The man who'd blackmailed Marysue and held her against her will for years. The man who'd made her mother complicit in horrible crimes in return for her safety. The man they had called *the colonel* before he'd moved up the ranks. Of course. If Teddy hadn't been so blind, so invested in a narrative that surrounded Yates and the blame that she'd placed on Clint and her parents' past, she may have been able to see the larger mechanics of Maddux's scheme at work.

Yates *had* been trying to help her, but once again she had misjudged his intentions.

She strained against the cuffs that bound her to the bed. She wanted to kill Maddux. Rip him apart. But she couldn't move. Nor could she summon enough telekinetic energy to blast apart the restraints or astral-project. "What have you done to my friends? My mother?"

Nilsson watched Teddy struggle. "So many questions," she said. "But you're in no position to demand answers, are you?"

"I disagree," Maddux answered. "This young lady has helped the cause so much already." He held up Miles's satchel. The Xantal. She thought of Yates's warning. She'd brought it right to Maddux. "The least we could do is give her some answers."

Teddy looked at the satchel. She knew that Xantal wouldn't be dangerous on its own, but it was a key to genetic research that would be lethal. But that could take months, even years, for Maddux to unravel. For now, she just needed to buy time. Time to gather her strength. Time for save her friends. Nick must be tracking them from San Francisco. Or Yates.

So she stalled. "Xantal blocks psychic ability. Why would you want it?"

Maddux said, "We had the same question as Whitfield. What if you could isolate the genetic information that made someone psychic?" He walked around Teddy's bed, and she jerked against her restraints in response. His teeth flashed in what Teddy supposed was a smile. "As you know, Eversley spent years developing this drug. Gene therapy is a subtle science. But the breakthrough was the virus. Eversley created one that affected psychics. We thought it was impossible. But this drug changes everything."

"Changes everything how?"

This time it was Nilsson who answered. "What if we could make psychics more psychic? More powerful?" Her pale eyes gleamed in the fluorescent lights. "What if this virus could deliver genetic material from other psychics to meld abilities? What if we could turn humans into—"

Maddux's gruff voice cut through Nilsson's speech. "That's enough."

No. Sector Three all over again but worse. So much worse. "You can't."

"But I can," Maddux said. "Thanks to you. For bringing this to me."

"Someone will stop you," Teddy said, heart pounding. "Clint will stop you." Her eyes stung, her throat burned. Every part of her felt like she was on fire.

Maddux passed the satchel to Stanton, then returned his attention to Teddy. "I'm afraid you're wrong again. As we speak, Clint Corbett and your friends are being loaded into a helicopter. I will inform

Whitfield that Corbett was the head of the PC. An undercover agent recruiting from the institution he led. Convenient, really." That sharp smile again, like he was congratulating himself on his own sick genius. "That I found him fleeing after I discovered he and a small group of recruits were the ones behind Miles's kidnapping. Unfortunately, their attempt at escape will be met with tragedy when their helicopter malfunctions and explodes over the desert."

Teddy's stomach flipped. This was Dara's death warning. The explosion. Teddy couldn't allow it. Couldn't bear it. Her mind raced, but in frantic, empty circles. She had trained for this moment, and yet she had no idea what to do next.

"Once Corbett's gone," Maddux continued, "Hollis will install me as permanent head of Whitfield Institute. With a steady flow of new recruits and a drug to make them even more powerful, I will have the strongest army in the world at my disposal."

Teddy looked at him. "You're out of your mind."

"Visionaries are often misunderstood."

"Visionary?" Teddy spat. "You're no visionary. This is about power."

"Just the opposite," he corrected. "When I put on this uniform, I swore an oath to support and defend the Constitution of the United States against all enemies, foreign and domestic. I am committed to that oath, to protecting this country from any person or organization meaning to threaten our democratic way of life."

"By subverting the processes that protect us all. Making yourself judge, jury, and executioner."

"This country faces daily threats. Threats that must be put down with equal force and determination. We are at war, whether our politicians in Washington want to acknowledge it or not. These vials contain the next step in modern warfare. The creation of a small, elite force trained to target and disable insurgencies before lives are lost. Sounds very similar to Whitfield, now that I think about it. We just have different methods."

Teddy scrambled for words. If no one was coming, she had to at least keep that helicopter from taking off. She sent a mental cry of distress to search out any of her friends' consciousness, but if they had tuned in to any channels, the frequencies were painfully silent. "That virus is dangerous. Xantal's not stable. We saw what it did to lab animals. To Miles."

"True," Maddux allowed. "In a perfect world, I would have preferred more time for testing. But as you know, this world is far from perfect." He gave a loose shrug. "At least now there will be no shortage of human subjects to test it on."

A chill shot down Teddy's spine. Exactly what Yates had warned. "You saw Sector Three. This will only end in disaster."

Maddux tilted his head as he considered that. "No. It won't end in disaster. I wasn't in charge at Sector Three."

Teddy opened her mouth to speak, but Jeremy stepped forward. "Sir," he said, "the helicopter is ready."

A rush of fresh panic tore through her. *No.* She had to stop it from taking off. "Don't do this," she said.

Maddux took a step back. He studied Teddy. "You're reasonably intelligent," he said. "It should be fairly clear that you have no options here. Don't forfeit your life. Work for the Patriot Corps. Devote yourself to fighting for the right side of history. Protect this country. And I'll give you all the answers you seek."

Teddy stared back, unable to hide her loathing. This wasn't a choice; it was blackmail. Her mother had been blackmailed into joining the PC. She'd done it in a desperate bid to protect her daughter. And yet here Teddy was, in Maddux's grasp nonetheless. She had spent so long looking: for Molly, for Marysue, for the answers Maddux dangled in front of her. Only now she recognized that the truth about the past came at a greater expense than she was prepared to pay: her friends, her freedom, her future.

Teddy did the only thing she could think of. She spat in Maddux's direction.

Maddux stiffened, took a pressed handkerchief out of his pocket, and wiped Teddy's answer off his uniform. "Very well. Then die here in the desert, as your friends will."

He turned to Nilsson and nodded. The woman lifted a syringe. She moved toward Teddy.

Teddy braced herself for the sharp pinch of the needle piercing her skin. Instead, the blonde pivoted at the last moment and injected the unconscious Miles with the syringe.

"No!" Teddy screamed, but she was powerless to stop it from happening. She'd failed to protect Eli, and now she'd failed to protect Miles. It had cost them their lives. It would cost all of them their lives.

As Nilsson and Stanton walked away, Jeremy stepped inside. "Guard them both until it's time," Maddux said. With that final order, the general left the room. The door slammed shut behind him.

CHAPTER THIRTY-EIGHT

EVERY TIME TEDDY HAD WALKED INTO A ROOM WITH Maddux, he'd made her skin crawl. Caused the small hairs on the back of her neck to stand on end. Made her stomach churn. She remembered the day she'd met him at Jeremy's New Year's party last year. His formal military attire. His hawkish dogma. His domineering presence. Her most basic survivalist instinct—her sixth sense, her gut—had told her *no*, but her mind had rationalized, and she'd ignored it.

Jeremy stood in the corner of the room, staring at her. From the day she met Maddux, Jeremy must have already been working for him. Part of the whole setup.

Teddy thought back to the Jeremy Lee she thought she'd known at Whitfield. Looked for something in his personality that she remembered, something she could use, something that might sway him over to her side. Unlike Maddux, he wasn't an egomaniac. False flattery wouldn't get her anywhere. But he was a quintessential misfit. Like all of them, he was lost and had seemed thrilled to be accepted as part of their group. Maybe that was something she could use.

"Jeremy, think about what you're doing. Maddux claims that the PC is protecting the world from the bad guys."

"That's right."

"How is killing your friends a good cause? What possible good will come of that?"

"There are always casualties of war. Collateral damage is regrettable but necessary."

Teddy's mind circled back to Molly. Out of all of them, Jeremy had cared most for her. "Like Molly? Where is she?" Teddy said, pushing harder. When Teddy had mentioned her name earlier, he'd reacted. Perhaps she could use that to her advantage now. Play on whatever sympathy he had left. "Or was she collateral damage, too, Jeremy?"

Jeremy's mouth twisted, in derision or pain, Teddy didn't know. He leaned over, hands on his knees.

"I thought you loved her."

He paused. For a moment he looked like he was going to tell her what had happened, but then Miles began to stir. Jeremy straightened. "What you don't realize, Teddy, is that there can't be *friends* at times like these. We're only what we can contribute to the cause. Your new *friend* here, do you realize what he can do?" He walked over to Miles and checked his restraints. "He's basically a giant conductor. A human coil that absorbs active energy and then transfers it. Not intentionally, of course. Or that well. He has no control over his powers."

"Sounds like someone else we know, doesn't it?" Teddy said, practically staring daggers at Jeremy, then looking over toward Miles. If only he'd had the opportunity to go to Whitfield. He might have learned to use his gift. She saw the small red mark in his neck where Nilsson had injected something.

"Not that it did her any good," Jeremy said.

Teddy brushed off his remark. That wasn't true. Whitfield had helped Molly. Teddy refused to believe otherwise. "What did Nilsson give him?"

"Triacetone—liquid explosive." Jeremy moved to the door. "Won't be long now." He turned back to Teddy, hovering at the door, then clapped his hands together. "Boom," he said.

That answer was worse than anything she could imagine.

The soft click of the door behind Jeremy sounded like a detonator.

Teddy lay helpless, scanning the ceiling. The PC had turned Miles into a bomb. Loaded his body with an explosive agent. When Miles woke up, once whatever power that was dormant inside him ignited, he would be the bomb that caused the helicopter to explode.

Unless she could come up with some way to stop it.

Henry Cummings's words in the quad came back to her in a rush: *You have to let it explode.*

No. She couldn't let any of this happen. She'd bent bullets and blasted a door off its hinges. She could summon what little energy she had left to get out of these restraints. She centered her thoughts, slowed her breath. Pictured the padded leather restraints weakening, pulling apart, the leather snapping—

The door swung open. A soldier stepped inside, his helmet riding low over his eyes, his manner brusque and efficient. No doubt ready to do his duty.

Teddy braced herself. Prepared to fight. Because she would. Fight to her—to all—their deaths. She wouldn't make the same bullshit deal Marysue had made.

They'd sent only one escort. That was a mistake she could take advantage of. Adrenaline coursing through her veins, she planned her assault. The moment he released her, she would deliver a sharp kick to the spleen, followed by a—

The soldier pushed back his helmet and looked at Teddy. "Theodora, I expected more from you."

Yates.

I expected more from you, she wanted to say. But she'd thought he'd been in on it. And now she was sure that he wasn't, she still couldn't figure out why he was here to help her. He would always have an agenda, and it would always be a secret one. Teddy's head pounded.

"Thought that bastard would never leave," he said.

"What are you doing here?" she sputtered, but Yates was already behind her, opening her restraints.

"I would think that's perfectly obvious, Theodora. I'm saving you."

Though the blood began to course back into her numb hands, she felt numb with disbelief. Once he'd finished, Yates moved to Miles. He put his fingers on Miles's neck, feeling for a pulse.

"They said he was alive." Teddy almost didn't want to know.

"It's faint, but he's still with us." He moved to untie Miles's restraints, but she grabbed his arm.

"He's going to die. We're all going to die."

"Perhaps. Perhaps not. Perhaps both."

Her head hurt. Her heart hurt. "Jesus, Yates! I don't have time for your messed-up nonspeak!"

"Or you could have all the time in the world," he countered. "Do you have the necklace?"

Teddy stared at him. "Of course I do, but I just traveled. I don't—I can't—I'm not powerful enough."

His eyes turned fierce. "This will go on and on," he said. "With Clint and you and your friends out of the picture, Whitfield will give Maddux control of the school. He will have an unlimited supply of young psychics to experiment on. Before long, he will have an elite army of superpsychics to do his bidding, working outside the law. But you can stop him before any of this ever happens. Before Maddux ever set foot on this base. Before your father was tortured and killed. Before your mother was blackmailed. Before I chose the wrong side."

"What you're suggesting is messing with time." Had this been his plan all along? She thought back to her mother in that room. How Teddy had tried to change the past and something had stopped her. Maybe the necklace itself. "I'm not supposed to—"

"Supposed to. Not supposed to. Who's the arbiter here? Clint?" Yates shook his head. "His rules are subjective. I'm talking about something bigger. What we are discussing is fate, what this has all been adding up to. What is the story you have seen? What has that necklace shown you about the past? That is what's important."

Teddy thought back to before she'd ended up in a hospital room, in a bunker, working with the person she'd thought was her enemy. She'd had to learn about her mother's bargain. She'd seen her parents in Sector Three, seen the bombing in New York unfold over and over again. If she stopped it all—

She wanted to save her friends, but Clint's warning about time travel was burned into her brain as hot as the necklace had burned into her skin moments ago: the risks were too great. They included her own life. Her own soul. She could mess with time in such a way that she'd never return.

"There have been other travelers, Teddy. They've done it. Go back in time to before all of this happened," Yates said. He handed her a gun. "Kill Maddux."

Other travelers. None her mother had met but . . . the Polson case. The traveler on the plane. He'd been from another time, Teddy knew. The weapon hadn't matched. The logistics were impossible. Travelers weren't supposed to rewrite history. But just because they weren't supposed to didn't mean no one had tried. Had this been what everything was leading to? This moment?

"Theodora," Yates said. "You know what you have to do. If you don't come back—"

Their eyes met.

"If I don't come back . . ." She could make sure everyone survived. But it meant taking a chance that she wouldn't. That was, after all, the point of Wessner's Secret Service lessons. She took out her mother's necklace. Turned it over in her hands.

Yates handed her a piece of paper. "I'd suggest returning here, if you could."

Teddy looked at the date, scrawled in handwriting she used to fear. Voices echoed in the hall. Maddux's soldiers returning for Teddy and Miles. It was now or never. Time to be a meat shield.

CHAPTER THIRTY-NINE

TEDDY'S PALM BURNED AGAINST THE AMETRINE STONE.
While parts of astral travel had become easier thanks to Clint's guidance, she still felt the same heat from the necklace every time she
jumped into a Pilgrim's Tunnel. This time, she welcomed the pain as a
reminder of what was at stake.

Teddy stood in front of Sector Three. The place looked different.
The walks were swept, the windows sparkled, and tidy plantings of
native succulents fronted the barracks and other buildings. Neat and
orderly. But that made sense. This was before the uprising that had
cost her father his life. Before decades of desert heat had reduced the
abandoned facility to ash and debris.

Teddy scanned the grounds, her hand tight around the grip of
Yates's gun, her index finger resting on the trigger guard, looking for
any sign of Maddux.

On a distant parade field, a unit of soldiers was being sent through
a drill. Nearby, a pair of privates unloaded supplies and carried them
into what appeared to be the mess hall. No one paid her any attention.
But then, why would they? From their point of view, she didn't exist.

The sound of laughter startled Teddy out of her thoughts. She
swung around. Marysue. Her mother, younger still than the last time
Teddy had caught her in the space-time continuum. She carried a small
bundle in her arms. Teddy's birth father, Richard Delaney, walked behind her. Her family.

Richard kissed Marysue on the forehead before turning away and walking toward Sector Three. Teddy tensed, knowing what waited for him there, even if he didn't.

She turned back to Marysue and watched her mother stumble over an uneven stone paver. She cursed and lightly kicked the stone. Teddy smiled. She would have done that, too. So much about Marysue was eerily similar—their build and appearance; the way she tilted her chin up, in seemingly unconscious defiance.

Teddy wanted to make herself known to her mother. Yates had given her a chance to change the future. But he had also given her a chance to confront her past.

"Marysue," Teddy called.

She turned in Teddy's direction. Her mother's eyes widened as she glanced at the gun in Teddy's hand. She backed up a couple of paces, protectively drawing the infant in her arms closer.

"Wait," Teddy said. She put the gun down and raised her arms as a sign that she meant no harm. "I'm—I'm a traveler."

Marysue froze. Shock showed on her features, coupled with wary disbelief. Suspicion. "You're from the future?"

Teddy nodded. As she looked at her mother's face, she realized that she didn't really *know* Marysue Delaney. Sure, she had studied the news articles. Read the files. Tracked Marysue's whereabouts. But she didn't know the woman standing before her. No way to predict what Marysue might do next. What if she sounded an alarm, put the base in some sort of military lockdown mode? But it was too late for what-ifs. There was no way to correct her slipup now.

The sound of a car in the distance. Teddy watched as it came into view. An army green jeep bounded toward them, Maddux riding shotgun with an even younger-looking Yates.

"I'm supposed to complete a mission," Teddy started, but her throat tightened. She didn't want to do this. Especially in front of her mother. "Someone told me that I have to come back here to fix things." She blinked. It was the option. The only option. She reached for the gun at her feet.

"Wait!" Marysue's eyes were trained on her.

Teddy's palm tightened on the gun's grip. Her hand shaking, she raised the weapon.

As she held her mother's gaze, Teddy could see all the ways they were different, on closer inspection: her mother's hair, a shade darker; the freckles on her nose; a scar on her forehead. How had her mother gotten that scar? In Sector Three? No, that was yet to come. As soon as Yates let Maddux out of that jeep, the terrible future would begin.

Marysue took a step toward Teddy. She raised her hand but stopped before making contact. "I've never met another traveler before, but . . . Whoever sent you on this mission. Those who don't travel will say that they understand it in theory. But they don't. They can't. It seems easy to go back to the beginning of things. To take our knowledge of the future and apply it to the past. Yates is always asking me . . ." She trailed off, clearly aware that she shouldn't share more information than necessary.

Teddy couldn't tell her even the half of it. But she didn't have time for theories. She thought back to Yates's instructions. He had asked her to go so far back in the past. Too far? There were so many twists and turns that could forever alter her future. So many things she couldn't predict.

Marysue continued, "If I were ever going to take the kind of risk I assume you're taking—let me be clear, I'm not saying I recommend it—I would stick as close as possible to your present day. Where did things go wrong with no hope of return?"

Teddy's voice shook. "I don't know."

"Then wait."

"I can't. I have to do this now."

"Now? Are you certain?" Marysue cocked her head. "I've always imagined traveling as being like a ball of yarn." She picked at the hem of her shirt as if to demonstrate. "Close your eyes and feel for the right string, the right time line, and it will take you where you want to go. What is the moment when you are willing to make the smallest change? That is the moment you are looking for." She took a step toward Teddy as if to reach for the gun; though they both know they couldn't touch, not really, everything in Teddy wanted her mother to do just that—to shoulder this burden, to make it better.

Teddy saw the truck pull around the corner of the field. She couldn't stop Sector Three from happening. She couldn't stop Xantal from being created. People would always try to use psychics to their own ends. She'd seen it happen once, twice, and it would happen again.

But she might save her friends.

She imagined the mess of the last few months, a ball of knots, of bad decisions so tangled it was impossible to see how to unravel it. If they never left for the base? Or earlier, if Miles had never disappeared outside Hyle, if she'd been focused on his safety and not on Yates? The answer came from the depths of her consciousness, and as soon as it surfaced, it rang strong, true, right. And in the voice of Henry Cummings, of all people.

Let it explode.

Teddy watched the truck pull out of sight. Clicked the safety into place. Released the tension in her arms. She could stop Maddux before this escalated. In her own time line.

Marysue nodded. "You've found it. Now don't let go of the string."

Teddy touched the necklace in her pocket. The IED at the holiday party. That's what Henry had been referring to. That was the bomb she had to let explode.

She and her mother looked at each other a moment longer. Time seemed to stand still, even though Teddy could feel her body being pulled back to the present. Everything in her fought to stay just another second. "Don't worry," Marysue said. "It will work out." For Marysue it wouldn't, or at least it hadn't yet. Teddy hoped it did.

"What do they say—everything will be okay in the end, and if it's not okay, it's not the end?"

Teddy nodded. She wasn't going to cry, goddammit. She felt the beginning of the crash back into her physical body.

Jesus Christ, not this again.

"It's not the end," Marysue said.

Teddy shook her head. "It's not."

Her body was being ripped apart as she plummeted back to present-day Sector Three. At least she hadn't passed out. Yates stood by her side. And he was furious. "Nothing's changed."

"You were the one preaching about fate," Teddy said. "I wasn't supposed to. The necklace took me to my mother." She searched her jacket pockets. Pilgrim's Tunnels were connected to objects. Objects were connected to time lines.

Find the thread. Pull the string.

Her grip encircled the metal frames.

"You didn't kill him."

She turned to Yates. "Not yet."

Teddy rooted in her pocket for the second object. Miles's glasses.

"That's not going to help," Yates said. "That's not a crystal."

Teddy shook her head. "It's not the crystal, not really." She tightened her hand on the glasses, felt the telltale burn. "It's psychometry, objects of daily wear. Miles is the key, not my mother."

She centered her thoughts, demanded the glasses to take her where she needed to go.

"It's not the end," Teddy said aloud. Both to herself and to Yates.

Take me to the holiday party. Hollis Whitfield's home, Thanksgiving Day.

The pressure and the pain enveloped her again and sucked her back in time.

CHAPTER FORTY

EVEN THOUGH IT WAS FAMILIAR, EVERYTHING ABOUT Hollis Whitfield's house felt foreign. A mansion perched on a cliff overlooking the sparkling waters of San Francisco Bay. Sleek modern furniture, contemporary art lining the walls. Well-dressed guests strolling through the rooms, catering staff offering drinks and hors d'oeuvres. Stuffy and self-important, every bit as *un*-Thanksgiving-like as Teddy remembered it. No football blaring from the TV, no friendly arguments over how many marshmallows to toss on the sweet potato casserole.

She'd done it. Used Miles's glasses to bull's-eye her way through time.

Teddy tailed her past self as she walked with Kate through the party. Watched as Kate scoffed and rolled her eyes. Teddy took a steadying breath, oriented herself in the moment.

This is when she tells me that Miles is Whitfield's grandson.

No one would notice a traveler here except her past self. So she needed to stay out of view until the right moment. She couldn't risk sending past-Teddy into full panic mode.

Teddy followed Kate and her past self inside, careful to stay a few paces behind. Her eyes locked on Maddux as soon as she entered Whitfield's lavish entryway. It would be easy to shoot him right there, but she had to wait for all the threads to weave together: the bomb had to go off, Whitfield had to see Maddux's involvement, Miles needed to know his own power.

She stationed herself in a corner, impatiently watching events unfold as she remembered. She saw Eli pour drinks at the bar. Watched Miles and past-Teddy making small talk. As if on cue, Teddy watched a woman cross the room and interrupt past-Teddy's conversation with Miles. The woman pulled Miles away to speak to other guests. Past-Teddy headed to the bar.

Go time.

Once again, Henry's words raced through her mind.

Let it explode

Though perhaps he hadn't consciously known it, Henry had been referring to the IED that the PC had planted at Whitfield's party. Teddy had to let it explode. That was the only way. Even Jeremy had said there were always casualties of war. He was right. Only this time, if Teddy pulled it off, the casualty would be General Maddux. A victim of his own collateral damage.

She felt a second's hesitation as she remembered Marysue's warning. Yes, there were risks, but they were worth it. They had to be.

Pull the thread.

Aloud, she said, "Teddy."

Sure enough, past-Teddy turned. Her eyes widened as she did a double take. Teddy caught her breath. How much had she known about astral travel in November? Could she have guessed what seeing her astral self *meant*? Incredibly enough, the only person in the room who could thwart her plan was . . . her. She jerked her head toward the hallway, indicating Whitfield's office.

Past-Teddy waited a second, then another. Considering. Then she turned without a word and entered Whitfield's office, uncharacteristically compliant. She hesitated near the door. "Am I going crazy?"

"No," Teddy said. "But after you hear what I came to tell you, you might think I am."

They returned to the living room. Teddy hoped she'd told her past self enough. It had been almost impossible to restrain herself from saying too much. She would have loved to warn her past self what would happen if she failed. That Eli would be murdered, that Miles would be kidnapped. That the PC would use HEAT as a cover for their actions. But that was too much information. No telling what past-Teddy would do if burdened with all that knowledge.

In the end, the only information she could give her past self was that Maddux was the leader of the PC, and the IED he planted at the party had to be used to take him out. She could clip only one of time's many threads. Any more information than that and she risked unknown consequences to her future time line.

Teddy looked on as her past self spoke with Eli at the bar. Watched him move out from around the bar, carrying a tray. He dropped a glass and bent to retrieve it, ducking beneath a skirted table that held a punch bowl. A second later, he came up empty-handed and moved away. She watched her past self peek under the skirted table.

But this time, past-Teddy didn't cry out to clear the room. She didn't telepathically reach out to warn Kate Atkins. She did exactly what Teddy had asked her to do. She walked toward Miles and suggested he go outside for a moment with his grandfather. Miles complied, and he and his grandfather stepped through the French doors, leaving them ajar.

The room's exit was wide open. Hollis Whitfield was safe.

Miles was removed from the site of the bomb. He wouldn't absorb the energy, wouldn't interfere with its detonation. It would go off exactly like Maddux had planned. And when the ballistics were analyzed, past-Teddy would have the piece she needed to connect the C-4 bomb to the PC.

Past-Teddy stood by the table, a look of panic on her face. She lifted the table skirt. When the bomb's timer reached three seconds, past-Teddy grabbed the IED and lobbed it directly toward Maddux and Nilsson.

Too late, Teddy noticed someone standing near the general. An innocent victim, a casualty of war, but that couldn't be helped. The IED detonated. Teddy watched the agonizing detail as a wave of intense pressure, accompanied by ear-splitting noise, knocked past-Teddy off her feet. Flames licked the ceiling. Glass shattered and walls crumbled.

Then Teddy felt a sharp pull at the center of her chest. The edges of the room began to fade. The glasses went hot in her hands, and the whole world went dark as she was plunged back into a Pilgrim's Tunnel.

CHAPTER FORTY-ONE

TEDDY WOKE TO THE FAMILIAR FEELING OF EMERG-
ing from utter darkness. Not blackout drunk, though. More like waking up anew. Her thoughts rose like helium, a gentle force moving
up, up, up. With this came the realization that she was warm and safe,
enveloped in layers and layers of soft downy feathers. If this was waking up without a body . . .

She stretched out her arms. She had arms! And she was in bed. For
a moment, she wondered if the whole thing—her race to Sector Three
to find Miles, the meeting with her mother on the astral plane, the decision to allow the PC's bomb to detonate at Whitfield's party—had
been a dream.

The bedroom was airy and bright, natural light spilling in from a
huge picture window. Beyond it was a view straight from a postcard.
Crisp blue cloudless sky, snowcapped mountains, and a pristine body
of water reflecting it all back. The kind of view only rich people could
afford.

She was back at Lake Tahoe.

Back in Whitfield's lodge. She recognized it by the vaulted pine
ceiling and sturdy crossbeams. But this wasn't the guest room. She
was in a king-size bed with the kind of soft, welcoming sheets that
made you feel like there was nowhere else you'd want to be.

Strange. Her last clear memory was watching her past self being
knocked flat by an IED. Forcing herself to take inventory, Teddy lifted

the duvet to inspect her own body. She was in an oversize T-shirt. Nothing was hurt, broken, or bruised. She looked at her feet and wiggled her toes. Pink nail polish. Where the hell had that come from?

She turned her attention to the steady whoosh of running water coming from the bathroom. Someone was taking a shower. She glanced around the room for clues to who it might be but saw only a man's blue shirt draped and a pair of jeans tossed over a tufted chair. Hmm. Definitely getting interesting. Maybe the siren call of the casinos on the other side of the lake had been too much to resist. Not exactly Vegas, but a girl had to make do. Maybe her night's winnings had included a sexy stranger who—

Then she saw something on the bedside table. A pair of round, wire-rimmed glasses.

At that moment, the water shut off and the door to the bathroom opened. There he was. Bare-chested, with a towel wrapped around his narrow waist.

Miles.

He squinted, trying to see. "You're up," he said cheerfully, as he ran his fingers through his damp hair.

"Miles?" She was too stunned to say anything else. He was alive. Her plan had worked. Of course, that wasn't the only shock. She was in his bed. Why was she—Well, okay. She could fill in the blanks, especially since he didn't seem at all surprised to find her there. This wasn't the first time she hadn't remembered what had happened the night before, although she didn't make a habit of completely skipping all the good parts.

He grinned. "You were expecting someone else?" He walked to the nightstand, grabbed his glasses, and put them on. Then he bent over and kissed the top of her head. "Sleep well?"

Teddy stared up at him.

Holy crap.

What would Pyro say?

"What's today's date?" she asked, aware that she had slammed back into her body after traveling back to Thanksgiving.

"Last I checked, Christmas was still December twenty fifth."

"It's Christmas morning?"

"And it sounds like you need some coffee. Come on, get dressed. I gave the cook the day off, told her we'd make our own breakfast." He dropped his towel, opened a dresser drawer, and pulled out a pair of boxers. And Teddy turned her head and blushed. Teddy Cannon blushed like some preteen because she was seeing her *supposed* boyfriend naked. But she'd skipped so many steps that Teddy couldn't begin to wrap her head around what the hell was happening.

Miles stepped into the boxers before grabbing his jeans and shirt from the chair. Even though she was embarrassed, there was something about this routine that pulled at her heartstrings, as if she'd been watching Miles get dressed like this for days. Maybe weeks. She tried to access a specific memory of when the two of them had become a couple, but she couldn't. And yet she couldn't shake the feeling this was real. The emotions attached to this moment felt deep and genuine. She and Miles were a thing. Not some holiday hookup.

"Come on, sleepyhead," Miles said. He grabbed a green and red sweater from the drawer and pulled it over his head. It wasn't a corny holiday sweater, like Pyro would have grabbed, but a soft cashmere crew neck in ruby red and deep emerald green. Even in her present state of mind, Teddy appreciated how beautiful he looked. Like a gift.

She glanced away and stared out over the lake. There was so much she needed to ask him. Clearly, whatever she had done at Whitfield's party had changed her present time line. She needed to get her bearings and understand this new world she had created. But she couldn't ask too much outright. She had to carefully feel her way forward.

"Uh . . . okay if I meet you downstairs?" she said. It wasn't that she felt self-conscious about dressing in front of him, it was that she felt like she *should* feel self-conscious about dressing in front of him. There was a part of her that felt very at home in this new life.

"I'll get breakfast started," he said, heading for the door. "Waffles or pancakes?"

"And after that?"

"Whatever you want. But I was hoping I could get you back on the slopes today."

Back on the slopes? Oh, come on. She hadn't actually been *skiing*, had she?

"I didn't mean for the rest of the day, I meant . . ."

"The rest of the break?" he asked. "Anything. As long as we get to campus by the time classes start, we can do what we want."

We? She studied his face, trying to understand. "You're coming back to school with me?"

"Why wouldn't I? My grandfather thinks it's about time I enrolled. And I figured you lot could be my private tutors and catch me up on what I missed first semester."

You lot. Plural. Teddy repeated the phrase in her head, letting the words fill her with hope. *Please let this mean my friends are alive.* That she'd righted the course of her time line and saved the people she loved.

"You mean me and Dara?"

Miles shrugged. "And Jillian. If we can drag her away from Eli. Kind of cool to start at a new school with a ready-made group of friends." He paused and cocked his head. "Are you okay?"

Eli. Teddy got out of bed and threw her arms around him.

It had worked. Everyone was okay. The end.

Miles backed up to look into her eyes, resting a hand on her cheek. "What's wrong?"

"I . . ." she said, and paused to find an excuse for her surplus of emotions. It was simply too soon to explain everything. "It's the holidays. I get a little nostalgic."

"Missing your family?"

She nodded. "And my friends. And school, believe it or not." Teddy let out a long breath. The only question was whether she should call Clint right away or wait until she got back to campus. There was so much she needed to tell him. About Yates. About her mother. And most important, about Maddux.

"Does that mean more skiing?" he asked.

Teddy laughed. "Maybe."

She looked around the room for a cell phone. She found one on the dresser next to a tall white vase, plugged in and fully charged.

"You didn't tell me what you want for breakfast," Miles said, pausing on his way out.

"Pancakes," she replied. Always pancakes. "I'll be right down. I just want to call Clint."

"Clint?" He stopped abruptly. Turned to look at her.

"I won't be long," she promised. "Just a couple of things I need to go over with him."

Miles stepped into the room and shut the door behind him. He walked across the floor toward her. He gently pulled the phone from her grip and put it back on the dresser. Then he took both her hands in his and looked into her eyes. Something was wrong. Very, very wrong.

"Teddy," he said softly, "I guess you're still a little confused. I know that happens sometimes when we lose someone we love, and when you hit your head as much as you tend to do."

Teddy rubbed the back of her head as a reflex. Miles studied the floor, clearly searching for the right words.

"Where's Clint?" she asked, her voice almost a whisper.

"Teddy, Clint is dead. He died at the party. He threw himself on top of the bomb. It took out Maddux and his aide as well. Thanksgiving Day, remember?"

It can't be. It can't.

Because if Clint was dead, that meant it wasn't the end. That meant it was her fault. Clint. The very person who had warned her that changing the past could have dire consequences.

She scanned Miles's face for some indication that he had misspoken.

"Your friend Pyro blamed himself," he said. "He took Clint's death pretty hard. That's why he left the institute. Said he should have been there to stop the bomb. That if he couldn't protect the people he loved, he shouldn't be in law enforcement."

Teddy sat down on the bed, her head in her hands. Miles sat next to her and rubbed her back.

"Don't you remember? You two fought about it."

She wanted to say: *Tell me. Tell me how it happened.*

Instead, she said: "It's my fault."

"No," Miles said. "You tried to save us all by tossing the IED away from the crowd."

Not exactly. But Teddy wondered if she could try again. If she could go back, keep Clint away, and everything would be okay. Clint wouldn't die, and Pyro wouldn't leave.

In her mind, she tried to find the right thread to pull, but each time she encountered another knot—she could save Clint, but what if she lost someone else? What if she got caught in an endless loop of saving one person only to lose another? Was that how the universe worked? Sacrificing one life for another in an endless code for the space-time continuum?

It was a conundrum she couldn't possibly answer. Worse, the one person she would go to for advice was the very person she had lost.

What sacrifices was she willing to make? The question had plagued her ever since Wessner's first class.

She didn't want to face this day. Or the next or the one after that. She wanted to crawl back into bed, burrow under the covers, and stay there. She was turning to Miles, trying to think of what she could say to him, when she felt a strange warmth radiating against the middle of her chest. At first the sensation was entirely foreign. But then she realized what it was.

The ametrine necklace.

Teddy pulled it out from under her T-shirt and looked at it in her hand. Then she wrapped her fingers around it and thought about the power it gave her. Suddenly, she felt flooded with hope. Because there *was* someone she could talk to. Her mother. Even if she didn't know Teddy as anyone but a fellow traveler. And in some way—some big, important way—that made her feel better.

"You okay?" Miles asked.

"No," she said. "Because it's not the end."

Teddy Cannon hadn't given up yet.